PLAYING
—WITH—
FIRE

Tangled in Texas

ALISON
BLISS

Entangled Publishing, LLC
2614 South Timberline Road
Suite 109
Fort Collins, CO 80525
Visit our website at www.entangledpublishing.com.

Select Contemporary is an imprint of Entangled Publishing, LLC.

Edited by Candace Havens
Cover design by Louisa Maggio
Cover art from iStock

Manufactured in the United States of America

First Edition October 2015

To my favorite cowboy of all time, Hubert Lyle.
Because women who don't believe in heroes have never met
my dad.

Chapter One

He strutted past me as if he owned the place.

A whole head taller than me, his height was nearly as intimidating as his broad-shouldered, well-muscled frame. The white straw Stetson he wore looked weathered from years of use, but the perfectly shaped hat fit his head as well as the name molded to the man.

Cowboy.

I couldn't forget his name, even if I wanted to.

No longer the cute sandy-haired boy on the cusp of becoming a man, his hair had darkened a little and his scrawny body had sculpted and toned itself proportionately in all the right places. But he hadn't noticed me then, and he wasn't about to now.

Long-legged strides pushed him closer to the computer area, showcasing the power of his thighs as his muscles flexed against his jeans with every step. When he pulled out a chair, his biceps bulged under the navy blue, long-sleeved shirt he'd rolled up to his elbows. Then he flicked a glance my way.

He held my gaze only for a moment—long enough to make my heart pound frantically against my rib cage—then focused on the pretty brunette reading across the room. As usual, he was on the prowl. It wasn't much of a surprise, though, given his reputation with the ladies. In fact, I doubted he could pick his most recent conquest out of a crowd of...*two.*

Even if one of them was a man. And dead.

Not that I knew from personal experience or anything. I mean, just because I'd met Cowboy before didn't mean I had slept with him. Though I was probably one of the few women in the entire Tri-County area who could pronounce *that* with a clear conscience.

Whatever. Didn't matter.

With a loud huff, I maneuvered around the circulation desk to the return bins, where I bent to gather a stack of books. Irritation coursed through my veins at the speed of light as I slapped one heavy hardback on top of another, forming a tall tower, until the weight of the last book smashed against my thumb. I winced and jerked my hand back, shaking the pain away.

"Damn it," I grumbled under my breath.

I closed my eyes and breathed out a sigh. Why was I suddenly so agitated over his very presence? It wasn't like I should be surprised to run into him. After all, Liberty, Texas was *his* hometown. Then again, the public library wasn't exactly the kind of place where a guy like him would normally hang out. If ever.

It was, however, a place where someone like me would

spend most of their time.

When the library's director had hired me two weeks before, I hadn't bothered to mention I would have done the job for free. Even as a child, I'd always spent more time in a library than my own home. It was the one place I felt safe. A place where I could get lost in another world, and my parents couldn't argue because they'd be forced to whisper. No fights ever broke out in a library.

And there was no shortage of love in one, either.

Nope. Not going there.

Arms fully loaded, I straightened and spun on my heel, bumping into a solidly built wall of…man. Strong hands shot out and grasped my shoulders to steady me as the books toppled to the floor. "Oh, I'm sorr—"

Emerald eyes stared back at me.

Oh God! It's him.

"Not your fault, darlin'," Cowboy said, flashing me one of his signature charming grins I remembered so well. "I didn't mean to sneak up on you. Let me help you with these, miss."

As I suspected, Cowboy hadn't recognized me. *Big shocker there.*

He kneeled and began gathering the pile of books easily into his muscular arms. The bulges in his arched back bunched and tightened with his every movement. Okay, so maybe I couldn't blame the ladies for throwing themselves at him. He was nice to look at.

"You okay, ma'am?"

His words shook me from my thoughts, and I stared blankly at him as I twisted my fingers into the flimsy fabric of my black tiered skirt. I gave him a quick nod. He grinned, then allowed his gaze to travel lazily over my body, examining me up and down, until his eyes finally zeroed in on my breasts.

With a high neckline, my cream-colored silk top covered my chest fully, though it didn't seem to matter to him. His green eyes twinkled with extreme confidence and blatant sexuality, which sent a familiar tingle skittering up my spine.

"You seem a little rattled. You sure you're okay, sweetheart?"

My fingers knotted together, cutting off the circulation, while my breath caught in my throat. Not only was he speaking directly to me and eyeing me like a tasty piece of candy, but he was referring to me in terms of endearments that sent a thrill up my skirt. Then he flashed me a very male grin that damn-near melded my panties to my body.

When I silently nodded again, he chuckled, straightened, and motioned to the books he'd retrieved from the floor. "Where do you want 'em?"

I stood there and stupidly pointed to the circulation desk, as if I couldn't speak. Which, at this point, was apparently true. *Great. Now he thinks I'm a mute imbecile.*

As he made his way to the counter, I followed, admiring his loose-gaited stride and the way his tight rear end filled out his faded Wranglers. The man was definitely a moving violation if I'd ever seen—

My heel caught on the rubber-back entrance mat beneath my feet, propelling me forward until I crashed into his back. He stumbled, but managed to hold onto the books while firming his stance to keep us from falling.

Pushing my palms against his stiff, muscular back, I quickly righted myself and regained my balance. But not before getting a whiff of his masculine, tangy scent. God, he smelled delicious. Thankfully, my 120-pound frame wasn't enough to bowl him completely over. Maybe he wouldn't even notice how clumsy I was.

"Darlin', if you wanted a piggyback ride, all you had to do was ask." He glanced over his shoulder with a teasing grin, then continued on his way.

Mortified, I closed my eyes briefly and let out a slow, calming breath as I fought the urge to fan my heated face. *Jeez, Anna. Get a grip already.*

When he reached the desk, he set the books down and turned to face me. "Maybe you can help *me* with something now. I'm looking for a book on fire accelerants. You know, like cleaners, paint thinners…that sort of thing."

"I know what fire accelerants are." I'd finally found my voice, but the words spit out at him, sounding snippier than I meant them to.

Wordlessly, he raised one questioning brow.

I bit my tongue and mentally cringed. What the hell was wrong with me? One minute, I'm checking out his ass, and the next, I'm being rude to him. Talk about mixed signals.

Silently, I motioned for him to follow and led the way, not bothering to read the signs labeling each aisle. I stopped abruptly and reached for a book—the one with the red spine—on the bottom shelf and shoved it at him. I knew it was exactly what he was looking for.

Before he could say anything, I hurried down the aisle, speed-walking away from him. Once I careened around the counter, returning to the safety of the circulation desk, I took a deep breath and stole a quick peek at him from a distance.

Unfazed by our exchange, Cowboy sat at an unoccupied table and opened the book I'd handed him. He glanced up briefly, but barely acknowledged me before focusing all his attention on the printed matter before him. Once he began reading, he didn't look up again.

Thank God.

I went back to work, shuffling through the returned books and inspecting each for signs of wear before scanning them back into the system. Then I organized them into neat rows on a metal pushcart to ensure they ended up back on the proper shelves in their rightful order.

A half hour later, Bobbie Jo appeared in the sliding glass doors of the library entrance, pushing a green stroller. Her shiny gold tresses and warm smile instantly brightened the room. She had been the one who introduced me to Cowboy all those years ago, and although she'd mentioned she might drop by, I hadn't expected *him* to make an appearance.

Apparently, neither had she.

When her gaze landed on Cowboy sitting alone and reading, one eyebrow rose and a grin played on her lips. But instead of moving toward him, she headed directly for me.

I slid around the counter to give her a quick hug, then wasted no time lifting her precious bundle out of the stroller to get a better look. "Aww, Austin looks adorable today."

The light blue cap and romper set matched perfectly. Well, if you didn't count the fair amount of drool wetting the underside of his chin, darkening the front.

Bobbie Jo smiled proudly. "He does, doesn't he?"

"Yes, he's quite handsome." I bounced him in my arms and tickled Austin's soft cheek. "By the way, thanks again for helping me get this job. I can't believe your mom is friends with the library director."

She waved me off. "Mom has been friends with Mary

Duncan since kindergarten, but we didn't have anything to do with it. You were perfect for the job. Even Mary said so. Just yesterday, she told my mom she could see you taking over the director position when she retires next year. Wouldn't that be cool?"

Sure. If I planned to stick around. But I didn't. Actually, *couldn't* was more like it. In six months, *he'd* be coming for me. So I had to make the most of my time here…while it lasted.

Alert and wide-eyed, the baby cooed at me, blowing spit bubbles and increasing his vocalizations as I made funny faces at him. Five-month-olds are so easily amused.

Then a shiver ran down my spine, and the hairs on the back of my neck stood on end. Someone else watched me. Only his eyes were like lasers searing into my skin.

I glanced at Cowboy and caught him grinning. My stomach dropped and my posture stiffened. I didn't know why it happened, but my wires had always crossed around him. My normal friendly, chipper demeanor was now anxiety-ridden and laced with nervous energy.

The little guy in my arms must've sensed how frazzled I'd become because, although I tried to focus my attention on Austin, he whimpered and poked out his bottom lip. I spoke softly and rocked him back and forth, hoping to soothe away his tension, as well as my own, but it wasn't working. "Sorry, Bobbie Jo. I didn't mean to upset him."

"Oh, Anna, don't worry about it. It's not your fault. He's been fussy since he started teething last week." She rooted through the diaper bag and handed the baby a liquid-filled plastic teething ring to chew on. He grasped it in his tiny hand, took it straight to his slobbery mouth, and chomped on it.

The teething ring seemed to be working until Austin hiccupped—hard enough to jolt his entire body—and startled himself. The surprise on his cute little face tickled me, and I forgot all about my nervousness...and my voyeur. I threw back my head and laughed.

Only after did I realize Cowboy still eyed me from across the room. And maybe it was the moronic way I always overanalyzed everything, but he seemed to be staring at me rather strangely. His eyes glazed over and the corner of his mouth twitched into a smirk, as if he were observing me with some sort of curious fascination or...*interest*?

For a brief second, I *may* have considered stealing the baby's soothing ring for myself. "Um, Bobbie Jo, why is Cowboy looking at me like that?"

She peered in his direction and shrugged. "Who knows why that man does anything. Wouldn't surprise me if he's over there imagining you naked."

My mouth fell open. "What? That's ridiculous," I said as my face burned with the heat of embarrassment. "I'm not the kind of woman men like *him* go for."

"Why do you say that?"

"Simple reasoning. Don't strapping young cowboys usually prefer their women how they like their horses—sleek, fast, and with a touch of wild?"

She laughed. A lot. "You've been reading too many of those romance books of yours. Sweetie, you're female and breathing. I'm pretty sure those are his only requirements."

I grinned at that, remembering my earlier thought about Cowboy's most recent conquest. "Well, he's not *my* type."

"What, you don't like hot, well-built men?"

"No. Um, yes. I mean…" I shook my head to clear the confusion I was feeling. "It's not that. I just don't like men who regard women as sheep. And knowing Cowboy, I bet he probably lines them up and shears the clothes right off them."

"Can't argue with that," she said, nodding in agreement. "In fact, I wouldn't be surprised if he's already imagined you naked twenty different ways by now." My stomach clenched tightly, and I frowned at the unwelcome sensation, making her laugh.

I shook my head adamantly. "Well, it's not going to happen. Not with me, anyway."

"Oh, come on. Don't tell me you're immune to Cowboy. That would be a first. Most girls have to claw through the hoards of women just to get him to notice them. After all, he's in the bachelor calendar, you know." She giggled at that.

"Bachelor calendar?"

"The local newspaper runs a contest where men from Liberty County compete to be in next year's calendar. Cowboy won a spot as May's bachelor."

"Like a beauty contest for men?"

"Basically," she said with a grin. "I mean, the winners get a photo shoot and everything. I'm surprised you haven't seen them yet. The calendars were released yesterday and the whole town has been talking about them."

"I guess I don't get out enough."

"Wait until you see what Cowboy… Uh-oh," she said, glancing over my shoulder with a grin. "Speak of the devil. Look who's coming."

Terrific.

He sauntered across the room, smiling at his five-month-old godson still cradled in my arms. Cowboy leaned lazily on the counter, gave me a quick nod, and turned his attention to Bobbie Jo. "Hey, beautiful. How's the little turtle doing?"

She heaved out an exasperated breath. "Would you please stop referring to Austin as a turtle?"

"Sure I will. Just as soon as he grows some hair."

I wanted to laugh, but bit the inside of my cheek instead. Cowboy's assessment of Austin's bald head and bug eyes was quite accurate—he *did* look like a turtle. Though I wouldn't dare tell his mother that.

Bobbie Jo rolled her eyes. Apparently, she was used to the insulting nickname. "What are you doing here, anyway? I don't think I've ever seen you in a library before. You lose a bet or something?"

"Very funny," Cowboy said, though he wasn't laughing. "No, Miss Nosey. I'm doing research." He held up the book I'd helped him locate.

"On household chemicals?" She shook her head. "Cowboy, when are you going to stop looking into that case? Don't you think it's time you let it go? It's been months already. There's nothing more you can do."

"Well, if I don't investigate that goddamn fire, then who will?"

My ears perked up. "Isn't that what the fire marshal is for?" I said it without thinking, then looked down quickly, keeping my gaze from meeting his. It wasn't like I *couldn't* speak around him. Basically, everything just came out sounding as awkward as I felt.

Cowboy's hand fisted on the counter. "I'm captain of the fire department, so that makes it *my* job. Besides, that jackass couldn't find his balls with both hands. He damn sure isn't going to solve this case."

Bobbie Jo touched his hand, offering him comfort. "I know you don't feel like he's doing enough," she murmured. "But your department's already so thinly staffed. And with the loss of your chief…"

I cringed, realizing which fire they were talking about.

"I hate to see you working so hard," she added. "You need to take a day off and catch up on your sleep."

I'd noticed the dark circles under his eyes, but had attributed them to late night bar outings I imagined he was accustomed to. But hell, what did I know? I also thought his nose looked a little more crooked than the last time I saw him.

"Today *is* my day off, and it's just now getting dark outside." Cowboy rubbed at the back of his neck, then glanced at his watch. "When the library closes in half an hour, I'll be heading home and hitting the sack." Then he grinned at Bobbie Jo. "What are you doing here? Checking up on me?"

"You being in a library is most definitely a newsworthy event, but no, I didn't come here to make fun of you. That was just a bonus." She smirked at me as she reached for Austin and pulled him into her arms.

No, Bobbie Jo, don't say it!

"I stopped by to see Anna. She moved here a few weeks ago."

Damn. She said it.

Cowboy's face warped with confusion. "Who's *Anna*?"

Bobbie Jo quirked a brow at his question, but gestured to me, anyway. His piercing gaze followed, and I gave him a fake, strained smile. Though he hadn't recognized me, it still hurt that he hadn't even remembered my name.

"I didn't know you were friends with Bobbie Jo." He glanced back to her and said, "Your friend and I bumped into each other earlier. Could've sworn I punctured her voice box or something. She barely said two words to me." He turned back to me and grinned. "You must not like strangers."

I chewed on my bottom lip, not sure what to say.

"*Strangers?*" Bobbie Jo laughed. "What, you don't recognize her?"

Her comment made Cowboy blink, and me wince. *Damn it, Bobbie Jo.* I wanted her to stop helping me.

His glittery green eyes scanned up and down my slender body, and I could only imagine the shades of red my face turned. "You know, you do look awfully familiar," he said easily. "Did we sleep together?"

Oh, good grief.

Bobbie Jo was patting Austin on his back, but froze mid-pat. "Seriously, Cowboy?" She gave him a stern, motherly glare. "You don't even know if Anna's someone you've had sex with?"

I cringed. Obviously, he thought sex with someone like me would be unmemorable. But did Bobbie Jo have to actually verbalize it?

When he just shrugged, Bobbie Jo shook her head in disgust, then placed the yawning turtle back into his green stroller shell. "After dealing with Jeremy earlier today, I don't even have the energy to smack you in the back of the head."

"You're still dealing with that shit stain?" Cowboy snarled. "Guess I'm gonna have to kick his ass."

She peered up at him in confusion. "For what?"

"For being a dick."

"Yes, he is. But he's also Austin's father…even if only in the biological sense." Bobbie Jo finished buckling her son into the stroller and straightened. "Look, I know he's your long-time rival, but is there ever going to be a time I mention Jeremy's name that one of Austin's four godfathers don't threaten to beat him up?"

Cowboy grinned. "Nope."

"Fine. But I don't want you or the other guys to do anything to him. I can handle Jeremy myself."

Glancing at the clock on the wall, I realized it was almost closing time and noted that the people milling about had greatly dwindled in numbers. I still hadn't even taken out the sack of garbage I'd left by the back door.

"Excuse me for a moment," I said quietly. "I need to take the trash out back before I close up." That would allow me time to settle my nerves.

After vacating the room I grabbed the bag of garbage, stepped out the back door, and tossed it into the big blue dumpster on the side of the library. I took a few deep breaths while fanning my hot face, then returned inside and rejoined Bobbie Jo and Cowboy just as she was about to leave.

"You know, darlin', you really do look familiar," Cowboy said to me as Bobbie Jo stored the baby's teething ring. "I just can't place how we met."

Of course, he couldn't. I sighed. "I could just tell you."

"Aw, now where's the fun in that?" Cowboy gave me a quick wink.

"Oh, Lord," Bobbie Jo said, rolling her eyes. She looked up at me. "Sorry I can't visit with you longer, but I need to get Austin home and ready for his bath. I'll call you tomorrow.

Maybe we can go to dinner or something this week."

"Sure," I replied.

Bobbie Jo pushed the stroller toward the door.

"Let me know if you want me to stomp Jeremy's ass into the ground," Cowboy called out after her.

She turned back long enough to give us a half-hearted wave, so I planted a smile firmly on my lips. But it was a ruse. The last few patrons had used the self-checkout scanner and had already vacated the library right before Bobbie Jo. That knowledge combined with the nervous energy zinging under my skin left me flustered. Deep inside, I was angst-ridden by the thought of being left alone in the same room as Cowboy.

To busy my trembling hands, I stood at the desk with my back to him, fiddling with a stack of flyers for a chili cook-off to be held over the weekend. I straightened the lime green papers until they were all neatly aligned with the edge of the counter.

Cowboy reached past me, brushing my body lightly with his, as he placed the book he held on the counter. "Mind holding onto this for me until tomorrow?"

The scent of his cologne lingered in the air. I turned toward him, carefully measuring him with my eyes. "You can check the book out."

"No library card."

"Oh. Okay, I can issue you one. I'll just need your driver's license and—"

"Won't work."

I paused, not entirely sure what he meant by his rude interruption. "All right. If you don't have identification, then a utility bill with your name and address will suffice."

"Sorry. No can do." He smiled at the puzzled look I gave

him. "I have identification, but very few people in this town know my real name, and I'd like to keep it that way. If I told you what it was, then I'm afraid it might be all over town by morning."

"Excuse me?" When he grinned at my surprised tone, I lifted my chin to portray my exasperation. "If you're suggesting I'd speak to anyone about the library's confidential records," I said, my tone bordering on contempt, "then you're—"

He raised his hands in surrender. "Whoa! Hold up, darlin'. I wasn't doing any such thing. Relax a little. Good Lord, are you *always* this uptight?"

My eyes widened. "I beg your pardon?"

"Guess so. Judging by your clothes, I should have figured that." Cowboy grinned and leaned one hip lazily against the counter next to me. Then he gave me a quick once-over and his eyes twinkled with shameless mirth, as if he were enjoying my exasperation…and proving his point.

I glanced down at my clothes and shook my head in disbelief. My black skirt fell respectfully below my knees and my long-sleeved blouse was buttoned all the way to my throat. I imagined my old-fashioned attire probably bored most men since it was about as stimulating as watching grass grow or a car rust. *Which is exactly why I wore it, you jerk!*

I gaped at him, not caring if he saw how offended I was. And I *was* offended. "Well, excuse me if I'm not dressed to your liking. I'm sure the kind of women you're used to shed their clothes whenever you enter a room, but as you plainly see, I'm *not* like most women."

When he stepped closer, I assumed he did so to intimidate me with his overwhelming masculine presence. I straightened my spine, ready to give it right back to him. But instead he said, "Did you know your blue eyes brighten when you're all fired up?"

"I don't care. And furthermore… Wait, what?"

As if he couldn't control himself, Cowboy reached up and removed the thick, unattractive lenses from my face.

I stiffened. "What do you think you're doing?" My low voice sounded almost breathy.

He didn't answer. Instead, he raised his arm and went for the clip in my hair. I tried to move away, but he blocked my escape route with his body, forcing me to stand in place as he freed the red strands I had twisted onto the back of my head. My wavy locks tumbled loosely around my shoulders.

Cowboy cocked his head, scrutinizing my new look, as I crossed my arms and drew my lips into a thin line to show my petulance. It only made him grin more. "You know, I was going to say you looked like an angel. But that's not quite right. With your fiery red hair, deep blue eyes, and that rebellious little pout, I think you look more like…a *fallen* angel."

"You're kidding, right? *That's* the best line you have?" I rolled my eyes and scoffed under my breath. "And here I thought you were actually supposed to be good at this."

He ignored my comment and leaned his chiseled face closer to mine, rubbing one calloused finger along my cheekbone. His deep voice took on a sexier note. "All that innocence and compressed sexuality wound up tight inside you…just waiting to be let loose."

I resisted the urge to blow out the breath I was holding. *Okay, so maybe he's better than I thought.*

In an attempt not to come across as weak or feeble, I lifted my chin, but my nerves wound tighter, electrified by the way he penetrated me with his green eyes. "And let me guess, you think you're the man to unlock it?"

"I'd damn sure like to try," he said with a suggestive shrug of his brows.

The smile he wore reached his eyes, and although I tried to maintain my composure, the natural charm he exuded drew me in.

I let out a quick, irritated breath. "My God! Bobbie Jo was right. You'll hit on any Homo sapiens with a pulse."

He blinked at me, then a grin broadened his face. "Is it my imagination or did you just confess that you're into chicks? Because if that's part of the deal—"

"Oh, Lord," I said, snatching my hair clip and glasses from him. "*Homo sapiens* is a species of bipedal primates, a group to which humans belong. It's definitely not whatever dirty thing your mind conjured—"

Before I finished my sentence, the glass doors slid open and a brunette with a short blunt haircut stepped inside. She was a gorgeous girl with an athletic body, most of which she showed off by wearing itty-bitty things she obviously had mistaken for shorts. She stopped in the doorway, put a hand on her pushed-out hip, and eyed Cowboy with irritation.

"Mandy…?"

"I thought that was your vehicle parked out front, Captain. Where the hell is your radio?"

"I didn't want it squawking while I was in here, so I left it in my truck. What does it matter? It's my day off."

"Well, you might want to get your ass in gear and come with me. We've got a problem." Mandy scanned the room until her gaze stopped on me. "Might want to bring her along, too," she said in a clipped tone before spinning on her heel to storm out.

"Hold up, Mandy. Where's the fire?"

She stopped in the doorway and looked back at us over her shoulder. "At the library."

Cowboy's head snapped to me, then back to Mandy. "But we're in the library."

"No shit," she said. "*That's* the problem."

Cowboy made it to the door before he realized I wasn't behind him.

As Mandy's words had sunk in, I'd panicked and my throat had closed, rendering me speechless. My stunned mind grasped the danger I was possibly in, but my frozen limbs couldn't seem to react to the notion.

"Hey, what are you waiting for?" he asked, staring back at me. "You plan on staying inside a burning building?"

My body bristled with fear, and a strangled sound released from my mouth as terror-inducing recollections and smoke-filled memories choked me. *No, I can't do this. Not again.*

I staggered a step forward, gripping the counter to keep myself upright, but I felt the blood drain from my face.

"Christ. What the hell's wrong with you?" When I didn't answer him, he moved toward me with an outstretched hand. "Anna…?"

He must've thought I was in shock. And hell, maybe I was. One second I was standing there in complete silence, frozen in place, and the next I was humming a tune under my breath to keep the painful, all-consuming memories at bay.

No doubt he was utterly confused by my reaction. Nothing was stopping either of us from evacuating the building.

Nothing, except me, that was.

His hand clamped onto my wrist. "Damn it, come on! Snap out of it."

Thankfully, I did. With one touch, he'd somehow grounded me back to reality.

Gathering my strength, I forced my legs to move as Cowboy tugged on my arm and headed for the door with me in tow. By the time we made it outside and caught up to Mandy in the parking lot, sirens were blaring in the distance.

"Those are our boys," Mandy announced proudly. "I was driving past when I saw the flames." She motioned to the side of the library, where an orange glow illuminated the dark alleyway. "At first, I thought you were here because of the fire, but then I looked through the window and saw you inside with a book in your hand. Don't know which surprised me more."

Cowboy gave her a petulant look. "What's on fire?"

"Oh, um…I'm not sure, but I think it's the dumpster. I called it in over the radio and had Reynolds grab my bunker gear from the station in case they needed any help."

"Good thinking," Cowboy told her.

Flashing lights swung across the parking lot asphalt as two wailing fire trucks pulled in and rolled to a stop nearby. Several uniformed firefighters spilled out and sprinted in the direction of the fire. A tremor ran through me. With Cowboy's hand still latched onto my arm, I had no doubt he felt the physical vibration reverberate through my body and into his.

Our eyes met briefly, then he glanced to Mandy. "Go suit up, Barlow."

"Aren't you coming, Captain?"

"No. The crew can handle this one without me."

Mandy hesitated, wrinkling her forehead in puzzlement, then ran for the trucks.

The moment she got out of earshot, I looked up at Cowboy. "If you need to go—"

"What happened back there, Anna? Why'd you freeze up?"

And just like that, reality smacked me in the face. There was no way I could explain it to Cowboy without telling him more about me than I cared for him to know. Or anyone else, for that matter. Like he said, news traveled fast in small towns.

"It was nothing. I'm sorry."

"No need for apologies, darlin'. I only want to make sure you're okay." When I didn't say anything in return, he dropped the subject and focused his attention to the firefighters in action.

Even though the reinforcements had everything under control, Cowboy kept a sharp eye on the men as they hustled back and forth between the trucks and the fire, laying hoses and opening water lines. They were obviously capable of handling themselves, but he stayed on top of them by occasionally shouting orders from the sidelines where he babysat me.

We couldn't see the fire from our position in the parking lot, only the orange glow coming from the side of the building. Every time the flames shot higher, red-hot embers released into the air and then dissipated, before the ashes floated away in the evening breeze. Although I was awestruck by the lethal beauty, the pungent smoke littering the air took me back to a time I didn't want to remember. I was still a little shaken, but the last thing I wanted was for Cowboy to witness one of my physical or mental meltdowns.

Moments later, the flickering light vanished. Judging by how fast the blaze dwindled, and what knowledge I had of fires, I gathered this one hadn't been very large. If so, he probably would've left me in someone else's care while he led his team.

No surprise there. He liked to be in control. And it was sexy as hell.

A young fireman approached us, suited up in his bunker gear. "Engine four crew is heading back to the station, Captain. The rest of us will stick around for a few and make sure the fire stays out."

"Sounds good. Tell Barlow to fill out a report and have it on my desk by morning," Cowboy ordered.

The kid nodded and headed back to the trucks.

"Come on," Cowboy said. "You can walk over with me, and we'll check out the damage."

Shock blasted through me, as if he electrocuted me. "No, I can't!" But then I glanced back to the side of the library where the orange glow had emanated, and my nerves shriveled back into their rightful place. "I mean…the fire."

He looked at me strangely. "Fire's out, remember?"

I exhaled a slow, calming breath. "Right. Uh…okay." God, he probably thought I was a lunatic.

I trailed behind him as we made our way to the side of the building, where the dumpster sat. As we neared the site of the fire, my steps dragged until I ended up stopping completely.

Mesmerized, I stared at the large smoldering metal bin, imagining the flickering flames as they surrendered to the force of the water the firemen had pumped into the dumpster. Then I made the mistake of shifting my eyes to the scorch marks on the library's exterior stucco wall. A building *I* had inhabited while the dumpster was burning. *Jesus.*

An involuntary shiver ran through me as my legs liquefied. I forced myself to stay on my feet, though, rather than drooping like a wilting flower. I could handle this. I had to. But as rattled as my fragile nerves were, I couldn't handle much more tonight.

Cowboy took a look inside the dumpster, shook his head, and then walked toward me. "Do you smoke?"

"No," I replied, wondering why he would ask me such a weird question.

"Any clue how the fire started?" Cowboy asked, glaring at me strangely.

"Why are you asking me? You're the fireman here."

"Because, if memory serves, *you* were the last person anywhere near the dumpster before the fire started."

Chapter Two

I gasped. "You think *I* started the dumpster fire?"

"Not intentionally, no."

Offended by his insinuation, I gawked at him. "You're accusing me of starting it by accident, though?"

He shook his head. "I'm not accusing you of anything. I'm just trying to figure out what happened, that's all." He pointed to the container. "When you took out the trash earlier, is this the dumpster you put it into?"

"Well, yes."

"Was it on fire when you came outside?"

I crossed my arms and glared at him. "Of course not."

"Did you see anyone out here? Anyone in the parking lot, maybe?"

"No, it was just…me." My eyebrow rose. *He can't possibly think I…*

Cowboy sighed in frustration. "Do you know what was in the trash bag you carried out?"

"Some half-eaten plates of food, used plastic cups, and stuff like that. It was left over from a board meeting earlier today. Nothing that would start a fire."

"But you don't know for sure?"

"Well, no…I…" The way he stared at me made me nervous, as if he really thought I started the blaze. "I didn't do it," I blurted out.

"Never said you did."

"You didn't have to." The way he was looking at me said plenty. All I wanted was to get away from his suspicious glare. I sighed warily. "Look, if you're done with me, I'd like to lock up and go home."

"Sure, but I'll need you to come down to the fire station first thing in the morning."

He might as well have told me he needed me to wash his truck while I was there. "For what?" I asked.

"I'll need to take down your statement."

"That's unnecessary. I can give you my statement now. In fact, I already did. It went something like this: *I don't know how the fire started.*"

"By morning, you might recall some detail you forgot to mention or remember seeing something you aren't thinking clearly about right now. It won't hurt to go over everything one more time tomorrow so I can add it to the report."

"This is silly. So I'm supposed to come down to the station to answer questions about a fire I know nothing about. All because you think I'm lying?"

"I didn't say that, either."

"To hear you tell it, Captain, you aren't actually *saying* anything. But I somehow get the impression I'm being treated as a potential suspect."

He frowned at me, breathing out a hard sigh. "Listen, it's nothing personal. You're new in town, and I don't know a damn thing about you."

And if I had my way, he never would.

"I just need you to come down to the station," he repeated. "It won't take long."

"Why can't you question me here, then?"

"Because I don't have any of my reports with me. It's my day off, remember? So if you'll just swing by the station in the morning, I can—"

"And if I don't?" I couldn't have him looking into my background.

His jaw tightened and his eyes widened a little, as if he were surprised by my reluctance to cooperate. "I can always have the sheriff pick you up and question you at the police station if you'd like." He grinned smugly as if daring me to try him. "That works for me, too."

An erotic image of Cowboy standing over me, berating me, while I was bound in handcuffs flashed in my mind, and my mouth went dry. "Fine. I'll be there tomorrow to answer the same stupid questions you've already asked me. But don't expect my responses to change," I said, turning to head back to the library entrance.

"One more thing, Miss...uh, Anna."

Jesus. He still didn't remember me. I groaned under my breath and shook my head, but kept on walking without looking back. "Sorry, *Captain*," I yelled. "You should've asked your question while you had the chance. Guess now you'll have to wait until tomorrow...unless you feel like giving the sheriff a call, that is." With that, I disappeared around the corner of the building and let out a deep breath.

I barely made it back inside to the circulation desk before the door slid open behind me and a booming, masculine voice belted out, "I wasn't through with you, yet."

My body jolted at the gruff tone. I tried to keep my senses, but something about his comment had pushed my buttons. I whirled on him. "That's too damn bad. So far tonight, you've accused me of sleeping with you, spreading gossip about confidential library records, and starting a dumpster fire. So if you think you can walk in here and bully me into answering any more of your idiotic questions, then...well, you're sorely mistaken." I waved him away with my hand. "Now if you'll excuse me, I need to close up."

Cowboy chuckled. "All right, I'll go. But before I do, I still need to ask you the question I came in here for. Will you hold the book for me or not?"

"*Not*," I snapped back, having my fill of his arrogance. "You can google the information you need."

He snorted. "Yeah, because we all know that everything you read on the internet is true."

"I'll make you a deal. I'll hold the book for you if you don't force me to come to the fire station to give you a statement."

His eyes widened at my request. "You know damn well I can't do that." Then he lifted a brow, confirming I had just made myself look even more suspicious than before.

Great, Anna. Way to go.

"Fine. Then you can take your chances that someone else might borrow the book before you," I said, veering the subject back in its original direction.

His jaw tightened and his eyes narrowed. "But if they do, I'd have to wait weeks before they'd return it."

"Not my problem. If you don't like that option, then I guess you'll just have to check it out like a normal person."

Cowboy sighed in frustration. "Look, no offense, but gossip has a way of traveling fast around these parts. I'd rather come back and read it tomorrow than have a library card with my real name on it." He flashed me another cheeky grin, clearly thinking his charm would get him exactly what he wanted.

"That's the most asinine thing I've ever heard," I told him, putting my hands on my hips.

"Silly or not, I'm not taking any chances. Now, will you just hold the damn book for me until tomorrow?" I couldn't stop the unsympathetic smile from forming on my lips. And he apparently noticed it, too. "You think I'm being ridiculous, don't you?"

"No, I think you're paranoid." And I *may* have been slightly impressed that he knew what the word "asinine" meant. "Besides, no one cares what your real name is. Anything is bound to be better than a name like *Cowboy*."

My comment must've caught him off guard because he released a chuckle. "Ouch," he said playfully. "Guess I shouldn't have asked." He cocked his head to the side and squinted at me, as if he were trying to figure me out. "You're one of those no-nonsense kind of gals, aren't you?"

I wasn't sure how to answer that. A part of me wanted to be as carefree as the next girl, but my past didn't allow me the luxury of playing games...especially with *him* of all people. Sure, I'd always had a fresh-faced, wholesome vibe going for me, but I was no pushover. Or an angel, fallen or otherwise.

My cheeks flushed so I started to turn away from him.

"No, I—"

But his fingers caught my chin and held me there as his gaze probed mine. A shiver traveled the length of my spine, and I was exhilarated by the sudden yearning and longing that came over me. I needed to get away from him so I could screw my head back on properly. But I only knew of one way to get him to leave…

A strangled sound left my throat. "Fine, I'll hold the book for you until tomorrow. But that's it."

Cowboy wore a triumphant grin as he dropped his hand. "Thanks. And I'm sorry if I overstepped my boundaries. I probably shouldn't have done that." Despite his words, the insincere look in his mischievous eyes told me he didn't regret it one bit.

"Seems to be a trend with you tonight," I said sarcastically, blowing out a hard breath.

"I'm going to get out of your hair now. Literally." He grinned with amusement, then turned and headed out the door.

Half an hour later, I was sitting in my blue Cavalier on the side of a dark road, grinding my teeth together. Only five stupid miles. That's as far as I got. Leave it to me to get a flat at night in the middle of nowhere without a spare. Actually, I had a spare. It just wasn't currently in the trunk where it should be. *Because I'm smart like that.*

My cell phone sat cradled in the console, but it was no use since I didn't have anyone to call. Bobbie Jo was my only option and I didn't want to burden her any more than I had to. Austin would already be tucked into bed for the night and she'd have to wake him just to come give me a lift home. She'd already said he was cranky because he was teething. No way could I do that to her.

It was bad enough I'd have to call her in the morning and ask her for a ride into town to buy a new tire, since my donut replacement wasn't going to last me very long. Besides, it wouldn't kill me to walk the rest of the way home. Probably less than two miles from where I pulled over, anyway.

As soon as I reached for the door handle, a big jacked-up truck roared up with its high beams on and parked behind me. Blinded by the bright lights shining in my rearview mirror, I reached over and hit my door lock button, praying to God it was a little old lady with a hankering for masculine monster trucks.

The door on the truck opened and a tall, broad, and bulky figure — definitely male — appeared in my side mirror, just out of reach of the lights and shadowed by the darkness of the surrounding forest. He headed toward my driver's side door, walking with the measured, deliberate steps of Satan's hockey player, Jason Voorhees.

Frozen with fear, I sat there staring straight ahead, yet watching him from my peripheral vision as he stopped next to my door. He paused. My heart beat faster, until he finally leaned down and tapped on the window.

Then I jumped.

"Anna…? You okay?"

Oh, for goodness sakes. This wasn't happening. I twisted my head to see Cowboy's smiling face staring back at me. I cracked open the window. "Um, I'm fine, thanks."

His smile faded. "Really? Because you don't look fine.

You look like you have a flat. Want me to change the tire for you?"

God. He's going to think I'm an idiot. I rolled the window back up, then reached over and unlocked the door before shoving it open and crawling out. "I don't have a spare. Well, I do…but I took it out of my trunk last Saturday."

His brows gathered over the bridge of his nose and he frowned. "Why would you do something like that?"

Not appreciating the condescending tone, Cowboy. "If you must know," I said, "I went to the flea market over the weekend to pick up some used books. There wasn't going to be enough room in the trunk for all the boxes, so I removed the spare before I left and forgot to put it back in."

"Where is it now?"

"It's lying on the ground next to my front porch. I figured I didn't need it and I was right…er, until now."

Cowboy shook his head and sighed in blatant disapproval. "You *always* need a spare."

Yeah, no kidding. "Yes, I guess you could say I learned my lesson. Thanks for not rubbing it in," I said.

A tiny smirk lifted the corner of his mouth. "Come on. I'll take you home."

"That isn't necessary."

"Oh, yeah? What would you like for me to do? Leave you out here all alone in the boonies so some weird fella in a hockey mask can slice ya to bits?"

Guess I wasn't the only one who thought like that. I smiled lightly. "Well, okay, when you put it that way."

I reached inside the car, grabbed my keys, my cell phone, and my purse, then hit the door lock button before swinging it shut. As I turned to face him, I caught the scowl Cowboy was wearing. "What now?"

"You didn't have to lock it."

"Yes, I did. I didn't want to come back tomorrow to find my radio had been stolen."

"Way out here? What do you take us country boys for…a bunch of hoodlums?"

I blinked at him in confusion. "But you were the one who just said you weren't going to leave me out here so a guy in a hockey mask could slice me into pieces."

"Yeah, but I didn't say he was going to steal the radio out of your car first. Christ, woman, give us a little bit of credit."

I didn't have much of an argument for that logic, so I bit my tongue.

He led the way around the back of my Cavalier to the passenger side of his much larger, jacked-up red Chevy. He opened the door and spent a moment clearing off the seat before turning back to me.

I started past him toward the cab, but Cowboy unexpectedly stopped me in my tracks by planting two large hands on either side of my waist. Caught off guard, I stood there staring up at him with wide, unblinking eyes, unsure as to what the hell he was doing. And from the way he hesitated himself, I wasn't sure if he knew, either.

The movement had brought his face close to mine, so close I felt his breath caressing my lips. The warmth of his fingers seared through the thin fabric of my skirt, but it was no match for the heated look he gave me. Moonlit eyes stared at me, twinkling with what seemed to be a mischievous thought, judging by the way the corner of his mouth lifted.

Was he thinking about kissing me?

Before I could contemplate the idea any further, Cowboy lifted me easily into the truck with one quick, smooth motion. *Guess not.* An unexpected surge of disappointment ran through me. But why? It wasn't like I wanted him to kiss me. *Liar.* The thought flashed through my mind so quickly it annoyed me. "I'm not an invalid, you know. I could have climbed in without assistance."

His hands, still on my waist, tightened their grip. "The last thing I needed was you lifting that skirt of yours to climb in while I was standing behind you." His eyes smoldered and his tone deepened. "Otherwise, you'd have something much bigger to worry about than whether or not someone took your radio."

His potent words delivered a pulsing ache straight to my nether regions, and the hot tang of desire bubbled in my throat. I swallowed hard as I buckled up, but didn't dare let out a breath until he shut the passenger door and strolled around to the driver's side. Once settled into his seat, Cowboy strapped himself in, and put the truck into gear without looking over at me.

"Where do you live?" he asked.

"County Road 1500. It's not too far out of your way, is it?"

"Nope. No problem. I pass right by there on my way home. If you want help with your tire in the morning, I could always swing by and—"

"No, that's okay," I said quickly. "I'll manage. Thanks, anyway."

"Suit yourself. But just in case, take this," he said, grabbing a business card from his console and pressing it into my palm. "My cell number is at the bottom." He cocked his left arm over the steering wheel and raised one brow. "So are you going to tell me what freaked you out earlier?"

Not no, but hell no. I bit into my bottom lip, then said, "It was nothing."

He measured me with his eyes, then grinned. "Yeah, I didn't think so." He checked his rearview mirror and eased onto the highway. No doubt his bullshit meter had just rocketed sky-high.

The awkward silence that followed made me self-conscious. What the heck were we supposed to talk about now? The weather? Politics or religion? My lack of a brain every time I was around him? *God, what's the matter with me?*

"Um, Bobbie Jo mentioned that you made captain at the fire department a while back," I said, using his promotion as an icebreaker. "Congratulations."

I expected him to smile, but instead, his brows furrowed, and large grooves formed in his forehead. He kept his eyes on the road. "Three months ago, to be exact."

He hesitated, as if he were contemplating not saying more, then continued anyway. "But I've had to take on the role of acting chief because the man who promoted me, Chief Swanson, died in a fire the same night. Guess you could say I haven't felt much like celebrating."

My stomach clenched into a knot and my heart shriveled as a dull ache crept inside my chest. It was as if someone fisted my heart in their hand and gave it a hard squeeze. "I'm sorry to hear that." And I meant it.

"Chief Swanson threw me a promotion party that afternoon. Then sometime before midnight, several 911 calls came in reporting a structure fire at his home address."

I didn't even try to speak. My throat had caved in, my natural physical reaction each time anyone mentioned anything about a blaze. What would I say—*I don't want to know?* No. That would be too harsh. Instead, I closed my eyes and hoped like hell nothing else tumbled out of his mouth.

"One of them was a neighbor who'd seen smoke coming from the rear section of the home. Engine one—the truck I was in—was the first one on the scene. We—" Cowboy stopped talking, so I opened my eyes and glanced at him. He ran a hand over his distraught face, as if he were mentally reliving the moment. "We tried to enter the house to search for survivors and fight the fire from the interior, but the flames had already spread into the walls and roof."

Why was he telling me this? According to him, I was nothing more than a stranger, even if I *had* technically met him before. So why ramble on and disclose things that were obviously so upsetting and personal to him?

"The conditions forced us back outside, where we stayed until the fire had been declared fully contained. Three hours passed before the fire marshal allowed us to search inside. Downstairs, we found the corpse of…a man."

Jesus, please stop. I wanted to tell him not to go on, that I'd heard enough, but my thick tongue wouldn't work, so I sat there cringing while he kept on talking.

"Upstairs, we found Chief Swanson's wife, Janet." His fingers gripped the steering wheel tighter. "Dead. With her wrists bound behind her back."

I gasped and covered my mouth. *Oh, dear God, the chief didn't…*

It was only the second time he'd looked directly at me since he began the story. "I know what you're thinking,

Anna. It's the same damn thing everyone thinks. But Chief Swanson didn't do it. He loved his wife. They'd just gotten back together after being separated for almost six months, and it was the happiest I'd seen him."

Confused, I lowered my gaze and finally found my voice. "P-people sometimes do…things."

"Not this," he said, adamantly shaking his head. "He wouldn't have hurt Janet like that. Maybe he wasn't a perfect husband, but the chief and I were good friends. I spent a lot of time with that man. I know he didn't do it." He sighed heavily. "Besides, none of it makes any sense. Why would Chief Swanson tie up his wife and leave her upstairs while he doused himself with an accelerant and…"

I wasn't sure if Cowboy didn't finish the sentence because he couldn't say the words or just didn't want to. Either way, I was relieved. "I'm so sorry. I'm sure it was tough. For *you*, I mean."

He nodded and turned onto my road. "The other firefighters are all part of my extended family. It's like someone telling me that my brother killed himself and his own wife when I know he didn't." He released a hard breath. "I just can't prove it."

I gaped at him, recalling the book I'd helped him locate. "That's what Bobbie Jo was talking about earlier?"

"There are no other leads. I have to know what happened that night."

Up ahead, the small white house I'd rented came into view. I nodded at it. "That's where I live, the one with the blue shutters."

He slowed, veered off the road, and rolled to a stop in front of my driveway to let me out. "Chief Swanson and his wife lived up the road, only about half a mile."

I remembered passing by the charred rubble of a home nearby and even stopped to take a closer look. But, at the time, I didn't know it had belonged to the chief. Dread flooded over me as torturous images flickered through my mind. I didn't need or want any more sleepless nights than I already had.

Instead, I wanted to get out of the truck and walk away from the horrible pictures flashing through my head. Get as far away from them as I could. But I sat there for a second longer, feeling like I owed Cowboy some sort of comforting thought in return for the roadside assistance he had given me.

"No matter what happened to your chief, I'm sorry for your loss. It had to be devastating for you to lose someone so close."

Cowboy gave me a quick nod. "You lost someone, too, right? In a fire?"

For some strange reason, I wanted to answer his question. But the moment I opened my mouth to do so, nothing came out. *Damn it.* Frustrated, I looked down and twisted my fingers together.

"You don't have to say anything. I just wanted you to know I understand and you're not alone."

I glanced back up, meeting his unwavering gaze. Then I realized what he'd been trying to do. He'd hoped that by talking about his traumatic experience, I would open up to him about mine. "I...can't."

"If you ever want to talk about it, I might be able to help. Who better than a fireman, right?"

"Thank you," I said softly. "I'll keep that in mind."

As I reached for the door handle, he cocked his head and said, "You don't like me, do you?"

Oh, hell. What could I say to that? I couldn't forget how Cowboy had snapped me out of my panicky state and suppressed my inner demons. Like some kind of fairy tale with a brave knight who had courageously slain the maiden's dragon and won her hand, as well as her heart. But I didn't believe in fairy tales. Or knights in shining armor.

Because the one man I trusted—a man who swore he was saving me—ended up taking the one thing I loved most in this world. That knowledge left me with a dilemma. And it had Cowboy's name written all over it. "It's not that I don't like you. It's just...well, I'm a little quiet, that's all." And I had no intention of starting something I couldn't finish.

"A little?" Cowboy chuckled at that. "Sweetheart, if you got any quieter, I'd check your pulse." He smiled at me. "You know, I joke that Austin looks like a turtle, but he's got nothing on you."

I blinked with confusion. "Did you just refer to me as a turtle?"

"Yep. That's what you remind me of. Judging by the way you acted tonight, I'd say you have a tendency to protect yourself by pulling in your limbs and head." Then he grinned sinfully. "Bet I'd have one hell of a time breaking you out of your shell."

I could only imagine why he'd think *that* would be fun. But I didn't want him—or anyone, really—scraping at my innermost layers. That wasn't what I moved here for. In less than six months, I'd be long gone. So the last thing I needed was to fool around with a handsome, exciting playboy. Especially one who was only looking for me to stroke his ego.

Probably among other things.

"Well, Cowboy," I said, shaking my wrist loose from his grip and hopping out of the truck's cab. "I guess that's just one more thing you'll never know about me. Thank you for the ride home."

I closed the truck door and stepped away before turning to wave good-bye, but I didn't miss the look he gave me. I'd only meant to discourage him from pursuing this venture any further. Unused to being shot down, Cowboy's stubborn eyes narrowed and one corner of his mouth tipped up, as if I represented some sort of intriguing challenge. One he intended to overcome.

To get away from the scrutiny of his riveting green eyes, I quickly spun and headed for the house.

He motored down the window on the passenger door. "Hey, Anna," he called out from behind me. "You're still going to hold that book for me, aren't you?"

I stopped halfway through the yard and glanced back. "Of course I am."

"Good. See you tomorrow, then…*Sparky*." He flashed me a smug grin, then drove away.

Waves of regret crashed against the barrier of my heart, breaching my defenses, and creating tidal pools of sorrow. I barely cleared the doorway into my home when I bent over, squeezed my arms across my middle, and felt hot tears streaking down my face. Not only had he used a nickname that had taken me back to a time I wasn't fond of visiting, but…

He remembered me.

Chapter Three

It was all so bare.

No flowers. No trinkets left in his honor. No proof of the lives he'd impacted. Only unruly weeds and climbing vines that had taken over the gravesite, covering the bottom half of the granite marker.

I avoided the stinging bull thistle while carefully clearing the other invading weeds, then removed the vines that clung to the solid gray headstone, revealing the rest of the sandblasted letters beneath his name that had been enhanced with black lithichrome paint.

In honor of a husband, a friend, and a hero.

Saddened by the words, I lifted myself from the ground and trudged ten feet away to gather some wildflowers into a nice bouquet. White heath aster and blue-eyed grass were the closest, but I bypassed them, opting for the Indian blankets I had spotted a yard away. They looked similar to a sunflower, but were smaller and had bright reddish-orange petals with yellow tips. I took my time gathering a small bundle, and with my gaze trained on the grass in front of me, solemnly strolled back to the grave.

I kneeled down once more, arranging the flowers neatly together before placing them at the base of the stone. I'd been there for almost half an hour and hadn't cried once, but that one little good deed filled my heart with sorrow and had my eyes brimming with blinding tears. The only reason I'd chosen those particular flowers was because they were also sometimes referred to as "firewheels" and I thought it was a gesture Chief Swanson would appreciate.

"I'm so sorry," I said, kissing my fingertips and pressing them lightly to his gravestone.

It wasn't until that moment I felt *his* presence behind me. Or maybe I'd detected the vibrations of his irritation. Because when I glanced over my shoulder and shaded my eyes from the sun, Cowboy was standing there, holding his white Stetson in a death grip, and frowning at me like I'd just slapped his mother.

"What are you doing here?" he growled.

I pushed myself off the ground and straightened, dusting my hands together to remove any loose debris. "Just paying my respects."

"Oh, really?" He nodded to Chief Swanson's grave. "Thought you'd only been in town for a few weeks? Last night, you failed to mention you knew the chief."

"That's because I didn't know him." *Not really, anyway.*

He gave me a strange look, one I assumed meant he wasn't buying it. "I just saw you kiss the man's grave and tell him you were sorry."

Christ, how long had he been standing there? "I *am*

sorry. Sorry something so tragic happened to him. Is that a crime?"

Cowboy's brow raised in suspicion. "No, but do you normally visit the graves of people you don't know?"

"When I feel it's necessary, yes." I moved past him, heading in the direction of my car. "Now if you'll excuse me, I have to go home and change my clothes before I go to work."

His stride was much longer than mine, so it didn't take him more than a second to catch up to me. "If you know anything about this case, you need to tell me."

I kept walking as he slowed his pace to match mine. "I told you already. I didn't know Chief Swanson."

"Yet I still find it odd that you're at a cemetery visiting a man you *claim* you didn't know." Cowboy placed his hand on my arm to still me. "I'm looking for his brother, Anna."

"Good for you."

"I'm serious, damn it!" His grip tightened, and my gaze lowered to his hand clasped around my elbow. With a frustrated sigh, he released me and ran his fingers through his thick sand-colored hair before slapping the white Stetson back onto his head. "Look, I promised the chief if something ever happened to him I would find Ned Swanson and hand deliver a letter to him. If you know anything—"

I scowled at him. "I told you I don't. I don't know this Ned guy, and I didn't know Chief Swanson. Why do you keep pushing me? I have no reason to hide anything from you."

"Oh, yeah? You didn't show up at the station this morning like I'd asked."

I rolled my eyes and started walking again with him on my heels. "That's funny, since I don't recall being *asked*.

I believe it was more of a direct order." I gave him a nonchalant shrug and silently thanked my lucky stars I had a good reason for not showing up. Answering his questions wasn't something I looked forward to. "I was busy. Sorry."

"Don't seem all that sorry," he stated, just as we reached the entrance to the cemetery. Our vehicles were parked in the grass of the circle drive, his massive pickup bullying my tiny Cavalier from behind. "If anything, I'd say you look relieved."

His accusatory tone sent my frustration swarming like bees fresh out of a fallen hive. "And you, *Captain*, shouldn't be so surprised I didn't show up. You knew I had to fix the tire on my car." I stopped when I reached my driver's side and cocked my head at him. "Am I right?"

"You are," he agreed.

"Then you know why I didn't show."

Cowboy glanced down and gave the new front tire a light kick. "Well, it's fixed now, it seems." He circled around me from behind, then leaned against the rear door next to me, allowing his mere proximity to smother me. "Who took care of it for you? One of the guys from Tony's shop over on Main Street?"

"Not exactly," I said, shaking my head. "I called Bobbie Jo to give me a ride into town, but she was already at the pediatrician's with Austin. So she called Jake and asked him to help me. He took the old tire off and drove me into town to buy a new one. Even put it on the car for me."

"Is he okay?"

My eyes widened. "Now you're accusing me of doing something to Jake?"

He grinned with amusement. "I imagine Jake's a big

enough boy that he can take care of himself. I was talking about my godson," Cowboy clarified. "Austin's not sick or anything, is he?"

Oh. Right. "No, I guess not. Bobbie Jo said it was just a well-baby exam."

"That's good." But Cowboy's words didn't match his expression as his brows knitted together. "Last night I gave you a card with my cell phone number. Any reason why you didn't call me instead of Jake?"

I shook my head again. "*I* didn't call anyone. Bobbie Jo did, remember?"

"Well, why didn't she call me?"

"I don't know. I guess that's a question for Bobbie Jo." I pulled my door open and moved closer to get in.

His arm shot out across the doorway, blocking me from sitting down. I turned my head to look at him and watched another grin tug at the corner of his mouth. "You have a little something…" He lifted his free hand and swept his calloused thumb across my bottom lip. "Right there."

My mouth fell open involuntarily at the intimate gesture. At first, I thought he'd made the whole thing up — possibly trying to charm me once again — but then I remembered touching my fingers to my lips at the gravesite. I glanced at my hands, which were still dirty from pulling weeds and picking flowers.

Reaching into my pocket, I pulled out a tissue and dabbed at my lips. "Um, thank you."

He dropped his arm and straightened his posture, suddenly looking very official. "We still need to go over what happened last night so I can add it to the report."

Guess he was trying to charm me, after all. I glanced at

the thin gold watch on my left wrist. "I can't right now. I'm going to be late for work." I slid into the driver's seat of my car and closed the door, looking back at him through the open window.

"It's only going to take a few minutes."

"Sorry," I said, starting my car. "The director is only covering for me until noon, and I still have to go home and change." The denim overalls I wore were comfortable, but way too casual to be deemed professional work attire.

He huffed out an irritated breath. "That fire happened only minutes after you put something in the dumpster. I have questions that need answers."

"No, what you're really saying is you think I started the fire last night."

Cowboy's jaw tightened as he gritted his teeth. "No, that's *not* what I'm saying."

"But I am your number one suspect, correct?"

His eyes burrowed into me and a muscle twitched in his jaw. "Look, this isn't some sort of witch hunt. I'm just doing my damn job."

"Fine. I'll get in touch with you...*after* I've spoken to a lawyer. In the meantime, I'm going to work so that I can do *my* job. Good day, *Captain*."

As I pulled away, he cursed under his breath, but I sighed with relief. At least he hadn't called me Sparky again. How did he even know about that terrible nickname, anyway?

After driving home to change and grab a quick sandwich, I made it to the library right on time. The director had a meeting at City Hall she needed to attend, so the moment I arrived, she made a beeline for the door.

Only ten minutes passed before Cowboy stormed into the library, hands fisted at his sides and a sour expression on his face. "Would you quit running away from me while I'm trying to talk to you?"

"As far as *I* was concerned, we were done talking. I told you I had to change and get to work."

His hard gaze immediately lowered, taking in the sight of my calf-length yellow sundress and white canvas tennis shoes, before darting back up to my face. "Do you always dress like this?" The way his eyes widened told me he hadn't meant to verbalize his thoughts and he was just as surprised by the unintentional insult as I was. "I mean...er, sorry."

So what if my work clothes looked like something out of Sandra Dee's closet? It wasn't like I dressed to please him. Actually, it was just the opposite. I dressed this way to keep men like him away from me. It was an added bonus that it was for his own safety...even if I kept that information to myself.

I shook my head passively, then started past him, insulted by his comment. "It's fine," I said drily.

He reached out and gently touched my arm to stop my movement. "Anna, I didn't mean that the way it came out. I just meant you have a good figure. I can see it, despite your clothes."

Silently, I glared at him.

"Uh, I mean...I can see through your clothes." Then he cringed and breathed out a few expletives.

"Good to know," I told him, my tone suddenly drought-worthy. I snatched up the book on the counter that he'd given me to hold the night before and shoved it into his chest. "Here's your book, superhero. Now maybe you can use your telepathic abilities to read my mind." I walked away from him and kept going until I'd crossed the room and put some distance between us.

From there, I studied him inconspicuously as I pretended to straighten the books on the shelf before me. I rolled my eyes. *Good with the ladies, my ass!*

Cowboy rubbed the back of his neck and shook his head as he carried the book to the nearest table and sat down. He opened it to where he must've left off the night before. Once he looked determined to focus on the task at hand, I reluctantly circled back and returned to the circulation desk... and to my own work. The stack of romance novels I'd devoured over the past week and brought back to the library were piled high on the desk, waiting to be checked back in.

During my teen years, romantic fiction had become my favorite genre, mostly because it was so much better than my own reality. The library's shelves brimmed with romance-filled tales of brave heroes slaying fire-breathing dragons and sweeping fair maidens off their feet. But I didn't need a dashing hero on a white horse to save me from anything. I could ride my own damn horse, thank you very much.

I'd given up on finding love. Not that I'd ever done much in the way of searching for it. With love, came loss. And I wasn't willing to lose—or readily give—another piece of myself to anyone. I'd seen for myself what kind of damage a man could do to a woman's mind, body, and soul. Much less a girl's heart.

A half hour went by before an elderly lady from the Genealogy Society approached my desk to schedule their monthly meetings for the Rotary Room. I smiled at her, then spotted Cowboy leering at me from ten feet away. Somehow, I had unknowingly blipped back onto his radar. My stomach twisted with nervousness as my trembling fingers wrote down the meeting dates the woman gave me.

After she walked away, I busied myself by filing forms into the bottom cabinet. Okay, so maybe I was ducking to keep him from looking at me. Whatever.

A few wispy strands of my hair slipped free from the clip on the back of my head and hung down in my face while I worked. As I pushed one back, I remembered the way Cowboy's fingers had grazed my cheek the night before and shivered. His slight touch had left me with a pleasant feeling, but it wasn't something I could allow myself to indulge in. Part of why I was steering clear of him and coming off downright antisocial like an ungrateful shrew. It was easier that way.

As heavy footsteps approached, I straightened in my chair, bumping my head on the desk. I winced and gave it a quick rub, glancing over to see if anyone else—basically Cowboy—had noticed. He tipped back in his chair, an amused grin playing on his perfectly stupid lips. The prick.

Ignoring his smug look, I smiled sweetly to the gentleman standing at my desk and offered my assistance. He was one of our regular card-holders and I'd seen him almost daily since I'd started there. Once I finished helping him check out a crime novel he'd reserved, the kind old man gave me a quick pat on my hand to thank me and moved along.

I glanced back to Cowboy and caught an odd look on his confused face. It was a what-the-hell expression, if I'd ever seen one. Setting his teeth, he rose from his seat, picked up his book, and headed in my direction.

My gaze immediately darted back to my computer screen.

"Mind if I pester you for a minute?" he asked.

"Did you have a question…about the book?" I kept my eyes forward and my tone polite and professional.

"I have a lot of questions, actually, but none are book-related."

"Then I'm busy," I replied, not showing even marginal interest in him.

"Anna…?" When I didn't answer him, he reached across the desk and brushed my arm, sending my nervous system into overdrive. I jolted out of my chair, which made his mouth contort into a perplexed frown. "Did I do something wrong?"

"No, I just…don't want you to touch me." *Jeez. When did I become such a liar?* "Now if you'll excuse me…" I walked away from the counter and headed down one of the aisles before he had a chance to follow me. I weaved through the maze of bookshelves until I came to a dead end in the back corner of the library.

Breathing heavily, I hid behind a bookcase, monitoring him discreetly through the shelves as he combed the aisles searching for me. I knew it was silly to hide. Like a child, really. But I needed a moment to calm my nerves and build some much needed courage, which only made me feel more foolish.

It was the same reaction I'd had at eighteen when I'd spent two weeks working as an activities coordinator at a nearby summer camp. Bobbie Jo had been a counselor, as well as one of my bunkmates, and the two of us had hit it off.

That's where I'd met Cowboy.

The guys' quarters sat on the opposite end of camp, but first chance Bobbie Jo had, she introduced me to "her boys," as she called them. Jake had been her boyfriend at the time, but the others—Ox, Judd, and Cowboy—were her best friends. It wasn't until later I found out she'd roped them all into applying as a counselor so they could spend their last two weeks together before Jake left for college.

Upon meeting them, all of them were nice, of course. But Cowboy had been the one who stuck out in my mind all these years.

Right after I'd stammered my way through the mortifying introductions, one of the other female volunteers had stopped by with a camera and asked us all to smile for a group photo. Without hesitation, Cowboy had winked at me, slung his heavy arm over my shoulders, pulled me close into his warm body, and grinned devilishly for the camera. That was the moment I'd fallen for Prince Charming himself.

After the photo, when he tried to disengage his arm, his gold watch had caught on my shirt sleeve, lifting it slightly and revealing a small patch of red skin on the inside of my arm. With heated cheeks, I'd quickly yanked my sleeve down and tried to hide it by fidgeting with my clothes. It was too late.

Cowboy had noticed and said, "What's wrong with your arm? You get into some poison sumac or something?"

When I didn't respond, he shrugged it off and flirted with the cute blonde behind the camera. I'd wanted to talk to him, make him see *me*, but hated the idea of drawing attention to myself. So I said nothing.

After that incident, I'd clammed up whenever he was near, which had only been a few more times. I decided avoiding him altogether would be my best option if I wanted to form coherent sentences for the duration of my stay. But that didn't stop me from spending the next two weeks stealing glances at him from the shadows of my cabin window while every girl at camp threw themselves in his direction.

When camp had come to an end, I'd exchanged information with my new friend, Bobbie Jo, and over the years we'd kept in touch, sending pictures and letters back and forth. That's how I'd received my own copy of that very photo—the same picture that had sat on my nightstand in a wooden frame for the last ten years.

Ridiculous, I know.

I'd told myself I kept it out where I could see it because it was the only picture I had of Bobbie Jo and I together. But in it, I'd gazed up at Cowboy with wide, admiring eyes and a full-on smile, while he looked straight ahead, unaware of the pitiful, lonely girl at his side. *God, I'm pathetic.* The arm slung over my shoulders in the photo had meant nothing to him.

Forcing out a deep breath, I slouched against the shelves and shook my head. So what if I felt foolish. Maybe I *was* a fool. After all, what woman in her right mind would still get butterflies in her stomach from just being near a man she'd had a crush on ten years earlier? Especially when the same man all but accused her of arson.

I sighed. *Me, that's who.*

"Do I have bad breath or something?"

I jumped, flailing my arms, then clutched my heaving chest. I wheeled around to see Cowboy leaning lazily against the shelf as he eyed me curiously. "Good Lord. Don't scare me like that!"

A triumphant grin played on his lips as he stepped closer. In an evasive maneuver, I tried to hurry past him, hoping to escape with my dignity somewhat intact, but he stepped in my path. "Anna, wait. I just want to talk to you for a minute."

I stopped, but refused to look him in the eye. "What do you want?"

"Well, to start off, I'd like to know what I did to deserve the cold shoulder from you. If I upset you by calling you Sparky last night — "

"No," I said, glancing down at my feet. "It has nothing to do with that."

It wasn't like Cowboy even knew the significance behind the camp nickname the other counselors had teased me with. He hadn't been there to witness my freak-out the night of the bonfire. Thank goodness.

Instead, he'd been sucking face with Kelly Deter in the woods. With both hands up her skirt, according to her testimony the next day. Bobbie Jo hadn't been at the bonfire, either. Probably because she'd been doing the same thing with Jake.

"If I offended you last night by asking you to come down to the station…"

I shook my head. "I wasn't offended. I just found the whole thing unnecessary. I didn't start the fire."

"Never said you did."

"No, but you insinuated I *could have*, which was close enough. I have no idea why you'd even think that, anyway. Do I look like the kind of person who goes around starting fires?"

He held up his hand, showing me the book on household fire accelerants. "You knew exactly where this book was located. The *exact* location."

"It's my job to—"

"I also remembered where else I've seen you," he interrupted, crossing his arms. "Last week, you were at the big brush fire we had out on County Road 320."

I sighed. I hadn't realized he'd spotted me. "I was driving past when I saw the smoke. I hardly think that's a crime, though. Lots of other people were stopping to take a look as well."

"Yeah, but you're the only one who climbed on the hood of her car with a pair of binoculars. Let's just say you stood out in the crowd."

I mentally cringed, but kept my face even. "So what? I was just curious. Nothing wrong with that."

"Well, add all of those things in with you dodging my questions and refusing to come down to the station, only to have me find you at the cemetery visiting a grave of a man you *supposedly* didn't know—one who happened to be my chief—and I think you can see why anyone would be a little suspicious."

"I didn't know him!" I whispered loudly.

He shrugged. "Maybe you did, maybe you didn't. But since you're avoiding my questions, it's not like I would know that, now would I?"

My eyes narrowed. "Fine. You want to ask me something? Then do it."

"Anything?"

I couldn't stop the irritation from leaching into my voice. "Yes, anything."

Cowboy didn't hesitate. "Why would you visit a dead man you don't know?" He lifted a brow, waiting for my answer.

My heart pounded furiously against my rib cage, as if it were sounding an alarm to alert my brain to Cowboy's underlying motive. He was obviously trying to make a connection between me and the chief. As suspicious as he already was, I'd be an idiot to give him any ammunition to use against me.

But I had said I would answer, and if anything, I was a woman of my word. Here goes nothing. "I—"

A loud siren suddenly pierced the air, rendering me silent. It was coming from the black pager on his belt loop. Thank heavens. His cell phone chirped three times in a row, and Cowboy glanced at the information on the screen. He cursed under his breath and handed me the book he held. "There's a bad accident out on the highway. We'll finish our conversation later."

He turned and, not looking back, hurried for the exit. As I watched him disappear from sight, only one thought entered my mind.

God, I hoped not.

Chapter Four

"Thanks again for inviting me to the chili cook-off," I said as I climbed into the passenger seat of Bobbie Jo's tan Ford truck.

"No problem. I thought it would be nice for the new girl in town to meet some of the other locals." She pulled out of the driveway and cruised down the dark narrow back roads, lined with thick red oaks and barbed wire fences.

Coming from the opposite direction, a car's headlights shined directly into the truck's cab. I glanced into the empty backseat and frowned. "You didn't bring Austin with you?"

"No, I was afraid the noise and lights might be too much for him, so my mom is keeping an eye on him. When I get back, I'm sure he'll be sleeping soundly in her arms. She hardly ever puts him down. Spoils him rotten."

"That's sweet she helps you with him."

Bobbie Jo nodded. "I don't know what I'd do without her. I mean, I guess I'd figure it out, but I'm glad I don't have to. If only Jeremy would…"

"Jeremy would what? Come around more, share the responsibilities, support his child, or maybe grow up and be a man?"

She grinned. "All of the above."

Up ahead, the bustling fairgrounds came into view and my eyes widened. Bright and colorful carnival lights flashed as swarms of people milled around beneath them. Bobbie Jo slowed the truck to turn left into the parking area where a man wearing a fluorescent orange vest directed traffic with a yellow cone-shaped wand. With a sly wink, he waved us straight ahead where there was a closer parking space. Bobbie Jo gave him a friendly smile.

Being raised in the anonymity of larger cities, I found it fascinating that the people recognized and knew each other so well in this close-knit town. From my understanding, most had lived their whole lives there, growing up together, then raising their families alongside one another. As new residents moved in, they were taken under the locals' wings and treated as one of their own.

I should know. I'd only been the librarian for two weeks, and I'd already been brought more home-baked goods than I could stand to eat. All the older women had formed their own unofficial welcoming party. Such a lovely gesture of the inherent kindness and goodness of the people in Liberty County.

Too bad I'd have to leave it behind in a few months.

Bobbie Jo maneuvered her pickup into a tight space where we both had to squeeze out just to ensure we didn't hit the truck doors on the vehicles on either side. We met at the tailgate. "Not much room to park," she said with a laugh.

"These things are always so packed."

"You were lucky your secret admirer over there reserved you a closer spot," I said, motioning to the guy directing the traffic.

"Fred? Nah, he's just a friend from school." She wrinkled her nose. "I can't bring myself to date a guy I grew up with. It'd be like dating my cousin or something. Gross."

I laughed and glanced toward the entrance.

Even from the parking area, the loud music vibrated inside my chest and something sinfully sweet permeated the air. My mouth watered. "I've never been to anything like this before."

"Ever?"

I shook my head. "I'm pretty sure my stepfather was allergic to anything fun. I…" I hesitated, not sure if I should say anything more.

Years ago, I'd vaguely mentioned to Bobbie Jo how I'd lost both of my parents in a tragic accident, yet I'd never gone into specifics about my strained relationship with my stepfather. But I didn't want to hold back too much. She was the first person I'd ever felt close to…and would also be the last.

"I went to the library for hours after school every day just to avoid going home. I never admitted to him that I enjoyed my time at the library because I was afraid he'd put a stop to it." Her eyes widened, and I realized how it must've sounded. "He didn't abuse me or anything," I quickly added. "My stepfather was just a lost, lonely man who lived every day of his dull life in a dismal state."

"God, that's terrible. He sounds like a miserable guy." Bobbie Jo paused thoughtfully. "Almost makes me wonder why he let you work at the camp all those years ago. I guess he thought it was all work and no play."

"Actually, I was eighteen and living on my own by then. He didn't have a say in what I did."

"You were living on your own...at eighteen? Jesus, Anna. I didn't know that. We were roomies and you never said a word."

I shrugged nonchalantly. "I wasn't going to burden you with my problems. Besides, it was fine. I was better off on my own. It may have been a little lonely for me at times, but meeting you at camp was one of the best things that ever happened to me. I wouldn't change a thing."

Then I remembered that our time together, as well as our friendship, was going to be coming to an end soon and my heart sank. My vision blurred slightly from the building tears threatening to fall.

Apparently, I wasn't the only one. Bobbie Jo's glistening eyes shone brightly in the blinking lights. "Now stop that before you make me cry."

I blinked back the moisture pooling in my eyes and offered her a sincere smile. Bobbie Jo was the only true friend I'd ever really had...even though I'd never shared my secrets with her. She had no clue our friendship would be ending, without warning, in just a few short months when I dropped off the face of the planet and moved to a place no one would ever find me. But it wasn't like I had a choice in the matter.

She giggled gleefully as she looped her arm through mine and dragged me toward the entrance. "Come on, you're going to love this."

We strolled into the fairgrounds as Bobbie Jo explained all about how a chili cook-off worked. The contestants were composed of teams from various local clubs and organizations. They gave themselves fun, clever names and even dressed the part. For example, the ladies of the Genealogy Society were dressed as sexy saloon girls and called themselves the "Red Hot Ladies," while the men from the Moose Lodge were dressed as meat market butchers and called themselves the "Blazin' Butts."

I couldn't help but laugh.

Since it was Friday night, the early start gave each group a chance to perfect their homemade dish before judgment day because each team's chili would be judged by a panel of pre-selected officials in a blind taste test on Saturday afternoon. I had to work the next day, so I wouldn't be able to attend, but it didn't matter. Throughout the entire weekend, they sold samples to the masses to earn money for their local club's individual fundraisers. Which meant we could be unofficial taste-testers while donating money to great local causes.

We started at the first chili vendor and worked our way down the line, purchasing small sample cups from each and comparing one's flavor, texture, and heat level to the next. The degrees in temperature ranged from sweet to spicy to holy-crap-I-think-they-slipped-me-a-habanero, and they all tasted amazingly different. Who knew there were so many different ways to make chili?

As we reached the last vendor, I froze in my tracks. Apparently, the firefighters had a booth and their long line brimmed with an overabundance of female customers. The firemen's team name was "Too Hot To Handle" and they were serving chili in their bunker gear. While they wore pants, suspenders, boots, and even their helmets, the brawny men all seemed to be conveniently missing their shirts. And the ladies didn't seem to mind.

That's when I recognized a familiar face behind the counter.

Mandy stood on the far side of the booth, beneath the tent, wearing the same shirtless outfit as the men, although a bikini top had been added to her ensemble. Not that the two little black triangles covered much more than her suspenders did.

She stood in front of a folding table lined with several stainless steel chafing dishes and used a ladle to transfer chili into small Styrofoam cups on a tray. She glanced up and smiled, then motioned for us to come around and join her inside the tent.

Bobbie Jo led the way through the hoards of half-naked firemen, while I followed closely behind her, carefully dodging muscular chests and bulging biceps. "Hey, Mandy," Bobbie Jo said as we approached. "Where's Cowboy? I figured he'd be here with you guys."

"He was here earlier, but he left. Said something about having a few women to entertain," Mandy responded with a wide grin. "By now, I'm pretty sure he's a little...*preoccupied*, if you know what I mean." She shrugged her brows a few times and then gave us a sly wink.

I mentally rolled my eyes.

A few women? My God! How many women does one man need? Then I remembered it was Cowboy we were talking about. Sadly enough, I really wasn't all that shocked.

Folding my arms, I huffed out an irritated breath.

"Oh, sorry," Mandy said, cringing as she stared back at me. "Anna, right? So you and Cowboy, huh?"

I choked on my saliva. "Um...w-what?"

Bobbie Jo laughed at my reaction, but Mandy seemed almost surprised by it. "Oh. When I saw you two at the library, you looked rather cozy, and then he mentioned he'd taken you home, so I assumed…"

All the blood in my body rushed to my cheeks. "Oh, God no." I shook my head, denying the ridiculous charge. "We're just…friends."

Mandy didn't look convinced. In fact, she smiled, as if she were under the distinct impression Cowboy couldn't possibly be "just friends" with anyone of the female persuasion.

"Heads up," a man called out. "Hot stuff coming through…and I'm not referring to the chili, ladies."

I turned to see a beefy fireman carrying a steaming pot toward me. Realizing I stood directly in his path, I muttered a quiet apology and scooted closer to Mandy's table to let him pass.

He veered around us and stopped at the end of the table, poured the bubbling chili into a metal pan, then covered it with a lid. The moment he glanced up, his eyes suddenly widened. "Oh, shit!"

Everyone around us stopped in their tracks and looked in our direction. Correction: *my* direction. Their mouths gaped open and their eyes bugged out. I blinked back at them, oblivious as to what caused their reactions, until one of the men pointed just to the right of me and shouted, "Fire!"

I wheeled around and gasped at the sight before me.

A pile of scorched napkins lay scattered across the tabletop while orange flames danced across them like a wanton stripper. Unable to move, I stood there, staring at the one thing I feared most.

Thankfully, Bobbie Jo hooked her arm around my waist

and pulled me aside as Mandy shot into action. Wielding a fire extinguisher, she pulled the metal pin and doused the flames, creating a fog around us.

Within seconds, the air cleared and the small fire was out. I'd barely had time to register any of it, and if it wasn't for the white foam making such a mess of the tabletop, I would've thought I had imagined the whole thing.

"You girls okay?" a nearby fireman asked.

Bobbie Jo answered him, but I couldn't bring myself to respond. The idea of a fire breaking out so close to me had kicked my nerves into high gear. Now that the danger had officially passed, my adrenaline crashed, causing my body to tremble.

"Hey," Mandy asked, staring at me with wide eyes. "Are you all right?"

"I, uh…yes. It just startled me, that's all."

Bobbie Jo stepped around me to take a better look. "What happened? How did the fire start?"

"I don't know," Mandy said, gazing at the mess on the table. "I guess the candle under the warming tray must've caused it. But I don't know how the napkins got near the flame. They were in a pile over there just a minute ago." She indicated a spot on the table right behind where I'd been standing and shrugged. "Maybe the wind blew them across the table." Then she glanced to me and smiled lightly.

It was a nice gesture on her part. Not only because there wasn't much of a breeze, but the tent was covered by tarps on three sides, which kept her conjured-up scenario from being a remote possibility. It was much more likely I'd bumped the table in my hurry to move out of the fireman's path as he carried the chili past us.

But had I?

I couldn't remember doing so, but that didn't mean it didn't happen. "I'm sorry if I did anything to knock those over."

"Well, we don't know what actually happened, so I wouldn't worry about it," Mandy said, waving it off with her hand. "Besides, what better place to start a fire than in front of a bunch of firefighters?"

After a few more minutes—and another apology—Bobbie Jo and I moved on and found some new entertainment. We rode the Ferris wheel and the Tilt-a-Whirl, as well as a few other carnival rides, which was something I'd never done before. Then we sat at a picnic table and shared a hot funnel cake covered in powdered sugar. Once that was devoured, I bought a paper cone of pink cotton candy and munched on it while we played a game of Ring Toss.

As I polished off the last of the cotton candy, I scanned the area for the nearest trash can and stepped away to throw out the leftover paper cone. When I returned, she grinned at me. "What?"

"I don't know how you can be so skinny the way you eat," Bobbie Jo said as we meandered past the beer tent. "Where did you even put that?" She placed her hand on her stomach and feigned looking ill. "After all the chili-tasting and the funnel cake, I feel sick just thinking about eating anything else."

I shrugged. "It really wasn't all that much if you figure one skein of cotton candy is only about forty-two grams of sugar. It's mostly air, really."

Bobbie Jo smiled and shook her head. "Only *you* would know how many grams of sugar are in cotton candy. You're like a walking encyclopedia." Then something caught her eye over my shoulder. "Oh, hey, there's Cowboy! Let's go say hello."

She didn't see it, but I cringed. "Um, okay."

We made our way through the crowd until we reached a booth where Cowboy sat with a large group of men. As we approached from the side, an extremely impatient hoard of women blocked the front of the table, all jockeying to be the next in line. They were giggly and several were trying to push their way to the front. Since all of these guys had their shirts on, I couldn't imagine what they could be selling that was so popular with the ladies. Then I glanced to the wall behind Cowboy and my mouth went dry.

A huge banner that read *Liberty County Bachelors* displayed thirteen calendar-sized portraits—twelve individuals and one group shot. The men in each individual photo were good-looking and had terrific bodies, but none of them were wearing much more than a pair of briefs, at best. And although I told my eyes not to, they zoomed straight to the month of May.

I had expected his to be red-hot and possibly a little brazen. But in the picture, Cowboy was facing forward in a standing position, wearing that sexy little smirk he was so well-known for, with his white Stetson covering his... obvious nakedness. Nothing I found appalling, indecent, or shameful. Until I realized both of his hands were behind his head. *Oh, my Lord.*

An overwhelming urge to examine the photograph up close consumed me. I squeezed my thighs together, but an immensely pleasurable ache hit me low and deep, taking me by surprise, and leaving me feeling empty and frustrated.

I seldom thought about sex. But his provocative stance brought it forefront in my mind, thrusting me out of my comfort zone. No doubt, my cheeks bloomed furiously with my discomfort.

Eventually, I scanned the other pictures, noting that none of the other men had taken their sexiness to the limit the way Cowboy had. Leave it to him to be the outrageous and wicked one in the bunch.

"Hey, ladies," he said with a grin. "Did you come to get a calendar? At the rate they're going, we're going to be sold out before the end of the night."

Bobbie Jo looked at me. "I haven't bought one yet. Do you mind hanging out for a few minutes? The line looks pretty long."

"No, that's fine," I told her, keeping my eyes from returning to Cowboy's picture in an effort to regain my poise. "I'll just check out one of the nearby rides while I'm waiting for you."

"You should buy a calendar, too, Anna," Cowboy said, giving me a wink. "I'll even sign it for you real quick before I go on my break."

The cockiness oozed from him. I doubted the man could even help it. But I didn't want a sexy man calendar. What I wanted was to forget I ever saw so much of his muscular frame lacking in the clothing department.

That's all I needed. To spend every waking minute staring at his naked form on my wall. "No, thank you." I turned to Bobbie Jo, putting my back to him. "I'll be back soon," I promised her.

"Okay," she said, though her tone said otherwise. She gave me a strange look as I meandered away.

I made my way over to a ride called The Swizzler and waited in line until the operator took the three tickets I held out. If I had to wait for Bobbie Jo to indulge in her single woman fantasies, then I was going to enjoy myself in the meantime. Besides, this ride looked like a fun one.

Once the worker allowed my group through the gate, most of them scattered in different directions. I walked across a metal platform to an unoccupied red bucket on the far end. My flat heels clacked across the metal grating until I stepped into the bucket and sat in the middle of the spacious seat meant for three. There was a lap bar, but I wasn't sure if I was supposed to do anything with it, so I waited. The operator of the ride had started walking on the opposite side, checking each bucket's safety equipment, and would eventually get to me.

But while I sat there alone, I caught sight of Cowboy leaping over the ride's fence and climbing onto the metal arm of the machine my bucket was attached to. "What are you doing? Are you crazy?"

"Just thought you'd like some company," he said, hopping down into my bucket and squeezing into the seat next to me. He made himself comfortable by throwing his arm along the bench behind me.

No way. Being in such close quarters with Cowboy was a delicious kind of torture, but one I could do without. I started to rise, but Cowboy pulled the lap bar toward us which automatically locked into place, forcing me to stay put. "What did you do that for? I was going to leave."

He smirked. "I know."

"You do realize I can just ask the operator to let me out, right?"

Cowboy stretched his legs out in front of him and smiled confidently. "Yeah, but you won't."

"You seem awfully sure about that," I challenged.

"Oh, come on. You wouldn't want to hold the ride up for the next kids in line, would you?"

My eyes cut to the line forming once again at the entrance, filling with children who were patiently waiting their turn with excitement in their eyes. I huffed under my breath and scooted away from him. "Fine. But stay on your side and I'll stay on mine."

Cowboy grinned again. "You haven't ever ridden The Swizzler, have you?"

Before I could answer him, the operator stopped by our bucket and tugged on the bar to make sure it was in place. "All right guys, we're ready to rock and roll," the man said as he made his way back to the control box.

Loud rock music blared from the speakers as the buckets started to move. They traveled slowly in a zigzag pattern at first until it built speed and momentum. With all the wind blowing, I was glad my hair was held back with a clip and not whipping wildly around my face.

But the one thing I hadn't anticipated was gravity. Each time the bucket swung to the outside of the ride's loop, my rear end slid on the cold metal seat closer and closer to Cowboy. I held a death grip on the bar to keep myself in place, but it was no use. Several laps in, my hips were pushed all the way up against his and the force of the ride's movement kept me welded to him.

At one point my hand even ended up on his chest to keep my face from pressing closer to his. He grasped my hand and held it lightly in his as I fought to keep myself from ending up in his lap.

He leaned closer and whispered into my ear, "Stop fighting it and just have fun already."

I sighed. It was no use, anyway, so I did what he suggested.

Even with my body pushing into his, I found that I was enjoying the rush of wind on my face and the exhilaration of the twists and turns. The rock music reverberated loudly into my chest as the bucket zigged and zagged in different directions, like we were being slingshot from one side of the ride to the other over and over again in some weird yet consistent pattern.

The unexpected thrill of speed and gravity had me smiling uncontrollably, but the excitement of being shoved forcibly into Cowboy's hard body for the duration of the ride was a buzz-worthy event in itself. He smiled and lowered his brawny arm from the back of the seat to behind me where it came to rest on my hip. I was essentially being cradled in his rugged arms...and I liked it. Maybe a little too much.

Our bodies generated heat, while the friction hardened my aching nipples. They poked through my blouse. I knew I should put some distance between us, but his glittering green eyes held mine, keeping me in place. The fast ride invigorated me, but Cowboy's incredible smile made me dizzy.

As the machine finally slowed, so did my heart rate. That's when all of my senses returned, and I fully realized the intimate position Cowboy and I were maintaining.

Startled by the pleasure I felt, I pushed away from him so abruptly that he frowned at me. "What's the problem?" he asked as the ride came to a full stop and the lap bar automatically disengaged.

"Don't you have to get back to peddling your calendars?"

I asked softly, wondering how the hell he managed to get past my defenses. I stood up and stepped shakily out of the bucket, still feeling a little wobbly from the ride. Or maybe it was from the way he had held me.

Cowboy followed me, but I kept going, pretending he was no longer there. Once we made it outside the exit gate, he grasped my arm gently to stop me from walking away. "Anna, why do you keep running away from me?"

Because I have to. "I'm not," I said, shaking my head in denial. "The ride is over and I'm moving on to the next one. But since I know you have to get back, don't let me stop you. Please tell Bobbie Jo I'll check on her soon."

With that, I turned and speed-walked away. I was in such a hurry to get away from him that I didn't even pay any attention to which direction I had gone. I'd somehow ended up on the backside of the gaming booths where the carnies had parked their big trucks and travel trailers.

The area was much darker and I had to be careful not to trip over the large electrical cables that powered all of the rides and were running across the trail. I thought about turning back, but I was too afraid Cowboy would still be there, so I kept moving forward, looking for a path that would cut through the booths and take me back to the other side.

I caught sight of a glowing light up ahead and quickened my steps, hoping I'd run into someone who could tell me how to get back to where I came from. But when I rounded the bend, I found it wasn't a light at all. It was a stack of wooden pallets…one that happened to be covered in flames.

I skidded to a stop. The fire wasn't large and looked to be contained, but my chest still tightened as turmoil sloshed through my veins. My heart rate accelerated, and my pulse roared in my ears. Every fiber of my being wanted me to turn around and run in the opposite direction. But I couldn't. I remembered how those all-too-familiar flames had ruined my life by taking something precious from me. I couldn't—no, I *wouldn't*—allow it to happen anymore. I welded myself in place.

Focus, Anna. I could beat this.

As I watched the orange tendrils lick at the sides of the wood and grow higher and higher, I became mesmerized by the dancing flames, and the urge to get a closer look came over me. Slowly, I placed one foot in front of the other until I was standing directly in front of the terrifying demon I'd feared so long.

I wanted to see inside the flames. Needed to understand how it worked in order to rid myself of my fear once and for all. But the heat from the fire was too hot to get any closer. Then the wind suddenly shifted and smoke surrounded me. My eyes watered and I choked on the toxic fumes. I barely registered the sound of my name as Cowboy appeared through the haze of black smoke.

"What the hell are you doing?" he shouted, scowling at me. "Move!"

But I couldn't. My sweat-dampened palms reached for him, but my feet weren't cooperating. He grabbed my arms as I clutched at his shirt, trying to hold myself up and keep from passing out from the amount of smoke I'd inhaled. "I...c-can't," I coughed out, feeling weaker by the second.

His firefighter training must've kicked in, because his face changed from a perplexed, what-the-hell expression to a look of sheer determination and confidence.

Without hesitation, he snaked his arm around my back

and lifted my wobbly legs out from under me, drawing me tight against his hard chest. My face buried into his warm neck, and my fingers dug into his broad shoulders as he carried me out of the smoke.

I gasped in a breath of clean air, and coughed it right back out. My throat burned a little from the effort. Cowboy kept moving with me in his arms until he had toted me twenty yards away, where some of the carnival workers had gathered and a fire truck had just pulled in. I remembered seeing it parked near the firemen's chili booth, and figured someone had probably notified them of the fire around the same time I'd stumbled upon it.

In full bunker gear, Mandy stepped out of the passenger seat. Her eyes widened, as if she hadn't expected to see me standing there. "Something wrong with her feet, Captain, or did you just feel like playing hero?"

"I don't know what happened," he said, concern lacing his deep tone, along with a smidgen of petulance at Mandy's remark. He looked at me, as if waiting for me to answer for myself, but I still couldn't speak. He nodded his understanding and told Mandy, "She just sort of…froze."

"Oh. I'm sorry, Anna," Mandy said, her tone registering her sincerity. "You seemed fine after the booth fire. I didn't realize—"

"What booth fire?" Cowboy asked.

"When Anna and Bobbie Jo stopped by our booth earlier, some napkins caught fire on the table behind Anna. We had to use a fire extinguisher to put it out."

Cowboy's suspicious eyes met mine once again and his jaw tightened. "Go see if Reynolds needs any help, Mandy."

She bit her lip. "Are you sure? I can help you with—"

"It's okay. Just go." His low, gruff voice wavered between confusion and anger.

Obviously, he suspected me of starting that booth fire. But I hadn't. Not really. Or rather, not intentionally. It was an accident, one that could have easily happened to any of us. Though I doubted he would see it that way.

I managed to loll my head back enough to see the orange glow once more and a tremor ran through me. Cowboy's arms tightened around me, drawing my attention back to him. Our eyes met briefly, then I began to hum. It was so low, I hoped he couldn't hear it over the noise of the loud music and the shouts of the carnival goers, but knew he probably felt the vibrations against his ribs.

Cowboy pulled his arm out from behind my legs and let my body slide down his until both my feet touched the pavement. Then he unknotted my arms from around his neck. I'd coiled around him like a boa constrictor, and apparently didn't want to let go.

He smoothed one large hand over my hair while the other rubbed at the back of my neck, soothing and relaxing me. "You're okay," he whispered gently in my ear. "I've got you."

That's when the humming stopped. I accepted his calming touch willingly and my heart rate decreased. I didn't know why he'd elected himself to be responsible for me. But he had. And I fully believed he wasn't about to let me down now.

Cowboy leaned me against the cold metal of the truck and used the strategic placement of his body against mine to keep me balanced upright as he opened the door and maneuvered me into the passenger's seat.

He reached past me and grabbed a navy blue jacket with a fireman's patch on the sleeve, wrapping it around my shoulders. Then he pulled an orange emergency kit out from behind the seat and flipped open the lid. A small silver tank and a self-contained breathing apparatus were inside.

The last time I'd seen my mother alive, she was covered in white skin-peeling blisters and wearing such a mask. "No, I'm okay." But he ignored me and tried to put the mask over my face, anyway. I shoved it away. "I said I don't need it!"

He gritted his teeth. "Wear the damn mask, Anna."

I shook my head. Beyond watery eyes and a slightly sore throat, I wasn't presenting any other signs of damage from the smoke. "I would, if I thought I needed it, but I'm not even coughing anymore. I don't have a headache, hoarseness, nausea, or mental confusion. Nothing to indicate I suffered smoke inhalation."

When his gaze dropped to my chest, swiftly and blatantly, my pulse quickened and my eyebrow rose. "What do you think you're doing?"

"Shut up."

"Excuse me?"

After a minute, he lifted his head, letting his eyes meet mine. "I was counting your respirations, not ogling your breasts," he said, pressing two thick fingers to the inside of my wrist to measure my erratic pulse.

I'd angered him, though I hadn't meant to. *It isn't my fault the playboy has a reputation he can't live down.*

My pulse must not have spiked as high as I'd thought, because he tossed the lid closed on the oxygen tank and put it away. Wordlessly, he pulled me against his chest, sharing his body heat. It wasn't cold out, but I was shaking and couldn't have resisted if I wanted to. His strong arms wrapped around me like a security blanket and the divine scent of his cologne permeated my nostrils, lending me comfort I hadn't known I needed.

Reynolds produced a water hose from nearby and doused the blaze while we watched in silence. Guess the contained fire was small enough they didn't need to bring out the big hose because, within minutes, the flames were out.

Cowboy pulled back, placing his hands on my shoulders and looking me square in the eyes. "Anna, why did you start the fire?"

Stunned, I blinked at him and shook my head adamantly. "I...I didn't."

His eyes narrowed with suspicion and his mouth pulled taut into a flat, thin line. He didn't believe me. Not only that, but there I was clinging to a man I now wanted to strangle.

Angrily, I tried to shift away from him, but he held me firmly in place, nodding to the site where the fire had been. "Then tell me what happened," he demanded, his tone bordering on frustration and fury.

"How would I know? I was with you, remember? I just left you back there. Why would you even suggest I had anything to do with—"

"There's a bottle of lighter fluid on the ground not ten feet away from where you were standing. It only takes seconds to start a fire using that. Besides, you were practically standing in the fire when I found you. I had to radio it in and then double time it up here to get you out of the smoke before you killed yourself. What the hell were you doing, anyway?"

"I was just..."

"Just what?" When I didn't respond to his question, he

raised his voice. "Answer the damn question."

"It doesn't matter. I didn't start the fire. That's all you need to know."

"Bullshit, Anna! This is the third fire in three days you just *happened* to be near when it started. I don't want to believe you had something to do with it, but what the hell else am I supposed to think?"

I narrowed my eyes.

"Hey, Captain," a young fireman said, approaching us and addressing Cowboy. "No injuries to report and the flames are out. But we found the source of the fire. You might want to come talk to him. He's on the side of the building over here and refuses to leave."

Cowboy and I gave each other a puzzled look and then stepped out of the vehicle to head in the direction the fireman came from. We caught sight of a man with a scruffy gray beard and ratty clothes leaning against a nearby fence. "Damn you, Dan!" Cowboy yelled, making me jump. "I told you to stop setting shit on fire."

The homely-looking man lifted his head and gave us a rotten-toothed grin. "Fuck you."

"Watch your mouth. There's a lady present."

The old man grunted. "Well, fuck her, too."

Cowboy must've heard my small intake of breath because he rolled his eyes and whispered, "Just ignore him. He's nothing but a grouchy, filthy-mouthed old man. He doesn't like anyone telling him what to do." Cowboy glanced back at the man. "Do you, Dan?"

Dan held up a middle finger on his grimy hand and said in a gruff, rancid voice, "Up yours, shit-for-brains."

"He's trying to provoke me," Cowboy explained.

"Whenever he wants a hot meal, Dan here does something illegal…like setting fires."

I shook my head in disbelief. "H-he did this *on purpose*? But he could've killed someone."

"Yeah, including himself."

The old man guffawed. "Quit talking about me like I'm not standing right here. I know my rights. You gonna have me arrested or what?"

Cowboy nodded. "The sheriff will be here any minute. You'll probably be stuck in a cell until Monday morning, and then you can go home to your wife."

"Heeeeeell, no." He shuddered. "Have you seen that woman?"

"Yeah, but *you* haven't," Cowboy told him. "You're only imagining what she looks like." I squinted at him, not understanding what he was talking about. "Dan's legally blind," he explained. "Has been for years."

"Oh. I see."

Dan stared stupidly at me. "Well, just rub it in, why don't ya? You damn kids nowadays don't think twice about making fun of someone with a handicap. In the good ol' days, children respected their elders."

As the sheriff pulled in, Cowboy said, "Your ride's here, old man."

Dan pushed off the fence and picked up an aluminum cane I hadn't noticed leaning against his right leg. Then he started toward the sound of the cruiser, swinging the cane back and forth as it clattered on the pavement, while mumbling under his breath.

I looked up at Cowboy, still confused. "H-he's not a vagrant?"

"No, but he's still a bum. Every time he pisses off his wife, she refuses to cook for him and kicks him out. Then he pulls this crap."

"So, he's the town drunk, then?"

"Dan?" Cowboy chuckled at the thought. "Nah. He doesn't touch the stuff. Besides, this place is too small for a town drunk. Instead, we all just take turns."

Before I could respond, the fireman named Reynolds approached. "All clear, Captain? Or do you still want us to have the sheriff take her in for questioning?" he asked, grinning in amusement.

Lightning flashed in Cowboy's eyes and he gave Reynolds a go-to-hell look, which prompted the young fireman to quickly turn and head for the hills.

I crossed my arms, glaring at him in disbelief. "You were going to have me arrested?"

Cowboy closed his eyes and let out a hard breath. When he opened them, the anger I'd seen in them was gone and only softness and sincerity remained. "No, I was just going to have him...talk to you, I guess. I thought maybe if it was somebody besides me asking the questions, you would—"

"What? Tell the truth? Because you still think I'm lying to you, right?" As he opened his mouth to speak, I knew an apology loomed on the tip of his tongue. But it was one I didn't want to hear. His fury may have dissipated, but mine had just kicked into high gear. I shook my head and pulled the jacket from around my shoulders, shoving it into his chest. "Here. I guess it's safe to say that I can go now."

He took the jacket and reached for my hand. "Anna, wait..."

"Just leave me alone," I said, walking quickly away from him.

Chapter Five

"**G**ot my book?"

I'd seen Cowboy come through the library doors, but had refused to allow myself to acknowledge him until he spoke first. Even then, I only reached beneath the desk and handed him the book with the red spine.

"Guess you're still mad," he said.

I continued ignoring him.

He braced his hands on the counter. "Are you going to at least let me apologize for last night?"

"No." I grabbed a couple of returned books I'd already scanned back into the system, rose and headed for the far aisles, away from prying eyes and bent ears.

He followed behind me, not giving up. "I talked to Bobbie Jo."

"Good for you."

"She vouched for you, so I'm letting it go…this time. I closed the report on the dumpster fire and chalked it up to an accident. She trusts you." His tone sounded almost angry about it.

I kept walking, but glanced over my shoulder at him, noting his questioning eyes and the way he held his mouth in a flat, grim line. Suspicion and mistrust lit up his perfect face like a flashing neon sign. "Yet *you* still don't."

He didn't even bother denying it. "Do you blame me? You avoid my questions every chance you get, and you won't stay in one place long enough for me to have a decent conversation with you." When I walked faster hoping to get out of everyone's earshot before he spoke another word, he said, "Damn it, Anna. Why are you always running from me?"

"I'm not. I'm— "

"Afraid I'm going to ask you out?" he asked, as if he were finishing my sentence.

My heart skipped a beat, but I pretended to be unfazed. I stepped inside an alcove and placed one of the books on the shelf where it belonged. "Don't be absurd," I said, lowering my voice.

"So it's okay for me to ask you out, then?"

"What? No, I...I didn't say that. Don't put words in my mouth." I marched down the aisle with him hot on my trail. "You're *not* asking me out."

"Why not? Since I closed the report, there's nothing stopping me from doing so."

"Doesn't matter."

He groaned. "What the hell is your problem with me?"

I stopped and turned to face him, lifting my brows. "You really have to ask that?" Then I moved further down the aisle.

"I'm trying to apologize for last night," he said from

behind me. "If you would just stand still long enough…" He grasped my shoulders and turned me to face him. "Look, I'm sorry. I was wrong, okay?"

"Fine. Apology accepted." I spun away from him and scanned the shelves. When I found the spot I was looking for, I slid the book back into its rightful place. I pivoted and walked toward him, then passed right by him on my way back to the circulation desk.

"That's it?" Cowboy asked.

I paused and looked back, shrugging nonchalantly. "What more is there?"

"Have dinner with me tonight."

My stomach fluttered and I smiled, but didn't hesitate with my answer. "No, thank you."

He sighed. "Why? Because of last night?"

"No, not because of that," I said, straightening a book on a nearby shelf.

"Just dinner. I'm not asking for anything more."

Yeah, sure…yet.

To say I didn't trust men was the understatement of the year. And Cowboy was definitely all man. Good-looking. Charming. The kind of guy who made hearts bleed in every female within a hundred-mile radius. Even with his lack of commitment and my plans to leave town, it would still never work between us. So why waste either of our time?

"I'm sorry, Cowboy, but my answer is still no."

His face twisted in genuine confusion, as if he'd never been told "no" before. He hesitated and then said, "It's because you think I'm butt-ugly, isn't it?"

I bit my lip to keep from giggling at him. He couldn't be "butt-ugly" if he tried. "No, that's not it, either. You just…

need to stop asking me out."

"Why? What did I do wrong?"

"You didn't *do* anything wrong."

"Then what? Am I too damn pretty for you? Come on, there's got to be something."

I sighed at his arrogance. "Listen, Cowboy, what you did for me last night was sweet and I appreciate it. But we both know you carrying me away from that fire wasn't some clichéd romantic gesture."

He nodded in agreement. "More like a caretaker helping an invalid get from point A to point B. So?"

"*That* is exactly my point. You're blunt, reckless, arrogant, and…frankly, a little conceited, which is something I'm not."

"Just spit it out already. I'm a big boy. I can take it."

I hesitated to tell him the God's honest truth, but I had to say something to get him to leave me alone. "I don't do short-term love affairs," I blurted out.

Clearly caught off guard by my admission, he blinked rapidly before a smile tugged at the sides of his mouth. "You mean sex?"

I closed my eyes and sighed, embarrassment flooding my cheeks. "Yes, of course I'm talking about sex."

"So what about *long-term* love affairs?" The inflection in his tone made his voice deeper, sexier.

I cracked one eye open and saw him grinning at me with a hand propped leisurely on the shelf beside me and the other at his waist, his thumb snagged in the loophole of his jeans. "Don't make fun of me."

"Darlin', I'm not making fun of you. I'm only suggesting something a little longer than what you were expecting." Then he shrugged his brows.

His cockiness pushed my buttons. "Okay, enough. Obviously you're used to flirty women throwing their wishful hearts at your feet and their willing bodies into your bed without you barely lifting a finger. But I'm...well, I'm not interested."

Wearing a sexy little grin, he stepped forward, forcing me to inch away from him until my back hit the bookshelf behind me. "Oh, really?" He actually sounded surprised. Arrogant jerk.

"Yes, *really*. I guess you find that hard to believe?"

"Sweetheart, as jumpy as you are around me, I don't see you doing either." His hands framed my face and his thumbs tipped my chin up. My breath hitched as his lips neared mine. "But the adorable way you're blushing and stammering all over yourself... Well, darlin', I'd say you have more interest than you're letting on." His emerald eyes twinkled with intimate knowledge of women's desires and a blatant invitation for me to test him on it.

An easy victim of wishful thinking, I licked my lips nervously and felt his breath warm them. A pulse developed between my legs as sexual undercurrents flowed rapidly through my veins. But lucky for me, it also heightened my sense of reality. Because a man like him wouldn't go for someone like me. Not unless he was getting something in return. Cowboy always wanted something he couldn't have. It was just the way he was.

That argument alone persuaded me to put an end to the standoff. It was self-sabotaging, I knew, but my heart and my mind threatened to form a conspiracy against me by sending me off to dangerous, Cowboy-infested waters. And that wasn't a depth I was willing to go.

I shied away farther, my back digging into the bookshelf, as I tried to put more distance between us. "I'm not a trophy, nor do I aspire to become a notch on someone's belt. I'm not the kind of girl who rolls out of a man's bed after one meaningless night of sleeping together."

He laughed softly. "I don't know about meaningless, sweetheart, but the sleeping part is not usually the way I do things."

I rolled my eyes. "You just don't get it, do you? I'm not looking for a fling."

"That's too bad," he said, settling his hands on the bookcase behind me, effectively caging me in. His masculine frame towered over me, forcing me to look up to see his eyes. "Because it'd be hot as hell watching you come unwound."

He brought one hand around and removed the glasses from my face, then reached up with the other and let my red hair fall out of my clip.

Again? *Seriously?*

It was nerve-wracking the way his gaze roamed aimlessly over my face and body. As if he were imagining me naked in his arms, writhing beneath him while he thrust into me. And that thought alone horrified me as much as it delighted me. *God, help me.*

I didn't stamp my foot, but I wanted to. "Are you done, yet?"

"Nope. Not even close. I want to know the real reason why you won't go out with me."

"Okay, fine." I crossed my arms to show my exasperation, but mostly to hide my body's response to his proximity. "You're someone who appreciates bluntness, right? You like to call a spade a spade?"

"Mmm-hmm." He was still smiling.

"The reason I won't go out with you is simple." I heaved out a breath and pushed the loose hair behind my ear, knowing I was about to wipe that smug smile off his stupid perfect face. "You're a king on a throne, and your sordid reputation with women is well-known throughout the land."

"What?" His brows lowered over his eyes and his smile dissipated. "*That's* your reason for not—"

"I'm not finished," I stated firmly, tapping my foot on the tiled floor. "Like I told you the other night, we're not a good match. Way too different, in fact. I'm predictable and dull and, without a doubt, you'd become easily bored with me."

His eyes softened. "You're not—"

"Not finished," I chastised, placing my hands on my hips. "I'm perpetually behind everyone else in most things, including fashion, and I'm a compulsive neat freak. I'm also logical and conservative."

"You probably recycle," he said with a smirk.

"Actually, I do. But then again, so do you." When he looked at me funny, I continued. "You recycle *women*. Use them up and toss them aside, leaving them for someone else while you wait for a new one to come along and replenish your stash."

"That's not true. I—"

"I'm still not through," I said, raising my hand to stop him. "Face it, Cowboy, we're nothing alike. Therefore, I think us going on a date would be futile and one hundred percent counterproductive." When he didn't say anything right away, I asked, "Do you understand what I mean by that?"

He tipped his hat back, and I could see the indignation

blazing in his eyes. "Being a southern redneck don't make me stupid," he drawled, clearly offended. I started to apologize, but he spoke up first. "Just one date."

"I'm sorry, Cowboy, but I have no interest in having dinner with you...or anything else for that matter. I don't want to be just another anonymous name on your list or another temporary playmate in your bed. For the last time, my answer is still no." Then I closed my mouth and bit down on my tongue before I did something stupid. Like change my mind.

We stared at each other momentarily before his jaw tightened and he said, "You done?"

I gave him a terse nod.

"Good. Then it's my turn." He relaxed into a seemingly more comfortable position. "First off, you should be less critical of yourself. You're not nearly as dull as you make yourself out to be."

"I'm not—"

"Not finished. I've got the floor, remember? You've had your turn."

I made a sweeping motion with my arm for him to continue.

"Second, allow me to put your foolish concerns to rest."

"Fine."

"You telling me that you're not my type is total bullshit, and you know it. You purposely make yourself unattractive to men with your long skirts and buttoned-up blouses. Hell, nuns wear less clothing than you do." Cowboy chuckled at his remark. "But let me assure you of one thing, sweetheart. Out of the two of us, the only one who mentioned anything directly related to sex is *you*."

My eyes narrowed at him. "What are you talking about?"

"Darlin', just because I make a flirty pass and ask you to dinner doesn't mean I expect to bend you over the nearest flat surface. That's your hang-up, not mine."

Oh God. He was right! He hadn't actually asked me for sex...yet. *Great.* So now *I* was the sexual deviant. How the hell had that happened?

"You would've eventually—"

"Not done," he said, pulling a page from my own book. "Let me tell you what else I know." He shifted his weight, as if he planned for us to be here a while. "Something about you is off. Last night you reacted to that fire the same as you do to me—you panicked. I don't know what it is or why, but there's something you aren't telling me."

I shrugged nonchalantly. "I don't know what you're talking about."

"You know *exactly* what I'm talking about. But lucky for you, I can help with both of those things. And that is not by any means me asking you for sex." Cowboy displayed a smug grin. "Not to toot my own horn or anything, but I'm a catch."

I rolled my eyes. "And modest, too."

"Anna, all I'm asking for is dinner. What we do—or *don't* do—afterward is completely up to you."

"Give me one good reason why I should."

"Huh?"

I crossed my arms and huffed. "Go on, tell me. Why me?"

He squinted at me. "Is this a trick question?"

"No. I really want to know. Why are you so insistent when I have repeatedly refused you?"

"You intrigue me."

I rolled my eyes. "You don't know enough about me to be intrigued."

He sighed. "See? No matter what I say, you're not going to believe me, anyway," he said, waving me off.

"That's because you're only saying what you think I want to hear. Why don't you try it again, but this time, throw in a little truth?"

Cowboy stood a little straighter as he glared at me. "Fine," he snarled. "You want to know why I asked you out? It's because…" He hesitated, then shrugged and turned away from me. "Never mind. This is stupid."

I stepped around him and faced him. "Why? Are you afraid to give me an honest answer? Or maybe it's because you can't?"

He threw his hands in the air. "Because I knew you'd say no, okay?"

I blinked, not expecting him to be so forthcoming.

"That *is* what you wanted me to admit, right? That I'm intrigued by you because you don't want anything to do with me." He hooked his thumbs into the loopholes on his jeans and ground out, "Does that satisfy your curiosity?"

Yes. Unfortunately. But it didn't change a thing.

Obviously, brushing off his advances hadn't worked. In fact, the whole thing had backfired. Even worse, his little speech had nearly coaxed a yes from me. But self-preservation demanded I end this once and for all. That left me with no choice but to bruise that precious male ego of his, which would require something drastic, since he had an ego the size of Texas.

"Come with me," I told him, turning to walk up the aisle. He followed behind me silently, but I felt his eyes burning into my back, the question looming in the air, as we neared the circulation desk. I veered around the counter and pulled my purse from the bottom cabinet. I took out my wallet, searching through it until I found my library card.

I scanned it, then picked up the book Cowboy had left on the counter and did the same with it. Only then did I shove the book into his hand. "There. I've checked the book out for you. It's due back in two weeks. There's a drive-up book return drop outside under the portico."

He glanced to the book, then back to me. "What's the catch?"

I sighed heavily, letting out the irritated breath I had been holding in my lungs. "In return, I ask that you don't come back into the library again."

Chapter Six

Cowboy had probably expected me to turn him down, not banish him from the library altogether. But the day before, I'd done just that. Lucky for him, today was Sunday, which meant the library was closed. Unlucky for me, I forgot to also ban him from my home.

It was almost dark outside when he pulled up, and I was stretching a garden hose across my front lawn. Fresh from the shower, I'd put on a white terrycloth robe and left my wet red hair hanging loosely around my shoulders. Both were decisions I immediately regretted, but I didn't detour from my mission.

By the time he joined me on the side of my little white cottage, I was doing something he undoubtedly found rather strange: watering my house. He stepped up beside me and glanced at the wet rooftop and dripping eaves. "Think it'll be ready to harvest by the end of the season?"

"What are you doing here?" I frowned, my face already

heated and my body vibrating with anger. "I thought I told you I wasn't interested."

Cowboy held up his hands in mock surrender. "Whoa. No need to get pissy. I just came by to talk."

"We did enough talking yesterday. Good-bye."

But he ignored me. "Where are your glasses?"

"Huh? Oh." I reached up to my face, realizing I didn't have them on. "They're reading glasses. I don't wear them all the time, just at work and…" I shook my head, feeling even more frazzled than I'd been before he'd shown up. "Never mind. I don't know why I'm explaining anything to you. You're leaving."

His brows furrowed. "What's wrong?"

"Nothing you need to worry about. It's my problem, and I'm handling—"

Loud, thumping music sounded from up the road. Within seconds, a dark blue Bronco appeared and pulled into the driveway next to mine. I put one hand on my hip and watched the Barlow brothers climb out, hooting and hollering, and carrying a brand new eighteen-pack of beer.

Sloppy. Rowdy. And drunk, as usual.

Joe Barlow wore his cap backward. Stray tufts of his dark hair poked out between his eyes, his sideburns, and the back of his neck. His dirty white tank top left his tattooed arms exposed, though I couldn't make out the red ink blob on his left bicep. As he rounded the hood of the Bronco, he guzzled the last of the beer in his hand, then crushed the empty can on his chest. His brother chortled at the sight.

Clay was shorter than Joe, heavily overweight, and laughed like a snickering hyena. He wasn't wearing a shirt and the too-tight jeans he had squeezed himself into only emphasized his large pot belly and tanned ass crack. A toothpick dangled from his yellowed teeth as he turned, set down the case of beer, and did something with his hands I couldn't quite make out.

There was a shrill whistle and a loud pop as a fire cracker shot through the air and over my house, leaving a trail of sparks in its wake. I threw down the hose and started for the two men. I'd made it halfway across the lawn when Cowboy caught up to me. To him, it must've seemed like a random burst of energy. He hadn't been there for the first round of fireworks before the brothers had taken off on their apparent beer run.

Cowboy latched onto my arm and shook his head. "Hold up, tiny. You don't want to do that."

I glared at him. "Oh, really?"

"Those guys are bad news. Most people—at least the ones in their right minds—tend to avoid them."

"And why's that?"

"Those boys are known bullies," he said, letting go of me. "They live to intimidate others, plain and simple. They were a few grades ahead of us in school, but I've known them my whole life. Even saw them in action firsthand when they got into it at The Backwoods with my captain the day of my promotion party. If you go over there, you're asking for trouble."

I crossed my arms and sighed. "So I'm supposed to keep quiet and do nothing?"

"When they were younger, Clay had an itchy trigger finger, taking a notion to shooting things with his BB gun just for the hell of it. Joe wasn't much better. He may be older, but he's always had a problem with authority. Ended up in jail more than once after a scuffle with the sheriff. You don't want to get mixed up with—" He glanced back at them and said, "Oh, shit!" Then he grabbed me and spun me sideways.

A *whoosh* sounded as something whizzed past us like a rocket, hit the side of my house with a loud thump, and exploded on impact. The fireball fell into the bush directly underneath, and the shrubbery instantly caught fire.

Joe and Clay burst into hysterics.

"You idiots! Watch where you're shooting those things!" Cowboy sprinted away from me, picked up my abandoned hose, and soaked down the greenery, as well as the side of my house.

Maybe most people in their right mind avoided the Barlow brothers, but I was no longer in mine. I marched across my yard and right into theirs, sticking my finger in each of their faces as if it were a loaded weapon. "That's it. I've had enough! Every night this week, you two have shot fireworks over my home."

Clay grinned. "So what?"

"*So what?* Are you kidding me?" Outraged, I flapped my arms and squawked at him like a hen. "It's a fire hazard. You could kill somebody doing something so stupid and reckless."

"Ah," Joe said, waving me off. "Why don't you shut up and go home?" He turned away from me, dismissing me completely.

But I wouldn't allow it.

I circled him and stepped in his path. "Look, I tried to ask nicely the other day, but you just laughed and ignored me. I won't sit back and watch you set my house on fire. If you don't knock it off this time, I'm going to…to…"

Joe's eyes narrowed at me. "You're going to do what?"

"I'll call the police."

Clay elbowed his brother in a "get this chick" capacity and chuckled. By now, anything I said would fall on deaf ears, so I spun around and headed back onto my own property to get my phone and make good on my promise. I wasn't sure if Joe caught a glimpse of the determination in my eyes, but he jumped in front of me, blocking my path.

"Get out of my way."

"And what are you going to do if I don't?"

Cowboy was still busy snuffing out the burning bush, but I wasn't willing to back down. I crossed my arms and glared at Joe. "You're already in enough trouble. Do you really want to add holding me hostage to the charges?"

He snorted. "Lady, you'd have to prove it first. Besides, I'm not in trouble for nothing. My dipshit brother shot the fireworks off, not me."

"True. But maybe when the cops get here, I'll tell them about the little side business you've been running."

Joe's brows rose slightly. "Uh, side business?"

I rolled my eyes. "You think I haven't noticed the multitude of cars stopping at your house at all hours of the night? It's obviously something illegal you don't want the sheriff knowing about."

He glared back at me. "What are you doing—spying on us?"

"Oh, please. Anyone with half a brain could figure out you're doing something shady over here. Did you really think you wouldn't get caught sooner or later?"

"Look, you little bitch—"

"No, *you* look!" I yelled, poking him in the chest. He

grunted, but stood his ground as I continued. "Since I moved in a few weeks ago, you two have been nothing but rude and obnoxious. You play your music too loud, you have friends coming and going all hours of the night, and setting off fireworks is dangerous. I'm not going to tolerate this crap any longer. I won't allow you morons to burn down my home with me inside."

In retaliation, he leaned over and grasped my arm in a bruising grip, his hands cold as ice. "You may not have much of a choice," he snarled.

"E-excuse me?"

"You heard me, lady. Better watch yourself. That sassy mouth just might get you into trouble one of these days. I don't know where you came from, but 'round here, neighbors who go buttin' their noses where they don't belong tend to get...*burned*."

My eyes widened at his insinuation, but I couldn't speak. I glanced in Cowboy's direction and realized that, although he'd finished putting out the burning bush, he'd been oblivious to the heated argument going on next door. Between the distance and the whipping wind rustling the leaves on the trees, he hadn't heard a single word.

With no witnesses, I had no way to prove what Joe said to me. Not only did he threaten me, but he chose the most terrifying way imaginable.

Fire.

A hoarse sob broke from my throat.

Shoulders slumped and fighting back the tears

stinging my eyes, I stood in their pea gravel driveway as the Barlow brothers disappeared inside their house, letting the screen door bang against the jamb behind them. Part of me wanted to march in after them and give them another piece of my mind, but the other part—a much bigger part—was afraid of what would happen to me if I did.

I glanced back over my shoulder just in time to see Cowboy toss the hose aside and cut across the lawn, heading in my direction. I swiped the tears that had dropped onto my cheeks and blinked to clear any additional moisture from my eyes. I couldn't let him see me like this.

By the time he reached me, I had taken a few deep breaths and calmed myself considerably, though I hadn't moved an inch.

"Where'd Tweedledee and Tweedledum go?"

I closed my eyes and swallowed hard. "They went inside." My voice cracked on the last word and I cringed. The last thing I wanted was for Cowboy to see or hear how they'd affected me.

"Anna…?"

I turned to walk past him, but he grasped my shoulders and held me there, his eyes searching mine for answers. No doubt they were still shiny from the tears that had been there moments before. "What happened?" he asked.

"Nothing."

His face hardened and his jaw tightened. "Bullshit. Tell me."

"It's nothing, okay? I told them I'd call the police if this didn't stop and…well, he threatened me."

I barely finished the sentence before Cowboy's intense eyes sparked with fury and his mouth twisted into a frightening sneer. "I'm gonna kill 'em," he said, dropping my arm and starting for their house in a full-on bout of rage.

"No! Please don't. You'll only make things worse." I grasped his arm, digging my fingernails into his skin to stop him. Not only was he outnumbered, but those two brothers were clearly unstable. I didn't want Cowboy to get hurt. "You can't go in there."

"Watch me."

"It wasn't a big deal. I doubt Joe even meant it. He was just being a jerk."

Cowboy paused. "What exactly did he say to you?"

"Joe told me…" I hesitated, but took a deep breath. "He said he would burn my house down…with me inside."

He blinked at me, as if he couldn't believe what he was hearing. Then lightning flashed in his eyes. "Those little bastards," he said, shaking out of my grip. "Stay here. I'll be back after I have a few words with them."

But I knew that was a lie. He wasn't going in there to do any talking. No, he was going in there with every intention of beating the hell out of them. I could see it in his stiff posture and the way his teeth gnashed together in anger. But I couldn't let that happen.

I jumped in front of him and put my hand on his chest. Like that did any good. He glared at it, pushed my hand aside, then picked me up and physically moved me out of his way. I was no match for his strength. It was the equivalent of me trying to stop a speeding train with my bare hands.

As he strode briskly away, I panicked and blurted out, "My mother died in a fire!"

The grief and sadness must've registered in my voice because he stopped in his tracks and looked back at me. A dull ache gnawed at my insides, dredging up an emptiness I hadn't felt in years. His withering stare softened and his eyes flooded with compassion and understanding. That was the moment the dam broke wide open. Tears dripped freely onto my cheeks and I wiped at them, smearing the painful memories down my face. Apparently it was enough to convince him I needed him to stay more than he needed to defend my honor.

Silently, Cowboy returned to me. For a moment, he just stood there with his eyes closed, as if he were willing himself to settle down. When he opened them, something else had taken the place of the anger. Something closely resembling sympathy and understanding. "Is that why you're scared of fire?"

I bit my lip to keep it from trembling as another tear rolled down my cheek. I nodded slowly.

Bridging the gap between us, Cowboy pulled me into his masculine arms. At first, I tried to push away, not wanting his pity, but he wouldn't allow it. He drew me back to him, and within seconds, I surrendered to the security of his strong hold, burying my face into his chest as little hiccupping sobs burst from my throat.

"Okay, just breathe." He smoothed one hand over my hair, then settled it on my lower back. "Slow and easy. Like this," he said, using his other hand to place mine against his chest, allowing me to feel the rise and fall of his even breaths.

He held me comfortably, giving me time to calm down, while he probably contemplated which one of the Barlow boys he was going to punch in the face first. Because when their screen door banged against the jamb again, Cowboy whirled around fast, fists clenched, ready for a fight.

Mandy Barlow had stepped outside on their porch with her short, blunt brunette hair and perky nose. She looked straight at me, her eyes registering concern, then flicked a glance at Cowboy. "Is everything all right?"

"Apparently, your brothers get off on threatening women."

"Oh God. I'm sorry," Mandy said, shaking her head. She directed her attention back to me. "Don't listen to them, honey. They're all talk…well, mostly." She offered a small non-committal shrug. "They may not use the sense that the good Lord gave 'em, but I'm sure they were only trying to scare you."

"Well, it worked," Cowboy said, his tone shifting from sour to downright caustic. "Give them a piece of advice for me, Mandy. Tell them that if they come near Anna again, they're going to answer to *me*."

Mandy bit her lip. "I don't think—"

"Tell 'em," he demanded. "Because if this happens again, we're going to see how they fare with someone a little closer to their own size."

She looked like she wanted to argue, but instead, she nodded silently and went back inside.

Cowboy slid his arm gently around my shoulders and softened his voice. "Come on, darlin'." He kept me tucked firmly against his side as he walked me home.

I was relieved he was no longer going after the Barlow boys, but hoped like hell Mandy didn't actually tell her brothers what Cowboy had said. It would be the equivalent of beating on an active beehive with a short stick.

Once we cleared my front door, I let out a sigh of relief. Just being back inside my small rental home, surrounded by my own things, made me feel better. Safer, even. My quaint cottage held only sparse, simple furnishings, such as a small flat-screen TV and an eggshell-colored love seat, but it was my comfort zone. *My sanctuary.*

I loved everything about it. From the plain white lace curtains adorning the living room windows to the delicate pink rose wallpaper in the narrow hallway. Not to mention the hundreds of books on the two huge bookcases which commandeered an entire wall behind my beige reading chair.

Cowboy raised a brow. "You read all those?"

I nodded. "I enjoy reading."

He lifted a romance book I'd left lying in my chair, scanned the title, and chuckled. "Sounds like some kind of guidebook for birth control, rather than a romance."

Mentally cringing, I moved into the tiny kitchen to keep from awarding him with the blush I felt slowly creeping into my cheeks. His boots clomped on the floor behind me, signaling he'd followed. I glanced over my shoulder and caught sight of him eyeing the steaming white teapot on the glass-top stove.

"I was preparing a cup of tea when I heard the popping sounds coming from outside," I explained, my voice shaking a little.

"Would you like a cup?" he asked.

I nodded and opened the cabinet nearest the sink, where I kept my good china and a small box of tea bags.

"Sit down," he ordered, reaching over me and taking them from my hands. "I'll get it for you."

Wordlessly, I obeyed his command and sat at the small round dining room table. I reached over and flipped the switch on an electronic warming plate that held a vanilla-scented candle in a glass jar, needing the calming Zen the aromatherapy would provide. Then I took a couple of slow, deep breaths.

It was hard to believe Cowboy was inside my home, much less making me a cup of hot tea. Every vision I'd had in the last week of him being here with me had always had way more to do with my bedroom than a kitchen. And the thought of Cowboy and me anywhere near a bed together made my heart race and my breath quicken. Not that I'd ever tell *him* that, though.

My irritating mind used the pleasant fantasy against me to slowly drive me insane. I'd be leaving in a few months. Besides that, Cowboy had never been attracted to me. How could he be? Especially now when I resembled a worn, wrung-out mop.

Standing outside in the wind had dried my damp hair, but now it felt like an unruly ball of tangled twine on top of my head. Drab, stringy, and no doubt completely unflattering. Then again, I doubted he'd even notice. Cowboy's only interest in me had to do with him bedding a woman who'd turned him down flat. That's what he'd said, after all: *I'm intrigued by you because you didn't want anything to do with me.*

Cowboy brought over two cups of the aromatic tea, placed one in front of me, and plopped down in the empty chair beside me with his cup still in his hand. He brought it to his lips and took a large swallow before cringing, making a god-awful face, and setting the cup down. He pushed it away from him. "That tastes like shit."

I dunked my tea bag a couple of times and cautiously took a sip from my cup. As I swallowed, the warm, fragrant liquid traveled down my throat, soothing me from the inside out. Puzzled, I shook my head. "There's nothing wrong with it."

"Tastes like dirt and grass."

I smiled lightly. "It's herbal."

He crooked his mouth and wrinkled his nose, as if he couldn't understand why anyone would drink the earthy stuff. Then his green eyes flickered to the flameless candle warmer, which apparently reminded him why we were sitting there together. "Do you want to talk about it?" he asked softly.

I didn't. Not really.

All the slow breathing I'd done earlier had helped lower my blood pressure and pulse rate, but I suddenly felt both rising once again. I'd carried the guilt over my mother's death with me for so long. Maybe it was time I let someone in and get it off my chest. But then I wondered what he'd think of me once he knew the truth, and the fear clamped my vocal chords into silence. Bringing the cup back to my lips, I took another sip and shook my head.

Cowboy's eyes narrowed in determination. He took my cup from me and set it aside, then he grasped my seat with both hands and scooted my chair around to face him. "Talk to me."

Guess he wasn't taking no for an answer.

I couldn't look directly at him. A long pause ensued until I felt calm enough to speak the words out loud. "I was… six years old at the time," I whispered, wringing my hands together in my lap. "My mother was cooking dinner while I finished my homework at the kitchen table. My stepfather had just called to say he was on his way home from work when the doorbell rang." I paused.

"Go on," he encouraged.

I swallowed hard. "My mom went to answer it. I...I should've stayed in the kitchen like she told me to...but I didn't." I was having a difficult time talking and shook my head in disgust as a fat tear dropped onto my cheek. "Had I stayed, I could have stopped the fire from happening. Things might've been different," I told him, my lips trembling with remorse. "S-she might still be alive." With that admittance, a sob tore from my throat and guilt stabbed into my chest, piercing my heart. Angry tears assaulted my cheeks, and although my hands flew to my face to fend them off, it was useless. The battle was lost.

Drawing me to him, Cowboy pressed his lips to my ear and made a shushing sound. He rubbed my back lightly, allowing me to release all the pent-up regret I'd held onto for so long. "I'm sorry, Anna. I should've trusted you from the beginning. I won't make the same mistake twice."

I squeezed my eyes closed. I was a coward. He trusted me...yet I still couldn't bring myself to tell him the whole truth.

When my cries finally died down, he asked, "Want to know why I became a fireman?"

His chin rested on top of my head, but he must've felt me nod.

"When I was thirteen, a single mother moved in across the street from my parents' home. She lived in a double-wide trailer and had three kids, all under the age of six—Danny, Lynn, and Suzie Q. Well, that's what I used to call her, anyway. The kids would come over on the weekends sometimes to play with my dog.

"One morning, I was out back working on my go-cart when I picked up a strong whiff of smoke blowing in the breeze. I'd circled the house trying to figure out where it was coming from, when I looked across the road and saw their trailer on fire."

My temple was pressed to his throat, and I felt him swallow hard.

"I knew they were inside and yelled for my mom to call 911 while my dad and I ran over and pounded on their door. It was locked, though. We couldn't get in. We knocked in a few windows and yelled, but no one answered. Every time we tried to enter, the smoke choked us and the heat from the fire burned our skin."

I pulled back and looked at him, wide-eyed. "They didn't make it out, did they?"

Solemnly, he shook his head. "I was there when the firefighters pulled their bodies out, one by one. It made me sick. The fast-moving fire had spread before their mom could wake up and carry them to safety. I stood outside that charred trailer and said good-bye to each one of those babies. They never even had a chance at life."

I studied his face. His eyes were glossy from tears that hadn't yet fallen. The cool arrogance he normally displayed was long gone, replaced by things I easily recognized. Grief. Sadness. Regret. Maybe we weren't as different as I thought.

"It's always tougher when it involves children."

"Yeah. But it's worse when you realize that if only you'd had the right tools for the job, they would all still be alive." He shook his head at the injustice. "That's only one of two reasons why I joined the fire department, though."

"What's the other?"

Cowboy grinned a little. "Danny wanted to be a fireman. That's all the kid ever talked about."

My heart squeezed as I smiled warmly at him. Without thinking, I leaned forward and pressed my lips to his cheek, surprising the both of us. He stiffened at the unexpected gesture, and I pulled back immediately. But his hand caught me behind my neck, stopping the motion.

His face lingered near mine, and his gaze landed on my mouth as I licked my lips with nervousness. Okay, anticipation. So I wanted to kiss him. Big deal. Who wouldn't?

But it wasn't a good idea. And, judging by his expression and the tightening of his grip on the back of my neck, it seemed we were both grappling with the decision to take the innocent kiss on the cheek one step further.

"Anna, I—" He lowered his gaze, his whole body becoming rigid. Cowboy's eyes widened and his mouth fell dormant.

At first, I wasn't sure what caused the reaction. Once my gaze followed his, it only took me a fraction of a second to realize what had taken him by surprise. My heart flatlined. My robe had parted on my thighs, baring them, and Cowboy had gotten an eyeful of much more than I'd ever intended for him to see.

Panicking, I grasped the skirt of my robe and covered myself, but his hands shot out and grasped mine. "Don't."

Before I could argue with him, Cowboy shoved my hands aside and carefully slid the fabric from my legs, revealing the large, irregular patchwork of ropey pink scars that marred my slim thighs. The unsymmetrical planes of skin were thickened with grotesque, disfiguring reminders of exactly why I avoided fire...and men.

As he focused his attention on my legs, my chest tightened with the strong urge to escape, but I was unable to move. The last person to look so closely at my deformities was the plastic surgeon who'd performed several painful corrective surgeries on me over the years in the form of agonizing skin grafts and laser resurfacing. That was, until I finally refused further treatment.

A tentative touch jarred me from my thoughts as Cowboy's hand fell lightly upon my right knee. His fingers inched upward, carefully considering the texture of each mark before tracing one blemish to the inside of my leg. His gaze heated as his fingers whispered over my deformed skin. Though there had been some nerve damage, and the skin in that area wasn't particularly sensitive, the sight of seeing Cowboy's hand between my legs caused me to tense and a strangled sound bubbled from my throat.

Our eyes met.

His calloused hand flattened, covering my thigh with warmth. He stopped exploring the marks, but didn't pull back. For a moment, we sat there in a deadlock, his hands on my thighs and neither of us moving. His face tightened with a cornucopia of emotions: anger, protectiveness, understanding, and pity.

I wasn't sure if I should say anything or not. Thankfully, he made the decision for me by releasing me and lowering his gaze, severing the intense connection between us. "I have to go," Cowboy volunteered in a hasty voice much deeper than before. "Right now."

"Oh," I said as my cheeks flushed. "Um, okay." I yanked the robe to cover my legs, while he extended the courtesy of looking away. I shot to my feet and faced away from him, not wanting him to see the disappointment and confusion in my eyes.

When I opened the front door and moved aside, he stepped through it and out into the warm night air. Darkness had fallen quickly, as it usually does when you're surrounded by nothing but trees and no streetlamps.

"Thanks for, um…listening, I guess."

"You're welcome." He started off the porch, without looking back. "Have a good night," he called out over his shoulder.

"You, too," I said softly, watching him stroll out to his truck.

Once he reached it, I closed the front door and leaned against it, blowing out a long, slow breath. I probably should've been relieved he hadn't pressed me for more details about the fire. And realistically, I didn't even know why I was bewildered by his reaction to seeing my scars. From the beginning, I'd predicted—if not projected—the outcome. Although he hadn't appeared exactly repulsed by them, he was obviously distancing himself from me, which was close enough to the same thing.

At least he'd demonstrated some compassion by not drawing out a long, awkward good-bye littered with excuses and insincere apologies. Not that it mattered, since I could already feel a stinging sensation as the first tear pricked my eye.

If I can't see past the scars, then why should he?

I was still leaning against the door moments later when someone rapped lightly on the other side. What the hell?

I opened it to find Cowboy filling the space with unnerving eyes, a strange look of desperation on his face, and his mouth held in a grim, firm line. "I should keep my hands off you," he said with a hoarseness to his voice.

"Um, okay." Guess he was more repulsed than I thought, because he was going ahead with the insincere apology, after all. "You came back to tell me *that*?"

"No, I forgot something." He sounded even more irritated than when I first opened the door.

"Oh. What'd you forget?" I started to turn to look for a set of keys or something else that could be his, but he gripped my arm to stop me.

"*This*," he said, spinning me back to him and covering my mouth with his.

Instantly, I froze.

Since I'd first met him, I'd always wondered what it would be like to be under that perfect mouth of his, and now that I was finding out, I stood there stupidly with my fish lips smashed against his in the most unflattering way.

But that didn't deter him. He moved his lips slowly against mine, patiently awaiting my response. And he got one. Within seconds, my passive lips became soft and pliant against his as our mouths began a seductive dance together. His warmth tempered my body, bringing it to just the right degree, until I melted into him, my fingers gripping his shirt as I kissed him back with no physical hesitation.

Mentally, I was still hesitating, though. "We shouldn't be doing this," I whispered between kisses.

In answer, his hands moved into my hair, tilting my head slightly to the right, as his breath tickled across my lips. "Open your mouth and shut up," he murmured, bringing my face back to his.

I did as he asked, and his tongue swept inside, delving

deep. My good sense flew out the window. He was warm and tasted like wild honey. The insistent rolling of his tongue against mine excited me more, enticing me to participate. Feeling braver than normal, I ran mine across his bottom lip and gave him a little nip.

He stilled.

At first, I thought I'd done something wrong, but my hand resting on his chest pulsed with the acceleration of his irregular heartbeat. Keeping his lips glued to mine, Cowboy spun me around with dizzying speed and planted me firmly against the door. Before I could say anything, he hungrily kissed me. His enthusiasm grew immensely, radiating off him with each insatiable thrust of his tongue, beckoning me with every curl.

His right hand moved lower, past my hip, and cupped the back of my knee, raising it to his waist. My robe lifted higher and left me feeling a breeze in places that shouldn't be breezy. I arched my hips forward to keep my balance, and the large bulge in his jeans rubbed against the thin fabric of my cotton panties. The delicious friction shot sparks throughout my body, and a purr-like sound rumbled from deep within my throat.

His warm fingers found their way to the back of my thigh, stroking and kneading, as he moved higher and higher. He used the position we were in as leverage to access an intimate part of me and easily slipped two fingers under my panties.

I was long gone. He could've taken me against the door with the neighbors watching for all I cared. But as Cowboy's fingers met damp flesh, he hesitated, then tore himself away from me completely. I could see in his lustful eyes it had taken everything he had to do so.

"One taste," he said, panting heavily. "That's all I meant to take."

Flustered, I swayed unsteadily as my breath synched to his. I had never felt so alive. "I…I'm discombobulated."

He released a shaky breath and squinted at me in confusion. "You're *what*?"

"Discombobulated."

Cowboy frowned with disapproval. "What the hell does that mean?" He stared at me intently, his gaze penetrating me so deep that my thighs trembled.

"It means…" That's when my sanity came back full force, and I realized what exactly I would have let him do to me against the door. Correction: what I *wanted* him to do to me against the door. No matter how good it had felt, I couldn't believe how out of control I'd let things get. "It means you have to leave," I said with exasperation.

"What? Why? Because you say weird shit and expect me to know what it means?"

"No, I just…need you to go," I told him, pushing him steadily out the door. Before I lost my godforsaken mind. Again.

He let me shove him out onto the porch, but he turned and grasped the doorjamb with both hands and leaned toward me with a smirk. "Discombobulated, huh? That's not one of those sex change operations or something, is it?"

Oh, Lord.

Without another word, I shut the door in his face.

Chapter Seven

From the shadows of the living room window, I watched as Cowboy strolled out to his truck, climbed inside, and drove away. My fingers feathered across my lips, still numb from the searing kiss we'd shared minutes before. A moment of closeness that had derailed me mentally, as well as physically…and yet, he'd barely even touched me.

But why had he touched me? And more importantly, why had he stopped?

As his taillights faded into the night, I took a ragged breath, closed my eyes, and wished for… What exactly? For him to come back? For him to have never shown up at all? I wasn't really sure. Or maybe I was and just wasn't willing to admit it to myself.

Regardless, I couldn't rationalize my behavior in a logical manner. Not when it had been nothing more than a self-indulgent whim. A fantasy, really. Clearly, the emotional cocktail of fear, need, wanting, and loneliness had played a giant role in me making such a poor, thoughtless decision.

I released the curtain, letting it fall back in place over the window as I plopped down on the couch and folded my legs under me. A frustrated breath escaped my lips. What the hell was I thinking, allowing him to kiss me, to touch me? It was Cowboy, damn it. I knew better than that.

Sure, ten years ago, I'd longed for him to notice me and look at me the way he did other girls. But he hadn't, and with good reason. I wasn't like those other girls. And now he'd undoubtedly seen that for himself.

Obviously, it had been a bad idea from the start, even if I'd seen some hidden layers to Cowboy, which made it harder to dismiss the strong, irrefutable attraction I felt toward him.

But that was one slippery slope I wasn't willing to climb. He may have kissed me senseless once, but if I had any brain cells left, I'd stay as far away from him as possible.

Then I sighed. Yeah, like that's going to happen. I hadn't stopped thinking about him since he'd left. Oh, hell. Who was I kidding? I hadn't stopped thinking about him since camp ten years ago.

In an effort to shake all lustful thoughts of Cowboy from my mind, I busied myself by cleaning up the kitchen. But as I picked up the teacup from the table, I remembered how tiny it had looked in his large, masculine hands. The same hands he'd gripped my thighs with as he… *Holy hell.* What was the matter with me?

Figuring I needed a change of scenery to clear my mind, I strolled back to the living room, where I dusted and re-arranged my bookshelves. I thought it was working until I caught myself organizing the titles by which male on the cover looked most like Cowboy. Damn him and his perfectly handsome, stupid face.

I needed to find something to keep me from thinking about that man. If it was even possible.

Frustrated, I planted myself at the computer desk and pushed the button to make the monitor light up. Unsure as to what I was doing, I cleared my mind and typed the first name I thought of into a search engine and hit enter. Thousands of returns popped onto the screen for Ned Swanson.

At the very least, it would definitely keep me busy. And help Cowboy in the process. Though he didn't seem to be the type to ask for help. But research was my thing. I worked in a library for goodness sakes. If I couldn't find the chief's brother for…a certain person—one who would remain nameless—then no one could.

It wasn't going to be an easy feat, that was for sure. But as I sat there clicking and typing my way into an oblivious stupor, my mind settled and focused on the task at hand.

Hours later, I lifted my head off the desk and rubbed my eyes. I must've dozed off because it was suddenly three o'clock in the morning. I hadn't found Ned Swanson, but I had some good leads to follow up on.

I turned off the computer screen and was heading to the bedroom when a clanging noise echoed outside my kitchen window. Raccoons were always trying to get into my trash cans, so I opened the front door, flipped on the flood lights, and stepped out onto the porch, hoping to scare them away.

But what I saw had the opposite effect.

A shadowy figure—a man, judging by the height and bulk—stood within the trees at the edge of my property, staring back at me. Frozen in place, I blinked rapidly as a chill ran up my stiffened spine. It was too dark to make out all of his facial features, but his intense eyes shone bright from the glow of the floodlights, much like a wild animal. No sooner had I laid eyes on him than the man took a large step backward and melted into the darkness.

I strained to search for movement among the woody area while listening for the sounds of snapping twigs or rustling bushes. But there was nothing, no evidence of anyone having been there. It all happened so fast, though. Had I imagined the whole thing?

Still, I stepped back inside, locked the door behind me, and picked up the cordless phone from its cradle. But who would I call? The sheriff? Cowboy? And what if I *had* imagined the whole thing? It wouldn't be the first time I'd seen something that wasn't really there. Almost nightly I had dreams that made no sense.

But this wasn't a dream and that wasn't something I wanted others to know about me. Not the police and especially not Cowboy. Besides, it could easily have been any one of my very few neighbors out on a stroll…on my property…through the woods…at three o'clock in the morning. I sighed and reluctantly set the phone back down. I'd be up all night thinking about a man, all right. Just not the one I had originally thought.

The following day seemed to drag on forever. I left work and headed home, planning to take a very long, well-deserved nap. As expected, the man in the shadows had plagued my thoughts all night, leaving me with an uncomfortable somebody's-watching-you feeling.

Even now, the hairs on the back of my neck stood at attention. It had actually kept me from thinking about Cowboy, which would've been a welcome relief if it hadn't been so damn creepy.

Before leaving for work, I'd walked the edge of the woods, looking for footprints or some evidence to suggest the visitor had been real. But I found nothing. Based on that alone, I decided that the whole thing had been nothing more than a figment of my overactive imagination.

I parked in my driveway and walked down to the mailbox before strolling inside. I tossed the mail on the kitchen counter, causing it to fan out as I kicked off my shoes. A small envelope with my name handwritten on the outside in big letters caught my eye.

Shifting the other mail aside, I picked up the envelope and flipped it over, searching for a return address. There wasn't one. No stamp, either, which meant that someone had placed it in my mailbox, rather than mailing it.

I opened it carefully, pulled out a small note card that had been tucked inside, and read the message. As my eyes scanned the words, I gasped and a twinge of dread ran through me. My thoughts went directly back to the supposedly non-existent shadowy man standing outside my home the night before.

Then I realized something.

I shook my head and almost laughed aloud at myself. With the messy scrawl and misspelled words, it didn't take a genius to figure out who wrote the note. After all, no one else would say, "*Play with fire and your gonna get burnt*," except for the two idiots next door.

It all made perfect sense.

Last night, I must've caught one of the Barlow brothers in the act of delivering the note to my mailbox. They probably hoped I'd get the ominous note today and storm over to their house so they could torture me with more of their idle threats.

But I wasn't going to play into their hands and give them the reaction they wanted. I'd just ignore it. And them.

Those two boys were known bullies who got their thrills by intimidating and terrorizing others, but they were also cowards, which made it difficult for me to believe I was in any real danger.

At least as far as the Barlows were concerned.

Almost a week later, I was sitting in the passenger seat of Bobbie Jo's tan Ford truck as she drove. She glanced at me warily. "You sounded a little upset on the phone. Is everything okay?"

I shrugged lightly. "I had a bad morning, that's all."

And that was the truth.

The note I'd found in my mailbox earlier that morning had irritated me, though it was only one of several I'd received over the past week. The Barlow brothers hadn't improved with their spelling any, but the lame threatening notes were starting to get on my nerves. I had a good mind to march next door, give them an ass-kicking, and possibly a lesson in good grammar.

Nor had Cowboy come back after kissing me almost a week ago. Of course, that *may* have had something to do with me throwing him out of my house afterward and slamming the door in his face. But still…

I wondered if my blatant sexual inexperience had shone through the moment our lips touched. Maybe that was why the persistent playboy hadn't returned. I mean, I'd kissed a guy before. Just not one who made me feel the way Cowboy did. Like I would willingly tear off my clothes and let him caress me any way he wanted.

And the thought terrified me. Because once I told him the whole truth about me, he'd hightail it. Never to be seen or heard from again. Though seeing how he'd disappeared already, I couldn't figure out how things would be much different than they were.

It was probably for the best. If I was smart, I'd take a lesson out of Cowboy's dating playbook by moving on and putting the whole experience behind me. It wasn't like I had much of a choice. Cowboy had already dropped off the book I'd loaned him in the outdoor return bin and hadn't been back to the library, either.

Another reason for my foul mood.

I'd told him that was exactly what I'd wanted. But if that were true, then why did my chest ache? And how come every time I thought about Cowboy's body pressing mine against that door, my knees went weak?

Damn it. I let out a frustrated sigh.

"Want to talk about it?" Bobbie Jo asked, pulling me from my thoughts.

"Nothing to talk about. I'm fine."

"You sure?" she asked, turning left into a driveway marked by a large wooden sign with faded black letters that read "Miller's Bird Farm."

I plastered on the most genuine smile I could fake. "Yep.

I'm great."

Bobbie Jo parked her pickup on a concrete slab in front of a large white house and shut off the engine. "Good. Then let's go inside so I can introduce you to the girls."

I opened my door and slid out of the truck as the distant sounds of birds, squawking and chirping, drifted to my ears. As I maneuvered around the front of the vehicle, I spotted a small flock of white and gray guinea fowl running loose nearby. Ignoring me, they scratched at the ground in search of insects.

"You'll love Floss," Bobbie Jo said, bringing my attention back to her. "She's the sweetest thing ever. And Emily... well, she'll grow on you," she said with a laugh.

I laughed, remembering the story she'd told me about how Emily and Jake had gotten together. Emily had entered Witness Protection, and Jake had been the FBI agent in charge of protecting her. Unofficially at that. While none of that was remotely funny, the wild shenanigans Emily had put Jake through were.

"I guess Emily's not causing any more problems for Jake now that they're married and have a baby," I said, stepping up beside her.

"Are you kidding? That girl is a handful. Lucky for her, Jake loves every minute of it...when she's not frustrating him to the point of throwing things."

One of my eyebrows rose involuntarily. "Isn't he a little too old to be pitching fits?"

Bobbie Jo smiled, then turned toward the back passenger door of the truck. "Jake wants Emily to behave herself, but that's like asking the sun not to rise." Her hand stilled over the door handle for a moment, then she shook her head and frowned. "He's a man, Anna. They *all* throw tantrums when they don't get what they want." She swung open the door to retrieve Austin from the backseat.

By the sound of her strained voice, I gathered she must've had another run-in with Jeremy. "Do *you* want to talk about it?" I asked softly, returning the favor.

"And ruin our good time?" Bobbie Jo snorted. "Definitely not."

I waited patiently as she pulled the baby from his car seat and shouldered his diaper bag. She'd dressed him casually in a simple, orange-striped onesie with matching socks and a thin blanket wrapped around him. It was a warm day, but the cool breeze kept it from being too hot.

"After we go see what the women are up to, we'll check on my boys and see what trouble they're getting into. They're helping Hank over in the pasture today."

Her boys? As in plural? Oh, no.

I glanced out into the field and caught sight of a group of men standing on the other side of the barbed wire fence in the back pasture. My gaze landed squarely on Cowboy as he stood from a crouched position and stretched his arms above his head, elongating his tall, muscular frame. The white T-shirt he wore lifted a few inches above his belt buckle, allowing me a glimpse of his well-defined, perfectly sculpted abs.

Oh, dear God. I wish I'd known he'd be here.

I wanted to appear nonchalant, but at the mere sight of him, my body betrayed me. Anticipation zinged through my veins. Butterflies fluttered in my stomach. I managed to swallow the knot in my throat, although as much as I was salivating, I wasn't sure how it was possible to feel so parched.

Then I noticed my nipples straining against my white cotton dress. One look at Cowboy and he was already screwing with my hormones again.

Bobbie Jo looked up as I crossed my arms over my chest and shivered. She quirked an eyebrow. "It's almost ninety degrees out here, Anna. Don't tell me you're cold."

"Um, a little?" My reply sounded like a question.

She reached into the backseat of her truck and pulled out a blue jean jacket, tossing it to me. "Here you go. Put this on."

"Thanks," I said, slipping the jacket on and cuffing the sleeves up to my elbows.

I was going to burn in hell for lying to my friend. Didn't matter, though. It was the equivalent to wearing a jacket in ninety-degree Texas heat, anyway.

"Hey, fellas," Bobbie Jo yelled out, waving at the men.

Cowboy turned his head toward us, did a double take, then a stoic expression crossed his face as he looked away. I was pretty sure I even saw his lips move inaudibly with something that very closely resembled "sonofabitch." I guess his interest level had cooled considerably since our last encounter.

Unfortunately, I'd seen this sudden change in attitude and behavior before in other men. And it always happened after each of them had witnessed one thing in particular: my scars. Which was going to make this fun get-together a complete and utter disaster.

Lovely.

I added the last pieces of cut-up raw bacon to the pot of pinto beans and washed my hands, admiring the antique milk glass bottles in the window over the kitchen sink. "Is there anything else I can do for you, Mrs. Miller?"

"Yes," she replied, never looking up from the potato she was peeling. "You can start calling me Floss."

I turned and smiled at her, though she didn't see it. The kind, little old lady sitting at the island in the kitchen was adorably sweet. She reminded me of Popeye's Olive Oil, except her hair was gray and she was shorter than even me. She kept her hair pulled into a tight bun at the base of her neck, and even through the handmade blue jean dress, I could see how stick-thin she was.

"Okay, Floss. Anything else I can help with?"

She pulled another potato from the bag and began peeling. "No, dear. You've been helping since you arrived. I think you've done plenty already."

"I can peel these potatoes for you. I'm happy to help," I said, reaching for one. "I don't mind at all."

She swatted my hand. Hard. "You sure don't," Floss stated firmly. "I said you're done. Now don't make me tell you again, young lady."

I blinked, not sure what to make of her harsh tone.

Unfazed, Floss went back to work peeling the potato. "You're a guest in my home, dear, and guests shouldn't be doing all the work."

Bobbie Jo sat at the nearby kitchen table with a smile on her face. "I warned you Floss was going to get onto you if you didn't sit down."

True. But she didn't say the old woman would turn physically violent.

Emily stepped into the room with one hand up her shirt, adjusting her bra. "Okay, I fed Lily, and she's out like a light."

"Do you need me to move Austin?" Bobbie Jo asked her. "He fell asleep on my shoulder, so I laid him in Lily's playpen."

"Nah. I put her in the bassinet and wheeled her over beside him in the living room. They look so cute sleeping next to each other."

"Aww," Bobbie Jo said, leaning to catch a peek of the little ones sleeping together.

"Bet you two mommas won't be saying that in another twenty years or so," Floss said, giving me a knowing smile.

"Oh, jeez," Emily said with a laugh. "Jake loves Austin like his own son, but he'll kill that boy if he comes anywhere near Lily after puberty."

"Cowboy swears it's going to happen," Bobbie Jo said, grinning.

At the mention of his name, I felt my body warm. "Well, they *are* so close in age," I told them, nodding in agreement. "It's probably kismet."

"Nope, it's all in God's hands." Floss winked at me. Then she gestured to a pitcher of iced tea and a pack of clear plastic cups on the counter. "Now that the babies are down for their naps, why don't you three take some iced tea out to the fellas? I'll keep an eye on the young'uns."

Emily lifted the pitcher as Bobbie Jo reached for the stack of cups, leaving nothing for me to carry. And I desperately needed something to hold onto with my shaky hands. I wasn't entirely sure I was ready to face Cowboy after what happened between us.

"I could stay behind and help with—" Floss cut her eyes

to me, daring me to finish my sentence. "Okay. Well, if you're sure…"

I was anything but.

To busy my trembling hands, I opened the back door off the kitchen and allowed Emily and Bobbie Jo to walk out first while I peeked over the railing. On the ground, the men all congregated around an old barrel-style smoker, where Hank was basting huge slabs of beef he must've put on the grill before we'd arrived.

Floss had introduced me to her husband, Hank, when he'd popped inside to grab what he called his lucky barbecue fork. I still wasn't quite sure what sort of "luck" a barbecue fork could hold, but I found him to be a charming man.

Jake ribbed his uncle about "rubbing his meat," while Ox and Judd stood off to the side, playfully arguing over which of them looked better in a Speedo. It wasn't hard to recognize either of them, since Ox was almost always the littlest guy in the crowd and Judd was the giant.

Cowboy lounged in a nearby chair with one booted foot kicked over the other. He stared out into the pasture, as if he were lost in deep thought, and was relatively quiet compared to the others.

I followed the girls downstairs, but as we reached the bottom, Cowboy was the only person who looked our way. He tilted a bottle of beer to his lips, but his eyes never left mine. Unaware of his watchfulness, Emily and Bobbie Jo turned and headed for a nearby picnic table. But I just stood there empty-handed, feeling as useless as I probably looked.

Cowboy's gaze burned into me, searing me from the inside out, as if he were reading my soul like a book. My gaze fixed on him, too, trying to decipher the hidden meaning behind the look he gave me, but I couldn't think about anything other than the way his lips had felt on mine the last time we were together.

A low whistle broke us from our trance-like state as Jake slapped him on the shoulder and snared Cowboy's attention. "Going to sit around all day ogling the women or are you going to give us a hand?"

"I wasn't ogling," Cowboy told him, glancing back at me to see if I heard, then his attention fell back on his friend. No doubt he noticed my blushing cheeks.

Jake grinned. "Yeah right. This is *you* we're talking about."

Cowboy glared at him. "I said I wasn't ogling!"

The surprised expression on Jake's face was enough to convince me I wasn't the only one who thought Cowboy overreacted.

"Damn it, Jake. Leave the boy alone," Hank said, closing in on the two of them. "If he said he wasn't ogling the girls, then drop it. Don't piss off the help."

As Jake walked away, Cowboy grinned at Hank. "Afraid I'd get mad and leave before saddle-breaking that horse of yours?"

"Nope. I know I can count on you, son." He leaned in a little closer, but didn't bother whispering. "Now quit ogling the women and get back to work."

The other men snickered.

Cowboy shot to his feet and tossed his empty beer bottle into the nearby trash can so hard it broke as it clanked against the other empties. Then he shook his head. "Everybody 'round here thinks they're a goddamn comedian."

He lit out for a swampy-looking pond at the back of the

property, probably to blow off some steam. Everyone sat silent and slack-jawed for a moment until Cowboy was out of earshot.

Then Ox said, "Man, who kicked him in the sac?"

I wasn't sure, but judging by Cowboy's avoidance of me all week, and his sudden annoyance after seeing me again, apparently *I* had. And considering the smile and wink Hank gave me as he plopped down in a nearby plastic lawn chair, the old man agreed.

Thank goodness no one else had noticed me standing there and could connect me to Cowboy's bad attitude or his sudden disappearance.

"Hey, fellas," Jake said, gazing directly at me. "Look who's here. It's Anna."

Crap.

The moment Jake mentioned my name, all eyes shifted onto me. Like he'd just crammed me under a very uncomfortable microscope. But even though I hadn't seen some of them in ten years, each of them had a smile on their face. At least *somebody* was happy to see me.

With the others on his heels, Jake headed directly for me and gave me a friendly one-arm hug. "I had no idea you'd be here today."

"Bobbie Jo talked me into coming at the last minute." I offered him a genuine smile. "By the way, I saw your precious baby girl upstairs. You must be so proud. Lily's a doll."

"Of course she is," he said with a wink. "She takes after her daddy."

Ox tapped Jake on the shoulder from behind. "All right, Barbie, move it along. You're holding up the line."

Emily chuckled from somewhere behind me, and Jake

glared at Ox. "If she starts calling me that, I'm going to kick your ass."

Ox didn't look concerned, though. He moved past Jake and leaned in to hug my neck and gave me a quick peck on the cheek. "Hey, girl," he drawled. "Bobbie Jo said you moved to our neck of the woods."

Ox moved aside to make room for Judd, who'd been waiting patiently for his chance to greet me. And he needed *a lot* of room. I'd thought it was impossible for him to get any bigger than the last time I'd seen him, but sure enough, he looked like he'd nearly doubled in size.

Judd swept me up in a big bear hug that cracked my back. "It's great to see you again, Anna."

When he put me down, I had to take an extra deep breath. "Thank you. It's nice to see you, too," I wheezed out.

"See, Jake?" Ox said. "That's how you take turns. Learned that in Kindergarten, ya know?"

"Shut up," Jake said.

Emily must've approached from behind me, because suddenly she was standing next to me. "Don't mind Jake. The bonehead's been grouchy for weeks now."

Jake poked Emily in her side, making her squeal with laughter, then wrapped his arms around her waist and nuzzled his face into her neck. "I'll show you a bonehead."

"Uh-uh-uh." She shook her finger at him. "The doctor said *six* weeks. You've got two more days before I'm allowed to—"

Jake clamped his mouth over hers, muffling out the last word.

"Did she say *duck*?" Ox asked, grinning.

Judd chuckled. "Nope. Pretty sure it was *truck*."

"Maybe she meant *luck*," Bobbie Jo said as she joined the group.

I shrugged. "Could've been *suck*."

Jake pulled his mouth from Emily's and everyone blinked at me. I blushed, realizing they took it differently than how I meant it. I was just throwing out a rhyming word like everyone else. Or so I thought.

Jake laughed and said, "I like the way you think."

"You would." Emily rolled her eyes at him. "Don't give him any ideas, Anna. The man's relentless as it is."

He winked at her. "Pot and kettle, baby."

She grinned at that and winked back at him. I could see why Emily was so smitten by her husband. Jake was as good-looking as ever with his dark hair and steely gray eyes. And as funny and beautiful as Emily was, I could definitely see why Jake had fallen so hard for her. I was glad to see he ended up so happy.

And Bobbie Jo stood next to them with a genuine, heartfelt smile on her face, proving how glad she was that Jake found someone else to love. As far as ex-girlfriends go, he couldn't have asked for a better one.

"So, Anna," Ox said, snaring my attention. "Didn't you live in Houston all those years ago? What brings you to our neck of the woods?"

I nodded. "There was an opening at the library, and Bobbie Jo was able to put in a good word for me. Her mother knows the director."

"You're a librarian?" Ox asked, letting loose one of his boisterous chuckles. For a tiny guy, he had one of the loudest, most entertaining laughs I'd ever heard. "Perfect job for you. At camp, you always had your nose in a book."

"Yes. I…um, suppose I did," I replied meekly, realizing that everyone—including Cowboy—probably remembered me as a boring, mousy girl.

"I didn't even recognize you when you first walked down the stairs," Judd said seriously. "Man, you sure have changed since the last time I saw you. You're all grown up."

Though I was sure he meant it as a compliment, I felt the familiar heat of embarrassment creeping up my neck as everyone stared at me. It was terrific seeing so many recognizable faces, although I'd always hated being the center of attention. It overwhelmed me and gave me the urge to stick my entire head into a book, rather than just my nose.

But I tried to play it cool. Even if my hands were feeling clammy and I was beginning to break into a sweat. The jacket I had on wasn't helping matters.

"So, what have you been up to all of these years?" Jake inquired.

"Not much, really," I said vaguely. "What about you guys?"

Jake's keen eyes fixed on me and he cocked his head, as if he knew I was deliberately taking the focus off myself and steering the conversation back to them. It's not like I had anything to hide. Nothing more than usual, anyway. I just didn't like talking about myself that much.

Hank pulled at his belt as he rose from his plastic lawn chair. "All right, boys. Break's over," he called out. "Let the womenfolk be. You can catch up with them over supper."

"Why not now?" Jake asked.

"Because I said so. You boys need to go find Cowboy. I'd do it myself, but it's too far of a walk. I have enough damn pins and screws in my knee to declare myself a robot."

"We could always get you one of those souped-up

scooters to drive around on the property." Jake grinned as he baited his elderly uncle.

"Those are for old people," Hank said seriously. "Now go find Cowboy and get to work. I don't pay you all to sit around."

Jake chuckled at that. "You don't pay us at all, you old coot."

"That's because I dock wages for smart mouths. Right now, all of you are dangerously close to going in the red and owing *me* some money."

The men rolled their eyes at Hank's idle threat, but they didn't hesitate to get moving. Bobbie Jo and I grinned as Jake leaned over and gave Emily a quick kiss and then whispered something in her ear that made her face light up.

As the boys walked toward the pond, Hank turned to me. "Honey, can I get you to do me a small favor?"

"Um, sure," I said warily.

"Floss needs some fresh eggs to boil for her potato salad. There's a stack of buckets along the far wall in the barn. If you would be a dear and get me one, I'd appreciate it."

"Absolutely. In fact, if you want I could even…"

I was just about to offer to gather the eggs for him, too, but Emily stood behind him, shaking her head violently. She flapped her arms like a chicken, then sliced a finger across her throat, as if we were playing some weird game of charades that I hadn't signed up for. I wasn't sure what any of it meant, but gathering the eggs didn't look like anything I wanted to be involved in.

"No problem," I told him, bewildered by whatever came over Emily. "I'll be right back."

Chapter Eight

Inside the musty-smelling barn, I'd just found a small bucket when Cowboy's voice sounded outside the door. Not ready to face him alone, I panicked, hurried into the nearest horse stall that was filled with a few hay bales, and ducked down to keep from being spotted. Thankfully, the stall sat against the back wall in the center of the room, leaving me a clear view of almost the entire barn.

My plan was simple: wait for him to leave, then do the same.

Through the narrow slats on the stall gate, I watched in silence as Cowboy stepped inside, followed seconds later by three shadows that turned out to be Jake, Ox, and Judd.

"Should've known you guys would follow me in here," Cowboy griped, clearly still upset. "It's not like you sissies have anything better to do than harass me."

He kicked a metal pail that clanged against the stall I was in. Startled by the loud sound, I jumped as the silver bucket shot out a few feet away from the gate and knocked over several wooden-handled shovels leaning against the wall.

Jake, Ox, and Judd stood in the barn doorway giving Cowboy a slow clap for his bad aim. I couldn't help but grin.

"You guys are dicks."

"Aw, come on, Cowboy. We're just playing around," Ox said. "Besides, when the hell did you ever start looking at Bobbie Jo like that?"

Judd chuckled. "Yeah, you looked like you wanted to rip her clothes off."

Not looking the least bit amused, Cowboy whirled on them. "You sick sonofabitches! That'd be like me screwing my own sister," he snapped, throwing his hands in the air. "And for your information, you bunch of nitwits, I wasn't looking at *her*. I was looking at… Aw, shit. Forget it."

Even though it made sense that if Cowboy hadn't been looking at Bobbie Jo, he would've been looking at me, Ox and Judd didn't catch on. I mean, obviously he wasn't referring to Emily. At least not while Jake stood there. But leave it to the FBI guy to be the only one to pick up on it.

"Anna?" Jake asked, raising an eyebrow to his friend. When Cowboy didn't answer, Jake laughed. Loudly. "Really?"

I ground my teeth together, offended by his question. *Thanks a lot, Jake.*

Then he added, "I mean, she's a cute girl and all. But since when did you become a sucker for a woman with a brain?"

That comment had me biting my lip and stifling a laugh.

Cowboy shrugged, but still didn't say anything.

Jake shook his head and grinned. "All right, Cowboy.

Spill it."

"Spill what?" Cowboy asked, shifting uncomfortably.

"I want to know what's going on with you and the woman who dresses like a grandma."

I cringed. This was *precisely* why people shouldn't eavesdrop.

Then Jake said, "You've been behaving strangely today and I'm betting it has something to do with Anna. You started acting funny the moment she showed up."

"I don't know what you're talking about," Cowboy said.

Jake sighed. "Don't play fucking games with me. Or with Anna, either. You know *exactly* what I'm talking about."

Cowboy leaned back, hooking one arm over the top railing of a nearby stall, as he gave the others a cool look. "I'm not interested in playing games with anyone."

"But you're interested…in *her*?" Jake asked, his expression souring.

"So what if I am? You got a problem with that?"

I blinked rapidly and felt my heart rate speed up.

"I do if you're leading her to believe that whatever's going on between you two will be a mutually monogamous relationship."

Cowboy shoved off the stall, shuffled a few feet away, and kicked at a clump of mud mixed with hay. At least I thought it was mud…until the barn's pungent odor of manure worsened. Then he spun around to face Jake, irritation lighting up his face. "I guess this is your way of telling me to leave Anna alone…all because you don't think I can be faithful to a woman."

Jake shrugged, unaffected by Cowboy's temper. "Just looking out for her best interests."

"And that isn't me, right?"

"Damn it, Cowboy. Anna's not like other girls you've chased. She's always been so sweet and innocent and…naive. From the looks of her, I don't think any of that has changed. I just don't want you to do anything to disrespect her."

Sweet and all, Jake, but you could've left off the part about me being naive. Jeez.

"So what you're really saying is you don't want me to soil her reputation. Why the hell would I do that?"

Jake gave him a get-real look. "If she takes a bath with a dog, he's not going to dirty only his half of the water."

Cowboy's face reddened and anger flashed in his eyes. He took three large strides and got into Jake's face, making my eyes widen. And Jake didn't back down. Ox and Judd shifted closer to the faced-off pair, as if they were readying themselves to break up a fist fight.

"When the fuck did you get so self-righteous, you bastard?" Cowboy snarled. "If it wasn't for Emily, you'd probably be out at the bar right now looking for some action."

"Don't confuse my string of morality with yours, jackass. And don't bring Emily into this, either. I'm not the one who went home with every girl who sashayed her ass in my face." Then Jake's voice deepened, doing the best Cowboy impression he could muster. "*Why buy the milk when I can get the pair of tits for free?* Sound familiar, asshole?"

Cowboy huffed out an annoyed breath, but backed down, stepping away from the other three men. He took his hat off and scrubbed his hand through his unruly sandy-blond hair. "Yeah, well maybe I'm looking to change my ways."

I blinked, not sure I heard him correctly. Or maybe

he didn't mean it the way it sounded. But if I pressed my cheek any closer to the slats in the gate, I was going to have splinters in my face. He couldn't have possibly meant...

They all stared blankly at Cowboy, and then a slow smile formed on each of their faces.

"What?" Cowboy asked, seemingly confused by their grins.

That's when the laughter began.

Jake let out a loud barking laugh, chuckling so hard that he held his belly and doubled over with tears springing into his eyes. Judd snorted and threw his head back, chortling himself into hysterics. Ox slapped his knee, hooting and cackling so much I was sure he would fall over any minute and roll around on the ground laughing.

At first, Cowboy didn't appear to appreciate their expressed humor. He looked like he was on the verge of having an aneurysm the way the vein in his temple kept popping out. But the more the others laughed, the more Cowboy's expression softened, until he ended up chuckling a little himself.

But I wasn't amused in the least.

"Never would've believed that line of bullshit in a hundred years," Jake said, still snickering. "Like some stuffy librarian would be the cause of *your* demise. You can't even keep your dick in your pants long enough to be serious about any girl, much less a mouse like Anna."

Cowboy tossed his hat back onto his head and glared at his friend. "You know what, Jake? Go fuck yourself."

Yeah. What he said.

Jake grinned wider. In fact, they were all smiling, looking quite pleased with themselves. "Oh, calm down," Jake told him. "We're just messing around."

Judd shook his head and squinted in confusion. "Why are you getting so mad, Cowboy? You got a real hankering for this girl or what?"

"No!" Cowboy's mouth tightened into a grim line before he released it on a heavy sigh. "Maybe."

I rolled my eyes. Obviously, he said that to shut his friends up. I didn't know why they continued to pester him about me, but I hated that I was stuck there listening to them talk about me like…like…well, like I wasn't there. Sheesh.

"Come on, Cowboy. You have no shortage of women wanting to jump into your bed. What the hell do you want with Anna?" Jake asked.

"That's none of your damn business."

"It is if you're going to hurt her."

"Yeah, and I'm genetically coded to do that because I'm not you, right?" Cowboy's tone was anything but friendly.

"Why her?" Jake asked gruffly. "Why not someone like Mandy? She'd be a better fit for someone like you."

"Someone like me, huh?" Cowboy shook his head, allowing irritation to show plainly on his pinched lips and narrowing eyes as he glared at Jake.

"Well, you said she propositioned you before."

"I think that was only to make some boyfriend of hers jealous. But you know damn well I don't fish in another man's pond. Never have. It isn't sportsmanlike and you tend to catch things you don't want." Cowboy shook his head at Jake. "I thought *you* of all people knew that about me. Guess I was wrong."

I felt bad being a voyeur to Cowboy's persecution. He hadn't done anything to deserve Jake being so hostile.

"Look, I don't know what you're getting pissy about. I just don't understand what you want with Anna."

"Because you think I'm only looking for a piece of ass, is that it?"

Jake raised one eyebrow. "Well, aren't you?"

"Ya know, I almost hate to deflate your already low opinion of me, but I'm not nearly the jackass you automatically assume I am when it comes to women."

Jake scratched his head and grinned. "Prove it."

"How the hell am I supposed to do that?"

"By leaving Anna alone so you don't end up humiliating her."

Cowboy marched over to Jake and shoved him. "Fuck you, Jake! Why don't you mind your own goddamn business and stay out of my relationship with Anna?"

"So you admit there's a relationship between you two?"

"Of course there is, you fucking prick! What the hell do you think we've been talking about all this time?"

Jake grinned, then chuckled.

Cowboy looked as puzzled as I felt. "What the hell's so funny?"

"You are," Jake said, still laughing his ass off. "You want this girl so bad, you can't even see straight."

What? What the heck was he talking about? Cowboy and I were just friends. Nothing more. There could never be anything more.

"Ya know, sometimes I fucking hate you."

That only made Jake hysterical. "See what I mean?" As his laughter came to an end, there was a brief silence. Then he said, "Funny how one woman can make everything around you look so different, isn't it?"

Cowboy rubbed at the back of his neck and grinned. "Like getting lost in my own backyard."

I cringed at that, knowing the feeling well myself. After all, it was exactly how I felt every time I was around him. But no matter what Cowboy said, he wasn't interested in me for anything more than a roll in the proverbial hay.

"Who would've thought Cowboy would get an itchin' for a girl with a brain," Judd said, grinning.

"Well, if Anna had half a brain, she'd run like hell from the likes of *him*," Ox said, thumbing over to Cowboy. Ox chuckled and shrugged his eyebrows suggestively. "So, Cowboy, you get her in bed, yet?"

I mentally gasped. *Hey!*

No wonder women had such a hard time trusting men. The callous asses were all the same. Always bragging about getting into a girl's pants. Guess it only proved what I'd thought all along.

Cowboy's eyes burrowed holes in his friend. "Shut up, prick."

"Shutting up now," Ox said, although he continued grinning.

"Damn," Jake said, glaring at Cowboy. "What's wrong with you today? You know we're just teasing. Anna's a great girl. Why are you being so overprotective and getting wound up?"

"Just drop it, okay?" Cowboy leaned back against a nearby stall barely in my field of vision and crossed one boot over the other in a comfortable-looking position. He sighed. "Look, she's got bigger problems than worrying about me chasing after her. She's having some problems with the Barlow brothers."

"Those turds?" Ox asked. "What the hell would they have against our sweet little Anna?"

Our? Since when had I become theirs?

"She told them if they didn't stop shooting fireworks over her house that she'd call the police on them."

"Shitfire!" Ox said, letting loose a high-octane laugh. "For a mouse, that girl has some brass balls on her."

Judd scratched his head and looked a little worried. "Cowboy, you tell her to be careful with them Barlow boys. Fires have been known to start around them."

Ox's comment had made me smile, but Judd's wiped it away and had my teeth worrying my bottom lip. I closed my eyes and took a deep breath.

"I'm taking care of it," Cowboy told them.

He was taking care of it? Yeah, right. By doing what— avoiding me?

"If you need any help…" Jake started.

"Yeah, yeah. I know where to find you, Mr. Hotshot FBI man."

"Look who's talking," Jake said with a teasing grin. "You've got all the women of Liberty County hot and bothered over that photo shoot you did. Not counting the ones outside of Liberty. I had three female agents in our Houston office ask me to get them autographed calendars. And one of them wants to know if the hat was photoshopped in. Pretty sure she's hoping to dig up an original proof somewhere."

"That shit wasn't photoshopped. Used the hat off my own head and placed it on my other head," Cowboy responded proudly, making the others chuckle.

I rolled my eyes. Of course he had. Because sexually violating a hat in order to get a rise out of women for the notoriety would be something only Cowboy would do.

"It was for a good cause," Ox stated. "Those three charities are going to receive way more funds because of what you did."

He did it to raise money for charity? I had no idea, or I never would have walked away from him at the chili cook-off without buying a calendar…even if I would have thrown it away to keep from eyeing it daily. *Damn.*

"All right, enough standing around gossiping like a bunch of hens," Jake said, smiling. "When are you going to go saddle-break that crazy fucking horse? Or are you going to make one of us do it for your lazy ass?"

Cowboy laughed. A lot. "Like any of you could?"

"How hard could it be?" Judd asked. "Don't you just mount up and hold on?"

"No, no," Ox said with amusement. "That's what Jake does with Emily."

My God. They were worse than a group of women when it came to gossip.

Cowboy and Judd chuckled, but Jake's mouth morphed into an irritated snarl. "Might want to watch how you're talking about my wife, asshole."

"God, why are you and Cowboy so sensitive today? You both on your periods or something? Jesus, Jake, you know we love Emily. Hell, we probably like her better than we do *you*. At least she's fun."

"Emily's not fun. She's frustrating. There's a difference."

Suddenly, a woman cleared her throat somewhere behind them. I hadn't seen her walk in, but I recognized the sound of her voice immediately.

Apparently, so did Jake. He silently mouthed the word

"Emily" to Cowboy and received a terse nod in return.

Then Cowboy beamed with a gleam in his eye, silently letting Jake know that he'd seen her standing behind him the whole time.

Jake turned around to face her, but kept one hand behind his back prominently displaying his middle finger to Cowboy. "Hey, honey."

"Don't '*hey, honey*' me, Jake," Emily told him. "So I'm frustrating, huh?"

"Just kidding around with the guys, baby."

"Uh-huh. Sure you were," she said, moving closer to Jake and into a position where I could see her through the gate. And she didn't look happy.

"Need something?" Jake asked, shifting his weight uncomfortably.

"Momma Belle just called and said she's on her way over. If you think you can hide out in here like you did last time while that crazy-ass woman feels me up again, I'm going to make sure she's the *only* one getting any action from me this week." Emily grinned wide. "Then you're going to find out exactly how *frustrating* I can be."

The other men all snickered, while Jake gave her a solemn, "All right. I'll be there in a minute."

Emily put one hand on her hip and cocked a brow at him. "Yeah, I've heard *that* before. I'm not kidding, Jake. If you aren't out here in two minutes, I'm cutting you off indefinitely."

"You wouldn't dare," Jake said, grinning, but eyeing her warily. "Because you can't do that to me without *me* doing the same to you."

"Oh, *Jakey*," she said with a sinister gleam in her eyes.

"You can't cut me off. You don't know *who* I'm getting it from." Then she sashayed out of the barn, giggling to herself.

"Emily, that better be a fucking joke!" Jake called out to her as she disappeared from sight. "Emily…?" He waited for her response, but there was nothing but silence. "Sonofabitch, that woman doesn't fight fair!" He stormed out after his wife.

The others had been doing a terrible job at keeping a straight face, but the moment Jake left the barn, they all keeled over with laughter. I bit my tongue to keep from joining them.

Once they got themselves under control and finally left, I grabbed the bucket I came for and slipped out the barn door as well.

I wasn't sure what to make of Cowboy's comments, though they replayed over and over in my head. Had he meant what he said? Or was it him just playing some kind of sick game? I couldn't bear to get my hopes up only to be let down when he realized he wasn't attracted to *me* nearly as much as he was attracted to *something he couldn't have*.

Trying to stay busy and away from Cowboy, I arranged the foam plates and plastic silverware in neat little piles. Hank rested at the picnic table, drinking a glass of sweet tea I'd poured for him. "Why don't you go over and join the others, honey? Floss is bringing the last few things down now, and I'm about to pull the meat off the grill. We'll be eating shortly."

I stopped adjusting food platters and looked up at him

warily.

He eyed me with what he must've thought was some understanding of the dilemma. "You don't have to be shy. We're all family and friends here, and we're always happy to have a guest join us."

I smiled at him. "Thank you. I'm glad to be here."

Hank was a sweet man, but I still didn't feel the need to confess the real reasons I was over there with him rather than with the others. Sure, one of those reasons was Cowboy. But the other had to do with something entirely different.

The fire.

Everyone hung out near the burn pit to ward off the swarming mosquitos. It had a stone edge and three thick logs sat in the center, covered with orange flames. Occasionally, the fire spit out embers with a crackle and a pop, but the group barely seemed to notice.

They looked content sitting in the flickering heat while having a quiet fireside chat. But I couldn't bear the thought of being that close. Especially after Cowboy accused me of starting the pallet fire at the chili cook-off. I preferred to stay right where I was, watching them all from a distance.

Hank stood and headed over to the nearby barrel smoker. Ox and Judd joined him, holding out large steel pans, while Hank filled one with barbecue ribs and the other with a huge chunk of brisket.

Jake lounged in the shade of a tree, holding his sleeping daughter on his chest, while patting her back lightly with his large hands. They looked so comfortable and peaceful.

Actually, everyone did.

Cowboy was the only one making any real noise. He sat on a plastic chair bouncing Austin on his knee in time to the *Bonanza* theme song, providing all the sounds with his mouth. I couldn't help but grin as he used the baby's tiny hand to crack an invisible whip.

When Bobbie Jo took Austin from him—probably to keep him from getting whiplash from the way his head was lolling around—Cowboy stood and walked away from the fire. He passed by Jake and paused long enough to rub the back of his finger lightly against Lily's cheek. It was sweet, the way he showed so much attention to the babies.

A clinking noise interrupted my thoughts, and I turned to see Emily putting some beer and ice into a cooler. "Hey, Anna. Do me a favor?" She handed me the empty beer box. "Throw this into the burn pit for me, will you?"

My mouth opened, but I froze in place, unable to answer her.

Cowboy stepped in front of me and looked straight into my eyes. He read my expression and gave me a little wink as if to calm my nerves. "I've got it," he said, then took the box from me before moving back toward the burn pit.

Relief washed over me, but it was only a temporary fix, since Emily stepped up beside me a second later and asked, "What was that all about?"

"Well, I…" I closed my eyes, not knowing how to tell her what Cowboy already knew. And it didn't help that it mortified me.

"Are you okay, Anna?"

"I…um, have this thing…about fire." I lowered my gaze and cringed. "It scares me."

"No shit?" Emily said, pausing to contemplate what I told her. "Did Bobbie Jo tell you about last summer when Jake hid me here to keep the mob from finding me?"

I nodded, hoping she wouldn't be upset with Bobbie Jo for sharing that bit of personal information with me.

"Well, even though Hank taught me to shoot a gun, I still hate the sound of gunfire. It makes me nervous."

"That's understandable after what you went through."

"Well, you must've had a bad experience yourself," Emily said.

I nodded, but didn't bother to elaborate.

"Don't worry about it. I know how hard it is to get over something like that. It takes time."

Bobbie Jo walked over, having left Austin in Ox's capable hands. "Lord have mercy. Did you see what Cowboy was doing to my child's head a minute ago?"

"If he does that to Lily, I'm going to sic Jake on him," Emily said, shaking her head with blatant disapproval. "She can't even hold her head up on her own yet like Austin can."

Maybe it was because he'd helped me only moments before, but I felt the need to defend Cowboy, even if I did agree that he was bouncing the baby around a little too much. "I think it's sweet the way Cowboy is with both of the children."

"Did I hear my name?" Cowboy hollered from across the yard. I glanced in his direction and he smiled wickedly at me. "Hey there, beautiful. Long time, no see."

Heat flashed through my entire body, but settled in my cheeks. No one had ever called me that before. Not that it meant much, though, since he called Bobbie Jo the same thing that first night I'd seen him in the library. And probably every other girl he ever crossed paths with.

"God, Cowboy. Do you always have to hit on all of our friends?" Bobbie Jo rolled her eyes. "Ignore him, Anna.

He'll eventually give up."

"What are you ladies talking about over there?" Cowboy asked.

Emily grinned. "Menstruation."

A horrified expression crossed his face, then he turned his attention back to the other men, making the three of us laugh.

"Works every time," Emily said.

"Poor guy's going to get a complex if you keep doing that to him," Bobbie Jo told her, still giggling.

"Serves him right," Emily said, shrugging it off. "We're never going to have other females to hang out with if he keeps sleeping with all of them and running them off." She smiled at me. "And I like this one."

All of them? Blushing, I somehow managed to smile back, though I couldn't look either of them directly in the eyes. "I, um… Thanks, I like you, too."

Both girls just stared at me, blinking, until Emily said, "Oh God! Not you, too? Holy hell. Can't that man keep his dick in his pants for more than two minutes?"

I shook my head, denying the charges. "No, he didn't… I mean, we didn't… Oh God." Embarrassed, I pressed my fist to my lips to stop them from flapping.

Emily huddled closer. "Okay, missy, we want the goods on you and Cowboy."

"No, *we* don't," Bobbie Jo quickly clarified.

"Okay, she doesn't. But I do. All the juicy, luscious details about you and the hunky fireman."

I dropped my hand and shook my head. "There's nothing to tell, really. He came by my house last Sunday and he sort of…kissed me." I quickly followed with, "But I haven't seen him since. Not until today, that is."

"What? That's such a jerk move," Bobbie Jo said. "I should give him a piece of my mind for acting like Jeremy."

"Oh, no. Please don't say anything." My eyes pleaded with her. "I just want to forget the whole thing."

"Why?"

"Because it was a mistake," I told her. "One that I won't be repeating."

"I'm sorry, Anna. He's acting like an ass. And I hate to say I told you so, but you can't say I didn't warn you. He's a great guy most of the time, but men like Cowboy and Jeremy are womanizers. Too hot-blooded to commit to a real relationship. It's that stupid *love 'em and leave 'em* attitude of theirs."

"It's okay," I said with a shrug. I felt stupid that I even thought for one second Cowboy had been serious about being interested in me. "It's not like I was expecting anything from him. And to be honest, I'm sure he looks at it the same way I do. We don't have a thing in common. He's probably forgotten all about it already," I said, though Cowboy's words in the barn still ran through my mind.

Bobbie Jo turned to Emily. "How did you know something happened between them, anyway? You have ESP or something?"

"Beats the shit out of me," she said with a shrug. "Anna looked guilty so I took a wild guess. After all, it *is* Cowboy we're talking about."

Chapter Nine

Just as we were lining up to fill our plates, a beat-up red Pontiac pulled into the driveway, parking on the concrete slab in front of the main house. The wrinkled old woman behind the wheel had fluffy white hair that made her round head resemble the end of a Q-tip.

But as she wrenched herself from the sedan, I mentally corrected myself. *Actually, more like a cotton ball.* There was nothing stick-like about the elderly woman's body. The white cotton sundress clung to her thick waist and the short sleeves showed all the slack, loose skin on the underside of her flabby arms.

No one, except for Floss, made any attempt to greet her. In fact, everyone was suddenly occupied or quiet and facing the opposite direction with stiff spines and breath-held lungs. I wasn't sure what to make of that, but I thought I'd better follow suit and busy myself, as well.

I wasn't paying attention when I reached for a foam plate

and accidentally bumped fingers with Cowboy. As our eyes met, I pulled my hand back quickly. "I'm sorry. Go ahead."

"No, ma'am," he said, offering me the plate in his hand. "Ladies first." Then he stood there, staring at me in silence as he waited for me to take it.

I accepted the plate and nodded a thank you, then moved over to the food table, where I added a small piece of brisket and topped it with some red-eye gravy that I'd helped Floss make earlier.

When I turned, Cowboy was back at my side, standing so close that his arm bumped mine. "I didn't mean to touch you," he said in a low voice.

"That's okay. I'll just move over a little."

"No," he said, frowning. "That's not what I meant." He set his empty plate down on the table and turned to face me as I reached for a yeast roll. "I'm talking about last weekend. I didn't mean to kiss you."

Flustered, I jumped as if he'd shot me, missed the rolls, and ended up raking the back of my fingers across the barbecued ribs instead. *Damn it.* Awkwardly, I balanced my plate in one hand while holding up two sticky fingers coated in a sweet-smelling dark red glop.

"That night, I didn't come to your house with any intention of putting my hands on you. Or my mouth. It just…sort of happened."

A shiver ran through me as the blood hummed in my veins. The memory of his hard body pressed against mine played over in my mind, tampering with my sanity. My teeth bit into my bottom lip, pulling it into my mouth as he had done that night, and I swore I could almost still taste him.

"I don't think this is an appropriate time to talk about

that…um, incident." I glanced around for a napkin.

"How about later, then? I could always swing by your place and—"

"No! I mean…I can't. I'll be busy later."

"Doing what?" he asked, his brow lifted with curiosity.

"I don't know…just stuff." Like trying to figure out what the hell was wrong with me.

"If you're upset because I avoided you all week, I was only trying to wrap my head around what's going on between us. We should talk about it. About *us*."

I continued my perusal of a napkin, while ignoring the fluttering in my chest. "There's really nothing to talk about, Cowboy. It happened and it's over. Let's just forget the whole thing."

"What if I don't *want* to forget it?"

"People don't always get what they want," I told him, just as I spotted the pile of paper napkins someone had placed at the end of the table on the other side of Cowboy. I nodded to them, silently asking him to hand me one.

He looked at the napkins and back to my fingers. Grasping my hand, he gave me a sexy little grin and said, "I *always* get what I want." Then he slid my fingers into his warm mouth. I tried to pull back, but he held me firm while sucking and licking the barbecue sauce off. Heat traveled from my cheeks into places lower in my body.

The suction of his mouth coupled with the erotic tongue action he performed on my fingers nearly had my knees buckling in bliss. Good Lord, the effect this man had on me. I whimpered softly.

When he was done, he kissed my knuckles lightly, gave me a quick wink, and said, "Enjoyed that, did ya? Next time we'll try whipped cream...and a different body part."

I quivered from head to toe, but didn't have time to speak.

The old woman who'd arrived moments before stepped up beside him and slapped him in the back of the head. "Behave yourself, you horn-dog. There'll be no hanky-panky at the dinner table, ya hear?"

"Yes, ma'am," Cowboy said, rubbing where she whacked him.

"Now, stop playing around, loverboy, and introduce me to my newest granddaughter."

Smiling, I looked around, but didn't see anyone near us. When I glanced back at her, I realized she was talking about *me*. I shook my head insistently and set my plate down on the edge of the picnic table. "Oh, no. You're mistaken. I'm not Cowboy's girlfriend."

"Horsefeathers! I saw how you two were fiddlefarting around over here and canoodling over the string beans while the rest of us starve to death."

Flustered, I tried to explain. "We weren't...ah, I mean, I wasn't..."

The old woman scoffed and pointed her finger straight into my face. Somehow it seemed deadlier than a loaded shotgun. "Young lady, you mean to tell me you let any Romeo with a wandering eye play coochie-coo with you?"

Great. What was I supposed to say to that? Speechless, I looked to Cowboy for help.

Thankfully, the lady turned her attention on him as well. "You trying to pull a fast one on me, boy?"

Cowboy chuckled, then put his hand on the old woman's shoulder. "Aw, settle down, Momma Belle. This is Anna.

My girlfriend." My eyes widened, but Cowboy just kept on grinning. "She's just a big *tease*."

Why, that little… My eyes narrowed. "No, I'm not!"

Momma Belle cast a glance my way. *Crap.*

I didn't see any other way around it but to play along. If I told her Cowboy and I weren't dating, she would think I was a hussy. Then again, wasn't that the kind of woman he normally dated?

I mentally sighed. *Oh, jeez.* "Momma Belle, of course I'm his girlfriend. I don't play…um, coochie-coo with *any* man without the promise of a commitment. I guess I thought you'd see right through such a silly notion." My eyes cut to Cowboy to make sure he got the message loud and clear, then glanced back to Momma Belle. "It's nice to meet you," I said, extending my hand.

But the old lady frowned at me. "Girl, do I need to break a switch off one of these oak trees and strap your legs good? You almost gave me a heart attack. Fossils my age don't have strong tickers, you know?"

Oh God. The woman had heart problems? "I'm so sorry. Are you okay? Can I get you anything? Maybe some water or something."

"Bless your heart, child, but I'm okay. Just need to sit down and rest my achy joints. When my dadgum arthritis starts acting up like it is, there's only one remedy that works." Momma Belle directed one gnarled finger toward her car. "If you'd be so kind, it's in a medicine bottle inside my purse on the floorboard."

I nodded and patted her on the hand. "Of course, I'll get it for you."

I started toward her car, but didn't get halfway there

when Cowboy caught up to me and yanked me to a dead stop in between two vehicles. "Tell her you couldn't find it."

"What?"

"Don't take Momma Belle her purse. In fact, toss it in the bushes and tell her she must've left it at home."

I gawked at him. "Why would I do that to that poor, sweet woman?"

"*Poor, sweet woman?*" Cowboy made a strangled sound of disgust with his throat. "That woman has the fangs of a rattler. If you let her, she's going to sink them right into that pretty little neck of yours."

Obviously, he was overreacting, so I rolled my eyes at him and continued to the car. I opened the passenger door on the red Pontiac and leaned in to lift the heavy black tote from the floorboard. As I straightened and turned, I bumped right into Cowboy, who was blocking my path.

He held his ground and frowned at me. "I'm serious, Anna. Don't take her that bag."

"Why are you being like this about a little old lady who needs her medicine? I know you can be arrogant and self-centered at times, but I never realized you were such an ass."

His eyes narrowed as he snatched Momma Belle's purse from my hands and rifled through it with a mad flourish. Clearly, he was searching for something in particular, but having a hard time finding it with all the junk stuffed inside. This lady was worse than Mary Poppins.

"What do you think you're doing? You can't just go through her personal belongings like that. It's an invasion of her privacy."

"Here, hold this," Cowboy said as he passed something to me.

My eyes widened as I stared stupidly at the small metal object in my hand. "I-is this a gun?"

"No, it's a bingo dauber that happens to resemble a small caliber weapon." Cowboy stopped rooting through the bag and glared at me. "Of course it's a goddamn gun." He shook his head and continued his search.

Okay, so maybe it was a dumb question. "Why is your grandma carrying a gun?" I asked him.

"That insane woman is *not* my grandma. If she were, I'd shoot myself with her…bingo dauber."

I gaped at him, appalled by his lack of sympathy and his cold-hearted behavior toward an elderly woman with health problems. "Jesus, what is wrong with you? You're being so… callous and insensitive."

"Oh, that's rich. Especially coming from the woman who won't go on a date with *me* all because she's heard a few bullshit rumors." Before I could respond to that, he found what he was looking for. "Aha!" He held up a small mason jar of clear liquid. "*This* is what Momma Belle calls her 'medicine.'"

I sighed with irritation. "Moonshine?"

Cowboy shook his head at me. "You know, for someone who is supposed to be so smart, you sure ask a lot of stupid-ass questions."

My eyes narrowed. "Okay, that's it! I've had enough of you and your demeaning insults." I yanked the purse from him and then snagged the jar from his hand, shoving it back inside the large bag. "If that old lady wants to drink moon-shine, then that's *her* business, not yours."

"That insane woman has no business drinking—"

"That's enough," I said, huffing at him. "Since I don't

see you over there wrestling the beer out of Hank's hand, I can only assume you're saying that because she's a woman... you...you...chauvinistic pig!"

"Oh, don't give me that women's lib crap. You know that's not what I meant."

Crap? Really?

"You know what? There's something seriously wrong with you." I blew out an irritated breath as I shifted the heavy bag onto my shoulder. "I can't speak for other women, but I, for one, am not amused by your ludicrous behavior, no matter how ridiculously charming you may be."

His lips settled into a wide grin.

I crossed my arms, not sure what to make of his expression. "Why are you smiling?"

He raised one brow. "Charming, huh?"

"Oh, good Lord. *That's* all you got out of this entire conversation?"

"So how *ridiculously charming* do you think I am?" he asked as he moved closer, his proximity suffocating me.

Oh, great. I hadn't meant to encourage him. "I...I don't." I shook my head vigorously as heat spread throughout my cheeks. "That wasn't what I meant. I was just trying to explain how ridiculous you're acting."

Cowboy chuckled softly and touched my cheek. "Did you know that your ears and neck turn red when you blush? You keep looking so sweet and adorable, I might have to kiss you again."

A tingle ran through me straight down to my nether regions, but I held my composure and placed my hands on my hips to show my exasperation. "You'll do no such thing." The wicked little smirk he wore had me worried, though.

"Oh, yeah?" he asked, stepping forward until his body brushed lightly against mine. "You sure about that?"

"Y-yes," I said, trying to sound convincing. "Because not only are there other people around…" I glanced around, realizing that the vehicles blocked their view of us. *Damn it.* "But because you're a gentleman."

He lifted a hand and curled it around the back of my neck, pulling me closer to him as his mouth opened and his breath touched my lips. In that second, my heart raced and my mind drew a blank.

Then I remembered what I was saying. "And I…I'm asking you…to keep your hands to…yourself." There. I said it.

"Darlin'," he drawled with a sly grin. "There's only one problem with that theory of yours."

"What's that?" I breathed out, desperately trying to maintain my composure.

"I never claimed to be a gentleman." Then he covered my mouth with his.

The moment his warm lips fastened over mine, my hands flew to his chest. I meant to push him away, I really did, but just couldn't bring myself to actually do it.

His tongue flicked out, running teasingly across my bottom lip, then slowly worked its way into my mouth. The moment his tongue touched mine, an electrical current ran straight down my center, and my knees buckled. I sagged against him like a limp ragdoll, boneless and lacking all mental capabilities.

Never breaking contact with my mouth, Cowboy's strong fingers slid over my ass, gripped it and lifted me back up, and steadied me against his strong frame. He nibbled at my bottom lip, sucked it into his mouth a little ways, then released it with a sharp nip that sent my nerves skittering throughout my body.

Although I didn't want him to stop, I *needed* him to. I couldn't breathe. My mind swam ferociously through a riptide of emotions that threatened to pull me under. Like I was choking on his overpowering testosterone and drowning in his masculinity. Overwhelmed by his very male essence, a shiver ran through me.

As our kiss came to a frustratingly slow end, I made the unfortunate mistake of sighing into his mouth, obliging him with the sound of my satisfaction. I felt him smirk against my lips.

Once we separated, he turned and walked back toward the house, throwing a quick glance over his shoulder. Probably making sure my legs hadn't given out again.

And he was grinning. *The smug bastard.*

There were always two sides to every face: the one people wanted you to see and the one they kept hidden. But I already knew what was lurking in Cowboy's shadows. He was a player. Always had been. Even his own buddies had called him out on that well-known fact in the barn.

Which meant that no matter what I'd overheard him say, I couldn't trust that Cowboy wanted to change. Nor could I bear the thought of him scratching an itch with me, and then moving on to some other unsuspecting girl. It wasn't a risk I was willing to take.

But explaining that to my surging hormones was a feat in itself.

After spending a moment gathering my wits, I returned to the picnic table where Momma Belle sat. Cowboy lazed in a nearby lawn chair, looking quite proud of himself, his long legs stretched out in front of him with one booted ankle kicked over the other. As I handed Momma Belle her purse, he eyed my shaky hands and smiled, obviously pleased that he'd had an effect on me.

She reached into the tote and pulled out the container of moonshine, then glanced up at Cowboy. "Lovely young lady you got here, whistle britches. Yes, indeed." She opened the jar, took a large swig, then sat back as she peered directly at my breasts. "Just ripe for the pickin', as my Earl would always say."

Cowboy grinned, but said nothing.

"Is Earl your husband?" I asked, sitting down beside her and hoping to take the focus off my boobs. Jesus.

"Oh, yes, deary. He was. Up until the big C hooked its claws into him and sank him six feet into the ground. I'm tellin' ya, folks can't always afford no high-falutin' doctor these days."

"I'm so sorry to hear that."

"No need to be sorry, girl. My Earl kept himself in good spirits and didn't go down without a fight."

"Yes, I hear having a positive outlook can be quite healing."

"No, dear. *Spirits*." Momma Belle tapped her nubby finger on the mason jar she was holding. "He took to making moonshine before he died. Said the white lightning was the only thing that helped keep the pain at bay."

"Oh." I smiled sympathetically. "Well, I'm sure you miss him a great deal."

"Sure do. My Earl was a hoot, even if he did sag in places I didn't want to look." She cackled at that and gigged me hard in the ribs with her wrinkled elbow before leaning closer. "He had two bald eggs down below and a thingamajig that wasn't much bigger than our billy goat's, but that horny toad was always trying to get in my britches."

My eyes widened, along with Cowboy's grin. The woman was clearly having one of those senior moments. "He…uh, sounds like a nice man," I told her uncomfortably.

"Hey, Anna, I saved your plate over here and your food's getting cold," Emily said, winking at me.

"Oh. Right. I'm coming."

Momma Belle gave me a cold-eyed stare. "Listen here, girl. We don't waste perfectly good food around these parts. Especially when you're nothing but skin and bones. Those arms of yours are like twigs, I tell ya. In fact, when I first laid eyes on you, I nearly poked you with a stick just to see if you were still alive. Now you go get that plate and eat every last bite, ya hear?"

"Yes, ma'am."

"Darn females nowadays," she mumbled to herself. "They just don't know nothing."

I practically skipped to Emily, hoping Momma Belle wouldn't follow. "Thanks," I whispered, accepting my plate from her.

"No problem. Come on, you can sit over here at our table. Just do yourself a favor and steer clear of Momma Belle from now on. The woman's bat-shit crazy."

"Tell me about it. She thinks I'm Cowboy's girlfriend."

Emily chuckled. "I wouldn't worry about that. Cowboy has *lots* of girlfriends."

Yeah, so I'd heard.

I followed Emily to a nearby table where Jake, Judd, Ox, and Bobbie Jo sat with their plates of food. I sat beside Judd, hoping his hulking figure would hide me from Momma Belle, and possibly Cowboy.

Judd lugged his meaty arm over my shoulders. "So, Anna, if you need anyone to show you around, I—"

"You're taken, jackass." Cowboy plopped down on the other side of me and scowled at Judd. "Or did you forget about Gina already?"

"Whoa," Judd told him, holding up his hands in surrender. "Chill out, buddy. All I was going to say is that I have a single buddy who would be happy to show Anna around."

"I'm sure the last thing the new girl in town needs is some bastard trying to get his hands up her skirt." Cowboy smirked, then raised a cocky eyebrow to me. "Isn't that right, darlin'?"

My eyes narrowed at the challenge in his voice and I couldn't resist the urge to respond. "Thanks for the offer, Judd. Sure, why not? I'd *love* to meet one of your single friends."

Cowboy's jaw tightened as he gritted his teeth, but he said nothing in return.

"So who's Gina, anyway?" I asked Judd sweetly, ignoring the warmth of Cowboy's hard thigh against mine.

Across from me, Emily smiled. "Gina is my friend from Chicago. She and Judd have been carrying on a long-distance relationship since last summer. Same as Ox. He hit it off with my friend Dale."

I glanced to Ox who was grinning at that. "You finally came out to everyone?" I asked, smiling with approval. "I'm so glad to hear that."

Cowboy's head snapped to me. "Wait a minute. You couldn't have known Ox was gay when you met him at camp. None of us knew. He was still hanging out in the closet back then."

I shrugged. "I had my suspicions. I'm usually pretty observant when it comes to people."

"Speaking of suspicions," Ox said, changing the subject. "Jake, I heard the FBI seized a couple of moonshine stills they found in the woods."

Jake finished chewing his food and swallowed. "Yep, three of them. We stumbled across them after someone reported seeing some weird lights in the forest at night. Next thing I know, we're getting calls about wild hogs acting strangely."

"Strange as in how?" Ox asked.

"They were stumbling all over the place and falling over. Apparently, they had eaten the discarded mash that the owner of the stills left behind. The damn pigs were drunk."

That got a chuckle out of everyone.

"I'm heading up the case, but beyond the three stills we uncovered, the inebriated swine, and the weird lights, we don't have a lot to go on." Jake shook his head. "We still don't know who the head bootlegger in the area is. I'm working on finding that out."

"I don't know if he ever sold any, but Momma Belle said that her husband, Earl, used to make moonshine before the cancer got him."

"Cancer?" Cowboy asked, surprise registering on his face. "Earl didn't die from cancer."

"Oh. When she said that the big C hooked its claws into

him, I just assumed—"

"Cirrhosis of the liver," Cowboy corrected. "The old man drank himself to death. Probably to get away from Momma Belle, right, *Jakey*?"

Jake shook his head. "Christ, I hate when she calls me that."

Bobbie Jo laughed and then turned her attention onto me. "Hey, Anna, we're all heading out to The Backwoods bar tomorrow night. Do you want to come?"

"Good idea," Judd said. "My buddy will be at the bar. You can meet him while you're there."

Cowboy lifted his head, and his heated gaze met mine.

I shook my head. "Oh, I don't know. I really don't think—"

"Come on, Anna," Emily said. "It's the first time I'm leaving Lily with Floss for the whole evening. I could use the moral support. Besides, it'll be fun."

With everyone staring at me, waiting for my answer, I couldn't bear to tell them no. "Okay, sure. I'd love to."

"Great," Bobbie Jo said with a smile. "The girls can get ready at your house together and meet up with the boys at the bar. How does that sound?"

Emily and Bobbie Jo smiled at each other and were obviously up to no good, but I didn't want to be the party-pooper. "That's fine."

"Good," Bobbie Jo said, winking at Emily. "It's settled, then."

The girls started cleaning up, but I just sat there, still trying to figure out what the hell I had just gotten myself into. I wasn't entirely certain, but I had a feeling I had been coerced into…well, something.

Jake rose from the picnic table. "Let's go help Hank clean the grill and then we can get to breaking that horse."

"*We?*" Cowboy asked, cocking one eyebrow.

Jake grinned. "You think you're the only one who's ever broken a horse, asshole?"

Cowboy laughed. "Shit. Jake, the only horse you ever broke was the one outside the grocery store that takes quarters."

"We'll find out in a few minutes, won't we?"

"Guess so," Cowboy said with a challenging nod and a glint in his eyes.

My gaze flickered to Ox and Judd, who both sat there grinning at Cowboy, as if they were subconsciously agreeing with Jake. As Jake started away, the others stood up, threw their trash away, and followed him, leaving me alone with Cowboy.

Feeling awkward, I rose and gathered my plate in my hands, but just as I started to leave, Cowboy said, "Anna…?"

I turned back to him. "Yes?"

"When I come by later, which kiss do you want to talk about, the first or the second?" The intensity in his eyes held my gaze, only making me more uncomfortable than I already was. Which apparently was something he enjoyed, since his tight-lipped mouth turned up into a full-on smirk.

But I'd had enough. "You really think you're something, don't you?"

"I'm more concerned about what *you* think."

"Trust me, you don't want to know what I think."

"Try me."

I cocked my head, realizing he was serious. "Okay. I think you're an egotistical ass, who behaves like a large child.

You can't have what you want, so you keep acting out until you get it. I also find your actions to be inconsistent with the behavior of a gentleman...not that you ever *claimed* to be much of one," I said, using his words against him.

Cowboy blinked and the smile fell from his face. "No, no. Don't hold back or anything."

I shrugged. "You asked."

"Well, at least admit that you enjoyed the kiss."

It was true that I'd found the lip-locking frustratingly hot and...well, if I were being honest, downright exciting. But I shook my head in denial. "Doesn't matter. It won't happen again."

Cowboy flicked a glance down my white dress and back up to the denim jacket I'd borrowed from Bobbie Jo. Then he grinned, as if he could tell my nipples were straining against the thin cotton beneath the denim. "Yeah, that's what you thought last week, too."

Chapter Ten

"Jake, don't be stupid! Let Cowboy break the dumb horse before you injure yourself," Emily yelled with frustration.

"Sweetheart, I'm not going to get hurt," he replied calmly.

Emily rolled her eyes and kissed the tiny baby girl in her arms on the forehead. "Say bye-bye to Daddy, Lily," Emily said sweetly. "Because after that horse kicks him in the head, Mommy's going to kill him." She took Lily's small hand and waved at Jake with it.

I chuckled at the stern look Jake gave her as he walked out into the pasture where Cowboy stood, holding onto the white palomino colt's halter. "I'm sure he'll be fine," I said, hoping to put her at ease. "Jake's never been one to take uncalculated risks casually."

But Emily chewed on her bottom lip with worry, and I had to force myself to keep from doing the same. Even for a colt, the handsome horse was tall, had a stocky build, and looked as fully mature as the stallion I could see grazing in the back pasture. It didn't help that I'd heard stories from Bobbie Jo about just how wild and unruly this animal could be. According to her, there wasn't a stall or gate in the barn that he hadn't already destroyed, earning him the name Ruckus.

Hank left the sidelines and approached Jake as he reached Cowboy and the colt. "You sure you want to do this, son?" Hank grinned wide. "A smart man doesn't step in the same pile of shit twice."

"Have to earn back my money somehow, right?" Jake held up a fifty dollar bill.

His uncle wasted no time in snatching the money from his hand, but sighed warily. "And here I pegged you smarter than this."

Jake grinned at the challenge. "We'll see, old man. You just be sure to cough up my dough, and yours, when I win this bet."

Hank shook his head as he returned to his seat in the green plastic chair. "I've told that boy a hundred times," he muttered as he sat down, "the fastest way to double your money is to fold it and shove it back in your wallet. He just don't listen." Then he grinned smugly. "The dipshit."

I grinned, mostly because I agreed with him, but didn't say anything. That Hank was a smart man.

"Okay," Cowboy said, addressing all the boys. "The rules are simple. One shot, no redos."

Jake didn't waste any time. He stepped into the stirrup and swung his leg over, mounting the horse. The animal tossed his head and side-stepped a little, but Cowboy held tight to his halter until Jake readied himself in the saddle. At his nod, Cowboy let go and stepped out of the way while Jake braced himself.

But the horse just stood there.

"Give him a little kick," Hank said, grinning.

Jake did, but the colt still didn't move. "What the hell's wrong with this dumbass horse? Why's he just standing here?"

"Must be those superb handling skills you claim to have." Cowboy gave him a teasing grin. "Almost makes me wonder why you have so many problems controlling your woman."

"*Controlling his woman?*" Emily passed Lily carefully to Floss and headed for the pasture. "Is that what you've been telling them, Jake? That you're trying to *control* me?"

Jake glared at Cowboy. "Of course I didn't say that. You misunderstood what he meant."

Emily stopped a few yards away from the fence and crossed her arms. "Is that what you were *'kidding around with the guys'* about in the barn? Because if so, I don't think it's very funny!"

"Damn it, Emily, stop yelling before you spook the—"

Suddenly Ruckus came alive under Jake, lurching and rearing up onto its hind quarters. When the horse came down, his back legs kicked out frantically, bucking wildly until Jake rolled off backward and hit the dirt hard. The palomino bucked a few more times before finally settling down about ten feet away.

Emily's eyes widened and we both gasped, but no one else seemed overly concerned that Jake had landed flat on his back and wasn't moving. He lay there, as if struggling to regain the breath that had been knocked out of him, although a deep, whiny moan came from his throat.

Cowboy ran over and peered down at Jake. "Hey, Darth Vader, get up." He chuckled to himself as Jake closed his eyes and winced. "Oh, come on. Time to wake up, sleepyhead."

When Jake managed to get his breath back, he glared at Cowboy. "Don't you have a mute button?" Then he reached for the hand his friend offered and pulled himself to his feet. After dusting himself off, Jake bent backward to stretch out his back, which must've been sore after the fall he'd endured. "One day, I'm going to kick that fucking horse's head smooth off his body."

As Jake's temper flared, Cowboy grinned and glanced to the other boys. "Who's next?"

As Emily checked her husband's back for bruises, Judd mounted up. Cowboy held the ornery colt until he received a nod from the new rider, then he let go once again. Maybe it was Judd's heavier frame that caused the horse to panic, but the colt bolted immediately and ran for the back pasture with Judd clinging tightly to the reins. The horse headed straight for the barbed wire fence and didn't look to be slowing down any.

"Shit. He's gonna get snagged on the fence if he gets thrown," Cowboy said, concern lacing his voice. "Jump off, Judd! Jump!"

Judd did. Face-first into the side of a large mesquite tree.

Cowboy took off running toward him, and without thinking, I raced out behind him to make sure Judd was okay. Ruckus came to a dead stop at the edge of the property near the fence line and grazed on the thick weeds.

Judd was sitting on the ground with a dazed expression

when we made it out to him. He had a cut above his swelling left eye and deep scrapes embedded into his cheek. His entire face leaked blood, which dribbled down onto his white T-shirt.

As we stopped in front of him, Judd said, "Cowboy? Is that you?"

"Yeah, it's me, you idiot."

Judd shook his head, as if to clear his vision. "I think the horse kicked me in the face."

"Nah. You just got bitch-slapped by a tree." Cowboy grinned at him, though I wasn't entirely sure Judd could even see it. "Just a couple of scratches. Nothing that can't be fixed. A little ice and some first aid and you'll be good as new. Come on, I'll help you up."

Couple of scratches? Judd didn't need an ice pack and Band-Aids. He needed a trauma team and a CT scan. Apparently, *I* was the only one who even considered seeking professional medical attention, though. Because as we walked him slowly back to the house, I spotted Floss waiting for us with a first aid kit in hand.

Cowboy and I deposited Judd in a chair for her and stepped back as Hank stood up to assess the damage. He pulled at his belt and chuckled. "Son, it looks like you got into a knife fight and you were the only sonofagun without a knife."

Unconcerned, Cowboy laughed and said, "Next."

But Ox balked at him. "You're crazy if you think I'm stupid enough to get on that mangy horse."

"Oh, nut up," Jake said, scowling. "Judd and I took our turns. Don't go growing a vagina on us now."

"Hey!" Emily and Bobbie Jo yelled in unison.

"That's because y'all are dumbasses," Ox said as he winked at the girls. He was rewarded with their smiles and laughter before turning his attention back to Jake and Cowboy. "I'm not about to get on that deranged-ass horse and have him throw me off into the pond. I sure as hell don't need to spend any quality time with Charlie after what happened to the last guy who hung out with him."

My eyes cut to Cowboy. "Charlie?"

Cowboy grinned. "The alligator in Hank's pond. Eats one little mob guy and suddenly Charlie's on everyone's shitlist."

Jake rolled his eyes. "Come on, Ox. This is bound to be one of the things on your bucket list. Might as well get it over with."

"You kidding?" Ox said, cackling. "The only item on my list of things to do before I die is to yell for help. I think I'll leave the horse-wrangling up to the expert. Right, Cowboy?"

Cowboy nodded and turned to Hank. "All these klutzes are about as worthless as tits on a bull. Guess I'll have to show 'em how it's done."

"At least one of you possesses a little know-how and are up for a challenge," Hank said before walking out to retrieve the uneasy colt that was still nibbling at the tall weeds near the back fence.

When he returned with the horse, Hank offered to hold him steady as Cowboy climbed on, but he declined and took hold of the reins himself. Cowboy walked Ruckus around in circles for a minute, then ran his hands along the colt's neck and body, as if acquainting the horse to his basic touch.

After circling the horse and rubbing almost every square inch of him, he stopped at the colt's head and stared straight into his eyes as he allowed the palomino to nibble lightly at his fingers.

"All right, enough already," Jake said. "You going to stand around fondling him all day or are you going to mount up?"

Cowboy just shook his head and continued running his hands gently but firmly over the horse's head, scratching him between the ears.

He whispered something to Ruckus that was inaudible to the rest of us, then moved to the horse's side where he put his foot in the stirrup and swung onto the colt's back. Straight-legged, he stood up in the stirrups and held tight to the reins, though the palomino made no attempt to move.

After a few bounces in the saddle, he gave the horse a little nudge in the flanks and steered the colt in a couple of figure eights. The content horse bobbed his head and swished his tail, but never bucked or tried to throw him.

Hank grinned and happily stuffed the wad of money in his hand into his shirt pocket. "Leave it to a real cowboy to get the job done."

Judd shook his bandaged head and winced. "That's because when we were kids, Ox and I tied him on top of a goat and made a fast learner out of him."

Ox chuckled at the memory. "Hey, Cowboy. What'd you say to that horse to get him to do that?"

A smile split Cowboy's face in two as he gave me a sly wink. "I told him not to be a jackass, or I'd kick his head smooth off."

The men chuckled, but Bobbie Jo shook her head as she turned and walked toward me, rolling her eyes playfully with a smile on her face.

"Guess he's a lot better with horses than he is with women," I told her.

"Not from what I hear." She grinned, and kept walking.

Cowboy dismounted and handed the reins to Hank, but turned to scratch the horse between the ears. Ruckus bowed his head, enjoying the attention, which gave me pause. I'd always thought Cowboy lacked depth, but the idiosyncrasies I'd seen in him lately, especially while watching him with the horse, had me wondering about something. If the horse trusted Cowboy, then maybe I could possibly do the same. Animals and children usually had a sixth sense about those things.

Cowboy strutted in my direction, displaying a dazzling mega-watt smile. "See? I didn't even get hurt."

I smiled at him, but lifted a brow. "How'd you really do that? What's the trick?"

"No trick. I just didn't bother mentioning that I've been working with that colt for months now." He stared deep into my eyes and his mouth twisted with a smirk. "In case you haven't noticed, I can be a very patient man when I need to be."

The next evening, I squirmed in the chair, feeling a little like I'd been raked over the coals as Emily finished up my makeup. It reminded me of all my fears and struggles in high school. If I'd known they'd hatched a subversive plan to give me a makeover, I would've forfeited the whole night.

"Stop touching your face," Emily chastised. "You're going to mess it up."

I'd vowed to stick it out, but I felt self-conscious and started to waver on that decision. "Do I really have to do this?"

After finding another threatening note in my mailbox earlier in the day, I didn't have the patience to take any more abuse...no matter the form.

Bobbie Jo sipped her wine. "I told you she wasn't going to go along with this willingly."

Emily frowned. "Don't be such a stick in the mud, Anna. You're ruining all our fun."

Ruining their fun? I'd just spent the last hour being poked and prodded. Where was the fun in that?

Bobbie Jo started to say something else, but her cell phone rang. She held up one finger as she answered it. "Hey, what's up?" She listened for a few seconds, then said, "How late are you going to be, Cowboy?"

Hearing his name, I looked over at her. He'd mentioned dropping by my house last night, but he never showed. That's what I got for getting my hopes up.

"We're at Anna's getting ready. Do you just want to meet us there?" Bobbie Jo paused a beat, then raised one eyebrow. "Okay, hold on." She passed her cell phone to me. "He wants to talk to you."

Emily smirked at me. "Nothing going on, huh?"

All eyes in the room were on me as I lifted the phone to my ear. "Hello?"

"Howdy, darlin'. Whatcha wearin'?"

"Um, well, I'm wearing a dark blue tunic top with a pair of black leggings and—"

Emily quickly covered the phone with her hand and gawked at me. "Are you telling him what you're *actually* wearing?" She removed her hand and keeled over with laughter.

"Oh…" I cringed. *Damn it.* That was obviously not what he had meant. God, I was such an idiot. "And nothing underneath," I said hastily into the phone while blushing at Emily's nod of approval and watching Bobbie Jo shake her head.

Cowboy chuckled. "Works for me." There was a slight pause on his end of the line. "Sorry I didn't make it to your place last night. Huge structure fire in a nearby county kept me busy the rest of the evening. I didn't get back to the station until late last night."

I didn't respond, afraid the disappointment I'd felt over him not showing up would register in my voice. Then he would know that he was getting to me.

"I'm running late tonight because I had a fire call. Gas leak on the other side of town. Still have to go home and shower, but I'll be there later. Save me a dance?"

"Um, sure."

"Sounds good. See you then."

I clicked off the phone and handed it back to Bobbie Jo. Both women in the room were gawking at me. "What?"

"Girl, you have it bad for that man," Emily said, smiling.

"No, I don't," I protested. "We're just friends, that's all. He asked me to save him a dance."

"Well, I didn't see him asking to dance with me," she said.

Bobbie Jo laughed. "That's because the last time you danced with him, Jake threatened to lop off a certain part of Cowboy's anatomy."

"He did not," Emily replied, rolling her eyes. "Besides, that was my fault. I was trying to make Jake jealous."

"Worked, too." Bobbie Jo grinned. "Only, it wasn't you dancing with Cowboy that had Jake so pissed off. That was all Jeremy's doing."

Emily shrugged. "Speaking of that jerk, what's the deal with you two, Bobbie Jo? I know he's Austin's dad, but you aren't seeing him again, are you?"

"Hell, no!" She shook her head. "Jeremy may be Austin's biological father, but he's not exactly what I'd call daddy material. After dealing with him for the past year, I'm pretty sure I'm through with men altogether. The only guy I'm interested in is this little fella right here." She dangled her keys from her fingertips, displaying a photo of Austin.

"But don't you want more kids someday?" I asked.

Bobbie Jo shrugged. "You know, I always saw myself with at least two kids, a boy and a girl. But every time I even think about having another baby, my uterus cringes."

I laughed at the mental image she left me with, and Emily joined in. "I'm sure you'll change your mind when the right guy comes along. Besides, Austin would probably like to have a daddy one day…a real one."

"He already has four of the best father figures I could ever ask for. I'm not worried about filling that role in his life. I doubt anyone could, anyway."

"All right," Emily said, taking a step back from me. "I'm done. Take a look and tell me what you think. But no making faces."

If she had to warn me not to make a face, I could only imagine how bad I must look. Bobbie Jo was smiling, though, so maybe Emily had used clown makeup. I stood and walked over to the full-length mirror in my bedroom and gazed at… *Oh!*

I didn't recognize the woman in the mirror. Stunned, I turned to face Emily. "Holy crap! You're a magician."

Bobbie wore a huge grin. "Look at how your blue eyes pop. And I love all the sexy red curls framing your face. Anna, you look beautiful."

Emily smiled proudly. "See? You're a total hottie! Now I'm going to have to dare you to do something crazy. Prepare to get wild tonight," she said with a saucy grin.

Bobbie Jo rolled her eyes. "Don't listen to her. Ever. And for God's sake, don't take her up on any dares. The last time Emily accepted a dare, she ended up in Witness Protection." Bobbie Jo wrinkled her nose playfully. "And we're *all* still paying for that one."

Emily laughed. "Hey! Don't make me go back to calling you Bobbie Jugs again." She glanced over at me. "Did Bobbie Jo tell you that she and I haven't always gotten along?"

No, but I could imagine why. "Not exactly."

"Oh, yeah," Emily said, nodding. "As far as I was concerned, Miss Cheerleader could've taken her pom-poms and shoved them."

I looked at Bobbie Jo for confirmation. "Really? That bad?"

Bobbie Jo smiled. "True story. But I didn't take it personally. I knew it was only because Emily was jealous that I had dated Jake before her."

"Well, I knew that much," I said, remembering our days at camp. "I always thought Bobbie Jo and Jake were the perfect couple." Bobbie Jo laughed before I even realized what I said. "Oh my God. Emily, I'm so sorry. Forget I said that. I don't always think before I speak."

Emily grinned, as if she wasn't the least bit concerned

with my verbal blunder. "Don't worry about it. It's fine. I do it all the time."

"That's no lie," Bobbie said.

As I turned to smile at her, my gaze touched on the mirror. In the reflection, I caught a glimpse of the window... and a shadowed face staring back at me. I gasped and spun around so quickly that both women jolted from their seats.

"What's wrong?" Bobbie Jo asked.

I glared at the window, but there was nothing there. "I, um...sorry. For a second, I thought I saw something outside."

Emily picked up her cell phone. "Do you want me to call Jake? He could come over and take a look around."

"No, it's okay. I think my nerves are just getting to me." Which I'm sure is exactly what the Barlow boys were hoping for. *Those bastards.*

Chapter Eleven

It was sometime after midnight when Cowboy entered The Backwoods. I would've known the exact time, but I had stopped checking my watch every five minutes, figuring he wasn't going to show up after all. Leave it to him to prove me wrong.

His gaze swept over the crowd until finally landing on our group hanging out near the end of the bar. The girls sat at the small round table while the men leaned on the nearby bar. Cowboy's eyes met mine and he smiled as he headed in my direction. But just as he reached me, a fresh drink slid in front of me and a large hand suddenly rested on my shoulder, snaring both of our attention.

Bubba Ray stood next to me, grinning sinfully at Cowboy. At first, I was puzzled by the odd behavior of the guy Judd had tried to set me up with, but then quickly realized that the methodically placed, proprietary hand on my shoulder and the shit-eating grin was done in an eat-your-heart-out manner. Bubba Ray was claiming me as "his."

As if.

Bubba Ray stood next to me, closer than I was comfortable with, but not violating any personal space treaties…as of yet. Though the way he'd been flirting relentlessly with me, I had already figured that by the end of the night I'd have to explain my hands-off policy to him.

With a scowl, Cowboy veered toward Jake and leaned on the bar next to him, motioning to the bartender.

Jake glanced up at him. "You're late," he said, loud enough that I could hear him over the lively country tune blaring from the overhead speakers.

"And you're funny-looking. So what?"

Jake smirked. "Need a dancing partner?"

"You're my boy and all, Jake, but I'm not dancing with you." Cowboy picked up the bottle of beer placed in front of him by the bartender and took a swig.

"Not with me, jackass. With Anna."

Cowboy glanced back at me and his mouth tightened into a firm, thin line. "So she decided to come watch the sinners eviscerate themselves, huh?" His tone was callous and he said it as if he hadn't known I'd been there all along. Then he shook his head and told Jake, "Nah, I'm good."

Jake gave him a strange look, but didn't say anything.

Cowboy hadn't even said hello to me when he walked up and now he was shunning me, which only made me feel more awkward and uncomfortable. So when Bubba Ray asked me to dance with him, I jumped at the chance to get away from the group…and Cowboy.

After a few laps on the dance floor, Bubba Ray and I took a break and passed by six of his buddies sitting at a table across the room. They invited us to have a drink with them, and since I was in no hurry to return to my own group, we sat down.

For a moment, I worried about sitting at a table surrounded by seven hulking men. But they were sweet and made me laugh. Apparently not all men were cocky asshats. Nice to know. But just as Bubba Ray put his hand on my arm and leaned over to whisper into my ear, someone snared my hand and yanked me out of my chair.

My eyes flickered up, meeting Cowboy's direct, unwavering gaze. But the controlled intensity in his eyes had nothing on the contemptuous expression he wore on his face. "Come on. I need a partner."

He dragged me toward the dance floor as I stumbled behind him, unable to keep up. I tried to pull my hand free, but it had no effect on him as he charged through the crowd. It was like playing tug-of-war with a pissed off bull. "Hey! I was in the middle of a conversation back there."

Cowboy stopped on the wooden floor, turned, and pulled me into his hard chest, wrapping a strong hand around my waist. "That wasn't a conversation. That was a full-on tactical assault by Bubba Ray. Women are sex toys to him."

I pulled back slightly and raised a brow. "Look who's talking."

"Hey, at least I respect women afterward."

"Oh, really?" I rolled my eyes as he led me around the dance floor. "If you had any amount of respect for them, you wouldn't sleep with them to begin with. At least not so soon. Maybe try spending a little time getting to know something about the woman, other than what kind of underwear she wears…or doesn't wear."

His firm hand tightened on my waist, and I could feel the aggravation in his fingertips. "Oh, that's rich coming from a woman who was letting Bubba Ray feel her up two minutes ago."

My feet stopped moving. "Excuse me?"

"I saw him touching you. You shy away from me every chance you get, but you'll let that fucking idiot put his hands all over you?"

"Put his…?" I shook my head, not believing what he was accusing me of, then the anger took over. "He touched my arm, you jerk!"

Irritation tightened his jaw. "Yeah, and it wouldn't be long before he was playing grab-ass with you and rolling you into his bed for a slumber party."

I dropped my hand from his as other patrons danced past us. "Bubba Ray's been nothing but a perfect gentleman with me, which is more than I can say for *you*. If you think there was anything going on between him and me back there, then you're more delusional than I gave you credit for."

"Yeah right," he scoffed. "That's why tonight you dressed up and put on all that heavy makeup—because there's nothing going on?" His eyes filled with hostility, and his lip curled with revulsion. "You know, maybe you're more of a liar than I gave *you* credit for."

Outraged, I barely had time to register what I was doing when my hand smacked across his face. I blinked, shocked by my own reaction. Actually, I wasn't sure who was more surprised—him or me. No matter. I refused to apologize for my behavior after the way he spoke to me. I turned and walked quickly away. He didn't even try to stop me.

I squeezed through the crowd, fighting back tears of

frustration, when I bumped a man's arm and spilled his beer on both of us. "Oh, I'm sorr—"

"You!" Joe Barlow stood there, looking none too happy and wiping his beer-soaked hand on his pants. "What the hell are you doing here? Now you're following us?"

"Of course not."

Clay peered around his brother. "Then what's a stuffy girl like you doing in a place like this? I've never seen you in here before."

"Not that it's any of your business, but I'm here with my friends." I motioned to where Emily and Jake stood talking to Bobbie Jo across the room, though none of them looked in my direction.

"You're with that FBI guy?" Joe looked at Clay, then back to me. His jaw clenched as he grabbed my arm and pulled me toward him, whispering into my face with his beer breath. "You better keep your damn mouth shut, if you know what's good for ya. If I find out you're talking to him about us, then you're going to see firsthand just how mean I can get."

I glanced down at his fingers clutching my skin, then made the mistake of trailing my gaze upward to the tattoo on his arm. A large red fire-breathing dragon covered the bulk of his bicep with its red tail wrapping the length of Joe's forearm and ending at his wrist. Bright orange flames shot from its mouth.

It only reminded me of their earlier intimidation tactics and made me wonder if I was the only neighbor the Barlow boys had threatened to burn out of her home. That's when I remembered something. Cowboy had mentioned the Barlows getting into an argument with the chief the day of his death. Also, the fire chief and his wife had lived only half a mile up the road from my home next to the Barlows' residence.

Was it possible they were involved in the deaths of the chief and his wife? The thought terrified me, but I couldn't verbalize my fear. The brothers would just feed on it.

Not wanting to show how scared of him I truly was, I met Joe's gaze directly and narrowed my eyes. "Let go of my arm."

He chuckled, not the least bit intimidated. "Who's going to make me?"

A rich male voice rang out from behind me. "Me, that's who."

I didn't recognize the voice.

Flustered, my head jerked in his general direction, wanting to get a look at the bystander who was brave enough to step in and stand in my defense. With just three little words, he'd drawn the defining line between the Barlow brothers and me.

The dark-haired man's chiseled jaw was held tight and his arms were crossed, as if he were waiting for the idiot body builder to release me on command. Something I didn't see happening anytime soon.

"Why don't you mind your own business, dickhead?" Joe told the man, waving him off with his free hand.

The unknown man smirked at that. "I'm making *this* my business. Let go of her. Now."

"And if I don't?"

The man took a step forward just as Mandy Barlow walked over. "Hey, guys. What's going on over here?" She took notice of Joe's fingers wrapped around my arm. "Joe, you stop it right now, ya hear? If you don't let her go this instant, I'm gonna call Momma and tell on you." She glared at her other brother standing on the sidelines. "On both of you."

"Aw, Mandy, we're just playing around," Clay said. "We weren't really gonna do nothing to her. Were we, Joe?"

Joe smiled at me, but released my arm. "Of course not. Just talking to her, that's all."

Mandy looked at me and smiled warmly. "Anna, right? You're Cowboy's friend?"

I nodded silently, though I was pretty sure Cowboy and I weren't friends after I'd slapped him in the middle of the dance floor.

"I'm sorry. I'll make sure these two don't bother you anymore." Mandy gestured to her brothers who were still in a stare-down with the stranger who had stepped in to rescue me. "Come on, fellas. Let's leave Anna and her...uh, friend alone now. You two have caused enough trouble for one night. It's time to go."

Clay grumbled under his breath as he followed Mandy toward the door. She stopped a few feet away, apparently realizing Joe hadn't moved from his position. "Joe! I said it's time to leave. Come on, or you'll be walking home."

Joe slowly backed away from the dark-headed man, though they were both still eyeing each other. I breathed a sigh of relief as the Barlow clan disappeared out the front doors, then turned to the man standing beside me. "Thank you for stepping in. That was very sweet of you."

"No problem, ma'am." He winked at me and offered his arm. "You seem a bit shaken up. How about I buy you a drink and show you the proper way a man should treat a lady?"

I considered his offer carefully. He seemed like an okay guy, but the last thing I wanted to do was lead him to believe that a drink would turn into anything more. I wasn't interested in pursuing a relationship — casual or otherwise — and was happy to go home alone.

Okay, so maybe that was a lie. No one wanted to be alone. Not really. I'd spent a lot of time alone after my mother died and wouldn't wish that kind of isolation on anyone. But the thought of taking off my clothes and bearing my soul to a complete stranger wasn't very appealing, either.

So maybe I did want some companionship, after all. Just not with *him*. Unfortunately, he was the only one offering me anything at the moment. I couldn't very well say no without coming off rude, could I?

Things had worked out in his favor with the brothers, but they easily could've taken a nasty turn if Mandy hadn't stepped in when she did. The Barlow boys didn't come off as deep thinkers so I doubted they'd have outsmarted this guy, but they definitely would've outnumbered him. The least I could do was have a drink with my rescuer.

"Okay, sure. Let's go get that drink." I smiled and laced my arm through his, allowing him to lead me away.

He ushered me to an isolated corner table at the back of the bar. I slid into a chair against the wall, expecting him to sit in the one across from me. Instead, he pulled it around and sat beside me, so close that his blue-jeaned leg rubbed against mine.

Politely, I shuffled my chair over an inch and shifted my leg away from his, though there really wasn't anywhere else to go. If his goal had been to corner me, then he had effectively carried it out. That alone made me a little antsy, but I tried to play it cool.

As he flagged down a passing waitress, I gazed across the room and watched Cowboy take a seat at the bar with his back to me. He seemed oblivious to everything that had transpired moments ago between the Barlow boys and me. It only took me mere seconds to figure out why.

A gaggle of gorgeous, skin-baring ladies flocked around him, smiling and giggling as he spoke to them. I rolled my eyes. No woman was safe. From what I'd heard, he damn sure had never considered any off-limits. That man should come with a disclaimer stamped across his forehead.

Then I grinned, considering how his disclaimer would read.

Warning: appendages of this virile male are under constant pressure. Prolonged exposure to him may result in rash behavior, absurdity, coarse language, doses of immaturity, and occasional fainting. This man may not be suitable for women of any age. Batteries not included…or needed.

"You got something going with him, huh?"

Startled, I tore my gaze from Cowboy and shifted it to the man sitting beside me. "Um, no, I…well, not exactly."

"Hmm. That's too bad," he said sarcastically. Then he stealthily slid his hand onto my thigh. He might as well have palmed a hand buzzer the way I jumped. "Whoa, calm down, honey. I won't bite." He shrugged his brows suggestively. "At least not unless you want me to."

"I'm sorry. I think you misunderstood my intentions. I'm

not available."

He winked slyly at me. "Oh, I know, sweetheart. That's what makes this so much fun."

Befuddled by his comment, I pushed his hand off my leg and started to stand. But before I could, he grabbed my wrist, pulled me forcefully against his chest, and locked his repulsive lips onto mine. He tasted of sour liquor and smelled like cigarette smoke, which made me want to gag. I pushed against him, but he wouldn't let go. So I dug my nails into his bicep and bit him.

Finally, he released me. The asshole.

"There," he said, taking a quick glance over my shoulder. "That should do the trick." I raised my hand to slap him, but he stopped me by grabbing it before it made contact. "Hold up, sweet lips. We're still waiting on the last party guest to arrive. Wouldn't want to start the show without him. Don't worry, though. He's on his way."

He wore a smirk that reeked of trouble as he nodded across the bar in Cowboy's direction. I hadn't known this guy was manufacturing a scenario for Cowboy's benefit. And after the way Cowboy had acted on the dance floor about Bubba Ray touching my arm, I didn't have to turn to know exactly what I would see.

Yet I did anyway.

One very fired up country boy wearing a white Stetson shoved his way through the wall of onlookers. His eyes, blackened with intensity, reflected the colorful strobe lights as one hundred and fifty inquiring spectators followed his movements. The surrounding chatter dropped to a whisper before a hush fell over the crowd, as if his sullen, ominous mood stunned the audience into a muted trance.

The indignant, disapproving expression on Cowboy's face spoke volumes as to his mindset. Between that and the other man's smugness over sampling my goods, this moment had all the elements of disaster. Hoping to petition Cowboy's sensibility, I ejected myself from my seat, squeezed past the man at my table, and stood in front of the demon spawn who had fueled Cowboy's anger with his outlandish shenanigans.

"Move," Cowboy ordered, the strength in his voice weakening my knees.

But I lifted my chin, daring him to make me. "No. You're not getting into a fight."

"Wanna bet?"

"Stop it right now. You're making a scene."

"I haven't even begun to make a scene…yet."

The man behind me stood and came up beside me, leering at Cowboy. "Hey, bub. You're trespassing. This is *my* side of the bar, remember?"

"That's because you're poaching," Cowboy said, glaring at him. "What do you do—cruise the bar, stalking our women, just waiting for a chance to make a move on them?"

Our women?

"What, are you jealous she chose me over you, dickhead?"

Cowboy started for him, but I put my hand to his chest to stop him. "No fighting. I mean it."

"Anna," he said, gritting his teeth. It was a one-word warning.

The way he said my name irked me. As if there was some sort of prize element involved. With their heated glares and ready-to-charge postures, they looked like two territorial bulls in rut. The only thing left for them to do was the embarrassing scratching of their private areas.

"This gentleman and I—"

"Gentleman, my ass," Bobbie Jo said as she pushed through the crowd. "What the hell did you do now, Jeremy?"

Jeremy? Oh, good Lord.

"He's Jeremy?" I said meekly, keeping my eyes from meeting hers.

Though I hadn't thought it possible, the already tense atmosphere heightened to an even more uncomfortable level. Rooted in a long-time feud, these two men had some bad blood between them. Bobbie Jo had told me all about the rivalry between her boys and Jeremy, which happened to be the chauvinistic chameleon I was protecting. At least I finally managed to determine the cause of Cowboy's extreme irritation.

"Yeah, this is the asshole who broke my nose with a beer bottle last summer," Cowboy sneered.

I thought his nose looked slightly more crooked than when I last saw him at camp. Guess that explained it.

Jeremy shook his head. "Why don't you shut the fuck up and quit crying about it already."

"Why don't you make me?" Cowboy said, pushing me aside and getting into Jeremy's face.

Taking prompt measures, I squeezed back in between them. "Guys, please. This situation doesn't warrant a repeat of whatever happened last summer. Behave yourselves and act like grown-ups."

Jeremy chuckled behind me. "You always let a woman tell you what to do, Cowboy?"

Hoping to throw a wrench into Jeremy's plans, I turned

to face him and poked him in the chest. "Stop goading him, you jerk. You're just looking for a fight."

He grabbed my hand and lifted it to his mouth, nipping it lightly. "Actually, I'm more of a lover than a fighter." His gaze roamed down to my breasts and he smirked. "Why don't you come home with me tonight and find out for yourself?"

Before I could even respond, Cowboy latched onto my arm and jerked me away from Jeremy. "I'm about a pecker hair away from kicking your ass, you sonofabitch."

Jeremy grinned wide and cracked his knuckles as four men at a nearby table stood up and joined him. "Let's see it then."

Ox and Judd moved closer, stationing themselves behind Cowboy as Jake maneuvered Emily and Bobbie Jo behind him. When Cowboy tried to shift me behind him, I dug my heels into the floor. "Move out of the way," he ordered. "I don't want you to get caught up in this."

"The hell I will." I shook his hand off my arm and turned back to Jeremy. "If you thought for one second that you ever had a chance with me, you're crazy. No wonder Bobbie Jo is tired of putting up with you. You're nothing more than a...a mooncalf."

Jeremy's eyebrows squeezed together in puzzlement as he looked over at Cowboy. "What the fuck did she call me?"

Cowboy shrugged. "Beats the hell out of me, but I don't think it was a compliment."

"Dear Lord." I shook my head in frustration. "I called you a mentally defective person."

"An idiot, in other words?" Jeremy asked.

Several women, including Bobbie Jo, giggled nearby.

Cowboy's laugh caught my attention and I looked over

my shoulder at him. "Why didn't you just say that to begin with?" he asked.

"What's the difference? I can't help it if this vile oaf doesn't understand basic English." I turned to walk away, but stopped beside Cowboy. "Unlike you, I don't have to settle a dispute with fists. I know how to use my mouth effectively."

"I know how to use your mouth, too," Jeremy said to my back. "Those pretty lips sure would make a great resting place for my dick."

In the blink of an eye, Cowboy launched himself at Jeremy, tackling him onto a nearby table that crashed to the ground beneath their weight. The two of them broke apart on impact, but that didn't stop the squabble. They wrestled with each other, both trying to gain a foothold to return to a standing position. When Cowboy finally managed to shove Jeremy away, they jumped to their feet and the entire bar erupted into a madhouse.

Women spread in every direction, scattering to avoid getting hit, while other men jumped into the fight and threw punches. I yelled for Cowboy to stop, but my words were drowned out by the ribald shouts of the men and terrified shrieks coming from the ladies.

Stunned, I stood in place and watched Jeremy land a jab to Cowboy's ribs that shoved him against the wooden banister of the dance floor. Reacting, Cowboy wheeled around and struck Jeremy with a well-aimed thrust of his boot and a punch to his chiseled jaw.

The dramatically chaotic situation worsened as more men closed in. Shoved back through the crowd, I lost sight of the others. That's when I realized I stood smack dab in the middle of something closely resembling a war zone without a single recognizable face in the bunch.

A dizzying number of glass bottles, broken chairs, and bloody fists flew around me. And the men who weren't fighting sure as hell weren't helping the situation. They stood on the outskirts of the entanglement, taking bets and shouting encouragements to the soldiers in battle, as if they enjoyed the entertainment.

Then I caught a glimpse of Cowboy swimming through the sea of people with his eyes focused solely on mine. He had a painful-looking bruise on his left cheek, a knot on his forehead, and a small cut over his right brow. Yet he kept a diligent watch on me as he swiftly and competently made his way toward me like his body was on autopilot.

Once he made it to me, he didn't waste any time sliding his arm around my waist and escorting me toward the side exit. As he pushed us through the crowd, he kept his body close to mine, insulating me from the splintering wood, shattering glass, and wild punches. Without a single word, he towed me out the door, through the parking lot, and lifted me into passenger seat of his truck.

Relieved, I let out the breath I'd been holding in. Sanctuary, at last.

As Cowboy maneuvered around the front of the truck to the driver's side, a horn sounded nearby. Jake, Emily, and Bobbie Jo were piled into the front seat of Jake's truck and waved as they pulled out of the parking lot. I'd forgotten all about them when the fight broke out, but they'd apparently waited outside to make sure we'd made it out okay.

We had, but the way Cowboy gave them a half-hearted, pissed-off wave and climbed silently into the driver's seat led me to believe this wasn't the shelter from the storm I'd originally thought. Not only was he pissed, but I had no doubt we were about to have an unavoidable discussion I wanted nothing more than to…well, avoid.

Cowboy started the truck and peeled out onto the highway. His fingers held the steering wheel in a death grip as his dilated eyes fixed on the dark road, but he stayed silent the entire drive. If his strategy was to wait me out, it didn't work. I wasn't looking forward to talking to him. And at the rate of speed he was driving, maybe I wouldn't have to.

The small cut above his right eyebrow wasn't bleeding, but the goose egg on his forehead and the large bruise on his left cheek were swelling more with every passing minute. I wanted to ask him if he was okay, but his white-knuckled grip on the steering wheel kept me from doing so.

Within minutes, he slammed to a stop in front of my house, jerked open his door, and slid out. Guess our night wasn't going to end quite as soon as I'd hoped. Still completely mute, he walked me to my front door and waited for me to unlock it. The moment I pushed it open, Cowboy said, "What's your fucking problem?"

I blinked at him. "*My* problem?" I asked, my tone littered with disbelief. "I'm not the one who started a riot in the bar."

"Yeah, well what the hell did you want me to do? Not only did that bastard put his filthy hands on you, but he also put his disgusting mouth on yours. Ya know, we call him 'Germy' for a fucking reason." Cowboy exhaled a hard breath, as if to calm himself down. "You expect me to just walk away after how he treated you."

"Really, Cowboy," I said, rolling my eyes. "How is it any different than the way you've treated me yourself?"

I started inside, but Cowboy braced his arm across the doorway, blocking my entry. "Wait just a fucking minute. I've never treated you like that."

I raised a brow to him. "Oh, yeah?"

"You damn well know I haven't. I've never forced myself on you. You wanted me to kiss you...both times."

"How do you know? Did you ask me?"

"Well, no. But I—"

"Exactly. And I do believe the second time I specifically asked you not to. But you didn't listen." I shook my head at him. "You men are all alike. You take whatever you want because you're so afraid someone else might get to it first. Well, I'm not a trophy to be fought over. Good night, Cowboy," I said, stepping inside as I swung the door closed.

But not before the toe of a boot slid inside.

Chapter Twelve

Cowboy shoved the door open. "I'm not done with you, yet."

"Well, I'm done with you." I spun on my heel and stormed into the kitchen.

His boots thudded on the tile behind me. He'd shadowed my movements because as I neared the sink, he grasped my shoulders and spun me around to face him. "Sonofabitch, Anna. Stop walking away."

I sighed in defeat. "What do you want from me?"

He dropped his hand from my arm and clenched his fist at his side. "One fucking date. That's what I want."

"No."

"Just dinner, nothing else."

"I said no."

Cowboy closed his eyes and counted to ten under his breath. "Darlin', I'm about to blow my fucking top. Never in my life have I had to beg a woman to go out with me."

I crossed my arms and looked at him in disbelief. "And what? You want a round of applause? A monument in your honor? How about a cookie?"

"No, I want an explanation."

"I don't owe you anything, Cowboy, an explanation or anything else for that matter."

His eyes glazed with fury. "You damn sure owe me something after the bullshit you've put me through for the last week."

I looked him directly in the eye and scoffed under my breath. "I already told you I wasn't interested in dating you. But you just won't listen. You're crazy if you think you can blame—"

"Shut up."

I blinked, registering what he said. "Did you just tell me to—"

"Damn straight I did. I'm tired of listening to your bullshit excuses. That story of yours about you not being interested has more holes than chicken wire. Every time I touch you, your body reacts to me. And you already know what you do to me. I've had the same goddamn boner for over a fucking week. And jerking off hasn't done a damn thing to relieve it. So why don't you do us both a favor and quit blowing sunshine up my ass."

My mouth had fallen open, but I managed to snap it shut. "You don't need to use your licentious language on me."

His brows furrowed. "In English this time?"

"You know…the…um, sexy talk," I explained, my face flaring with heat. "Stop it. You're embarrassing me."

His expression lightened as he grinned with amusement, obviously delighted by my discomfort and not exhibiting the least bit of remorse for his behavior. "Darlin', I hate to tell you this, but there's no one else here."

I straightened my spine and took on a chastising tone. "Doesn't matter. Someone has to teach you proper etiquette."

"Oh, fuck me," Cowboy groaned, shifting the bulge in his crotch and shaking his head. "I can't believe I'm getting all hot and bothered for a woman who acts like an old-fashioned schoolmarm."

I glared at him. "Why don't you just leave me alone, then? Lord knows I've asked you to several times."

He closed his eyes and pursed his lips. "Because I can't, okay?"

"What do you mean you *can't*?"

"You're like a...drip on a leaky fucking faucet. You know, where at first you don't notice it, but once you do, it's the only damn thing you can concentrate on."

"So now I'm a drip?"

"No. That's not what I... What I mean is..." He pinched the bridge of his nose as the delivery of his lines stilted. "God, I'm fucking this up." He took a deep breath and looked back at me. "Don't you get it? Anna, I want you."

My stomach twisted into a knot, and I clamped my eyes shut, trying to block out his words. A sickening wave of nausea washed over me. Though I wasn't planning on staying much longer, the thought of having Cowboy at least once was enough to tempt me. It was a fantasy I'd played over and over in my head many times before. But could I actually do it? Could I allow myself one night with him, knowing it would mean more to me than it would to him?

No. I couldn't possibly torture myself that way. To even

consider it meant he'd already gotten under my skin. But to grant him one night would only ensure that when my time was up, I'd leave with nothing more than fond memories and a broken heart.

So instead, I said the one thing that would put an end to his relentless pursuit. "Cowboy, I didn't move here with any intention of finding a relationship. Even if I had, I'd want one with substance, one that means something. Not a fling with someone who wants to take care of his...er, baser needs. I'd need a commitment."

"So that's what it all boils down to, right? You think I'm in it for the sexual reward? Like some sort of test to my manhood? I'm not, I swear." He measured me with his eyes, his face serious.

Jeez. Would the man go to any lengths to get a woman in his bed? "You don't have to pretend you're interested in anything more than a one-night—"

His hand shot out and grasped my upper arm. "Where the hell did you get a lame-ass idea like that?"

I squirmed to free myself, but his grip only tightened. "That's what you've been after since day one, isn't it? To get me out of my clothes?"

"Of course not."

I raised a questioning brow.

"Okay, so maybe I've come on a little strong. But when it comes to you, I can't help myself. I've never met anyone like you. You challenge me in ways no other woman ever has." He lessened the strength of his hold on me. "I want you to give this thing between us a chance."

"You just see me as some sort of prize to be won because I'm the only girl who's ever turned you down. You said so yourself."

Cowboy's posture stiffened and a vein throbbed in his temple. "Maybe that's how it started out, but you're not just some woman who turned me down. If I only wanted to have sex with you, I'd have taken you against the door when I had the chance." I opened my mouth to argue, but he continued. "Don't even bother denying it. Because, darlin', we both know I damn well could have," he said, a sly grin forming on his perfect mouth as his intense eyes focused on mine.

A lump formed in my throat and my stomach twisted into a knot. The heat from his gaze alone had me clenching my thighs together.

"Look, I know I'm a piece of shit who doesn't deserve someone like you to give me a chance," he said, keeping his voice controlled and his tone even, "but I'm asking you to anyway. You're more than a passing interest for me."

That was the moment it dawned on me.

I blinked at him in fascinated horror, as if I were watching a speeding car driving headfirst into a brick wall. He wasn't asking for a one-night stand at all. Cowboy was asking me for a *relationship*, the very thing I'd just told him I wouldn't settle for less than. *Crap.*

I hadn't been prepared for this and wasn't sure what to say, so I shook my head adamantly and said, "I'm sorry, but you're…not my type."

His control wavered as he sneered. "Why? Because I'm not Prince Fucking Charming on a white goddamn horse? You think I can't measure up to the heroes in those fucking romance books you read?"

"It's not that," I told him, my eyes avoiding his as my body trembled. "I…I just don't want *this*."

God, I wanted this…and so much more.

He gritted his teeth. "Anna, you're going to have to do better than that if you think you have any chance at convincing me you don't want me. What the fuck are you so afraid of?"

"Nothing." My voice cracked under the pressure.

"That's bullshit and you know it," he ground out, pulling me to him.

My hands flew to his chest and I struggled to push him away. "No, I can't." He held enough power over my emotions to make me change my mind and tell him the truth, but I couldn't let that happen. I couldn't put anyone else at risk… especially him. I wouldn't allow him to make himself a target for the man I knew would soon be coming for me. Because he *always* came for me.

One of his hands held my waist firmly as the other pushed a strand of my hair back and slowly moved down my neck until his palm rested above my left breast. "You feel that—the way your heart pounds against my hand and your body trembles under my touch? Don't tell me it's nothing."

It was something, but… "I…can't do this. Not to *you*."

"Then talk to me, Anna. Tell me what's stopping you."

"I just don't want you to…touch me." Tears welled up in my eyes as my voice broke.

His jaw tightened and his mouth turned into a frown. "What is it about me touching you that scares you so much?"

"Nothing. It doesn't," I said quickly, adamantly denying it. I pushed against him, hoping he'd release me. I needed to get away from him. Now. His grip only tightened. I was going to have to tell him something or he was never going to stop pressing for the truth. "I'm afraid you'll stop, okay?" Having blurted out the one thing that bothered me most about leaving, I blinked and a fat tear landed on my cheek. But I managed to cover up the truth by giving him something that would make complete sense. "M-my scars…"

"Darlin', I've already seen your scars, remember?"

Sniffling, I lowered my head, unable to look him in the eye. "Yes, but not the full extent of them."

"Doesn't matter. When I look at you, I don't see scars." He lifted my chin with one finger and used his thumb to wipe away the tear. "I only see *you*. And whether you believe it or not, sweetheart, you're beautiful. If you haven't noticed, I haven't wanted to stop touching you since I first gave in to the notion."

"But you did. The night you first saw them, you touched them, and then left."

Cowboy's green eyes glittered as a muscle twitched in his neck. "Darlin', the *only* fucking reason I walked out on you that night was to keep my dick from tearing through my jeans to get at you."

My heart squeezed painfully tight in my chest. Contemplating a one-night stand with Cowboy was one thing…even if I couldn't bring myself to tear my own heart out that way. But the moment he clarified he wanted more from me, I was lost. Yet I couldn't ruin his life by letting him get closer to me. I needed to end this now by telling him I was leaving because I was in danger. I had no choice. Only then would he understand.

"There are other things you don't know about me. Things that matter. You have no idea what you're getting yourself into. I'm not a whole person." More tears flowed down my cheeks as I tried to make him understand. "I'm…broken."

His gaze flickered over my face as his mouth set in determination. He ran his fingers along the nape of my neck and leaned into me. "Then let me fix you," he whispered.

Unexpectedly, his mouth crashed against mine, sending my heart scrambling around inside my chest, searching for purchase. Sweet warmth pooled low in my belly as he parted my lips and sank deeper into me with his tongue. I plunged my fingers into his thick, wavy hair, knocking his white Stetson off his head. But even then, he didn't stop kissing me.

The hand he held over my breast twitched, but he quickly moved it to my waist. I had no doubt it was to keep himself from shifting a little lower and stroking the pebbled nub pressing into his chest. Because he undoubtedly would look like a fool if he told me this wasn't sexual for him one minute, then fondled me the next.

But no matter what lies I'd told him earlier, I craved his touch. Wanted it more than the air I breathed. No one had ever made me feel as alive as Cowboy, and I needed to feel his warmth against my bare skin. *Just once...*

In that moment, my reservations slipped completely away, no longer allowing me to keep myself at a distance. I grabbed his hand and moved it back up, covering my left breast.

Cowboy's mouth murmured against mine. "What are you doing, sweetheart?"

Hell if I knew. "I need to feel your hands on me."

"Christ," he groaned. He pulled his head back and searched my face for answers. "You sure about this?"

"God, yes," I rasped. In a gutsy, liberating move, I grabbed him by the collar and pulled his mouth back to mine, eager to have another taste.

It was a mistake, losing my composure that way, letting him tamper with my heart. But I couldn't stop myself. He forced me to feel things I didn't want to feel. And it was soul-shattering.

But Cowboy didn't do things half-assed. His hand dove under my shirt, roughly pushed my bra up, and cupped my naked breast. He thumbed over my sensitive nipple and gave it a pinch that stopped somewhere short between pleasure and pain, sending chills through me.

As I gasped, he took full advantage of my open mouth and plunged his tongue inside. A small whimper escaped my throat. He pulled back a little, allowing his lips to move against mine, as he whispered, "Fuck. I'm addicted to the way you taste. You don't know how beautiful you are." Then his lips claimed mine once more.

His hand grew more persistent as my nipple tightened beneath his calloused fingertips. I moaned into his mouth, pleasure zinging through my veins with every touch. His ravenous hunger consumed me, leaving me dangling limply in his arms.

By the time his teeth moved to nibble on my ear, I was panting and clinging to him like static, half out of my mind in some weird, altered state. And he must've known because he used it against me.

"Anna…?"

"Mmm-hmmm."

His lips brushed against my earlobe as his warm breath caressed my neck. "Dinner with me. Tomorrow night."

And just like the colt he'd whispered to, I was tamed into submission, unable to speak. I meant to shake my head, but instead found myself nodding. The moment I agreed, he released me and I staggered backward, swaying on my feet while feeling a little frayed around the edges.

He only looked more pleased with himself. "You okay there, sweetheart?"

No. "Yes."

He chuckled and gave me a wolfish, smug grin. "Good. Then I'll see you tomorrow night." Cowboy lifted his hat from the floor, placed it on his head, and then tipped it as he gave me a quick wink. "Pick you up at seven." With that, he turned on his heel and walked out.

What the hell just happened?

After spending three hours on the computer trying to figure out the puzzle of Chief Swanson's missing brother, I sighed, turned off the screen, and headed to bed. For a second, I thought I'd found him, but quickly realized my mistake. The old photograph had been of Chief Swanson when he was younger and his name had been misprinted. That small setback had cost me precious time and frustrated the hell out of me. I was starting to doubt if I would ever find Ned Swanson.

Which was the exact reason I hadn't bothered to mention it to Cowboy. I hadn't wanted to get his hopes up if I couldn't find the man before I left town. With only a few short months to go, I'd have to pick up the pace. Otherwise, Cowboy would have to go at it alone.

Like I'd be when I leave this place. *Alone.*

I slid under the covers and turned off the bedside lamp,

plunging myself into darkness. Unable to get comfortable, I rolled over onto my stomach and huffed. Did he mean what he'd said about seeing what was between us? I mean, he had me right where he wanted me…yet he still backed off. Annoyed, I leaned up and punched my pillow and then flipped over onto my back. Maybe I should call the whole date-thing off.

Hell, when it came to Cowboy, there were just no guarantees. I'd learned that lesson back in summer camp while living vicariously through Kelly Deter's tales of her intimate moments with Cowboy. Only one day after he'd had his hands up her skirt, he'd dumped the poor girl and moved on to some other unsuspecting victim of his charm.

As I imagined the other women had been, I was too easily distracted by the crook of his finger and that sexy smirk of his. He'd made me feel special, and I hadn't been able to ignore the burning-hot desire bubbling under my skin. Before I even realized what he was doing, he'd turned me into a hopeless puddle of confusion and I'd accepted his offer of a date. *Damn him.*

But I wasn't naive enough to think the moment he talked me out of my panties he'd stick around for anything resembling a relationship. Hell, he'd be gone before my breathing regulated. But if that's what it took for him to get me out of his system, then so be it.

The mere thought of having sex with Cowboy had me blowing out a hard breath. From the first moment he'd kissed me, I'd spent countless hours struggling to control my impure thoughts.

Even now, a warm, tingling sensation spread throughout my lower body and my forehead broke into a full-on sweat.

The room suddenly had become unbearably hot, sweltering even. *Jesus.* The man wasn't even here and he had me all hot and bothered. I kicked the bedspread off and rose from the bed.

If I planned to get any sleep, I needed to erase the memory of what his hands and mouth had done to my body. As if I even could.

I staggered toward the back door in search of some fresh air. I opened the door and stepped out onto the back porch, smiling at the sound of an owl hooting in the distance. My hair swayed in the balmy Texas breeze as my gaze followed the silver sheen of moonlight slanting across the wooden deck and onto a pair of…*cowboy boots?*

My smile deteriorated as my heart pounded furiously against my rib cage, plundering my sense of security. The scent of mint and tobacco overwhelmed me. I didn't want to look up, but I had to know if what I was seeing was real. I swallowed hard as my eyes lifted.

About five feet away, lurking in the shadows, stood a dark-skinned man with long black hair. He stared back at me, piercing me with his intense golden eyes. The frown he wore turned into more of a sneer. I gasped.

Then he reached for me.

I didn't even have a chance to run before the stars in the night sky swirled in my vision and the darkness overtook me.

The repetitious scratching irritated me, but it was the sulfuric odor that had awakened my senses. *He* was here. I could feel him beside me, even if I couldn't see him. I blinked in the dark, searching for his figure, but was unable to find him. The scratching sounded again and fire exploded in front of my face in the form of a lit match.

A familiar fear rushed through my veins as the flame was extinguished with one alcohol-infused breath. The same breath I remembered from my earliest childhood memories. But was he gone?

No, he was still here. Always here.

When a man's voice called out my name, I shot straight up. My eyes widened and swept the dark room, searching for two men: the dark-skinned man with the golden eyes and the man who had a starring role in my usual recurring nightmare. But they were nowhere to be found.

It wasn't the first time I'd awoken in a panic and wondered if what I'd seen in my vision was real. Yet this time was different. The dark-skinned man on the porch had never been a part of my dreams before.

I shivered, although my bedspread covered me to my waist. As the terrifying images trapped inside my head replayed, my heart raced and tears pricked my eyes. I took shallow breaths to calm myself and shook my head. "It couldn't have been a dream," I said out loud, trying to convince myself I wasn't crazy.

Yet, there I was, in my moonlit bedroom...alone.

Chapter Thirteen

After a long, mostly sleepless night, I'd finally resigned myself to seeing the date through. I wasn't sure exactly how well the night with Cowboy would go, but I needed to do this for myself. Too many times I longed for a man to find me desirable and treat me as he would any woman. I wasn't about to pass up a once in a lifetime opportunity.

Things were about to get very real, very fast, and I needed to be ready.

I spent the day primping and preparing myself for our date. I'd cleaned my house, washed my sheets, showered, and painted my toenails a pretty shade of coral. Not to mention my trip into town to buy the biggest box of condoms I'd ever seen, that were now resting on my bedside table. Just looking at them made me nervous.

Actually, that wasn't entirely true. The note I'd found in my mailbox on my way to town had me slightly off-kilter before I'd even picked up the condoms. It said, *"Think your hot stuff now? Wait 'til the fire starts."* The glaring grammatical issue on the crinkled paper was the least of my concerns.

The Barlows' threats were becoming more serious each day. I was no longer certain ignoring them was the best course of action, though I doubted confronting them would do the situation justice. So, for tonight, I'd decided to put it out of my mind and tackle only one thing at a time. Starting with Cowboy.

I smoothed out the wrinkles in my pale blue, flowery sundress and slipped on my white sandals. I wasn't sure what to wear for a one-night stand, so I just went with something simple and feminine. It was a safe bet. I'd never seen Cowboy in anything other than jeans and a T-shirt, so anything more than casual would be considered way overdressed.

When a truck rumbled to a stop outside, I tousled my loose hair one last time, checked my makeup in the mirror, and hurried to the door. I even waited for him to announce his arrival before opening it, just to keep from looking too eager.

The moment he knocked, I swung open the door and stepped directly into *The Twilight Zone*. Someone looking an awful lot like Cowboy stood in my doorway with a bouquet of pink roses. Except this guy was wearing a blazer, had his hair combed to the side, and was missing a cowboy hat.

What the hell?

He grinned at me. "Hey, ready to go?"

"Um, okay." It sounded more like a question looming in the air. "Let me just put these in some water first."

Cowboy waited at the door for me, whistling a tune I didn't recognize. He was certainly in a good mood. But then again, what guy isn't if he thinks he's about to get laid?

When I finished, I headed outside and he waited as I locked up. Once I turned back to him, he wordlessly offered me his arm and led me down the stairs and out to his vehicle. The red truck glinted in the fading sunlight, bright and shiny, as if he'd recently washed it.

Cowboy eyed my loose red strands before his gaze met mine and he grinned, as if he'd just noticed I wasn't wearing my glasses. "By the way, you look beautiful tonight."

"Thank you. So do you. I mean, you look very handsome."

He held the door for me as I climbed inside and buckled up, then gave me a wink before closing it. I watched as he strutted around the front of the truck to the driver's side, resembling a peacock proudly displaying his feathers. But, in this case, Cowboy was showing off his newfound gentlemanly behavior.

Silence sat between us for the first few miles. I spent most of that time sneaking peeks of his meticulously combed hairdo and uncomfortable-looking blazer and wondering what it all meant. The novelty of it all confused me. I yearned to run my fingers through his hair to mess it up and pull his blazer off in protest to see his broad shoulders I loved so much.

"I wasn't sure where you wanted to go for dinner, so I thought we'd just go somewhere close by."

"Oh." I couldn't stop the disappointment from leaching into my voice. Guess he was in a hurry to get back to my place.

"Is that okay? I just thought you'd be more comfortable that way."

Yeah, right. "It's fine."

"Are you sure? I could call and get us reservations

somewhere else, if you want," he said, lifting his cell phone from the truck's center console. "It's last minute, but I'm sure I could find us something."

"No, really. It's okay." I gave him a quick smile. "I'm just a little surprised, that's all. I figured a guy like you would have this dating thing down to a science."

He glanced over at me. "A guy like me?"

"You know, someone who dates a lot of different women."

Cowboy turned left into the parking lot of a restaurant called Junior's Diner, which resembled a big red barn, and parked in the front row. "I think we have different definitions of what a *date* is."

My cheeks burned with the heat of embarrassment, so I removed my seat belt to avoid looking in his direction. "You know what I mean."

Cowboy opened his door and stepped out. "Yeah, I do," he said, sounding perturbed by my remark. After marching around to my side, he yanked open the passenger door and took my hand in his to help me out. "And just for the record, I haven't been with nearly as many women as you think I have."

"Really?" I climbed out of his jacked-up truck and my eyes grazed over his face, searching for signs of sincerity. "Because I heard you were quite the—"

"Hey, manwhore!" someone called out, redirecting our attention. Emily stood on the nearby curb with an amused grin on her face.

Cowboy narrowed his eyes at her intrusion. The look he gave her was priceless: no parts embarrassment, all parts aggravation. Then he turned back to me. "We'll finish this conversation later."

I smiled. "All right."

"What are you two doing here?" Emily asked, squinting in confusion.

Cowboy hesitated. "We're…uh, just having dinner."

As we approached, Jake met Emily on the curb and his gaze landed on his friend. Jake's eyes widened as he gawked at Cowboy's attire and neatly styled hair. "What the fuck happened to you?"

I bit my lip to stifle my laughter and to keep from smiling, but Emily didn't. She chuckled out loud without any reservations at all.

"Since when the hell did you start wearing blazers?" Jake asked.

"What are you, the fashion police?" Cowboy retorted. "Guess that's what the FBI stands for: Fashion Bureau of—"

"Yeah, yeah. Knock it off."

Cowboy gritted his teeth together, then relaxed his jaw. "What are you two doing here?"

"We're celebrating," Emily said, gleefully. "It's been exactly six weeks since we've been able to have se—"

Jake covered Emily's mouth and gave her a stern look. "Since we had Lily." Then he removed his hand.

Emily rolled her eyes. "Oh, because they haven't heard the word 'sex' before. Jesus, Jake. You're such a prude sometimes."

Apparently, I was, too. My face had warmed enough that I was pretty sure everyone could see my blushing cheeks from a mile away. Though I liked Emily a lot, being around her in a small group made me nervous. You just never knew what would fly out of her mouth next.

"Well, since we're all here, why don't we sit together?"

she asked.

Crap.

"Emily," Jake said, lowering his voice. "We should leave them alone. I think they're on a date."

"*Date?*" she repeated, wrinkling her nose. "Since when did Cowboy actually start dating? I thought he only had one-night stands." Then she laughed. A lot. Sometime during her fit of laughter, she must've realized that no one else had joined in and that there was some awkward tension buzzing from the rest of us, because she stopped giggling. "Oh God, I'm sorry. I didn't mean it to come out sounding…well, you know."

I gave her a nonchalant shrug and a soft smile. "It's okay. Why don't we just go in and enjoy ourselves?"

"Sounds good," Jake said, moving past us through the entrance.

Cowboy took that as his cue and entered as well, while I followed behind him. As I passed by Emily, she mouthed an apology to me and I gave her a nearly imperceptible nod to let her know I wasn't angry. Then we followed the men inside.

I'd never been to Junior's Diner before, but I loved the atmosphere. The restaurant had a western decor with Old West paraphernalia tacked on every wall. Antique saddles, old spurs, and rusted horseshoes surrounded us.

Jake picked a table in the center of the room. "This okay?"

Cowboy nodded his approval and we sat on one side as Emily and Jake took the other. I'd barely planted my butt in the chair when a pretty young woman approached us while digging in the purse she had strapped over her shoulder.

She stood on Cowboy's opposite side and giggled shyly.

"Would you mind giving me your autograph?" she asked, whipping out a pen and a pocket-sized version of the Liberty County Bachelor calendar.

"Uh, sure," Cowboy replied uncomfortably. He shifted in his chair as he flipped to the month of May and scrawled his name across his racy photograph before handing it back to her. "There ya go."

"Would you sign mine, too?" Another woman popped up beside him, holding out a pocket calendar, looking hopeful and eager.

Cowboy smiled politely and gave her a nod as he took her calendar and administered the same treatment to it as the one before. But as he handed the woman back her calendar, another took her place. She held out a Sharpie and smiled flirtatiously at him. "Would you mind?"

"No problem," Cowboy answered, waiting for her to hand him her calendar.

But instead, she bent down, practically shoving her cleavage in his face. "Just sign anywhere you like," she purred with a blatant sexual overtone.

My eyes widened. Though it was rude for her to hit on my date, especially right in front of me, I didn't say anything. I had no claim on Cowboy and wouldn't pretend like I did. But Cowboy glanced over at me with uncertainty in his eyes, as if he wasn't sure how to handle the situation any more than I was. So I did the only thing I could do to put him at ease. I pretended to be oblivious to the woman's request by starting up a neutral conversation with his friends.

"Emily, did you have a good time last night?"

"Yep. Especially when you slapped the crap out of Cowboy. I'm guessing that wasn't a love tap you gave him on the dance floor."

I cringed. *Well, that didn't work out in my favor.* "Oh. You saw that?"

The woman standing there giggled, though Cowboy clenched his jaw. He quickly signed his name on her forearm and handed the marker back. "Sorry, I'm on a date. Best I can do." The woman sighed, disappointment tugging at her features, but retreated without another word. As she walked away, Cowboy mouthed a silent "sorry" to me and draped his arm on the back of my chair.

"Are you kidding? Everyone saw it. No doubt Jeremy did, too. That's probably the reason he targeted you. Jeremy's an ass like that. But then again, I guess he isn't the only one," she said, directing her attention to Cowboy with a suspicious gleam in her eye. "You must've done something pretty bad to cause our sweet little Anna to have that reaction."

God, I wish everyone would stop calling me that. It makes me sound like a four-year-old.

Cowboy's gaze cut to me, but I just lifted a brow and shrugged. Technically, they were *his* friends first, and if he wanted them to know, then he should be the one to tell them.

He combed his fingers through his hair, as if he were contemplating what to say. "I sort of…called her a liar."

Emily's eyes widened, but Jake chuckled and said, "That was your bright idea? To go over there and insult her? Jesus, Cowboy. Talk about open mouth, insert boot."

"Shut up," Cowboy sneered, firing daggers at Jake with his eyes.

Emily cringed, then leaned over to her husband. "Um, Jake, why don't we go look for the waitress?"

But he was oblivious to the reason for her request. "You

do know in here the waitresses come to the table. We don't have to go look—" The contemptuous glare Emily gave him finally sank in. "Oh. Okay, sure."

The moment they walked away, Cowboy grasped my hand in his. "I'm sorry. I guess I'm not very good at the whole dating thing. Tonight's not going at all the way I planned."

"That's okay," I said, giving him a genuine smile. "To be honest, I haven't been on many dates before so I didn't have any pre-conceived notions." Not about the dinner portion of our date, anyway.

Cowboy's brows furrowed. "My original idea was to take you by horseback down to Rickety Bridge, have a picnic, and then we could have cooled off in the old watering hole, but I wasn't sure if you would think it was lame or not."

"Actually, it sounds wonderful, but I…well, I don't swim."

"That's okay. I could teach you," he offered, looking hopeful.

"No, that's not exactly…um, what I mean is, I know how to swim. I just…" I peered down at our hands as he linked his fingers with mine.

"You don't want to get into a swimsuit?" he asked. When I nodded silently, he reached over and tilted my chin up until my eyes met his gaze. "Darlin', the only person here who is bothered by your scars is *you.*"

His words warmed my heart, melting the tension. The sincerity in his voice and eyes left little doubt that he was telling the God's honest truth. He didn't care about my scars. And the sheer notion sent endorphins rushing through my system, filling me with relief.

Until he winked and added, "Besides, who needs swimsuits?"

I sighed inwardly as Jake and Emily returned to the table with a waitress who handed us menus. She was an older woman but she chewed and smacked her gum as loudly as any teenager. She took our drink orders, shoved her notepad into her apron, and pulled out a pocket calendar of her own.

Sheesh.

Before she could even speak, I rose from my seat. "Excuse me for a moment," I said, heading in the direction of the restrooms. I didn't really need to go to the bathroom, but I couldn't sit through another moment of these women stroking Cowboy's ego. No wonder the man was insatiable. He had women coming out of the woodwork to get to him.

In the small room, I checked my makeup and hair in the mirror and then washed my hands. I waited a few more minutes, then left, working my way back to our table. But halfway there, I bumped directly into a tall, broad Native American man wearing a black western shirt with white pearl snaps who smelled eerily of mint. I started to apologize, but the moment my gaze met his, the only thing that left my throat was a strangled gasp.

Oh my God! It was him.

Last night, I hadn't realized he was a Native American, but standing before him now, face-to-face, I had no doubt this man was the very same man I'd seen on my back porch. His long, silky black hair was braided this time, but I recognized the minty scent of the chaw of tobacco he held in his bottom lip and the golden hawk eyes sliced into my soul.

But that was a dream, wasn't it?

The dark-skinned man blinked at me, almost as if he… recognized me, too. Then an unpleasant scowl appeared on his face. "Don't scream," he ordered and put his hand on his hip, which showcased a large knife in a brown leather sheath.

Jesus! It hadn't been a dream. So I did what any intelligent woman would do in that situation. I screamed.

The sound could've shattered glass and basically did, since a young waitress passing by dropped the drink-filled tray she'd carried. Shards of clear glass lay on the wet tile floor at her feet as everyone in the restaurant—including Jake, Cowboy, and Emily—jumped to their feet. Cowboy came running toward us, but since the man in front of me was armed, I didn't bother waiting for him to arrive.

I grabbed the first thing I could reach on the nearest vacant dish-covered table and pointed it at the man in front of me. The corner of his mouth lifted into a tiny smirk. To him, it may have only been a dirty butter knife. But to me, it was a deadly weapon, one I planned to gouge his eyes out with if he came any closer.

"Anna...?" Cowboy stopped beside the man and held up his two hands, as if surrendering. "Sweetheart, what are you doing?"

"Who are you?" I demanded.

"It's me, Cowboy."

"Not you. *Him.*" I nodded toward the burly Native American.

The two men exchanged casual glances, but the Indian spoke up first. "She saw me last night."

Cowboy blinked in surprise, then shook his head. "What the fuck do you mean she saw you? You're a goddamn tracker, Junior. You're supposed to be good at this shit."

Junior? As in the owner of Junior's Diner?

The man named Junior gave Cowboy a death stare. "She

caught me standing on her back porch and fainted. I caught her before she fell and carried her back to bed. You could have warned me she doesn't sleep."

"What do you mean she doesn't sleep?" Cowboy asked him. "Of course she does."

"Not for more than two hours at a time on any given night."

Cowboy wore a perturbed expression. "Then what the hell is she doing if she's not—"

"Stop talking about me as if I'm not standing right here."

Cowboy's hard gaze landed on me, but his tone softened. "Why aren't you sleeping?"

I placed the dirty butter knife back on the nearby table. "That's none of your business. Why are you having me followed by your…er, friend?"

"He's not following you. He lives about a mile up the road from your house and I asked him to keep an eye on you."

"Well, you should've cleared that with me first."

"I didn't want you to worry. I told you I'd handle the situation with the Barlow boys, and that's what I was doing. You don't have to lose any sleep over them."

"Look, I appreciate your concern, but you can't have someone watching my house and not tell me. This gentleman…Junior, is it? He's scared the devil out of me twice already."

With wide eyes, Cowboy tossed Junior a dumbfounded look. "*Twice?* Christ, Junior. Maybe next time I should get Big Jim's three-year-old twins to ride their tricycles over to her house and keep an eye out. They're low enough to the ground that she might not have spotted them," he said, rolling his eyes. "Some fucking tracker you are."

Junior's eyes narrowed and his voice held a menacing tone. "If you want to know what it feels like to be skinned alive, keep talking."

I shuddered visibly.

"It's okay, Anna. Junior's just spouting off. He wouldn't really do it."

With a lethal gleam in his eye, the big Indian put his hand directly on his knife at his side and cocked an eyebrow at Cowboy. I don't know whether Cowboy believed what he said or not, but the color suddenly drained from his face as he gave Junior a weak smile.

Junior wore a stone-cold expression, but it softened as he shifted his gaze onto me. "You didn't see me twice."

"Yes, I did. I saw you about a week ago standing at the edge of my property. You were watching me from the tree line."

"Wasn't me," he said, his mouth grim. "Last night was the first time I'd ever dismounted from my horse and approached the house. Had to be someone else."

Cowboy must've believed him because his eyes immediately lit with concern. My heart leaped into my throat and my knees wobbled, but I steadied them. This was not the right time to have a nervous breakdown. Not that there ever was a good time for that.

I glanced around the room, realizing all eyes were on me. Between the threatening notes that had me on edge, the disastrous date gone wrong, and the events of last night's public embarrassment, I couldn't take any more. "Cowboy, w-would you please take me home? I think I've caused enough of a scene tonight. It's probably a good idea to—"

"Go back to our house and order pizza," Emily chimed in. At first, I thought maybe she had something in her eye, but then I realized it was an exaggerated wink. She obviously thought she was somehow helping me out. "We have alcohol," she whispered. "Lots of it."

I'd never been much of a drinker, but I was suddenly parched, imagining that this was how it felt to think, "God, I could go for a drink about now."

Emily stood on the other side of her dining room table, holding up the bottle of white wine. "More?"

"Why not? One more glass won't hurt." I pressed my cool hand to my hot cheek and swayed a little in my chair. Nope, I was definitely not hurting…anywhere.

Cowboy grinned. "Darlin', maybe you should slow down a little."

"Oh, please!" Emily shrieked. "Since when did you not know how to have fun? Don't tell me Jake has finally rubbed off on you."

"Hey!" Jake said, clearly offended. "I'm lots of fun." He leaned over the table and snagged Emily's top with one finger, pulling her to him. Then he took a quick peek down her shirt and grinned. "See? Fun."

Cowboy stood up fast. "Okay, I think it's time for us to go and let you two have some alone time."

"It's fine," Emily said, waving off his comment. "Floss is keeping Lily until the morning. I pumped breast milk by the bucketful earlier today just so Lily wouldn't run out in the middle of the night."

"Still, it's your first night alone since you had Lily," Cowboy said. "I doubt you two want to spend it with us."

"Hold up," Jake told him. "I wanted to show you our new bay mare out in the barn real quick. Won't take but a few minutes."

"All right." Cowboy glanced at me. "I'll be right back to take you home."

The knot in my throat wouldn't allow me to answer him, so I just nodded an okay and took a large gulp of my wine.

"Don't be out there too long, Jake," Emily said with a quick wink. "Since they're leaving, I have *plans* for us... something that might involve pickles."

Jake gave her a quick kiss on the lips and headed for the door, wearing a huge grin. "I'm feeling a little lazy tonight. Might let you do all the work," he teased.

Emily smirked at him. "So what else is new?"

Cowboy chuckled as Jake stepped out the door, mumbling under his breath.

I waited until the door shut behind them. "Pickles?"

Emily laughed. "Jake won't allow me to eat pickles in front of him anymore. My entire pregnancy, he swore I was torturing him."

Normally, I would've blushed and stammered all over myself after a sexual innuendo such as that, but the alcohol in my system lent me some perspective. Instead, I broke into a fit of giggles.

"About time you loosened up," Emily said, smiling. "Now would you mind telling me what's going on between you and Cowboy?"

"We're friends." My cheeks grew warmer, so I took a sip of my chilled wine.

"Uh-huh. And Jake and I are brother and sister," she said. "Has he tried to undress you yet?"

Nearly swallowing my tongue, I choked at her bluntness and let out a little cough. "Um, not exactly." I wasn't aware that having a conversation with Emily would lead to such an intimate discussion, but maybe it was a good thing. She obviously had more experience with men than I did and could probably give me some fascinating advice on how to handle the situation with Cowboy. "If anything, he pulls back whenever we start to…you know, do stuff."

Emily's face warped with genuine confusion. "Really?"

"You seem surprised by that."

"Well, it *is* Cowboy we're talking about. Hmm. Guess that puts a whole new spin on that fireman saying, 'Find 'em hot, leave 'em wet.'"

We both laughed at that, and the sudden camaraderie put me at ease. Emily was impulsive and wore her blatant sexuality on her sleeve like a badge of honor. No wonder Jake couldn't keep his hands off her. All the sexual energy buzzing in the air between them after their ten minute round of under-the-table touching hadn't gone unnoticed.

But I wasn't Emily, and there was nothing wildly sexual about me. "Most men are simply not attracted to me. Not that I've given them much reason to be."

"What? That's ridiculous! You're much hotter than you give yourself credit for." She shook her head in disbelief. "You have the most amazing blue eyes I've ever seen. And look at that gorgeous red hair of yours. Any woman would kill for that shade of natural red."

"But I dress like an old maid," I said, averting my eyes to avoid showing her how embarrassed I truly was.

"Well, Cowboy doesn't seem to mind." I glanced back to her and caught an unreadable expression on her face. Then Emily grinned at me. "I think he likes the primness. You could probably curtsy and cause him to ache in places he never knew existed."

I shrugged lightly. "I don't know about that."

"Well, I do. Cowboy is well-known with the ladies for his insatiable desire. If he's not jumping in the sack with you, especially when you're offering, then there's something more going on."

It was true I'd seen oddities in his behavior that didn't coincide with the rumors I'd heard. But that couldn't possibly mean anything, could it?

"I don't know. I think we're just circling each other, trying to figure out what's about to happen. I'm not sure how to take things to the next level."

Emily leaned toward me. "You want to seduce him?"

I felt compelled to answer her honestly, but there's nothing like being asked a direct question that makes you lose confidence. So I chewed on my lower lip and nodded.

She grinned at that. "Anna, just think of this as sexual warfare. Panties are your weapons."

"Chalk this up to cluelessness, but how do I go about getting to that part?"

"That's easy. Just give him a sexy look and you'll be knocking boots with him in no time. Here, try one on me and I'll tell you what I think."

"You want me to—"

"Yep. Give me your sexiest look," she encouraged. "Then I'll judge if it will spark his libido."

"Okay. Um, here goes." I breathed out a slow breath and

relaxed my face. Then I cocked my head to the side, batted my eyelashes, and smiled wide, teeth showing.

It must've went horribly wrong because Emily wrinkled her nose and cringed. "Um, yeah, that's not sexy. Creepy, maybe, but definitely not sexy."

I covered my mouth and giggled with embarrassment. "I don't know what I'm doing."

"That was obvious by your epic fail of turning me on."

I rolled my eyes. "I wouldn't have turned you on, anyway."

"Oh, I don't know about that. You are pretty cute." She leaned closer and toyed with the stem of her wineglass, licking her lips as she lowered her chin and looked up at me beneath her dark lashes.

The sudden change in her demeanor had me stammering. "I…um…"

Emily sat back in her chair and threw her head with a laugh. "I'm just messing with you."

I breathed a sigh of relief. "Thank God. I thought you were flirting with me."

"Exactly," she muttered, taking a sip of her wine. "You saw how I did that, right? You can totally do it, too. Just practice a little. Then Cowboy won't know what hit him. He'll have to be carried out on a stretcher."

"But what do I do in the meantime?"

"Have another glass of wine for the extra boost of courage and then show him your panties. The rest will fall into place."

"Are you sure?"

Emily grinned. "As Cowboy would say, 'God always takes care of helpless creatures.'"

Chapter Fourteen

Cowboy snagged my house keys from my hand and unlocked my front door, pushing it open and stepping aside to let me enter. He followed me inside and shut the door behind us, then tossed the keys on the small entryway table.

To steady myself, I pressed my back against the wall.

Once he turned back to face me, a slow grin lifted his cheeks. He stepped closer, allowing his warm body to lean into me as his firm mouth dropped over mine. His tongue slid along my bottom lip where he then nipped gently. A feverish frenzy coursed through my veins.

My hands moved over his rib cage and onto his back, feeling the hard-packed muscles tighten beneath my fingertips. His hands traveled up my arms to my neck as his knee parted my legs, sliding my skirt up between my thighs. Within seconds, my nails were digging trenches into his shoulder blades.

Moments later, he slowed things down and rationed his touches, then stopped altogether. He backed away slowly. "We should probably dial it down a little before we do something you'll regret." Then he plopped down on the sofa and blew out a breath.

A sinking feeling came over me. "Me…or *you*?"

My remark gave him pause, and his eyes flickered in my direction. "Of course I mean you. Why would *I* regret it?"

I sat beside him on the couch. "I don't know. But you seem awfully sure that I would. Maybe you're the one with the issue."

"No, of course not."

"Good." I leaned closer to him and brushed my lips over his ear, but he only stiffened. "Maybe I should go slip into something a little more comfortable."

He swallowed hard and pulled at his shirt collar. "Yeah, sure. Go ahead. I'll wait here."

I rose and wobbled toward my bedroom, pausing in the doorway to look back at him. He faced away from me and was eyeing a framed art canvas on the wall, as if he wasn't the least bit concerned with my intentions.

I don't know what I'd expected. Hell, I thought I knew what *he* expected, but apparently I was wrong. Or doing something wrong. His preoccupation unnerved me almost as much as what I was about to do. Most men—at least the ones in their right minds—paid attention when a girl said she was going to take off her clothes.

In the bedroom, I stripped off my clothes and changed into a long white satiny nightgown and slipped on a matching silk robe.

"I should get going," he called out from the living room.

"You probably want to get to bed."

He looked up as I came around the corner, and his mouth dropped open. The robe barely covered my shoulders and I had purposely left it open in the front, allowing the negligee to peek through.

"Funny that you mentioned that," I stammered, feeling my entire body blush beneath the robe.

Cowboy stood up, but he didn't come any closer. If anything, he looked like he was about to hightail it for the front door. "Anna, if I didn't know any better, I'd think you were trying to proposition me."

"And that's a problem?"

"No. I mean, yes."

The uncertainty in his voice worried me. "Well, which is it?"

Cowboy looked a little lost for words, but finally shook his head. "Yeah, it's a problem." Then he muttered a few expletives under his breath before looking back at me. "I can't...I mean, we can't..."

"Oh." Feeling like a presumptuous idiot, I turned away from him and quickly closed my robe, crossing my arms over my chest to keep it in place. *What the hell was I thinking?* He'd obviously changed his mind about us.

"Anna, wait." He stepped up behind me and placed his hands on my shoulders. "It's not what you think."

"It's okay," I said, holding back tears of embarrassment. "You don't have to explain anything to me. I get it."

"Do you?" he asked, sounding painfully unsure. "You've been drinking and aren't thinking clearly."

"I understand the difference between a man who wants me and one who obviously doesn't."

"That's not what I meant, Anna. I was only talking about the alcohol. That's the reason we can't do this. When we do, I want you to be sure, and I'm not entirely convinced you are."

I turned around and looked into his eyes. "You think I'm throwing myself at you because I'm inebriated?"

He grinned. "Even drunk, you can't stop using big words."

I dropped my gaze and looked away. "This is embarrassing enough. You don't have to make fun of me."

"Darlin', I'm not poking fun. I think it's adorable the way you talk." Using one finger, he lifted my chin. "Look, your first time should be special. Not some post-drinking binge decision."

I blinked at him in horror. "What?"

"I don't mind being your first, Anna. But not like this. I know you're probably nervous about being with a man, but we don't have to rush into having sex."

"You know, you have a really infuriating and insulting concept of me," I told him, crossing my arms once again.

"Sweetheart, I'm not trying to make you feel bad about being inexperienced. I'm just trying to tell you it's okay. You don't have anything to be embarrassed about. It's not a problem."

"Apparently, Houston, we do have a problem." I pursed my mouth, trying to control my temper, then blew out a breath at his puzzled look. "I'm *not* a virgin."

The shocked look on his face was almost laughable. And I probably would've laughed if it hadn't been for the annoying way he was staring at me. As if I were tainted or something.

I shook my head with irritation. "Your silence is deafening."

"I'm just a little…surprised, that's all."

And disappointed, perhaps? Was that what he wanted from the beginning? "What does it matter, anyway? It has no bearing on—"

He shoved to his feet and started pacing. "When?"

I gave him an ill look. "It wasn't recent, if that's what you're asking."

"So this whole time, you've been acting innocent and toying with me?"

"Toying with you?" Confusion filled my head. "What are you talking about?"

"Your shyness about being touched, the virginal wardrobe, and the whole insecure schoolgirl routine you put out there. It was all an act?" He paced behind my couch for several beats. "Hell, woman, you might as well have been winking at me in the dark."

"Well, I'm so sorry if you didn't see my tramp stamp posted clearly on my back," I said.

"Jesus Christ, now you have a tattoo?"

Oh God. This was getting ridiculous. I stood and swiveled toward him, blowing out a hard breath. "No, you're missing the point entirely."

"Then maybe you better explain it to me."

"That's just it, Cowboy. I don't owe you any sort of explanation just because *you* assumed I was a virgin. If you wanted to know, then you should've asked."

He gaped at me. "I didn't just make that shit up in my head," he yelled. "You pretended to be innocent."

"I didn't pretend anything," I said, insulted by the accusation.

"Look, I'm not upset that you aren't a virgin. I'm just not

real keen on the idea about another man putting his hands on you. Especially when that bastard was married."

"Married? What are you talking about?"

"It was Chief Swanson, wasn't it? That's who you were sleeping with?"

"What? No. Of course not." I shook my head in disbelief that he would even think such a thing.

"Look, I already know he was sleeping with someone else before his wife came back in the picture. He dies and then suddenly you show up in town, claiming that you don't know him, yet I find you at his grave kissing his headstone and spouting off apologies."

"I already told you I didn't know him," I shouted, letting the anger consume me. "Excuse me if I don't go around screwing strangers, like *you*—" I cringed internally at the words that had slipped out.

"You done yet?"

"No. I'm. Not." I pushed back my hair and blew my bangs out of my eyes. "To quell your curiosity, I lost my virginity a long time ago. I don't know why you consider that such an affront to your masculinity, but if it's such a problem that I'm not the pure woman you assumed I was, then I don't need you."

"So you expected to drop something like this on me and not allow me to have time to process it?"

"There's nothing to process. My past experiences are my own, and unless you're willing to bare your dating lifespan to me, then it's none of your business what I did or who I did it with."

"Fine!"

"Fine!" I yelled back.

He grabbed his hat off the coffee table, turned on his heel, and stormed out to his truck. Throwing it in drive, he peeled out, spitting gravel across my lawn while stirring up a cloud of dust. Stumped by his anger, I slammed the door and sank into my couch. *Well, just great.*

I'd thought the night would've ended differently. Prince Charming was supposed to sweep me off my feet and carry me to bed. But that just goes to show why I'd never believed in fairy tales to begin with. *The prince isn't always charming and the princess isn't always a virgin.*

The next night, Bobbie Jo and Emily squeezed through the crowd of the bar and hurried toward me. They took a seat at the little round table in the corner that I'd been holding for us.

"We got here as fast as we could," Bobbie Jo said. "What's wrong?"

"I just needed someone to talk to."

"But you said to come quick," Emily said. "What's the big emergency?"

"Well, I…uh…" I closed my eyes and took a deep breath. "I want to have sex with Cowboy," I blurted out.

Emily laughed. "Who doesn't?"

"No, let me rephrase. I'm *going* to have sex with Cowboy…er, well I thought I was, anyway."

Bobbie Jo shook her head. "Oh, Lord, I can't believe you drank the Cowboy Kool-Aid." Guess Emily hadn't filled her in yet.

"It's always the quiet ones," Emily said, grinning. "So I

guess last night didn't go as planned?"

I blushed, not knowing how to explain the situation to them and maintain any bit of dignity I had left. "I think I made a mistake."

"What do you mean you made a mistake? What'd he do to you?" Bobbie Jo asked, looking like she was about to send out an all-girl mob to remove Cowboy's testicles.

"He didn't do anything. That's the problem." My cheeks grew hotter. "I tried to seduce him and…well, he rejected me."

Both girls blinked, as if I'd just told them aliens had taken over the planet. "Really?" Bobbie Jo asked.

Emily shook her head adamantly. "I didn't think he was capable of turning down sex. Are you sure he understood what you were offering?"

"Oh, he understood, all right. And he turned me down flat."

"Well, then it's his loss. Right, Bobbie Jo?" Emily paused, waiting for a response, but when none came, she elbowed her friend. "Bobbie Jo?"

"Really?" Bobbie Jo said again, clearly still not believing Cowboy shot down a female offering him sex.

I sighed. "Who am I kidding? Obviously, I'm the first girl he's ever turned down. Whatever. It's not like I would really know how to please a man like him, anyway."

"Oh, sweetie," Bobbie Jo said, her eyes filling with pity. "You don't have to be embarrassed by your shortcomings in that department. We've all been a virgin at some point, Anna. It's natural to want to—"

"Why is everyone assuming I'm a virgin?"

Emily keeled over with laughter. "Holy shit! You're

not?"

God, I wished I had a hole to crawl into. "You know, just because I don't look like one of those centerfold girls doesn't mean I haven't had offers." I rose from my chair and grabbed my purse. "Never mind. This whole thing is embarrassing enough without being laughed at."

Emily looked like a dog that had done something terribly wrong. Her eyes widened as her mouth drooped into a frown. "Oh, Anna. I'm sorry. I didn't know you were this upset. Please don't go." Her warm hand captured mine. "I'm probably not the best one to talk to about this stuff. Maybe I should leave and let you talk to Bobbie Jo alone."

I plopped back down into my chair. "No. It's not you. I'm the one who should apologize. I guess I'm still a little worked up from my encounter with him last night." And possibly even more on edge after finding another hostile note with horrid grammar in my mailbox earlier today: *Bridges don't burn theirselves.* I shook it off, not allowing the dread to consume me. "I'm letting all my fears and self-doubts control my emotions. I'm sorry."

Emily shook her head and gave my hand a squeeze. "Sweetie, there's nothing to forgive. I'm sorry I assumed anything about you. It wasn't fair."

"Me, too," Bobbie Jo said. "And I'm guessing Cowboy made the same assumption?"

I nodded. "Yes, but I told him the truth and he got mad. Then he stormed out. I don't really know what happened. I thought maybe you two could shed some light on what I did wrong."

Bobbie Jo huffed out a breath. "Listen to me, Anna. You did *nothing* wrong. Maybe he was just as surprised as we were and had a bad reaction."

"Yeah, like a coping mechanism," Emily agreed. "He's probably kicking himself in the ass right about now."

"Well, he's not the only one," I told them. "I felt like such a fool for throwing myself at him like I did. Especially after what I went through the first time."

Bobbie Jo looked puzzled. "You threw yourself at him before last night?"

"No. I meant…the last time I was with a man, the one who took my virginity." I covered my face with my hands. "Oh, gosh. I swore I was never doing it again."

"Technically, you aren't," Emily said with a grin. "Losing your virginity, I mean."

"She gets the point," Bobbie Jo said, rolling her eyes. "I think she meant sex. Right, Anna?"

"Yes, I meant sex. I…don't like it."

"What?" Emily shouted, stiffening in her seat. "What the hell do you mean you don't like sex?"

I put my hand over my heart and felt it beating fast inside my chest. These women were my friends, but I knew it would be hard to tell them what I'd hidden inside me for so long. "I had a bad experience…the first time."

"Do you want to talk about it?" Bobbie Jo asked softly.

I nodded, but was reluctant to speak. I'd never mentioned it to anyone else before now. "I went on a few dates with this guy and was afraid he would get frustrated and possibly lose interest if I wasn't willing to…well, you know."

"Anna, did he hurt you?" Emily asked, blunt as usual.

Bobbie Jo gave her a sour look.

"It's okay. I should've seen the red flags. He never really seemed to care about what I wanted. Everything was always about him. He chose which restaurant we went to and which movie we watched together. And by the fifth date, when he pressed the issue, I just…well, I didn't want to be a virgin forever and thought maybe it was better than nothing."

"No," Emily said adamantly. "Better than nothing is *not* good enough."

"He took advantage of your sweet vulnerability, Anna. No man should ever do that to a woman," Bobbie Jo added.

Shame trickled throughout my body. "I didn't enjoy it. Not that I expected to since it was my first time. But I wanted him to stop. He was too rough and was hurting me, but I didn't say anything. I just wanted the whole encounter to end quickly." I visibly shuddered and closed my eyes. "I wasn't aroused. Not really. But he just kept poking and stabbing at me. I just lay there until he was finished and finally rolled off me. It was the most humiliating moment of my life."

"You have nothing to be ashamed about," Emily assured me. "That guy was an asshole. Don't keep yourself from having a relationship—sexual or otherwise—with someone else because you're afraid that they'll be the same way. This time, you just need to make sure it's with the right person."

"Is that your way of saying you don't think Cowboy is the right person?" I asked.

Bobbie Jo smiled. "Do *you* think he's the right person? Because that's really all that matters."

"That, and the fact that he's the Legend of the South," Emily said, winking. "After all, that *is* what women around here say about him. He's supposed to be a wonderful lover. Might be a wise move to get a lesson from the master." She laughed a little. "Anna, have you ever had an orgasm?"

"Emily!" Bobbie Jo yelled.

"No," I answered honestly, not giving her time to retract the question. "No man ever gave me one."

Emily's eyes widened slightly. "Well, why the hell are you waiting for a man to give you one? No one knows how to please *you* better than yourself. Give yourself one."

Bobbie Jo shook her head. "I can't believe I'm saying this, but Emily's right. You can't show a man what you like if you don't really know yourself."

"And faking an orgasm isn't going to do him any favors," Emily added. "It would just be you cheating yourself out of pleasure. You need to communicate what you want."

"So, um…have you two ever…"

"What? Masturbated?" Emily leaned back in her chair with a huge grin. "Yep. In fact, I handcuffed Jake to the bed last night and let him watch. He loved it."

"Oh God!" Bobbie Jo laughed. "Ever heard of TMI? You know I'm going to make fun of Jake for that one."

"Don't you dare! He'd kill me if he knew I told you that."

I giggled. "What about you, Bobbie Jo?"

She grinned. "Are you kidding? I'm a single mom to a five-month-old. There's not exactly a line of men banging down my door at the moment. I'm basically dating my vibrator."

Emily and I laughed, but Bobbie Jo turned serious. "This is the thing, Anna. Whether it's with Cowboy or someone else, don't assume that because you sleep with someone that he'll fall in love. You see what I'm going through with Jeremy. It's not a fun situation to be in. Be careful."

"I agree," Emily said, nodding. "Some men are dogs and are always sniffing around for the next female in heat."

"So, you're saying that's what Cowboy is doing?"

The girls glanced at each other and smiled. Then Bobbie Jo said, "No, I think you scared that hound dog up a tree. He probably anticipated a longer wait, but you put a stop to the chase and offered him up the reward. Now he doesn't know what to do about it."

"Maybe I should call him and —"

"God, no!" Emily shouted. "Jesus. Don't make it so easy for him. For a man like Cowboy, it's all about the chase. This time, he just barked up the wrong tree. If I've learned anything about him over the past year of knowing him, he's probably at home right now, scooting his ass on the floor in circles trying to figure you out."

"She's right, Anna. Let him stew for a while," Bobbie Jo suggested. "He'll come pawing back at your door when he's ready."

Feeling a little unsure and apprehensive, I looked down and tangled my fingers together in my lap. "About that…" I said, lifting my head as my eyes glossed over. "There's something else I haven't told you, yet."

Chapter Fifteen

Three days passed before a knock sounded on my door. Actually, it wasn't a knock. More like a persistent banging. I slipped on my robe and pulled the wet towel from my still-damp hair, then went to answer it.

"Hold on a second," I yelled as I made my way through the house.

After receiving two more ominous notes over the past few days, I sure as hell wasn't about to swing open the door for just anyone. Even if it was only late afternoon. I hadn't mentioned the notes to anyone because it was silly to worry my friends for nothing, but the threats had become more volatile. Since I was largely ignoring the Barlow brothers' attempts at intimidating me, I was positive it wouldn't be long before they tried something different to provoke me into a reaction.

But when I glimpsed through the peephole, it wasn't the troublesome neighbors staring back at me. With a huff, I threw open the door.

Cowboy filled the doorway wearing his gray plaid button-down with the pearl snaps, which was only halfway tucked into the waist of his jeans. The hem of his pants sat on top of his boots, as if he'd thrown his clothes on in a hurry.

I crossed my arms. "What do *you* want?"

"We need to talk," he said, brushing past me into my living room.

My eyes narrowed at his intrusion. "Why?"

But he didn't seem to notice the irritation in my stance or my voice. He was too busy pacing around in circles beside my couch with a sour look on his face. I shut the door, but I didn't move toward him.

"Come sit down," he ordered, red-faced and still pacing the floor.

"I'm happy to watch the volcano erupt from here, thank you very much."

He stopped moving and looked directly at me. "Okay, fine," he grumbled. There was a slight pause as he cleared his throat, readying himself to say whatever he came here to tell me. "I didn't mean to walk out on you the other night."

"Oh, you mean after your little tantrum?"

"It wasn't a tantrum. You just caught me off guard. If you hadn't led me to believe you were a virgin, I would've—"

"You would've what? Tried to get into my pants sooner?" I shook my head and a disgusted sound gurgled from my throat. "You have a lot of nerve putting all this on me. I never told you I was a virgin. If you assumed that, then... well, that's on you."

I tapped my foot, waiting for his response, but he hesitated as he rubbed at the back of his neck. "You're right. I'm sorry. I didn't come here to blame you. I came here to rectify my mistake."

"You turned me down, Cowboy. So what…now that you're ready for me, I'm supposed to just roll over and let you have your way with me?"

"Christ, no. That's not what I meant." Cowboy shrugged. "I just meant that I came here to apologize for my behavior. It was uncalled for."

I moved away from the door and sat down on the couch. I didn't know why, but I felt the need to explain my situation to him. "Look, I had a bad sexual experience. Someone abused my trust and…well, he did things that hurt me. I don't want to go through that again."

"Some bastard hurt you? Tell me who the motherfucker is and I'll kill him." Cowboy blew out a deep breath and lowered his voice. "I'm sorry…that he hurt you, I mean." Despite his soft tone, Cowboy's hands fisted at his sides and his body vibrated with anger. He wasn't sorry. He was pissed.

"Thanks, but it's in the past, and I don't want to dwell on it." I glanced up at his eyes and felt the first dagger of pity slice into me. "Stop looking at me like that. I didn't tell you so that you'd feel sorry for me. I just wanted you to understand."

He nodded, but didn't speak.

A rush of heat flooded my cheeks, but I needed to be honest with him to avoid any more misunderstandings. "Listen, I don't have the kind of, um, experience you do." I gestured to a pile of books across the room on an end table—books I'd spent the last three days reading. "I checked out some self-help books from the library and spent the last few days going over them."

Cowboy walked over and lifted a book from the top of the stack. "You're reading a how-to manual on sex?" he asked, clearly shocked by the revelation.

I cringed, but it was too late to turn back now. "I bought some DVDs as well. They're all about self-empowerment for women in the bedroom."

He glanced at the DVDs sitting on the entertainment center, and he blinked. The top one's cover displayed a nearly naked woman with a man's hands covering her breasts. "So what you're basically telling me is that you're reading sex books and watching porn?"

"No! Of course not." I closed my eyes and sighed. No sense in getting defensive. "I was doing some, um, research."

He looked at me as if I were crazy. "On sex?"

"Yes." I blushed again. "I wanted to prepare myself. And I didn't want to be...ineffectual for you."

His brows lowered. "Translation?"

God, this was so embarrassing. "I didn't want to be bad in bed," I said then sighed, thinking this conversation hadn't gone over as well as I thought it would. "It's just that...well, I felt stupid asking you to train me."

"Train you?" Cowboy looked puzzled over my choice of words. "Hold up, Anna. Sex isn't about *training* anyone."

"Oh, yeah? Well, then how else would I find out that if you massaged a man's perineum while performing fellatio he would ejaculate faster?"

The stunned look on Cowboy's face lasted only seconds, then he grinned. "Darlin', you don't learn by reading clinical descriptions. You learn by doing what feels good."

I nodded in agreement. "Oh, I know! I did that, too, by experimenting on myself."

He rubbed a hand over his face as he contemplated what I'd said. "Did you just tell me you masturbated?"

I lowered my gaze briefly, wondering if that was something he found repulsive. "I mean the things I read were sort of arousing, and I wasn't sure about a few of the sexual maneuvers and all the endless variations, so I...well, yeah."

"Jesus." Cowboy looked up at the ceiling with what possibly could've been exasperation. "What the hell is wrong with you women these days? I thought Emily said some derogatory things, but..." His gaze lowered onto me. "She has nothing on *you*."

"Actually, Emily was the one who suggested it."

"Oh, hell. Why am I not surprised?" He shook his head, then kicked off his boots. "That's it. No more books or DVDs." He pulled at his shirt until the buttons unsnapped and then he slid it from his shoulders and tossed it onto the couch next to me.

"What are you doing?"

"I'm doing you a favor. Don't worry, I'm not going to touch you, and you can stop whenever you want, but the only way you're going to learn about a man's naked body is by seeing one in person. And I'll be damned if I trust anyone else to do *this* with you." He opened the button on his jeans and slid down the zipper. "Consider me your willing test subject."

My gaze dropped to the small line of hair running into his pants. His lack of underwear had my cheeks heating again. He tossed his hat onto the couch and then pushed his jeans down with one hard shove.

I gasped and my hand flew to my chest. "Are you insane?"

Without a word, he stripped off his jeans and socks,

leaving him completely nude and wielding a very large, rock solid erection. I tried to keep my eyes on his face as he paraded through my living room in the buff and made his way through the open door to my bedroom.

He was completely comfortable with himself as he crawled onto my bed and lay down, propping his head with my pillow. "You coming?" he asked.

It was a disarming gesture, one that left me speechless. But I had to admit that he provoked my curiosity. Maybe it was the lunacy of the situation or the psychological thrill of doing something so sinful. Or maybe it was just the way he, with his tight muscular ass, had climbed onto my bed while he offered up his delicious body for exploration. In any case, he had issued me a challenge.

I edged closer to the bedroom door, keeping my eyes on his. "Cowboy, I don't think—"

"That's the problem right there. Stop thinking."

My gaze drifted downward. "Sort of hard to do when you aren't wearing underwear…or anything else."

"I go commando all the time," he said nonchalantly. "Not a big deal. Now come in here and take a good look. I promise to keep my hands to myself."

"I…I can't."

He picked his head up to get a better look at me through the open doorway. "Anna, you said you wanted to learn, right? Just pretend this is an art class, and I'm your nude model."

With his spectacular chest, wide shoulders, and his other manly attributes, that wasn't so hard to picture. But this wasn't an art room filled with other artists all staring at the man on my bed. It was just me. Us, actually…in a terribly intimate setting. And if he was the one lying spread-eagled under the glaring, dome-shaped light in my bedroom, then why did I feel like I was the one who was exposed and vulnerable?

"Yes, but…"

A smile played on his lips as he leaned back and put his hands behind his head. "Reckon you have yourself a live study at your disposal."

To his credit, he was in excellent shape. And definitely willing. But I wasn't entirely comfortable staring at his naked form spread gloriously across my sheets. Especially when he was visually excited. Then again, if he didn't feel ashamed, why should I?

I bit my lip, feeling painfully inhibited. "I can do anything I want?"

"Darlin', you have my permission to do whatever your little heart desires. Well, within reason. No crazy bondage shit, okay? I don't like the idea of being trussed up like some rodeo calf. Now get over here." He patted the spot next to him on the bed.

I walked slowly into the room, keeping my gaze locked onto his, rather than his other male parts as I neared the bed. He smiled at me. "Sweetheart, it's okay. Really."

"If I do this, I think my moral compass is going to go way off the mark."

He chuckled. "Nah. You're overanalyzing it. Just look at it this way. If I'd have slept with you when I had the chance, you would've already done a lot more than this."

"True, but still…"

Cowboy reached out and took my hand, pulling me down into a sitting position next to him. "Let me earn your trust, Anna. The bastard who hurt you didn't deserve it, but I want to show you that I do. I'm not him, and I won't hurt you. Ever."

"I know that. It's just…well, I don't know what to do."

He gave me a wink, then flattened my palm against his chest. "Start here," he said, guiding my hand down to where his erection curved over his belly. "And work your way down…to *this*."

Holy hell.

I jerked my hand back. "Um, maybe we should start a little slower."

"Suit yourself," Cowboy said, laughing at my reaction.

"If you're trying to embarrass me, it's working."

"Darlin', I'm not trying to embarrass you. All I want is for you to feel more comfortable with me and less self-conscious about yourself. Trust me when I say that there's nothing you can do here that's wrong." Cowboy rested his head back on the pillow and closed his eyes. "Just think of it as therapeutic massage," he instructed.

"Am I being graded for this, teacher?" I asked.

He smiled. "Don't worry. I'm grading on a *curve*." Then he cracked one eye open to make sure I got his stupid joke. The humor helped ease the stress and humiliation coursing through my veins.

I shifted closer, folding my knees beneath me. My hand reached back out to touch his stomach, but I hesitated.

"Do you want me to talk about the weather or something to calm your nerves?"

"No. Just…be quiet. And close your eyes. I can't concentrate with you talking and looking at me."

"Yes, ma'am," he said, wearing a huge grin.

Most likely he was surprised I was actually going through with his ridiculous idea. Or maybe he thought I wouldn't and that's why he was so amused. But I'd never been able to inspect a man's nude body—especially one as fully equipped as Cowboy's—at my own leisure before. So, in the name of research... Okay, maybe that's the excuse I'd used to convince myself.

I lowered my hand gently onto his stomach. His muscles flinched under my unexpected touch. For a moment, I wondered if my hands were cold. Probably. I didn't feel cold, but it would explain why my whole body was shaking. Then again, that could easily be my nerves jumping as my hand traveled over his well-defined abs.

As I placed my other hand on him, I glanced down at his narrow waist and my gaze followed the muscle definition down the length of his nicely toned body. He was still fully aroused, which only made my skittishness return.

My straying hands lingered in designated areas, a safe distance away from his... *Nope. Not going there—yet.* But even though I enjoyed the hardness of this fine male specimen under my hands, I was beginning to feel uninspired.

I traveled a little farther south and checked his face for any signs of embarrassment or him wanting to turn back. Nothing. No blushing cheeks. No shocked, what-do-you-think-you're-doing look. He just reclined with a tiny smirk curving the corner of his mouth while prominently displaying an erection the size of a torpedo.

Obviously he knew I was avoiding his... *Penis? Member? What the hell do you call those things? Oh, come on, Anna! Go for it already. You want to touch his...dick.* Feeling weak at the thought, I shifted my weight forward, leaning into his muscular thigh. "I'm going to…um, do something different now."

Cowboy's grin widened, but his eyes stayed closed. "Whatever you say."

Stretching out my hand, I concentrated intensely on the descent of my fingertips until I reached my destination and curled my fingers around the base of his shaft. The moment I grasped him, Cowboy's entire body stiffened and his penis twitched.

I froze, not sure what happened. "Did I do something wrong?"

"Not at all." He groaned, then relaxed his body. "Just caught me a little off guard."

"I warned you first."

Cowboy chuckled. "That you did. But I didn't realize you were just going to…er, grab the bull by the horns. I thought you'd ease into it a little more."

"So what I did wasn't enjoyable?"

"Anna, you're holding my rock-hard dick in your hand. What part of any of this do you think I'm not enjoying?"

I coughed to stifle the laughter bubbling in my throat. "Right."

"Now, stop second-guessing yourself and just do what-ever you want."

Throwing caution and inhibition to the wind, I intuitively gave his swollen member a tight squeeze. He moaned under his breath, and the sound alone filled me with a renewed sense of confidence. It confirmed that I could elicit a response from him at will. A very positive one at that.

I caressed him slowly in what I deemed a vaguely sensual manner—something I observed on the DVDs I'd watched.

He lay quietly, eyes still closed, while I touched him intimately, calculating every robotic move I made. My touches became more fluid as my fingers traced over his thickness and I delighted myself in the bumps and ridges under the smooth, silky skin.

"You're so hard," I said, then blushed a little as I realized I spoke out loud. "I mean, you have a lovely, um…" *Damn. I still can't say dick out loud.*

I found certain motions took him to a higher aroused state. Direct contact made him grow thicker and longer, which I hadn't thought possible, while my hand pumping his shaft deepened the color of his helmet. Every moan, every grunt he released, hit me low and deep, sending ripples of pleasure cascading throughout my body. Then I tried this contract and release variation on him that I'd read about.

A quiver ran through him and his eyes flew open, wild and burning with need and desire. "Don't overdo it," he managed to say, "or this demonstration won't last very long."

I smiled sweetly at him, but a dirty little giggle left my lips. I couldn't help it. I loved the look of immense pleasure in his eyes.

At this point, I felt like an artist, harvesting my creativity and experimenting freely with his "materials." And my eagerness to please didn't want to lessen the severity of his symptoms. Nope, I wanted to magnify them, even though I knew his self-control would be tested.

So I sloped my hand underneath him, investigating the underside. His stomach flattened as I cradled him, cupping his balls in my palm and savoring the different textures while kneading him gently. Then, in slow motion, I leaned forward and dropped my moistened lips over the tip of him, tasting him for the first time.

A guttural moan left his lips. "Oh, Christ."

Then he groaned as I dragged my lips all the way down until his head hit the fleshy part of my throat. Out of the corner of my eye, I watched his hand fist my comforter. "Anna…you don't…have to do that."

I pulled my head up, allowing my lips to linger just over him, and he sucked in a breath. "I want to," I whispered and lowered my head again.

My tongue swirled around the head, and my lips tightened around his shaft, working their way back down to the base of his penis. He breathed heavily and twisted his fingers into my hair. Judging by his hesitation, I could tell he was resisting the urge to thrust upward into my awaiting mouth. *Damn, he's really struggling…and I love it!*

Instead, he pulled me back firmly. "You have to stop. Now!"

I blinked. "Was that okay?"

"Darlin', that was a hell of a lot better than just okay. Jesus. I have a strong desire to spank you right now. But I think I need to steer my thoughts to something pure for the time being or this little experiment of ours is going to end with an explosion." He released a heavy sigh, then said, "Where the hell did you learn to do that, anyway?"

It was a rhetorical question, and was obviously meant as a compliment, but I smiled proudly as I answered him. "I practiced."

Cowboy bolted upright and fire flashed in his eyes. "What? With who?"

My grin widened at his reaction. "No one, silly. I practiced that move on a banana."

He blinked at me, but I didn't miss the look of relief that washed over his face. "My God. The woman's touching herself and giving a banana head," he said to no one in particular. "Then she has the nerve to call me silly." He shook his head in disbelief as he glared at me. "Got anything else in your bag of tricks I should know about?"

"Can I show you?"

He considered my question thoroughly before giving me a reluctant nod and lying down once again.

I lowered my head and licked him again. He groaned and the sound came out as an abrupt, one-word warning. "Anna."

"Just wait," I told him, wetting his tip with my tongue. "It gets better…well, so I've read." My fingers slid slowly down the long ridge on the underside of him as I took him into my mouth once more and ravished him mercilessly.

"Sweet Jesus, you're killing me," he said, putting his hand on the back of my neck.

At first, I thought it was to impede my motion, but quickly realized he was steadying himself by anchoring his hand in my hair. A sense of satisfaction washed over me as he fought for control mostly because I wasn't nearly done with him. Keeping firm continuous suction, I allowed my fingers to gradually move lower until they reached the sensitive spot between…

"Holy mother of—" He paused to swallow hard, then touched the side of my face. "Anna, you have to…oh God… Stop!"

At his insistence, I pulled back and poked out my bottom lip. "I don't want to."

"But I need you to." He sat up and ran a hand over his

distraught face. "I never meant for it to go quite this far. If this continues, I'm not going to be able to keep my hands to myself like I promised."

I shook my head. "I…I never asked you to keep your hands to yourself. I want you to touch me. I mean, if you want to."

"Are you sure?"

"Yes."

"We don't have to—"

I put my finger to his lips. "Shhh."

He reached up and settled his hand around mine, kissing it, as he gripped my fingers tightly. "Anna, I'm not going to last long after—"

Still sitting beside him, I leaned forward and pressed my mouth against his to shut him up. When I was sure he wasn't going to say anything else, I released the hold I had on his lips and backed away. I untied the knot in my robe with trembling fingers, inviting him to touch me, but his hand grasped mine once more.

He stared into my eyes, probably looking for reassurance that this was what I wanted. He must've seen whatever he was looking for because he slid the robe from my right shoulder. Cowboy took his time undressing me, kissing every inch he exposed, as small rumblings of pleasure vibrated from my throat. His lips nibbled at the subtle curves of my neck and shoulders as he dropped my robe to the floor.

When my hands shot out to cover my marred skin, Cowboy grasped them and pushed them away. "Uh-uh. If we're going to do this, then I get all of you. No hiding." His gaze lowered onto my breasts and then trailed lower to where the large ropey scars covered my hips and thighs. He reached out and touched them, moving his hands over them slowly, as if he were measuring their length. "God, you're beautiful," he said, his green eyes darkening with lust.

My legs trembled, but I didn't know if it was from his slight touch or his words. No one had ever looked at me like that before. Like he wanted to devour me. And as his fingers feathered over my skin, moving upward, my nipples tightened. Cowboy idly rubbed his gentle hands over them. Then he lowered his mouth and curled his tongue around one, and a marvelous tingle ran through me. Like an electric buzz amplified by an incredible physical sensation.

As his lips returned to mine, his hand skated lower, cupping me between my legs. I jolted as he drew his finger up my center. He stopped kissing me, but his mouth lingered near mine. His eyes were mad with desire, and his hot breath intermingled with mine. "Sweetheart, are you sure you want to do this?"

"Hell, yes."

He smiled wide, pushed me backward onto the bed, and covered me with his body. "Good. Because it's my turn to show *you* a few things."

Nibbling at my lips, Cowboy wiggled his finger into my soft, pliant folds. The whimpering sound that left my lips pleaded with him to give me more, and he obliged. Slowly and smoothly, he inserted his finger, penetrating me, and I gasped into his mouth.

There was a sweet, slow buildup of pressure. My wetness increased as he played with me a bit more. Then he slid down my body, crouched between my legs, and gave me one of his famously sexy smirks. "Darlin', I'm about to introduce you to your most favorite thing in the world from now on."

His face pressed between my thighs, and his tongue found my core. My heart beat faster at the new sensation, and I even tried to worm away from him. "Uh-uh. The best part is yet to *come*," he said, chuckling at his play on words. "Let me finish you off." Then he grasped my hips and buried his tongue further into me, pleasuring me once again.

As he used an incredible lick, nibble, suck variation on my sensitive area, a tremendous amount of pressure formed, spreading warmth throughout my abdomen. Memories of being caught under a blazing wooden beam clouded my mind. But this time, it was as if I were burning from the inside out. My respiratory rate increased until I was full-on panting. I shuddered and bucked my hips wildly. *Holy shit!*

Cowboy braced himself by gaining purchase with his feet on the floor as involuntary spasms wracked my body. My legs molded around his head, but he cracked them open and drove me up again.

After the second orgasm, my hands twined into his hair. "Cowboy? Please...I need you to..."

"What, baby? What do you want?" He wanted to hear me say it.

"I want you inside me."

Obviously quite pleased with himself, he chuckled at the desperation in my voice and rose to a standing position. "I'll be right back. Let me get a condom."

I reached over, slid open the drawer next to my bed, and withdrew one. As I handed it to him, he caught sight of the large box I'd pulled it from and grinned. Seconds later, he was crawling up between my legs, condom in place, as he kneed my thighs apart.

"Don't worry. I'm going to take it slow and easy. I'll

make it feel good for you."

I didn't bother to tell him I was already feeling pretty darn good.

Sliding his hands over my shaky knees, he spread my legs wider and positioned himself at my entrance. Slowly and gently, he increased pressure until he entered me. I tensed up.

He groaned. "Jesus, Anna, maybe we should stop."

"No, don't."

"You're really tight. I don't want to hurt you," he said, shifting his weight a little.

I shook my head. "You're not. Keep going."

But he must've known I lied by the way I closed my eyes and braced for the burning sensation of being stretched by his large member. "Look at me, honey."

I did, but not before latching my ankles around his hips and pulling him slightly forward, laminating him to me. I gasped at the increased penetration and the uncomfortable fullness, while he swore under his breath. He stalled and balanced himself over me, probably afraid to move in case he hurt me more.

"I need this. I need you," I pleaded with him. "Please don't stop now."

Determined to give me what I needed, he slowly increased the heavy pressure until he was seated fully inside me. He leaned down and brushed my hair away from my face. "You okay, sweetheart?" Once I nodded, he kissed my forehead softly and said, "It's going to feel much better in a second."

It was a snug fit with a lot of heightened sensitivity—on both our parts, judging by his low, pleasure-filled grunts—but soon he was rotating his hips and gradually moving in and out. Suddenly, as he predicted, the pain vanished and was replaced with a new sensation, a better one. Beneath him, my body shimmied against his until I was undulating like crazy and speeding up the rhythm he had set.

"Are you going for extra credit, young lady?" he teased.

I grinned at that, but thrust my hips again, matching his every stroke. He lifted my ankles, holding them at hip level while he continued to spur me on to new heights. When he couldn't stop me from gyrating my hips, he draped my legs over his shoulder in an interesting new position.

"Darlin', slow down. I want to make love to you for longer than three minutes."

I ignored him, enjoying the sensation of him digging his fingers into my hips as he tried to slow my movements. He took my mouth forcefully, probing his tongue inside, as he rocked his hips into mine, thrusting deeper inside me. Flesh pounded against flesh as he tried to control my eagerness and keep himself from going over the edge. When that didn't work, he pressed my knees into my chest and made shallower thrusts.

He was still inside me when the orgasm overtook me and my contractions milked him to his own. His jaw clenched tight and the veins in his neck protruded as his release rendered him immobile.

Finally, he collapsed next to me and patted my bare bottom. "Fuck," he said, blowing out a hard breath. "You've got to show me those videos you've been watching." He panted heavily and ran his fingers through his sweat-soaked hair. "Then we're going to have a cram session with those books. Holy shit!"

Chapter Sixteen

Early the next morning, I awoke curled into a hard chest with an arm tucked firmly around me as a large hand stroked leisurely down the curve of my spine. I reveled in the sensation of his rough, calloused fingertips traveling over my smooth bare skin and let out a small sigh. I hadn't slept that soundly in years.

Cowboy shifted to look at my face, apparently checking to see if I was awake. When he saw my eyes open, he grinned. "Morning, darlin'."

The sun hadn't risen fully, but soft blue morning light illuminated his too-good-to-be-true face. *He stayed?* All night? I gazed into his twinkling green eyes and smiled sweetly at him. "Good morning."

I had to be at work by ten o'clock, but I didn't care. All I wanted to do was snuggle back in and sleep the day away wrapped in his arms. Because when he did finally leave, he wouldn't be back. This moment would be our last together and I never wanted it to end. Nothing could ruin this for me.

For a moment, he was silent, then he said, "I didn't know you had a photo of us at camp."

Crap!

I'd forgotten all about the framed print sitting on my nightstand. Had I known he'd wind up in my bedroom yesterday, I would've shoved the picture in a drawer or closet. "Bobbie Jo sent it to me."

"We were young. I was a cocky little bastard back then." He chuckled. "Not that I've changed all that much since." I grinned, but my mouth melted when he added, "And look at you. So sweet and innocent and…completely infatuated with me."

Kill me now. "Oh, stop it. Just because I was looking at you in the photo didn't mean I was infatuated with you. Maybe I was just stunned by your arrogance and your—"

"Impressive boner?"

Shocked, I glanced over my shoulder at him as a smile erupted on his gorgeous face. "You did not have…one of *those*."

His hand moved lower and massaged my rear firmly, grinding my pelvis against his rapidly hardening length. "No, but I damn sure do right now."

A rush of heat climbed my neck and flooded my face. I did the coy look-away thing, not wanting him to know how much his words and actions affected me.

When I tried to pull away, he wouldn't allow it. He grasped my chin with his free hand and tilted my face back to his. "What's this?" he asked, brushing a finger along my cheek. "After all the things we did last night, you're *still* blushing?"

I shook my head. "Don't do that."

"Do what, darlin'?"

"Don't humiliate me."

"Wouldn't dream of it," he said with another grin as his finger doodled lazy circles over my collarbone. "Though I do like it when you blush from head to toe. Everything on you turns pink. Your neck, your ears, your…" He glanced down at my nipples and they instantly hardened. His eyes darkened with desire.

Gently, he flicked the bud with the tip of his finger. It tightened even more as a tingling sensation rocketed through my body.

"Hmm. Interesting," he noted casually, as if he hadn't realized he'd just awoken hundreds of nerve endings in that one touch.

With warp speed, he rolled me onto my back and draped himself halfway over me, being careful not to crush me under his weight. He ran his tongue around my nipple, doing this little suck-nibble thing with his lips and teeth as his hand traveled farther south. By the time he reached the notch between my legs, my chest had already expanded with an inhaled breath. Surely he couldn't want to do it again, could he?

His knuckles brushed my nether region and he whispered, "Open your legs."

Guess so.

I started to do as he asked, but stopped, remembering the thick baseball bat digging into my hipbone. As much as I would've loved to play ball with him, my muscles were already deliciously sore from last night's overtime innings. And it wouldn't be fair to invite him up to bat only to let him strike out before reaching home plate. God, why was I thinking in baseball terms?

His fingers wiggled into the crevice between my thighs and moved upward, but I squeezed my legs together and bit my lip. "Um, Cowboy?"

He chuckled softly under his breath. "Don't worry. I'm not asking for anything in return. I just want to make *you* feel good. Now be a good girl and do as I asked."

Reluctantly, I relaxed my legs, allowing them to fall open. His fingers traced carelessly over my flesh, moving up my thigh, until they reached their destination. The moment he found me, he kissed my mouth. Once. Twice. Then he deepened the kiss, pulsing his tongue against mine, as his fingers provided gentle stimulation.

His thumb settled over my clit and kept a firm pressure as he slid two large fingers inside me. I gasped into his mouth from the sheer electric shock that jolted through my system in lusty waves of pleasure. I closed my eyes, but could feel his grin against my open mouth as he worked his fingers in and out of me.

When he suddenly froze, I opened my eyes to find him staring at me. "Why are you looking at me like that?"

"You're so…responsive," he said, slowly twisting his fingers deeper inside me. "It's like seeing an invisible girl come to life before my very eyes."

Physically, I couldn't pretend the power of his touch and the intensity in his eyes hadn't affected me. But mentally, I cringed. Telling a woman that she's only visible when she takes her clothes off wasn't my idea of a compliment. At least not a good one.

Suddenly, his watchfulness affected me more than his

fingers did…but not in a good way. "Stop looking at me like that."

"Like what?"

"I don't know…like you're a hungry carnivore about to gobble up your prey."

"Hmm. Good idea," he said, sliding his fingers out of me. "I like the way you think." He grasped my hips and rolled onto his back, taking me with him, until I was straddling his bare chest. "Don't move," he ordered firmly as he lifted me up just enough to slither down the bed until his face stopped between my thighs.

Holy hell. "Um, Cowboy?"

He ignored me. Hell, he didn't even pause. Slow hands made their way up the inside of my trembling thighs. When he touched me intimately, my body jerked from the contact. He worked his two thick fingers back inside me, slow and deep, and lapped at my swollen clit with his tongue.

My heart stalled as my knees locked into position around his head and my hands fisted his hair. I think I even whimpered a little.

He stopped momentarily. "Darlin', I'm not going to have any hair left if you keep pulling it all out."

Closing my eyes, I let go of his hair and breathed out a sigh. "I need you to stop for a moment."

"Uh-uh," he said, nipping into the flesh of my right thigh and sending sparks through my central nervous system.

I started to move off him, but he gripped my hip with his free hand. "Whoa! Where do you think you're going?"

"Stop, please. Just for a second." Reluctantly, he released me and let me move off him. I turned around quickly and mounted him again, climbing astride his shoulders and situating myself over his mouth in the opposite direction. "If you don't want me to pull all of your hair out, then you're going to give me something else to hold onto," I said, taking a firm hold of his manhood.

He released a guttural groan and swore under his breath. "Christ, Anna."

I smiled at the strain in his voice and pumped his throbbing length in my hand, working it with the same pace as his tongue. I took in the planes of his body and nibbled on his stomach, giving him love-bites that left teeth marks. When his body stiffened, I considered apologizing for them. But his erection grew stronger in my hand and I got the message: no apology needed.

The sounds of his grunts delighted me as he dug his heels into the mattress. The vibrations his mouth provided sent me into overdrive, and my hips swiveled in circles, grinding into him as he continued to coax me to euphoria. Fingers here. A nibble there. Tongue everywhere.

When the blinding orgasm he facilitated hit me, I dropped my mouth over him and swallowed him whole. His hand shot downward and clasped my head, his fingers twining in my hair, as he tried to deter me from my mission.

"Anna…God… You need to stop. I'm about to—"

The only answer I gave was firmer suction as I took him deeper into my throat. I knew he *tried* not to thrust, but he did a little, anyway.

Quivering beneath me, Cowboy gripped the back of my thighs to steady himself as he vocalized his completion in grunts and groans and let himself go.

I came out of the bathroom swaddled in a robe with my wet hair wrapped in a white towel on top of my head. Cowboy still lay on the bed in all his blatant nudity while already sporting another massive hard-on. I shifted my eyes away, but my face flushed. "Oh, I guess I thought you would've gotten dressed by now."

He chuckled. "Can't seem to get past that shyness, can you?"

"I'm trying," I said softly, keeping my back to him.

"Turn around, Anna."

"Uh-uh."

"Come on, darlin'. I want to see your pretty little face."

"Fine." Begrudgingly, I did as he asked, but kept my gaze above his waist. "There. Happy now?"

He grinned wide. "Sweetheart, if you keep twisting your fingers in your robe like that, you're going to break them off."

I settled my hands at my side. "Sorry. Nervous habit."

Cowboy shook his head. "I just don't get it. Why does seeing me naked make you so nervous? You weren't this jittery when you were sitting on my face a few minutes ago."

I gave him a stern look. "Do you have to refer to it as… *that*?"

"Well, what the hell do you want me to call it? It's what you were doing…and you *liked* it." He licked his lips and winked lewdly at me. I rolled my eyes and wheeled around to return to the bathroom, but Cowboy shot off the bed and clasped his hands around my waist, turning me back to him. "All right, I'll stop, I promise."

"No, you won't. You'll keep saying things like that because that's who you are."

He smiled at that. "Okay, probably. But I'm not trying to embarrass you. I'm trying to understand how one minute you're a sex kitten and the next you're like a virginal blushing bride on her wedding night. It just doesn't make any sense."

I shrugged nonchalantly. "I was raised by my stepfather. We didn't really talk about sex, or anything else for that matter, openly. It was very much *his* household, and he never let me forget it, either. I always knew that the day I turned eighteen I would have to find somewhere else to live. That's why I started working at the summer camp when I turned sixteen. I had to save money, but needed a job that didn't interfere with school. When school started back up, I babysat in the evenings to help get me into my own place."

Cowboy's jaw tightened. "All because that bastard kicked you out?"

"I wasn't his responsibility. After my mother died, he was nice enough to take me in and keep a roof over my head until I became an adult. It's more than most foster kids get."

"You don't have to make excuses for him." His voice lowered and his eyes narrowed. "What he did to you wasn't right."

"Maybe not, Cowboy, but I understood why looking at me every day was so painful for him."

"Because you weren't his?"

"No. Because I look just like my mother." Lowering my head, I opened my mouth to speak, but nothing came out. So I tried again and managed to find my voice, even if it was a little shakier than before. "I reminded him every day of what he lost, and he hated me for it. That's part of the reason I spent so much time at the library when I was younger."

"It was a place to hide out...from him?"

"Yeah, I guess so." I lowered my gaze. "Anything to make it easier for him to—"

"Goddamnit. What about him making it easier on *you*? You were just a kid."

I glanced back at him and shook my head. "It doesn't matter. My stepfather provided for me when I had no one else." My voice cracked with the desperate need to make him comprehend the guilt and shame that overwhelmed me. "He lost someone he loved dearly—my mother—and it broke him, but he didn't abuse me or anything."

"Neglect is a form of abuse, Anna."

I didn't expect him to understand why my stepfather treated me the way he had. But since I was responsible for my mother's death, I couldn't blame the man for hating me. For years, I hated myself.

I sighed heavily. "I don't want to talk about this. It's in the past and it doesn't matter anymore," I told him, hoping to change the subject. "Why don't you go hop in the shower while I run out and get my mail? I forgot to check it after you showed up yesterday, and I still have to get ready for work."

He frowned, but didn't press the issue. "I can go out and grab it for you, if you want."

My eyes glanced up and down his nude figure and I plastered a grin on my face. "Not like *that*, you can't."

"All right, fine. I'll shower, and *you* get the mail." He leaned down and pressed a sweet kiss to the corner of my mouth and then turned and walked toward the bathroom, the muscles of his tight buns flexing with the motion. Within seconds, the water was running while he whistled a low tune.

I had a good mind to sneak over to the door and watch

him soap up that magnificent, firm body of his, but thought better of it. Knowing Cowboy and his insatiable nature, he'd probably pull me into the shower with him and have me do it for him. Although it wasn't the worst thing that could happen to a girl.

No, Anna. *Damn it.* Mail first. Otherwise the "male" will have his hands all over you making you forget…well, everything. I released a long, slow breath and headed for the front door. Being responsible and logical really sucked sometimes.

When I stepped outside, I squinted in the bright morning sun as I strolled across the yard to the end of the driveway where my weathered mailbox sat just off the road. I grabbed the stack of mail inside and headed back to the house, shuffling through the pile of bills and junk mail as I walked.

I'd just stepped back inside and kicked the door shut with my heel when I noticed a small envelope stuffed between two coupon ads. My name was written illegibly on the outside in something that resembled a child's handwriting. *Just like the others.* I tore it open and quickly read the note inside just as Cowboy called out from the bathroom, "Hey, darlin', where are your towels?"

My body stiffened. I'd been so preoccupied by the stupid note that I hadn't noticed he'd turned the water off. "They're…um, in the cabinet next to the shower." I hurried to stuff the paper back inside its holder and looked for a convenient place to hide it. "On the top shelf."

I shoved the envelope down the back of the couch in between the cushions and had just pulled my hand free when Cowboy stepped out of the bathroom wearing only a white towel tucked around his waist. Droplets of water dotted his skin and dripped from his short hair.

"I found them before I even finished the question," he said, grinning.

Skittishly, I turned toward the kitchen, keeping my back to him as I placed the rest of the mail on the counter in front of me. "I...uh, okay."

A beat went by before he said anything. "Something wrong?"

I shook my head. "No, nothing." I closed my eyes as I felt his presence behind me. "You just caught me off guard." I felt his arm brush against mine, but it didn't close around me like I thought it would.

"Then what's this?" My eyes shot open and I saw him holding the note up in front of my face. Fear raced through me at the thought of him confronting the Barlows. Panicking, I made a quick grab for it, but he jerked his arm back. I spun around to face him as he turned the envelope over in his hand. "Who sent you this? There's no address or anything, only your name."

"Just leave it alone, okay?"

"Anna."

I swallowed hard at the stern tone of his voice. "It's nothing, really. I've just been finding some notes in my mailbox on occasion. I guess the Barlow boys are leaving them."

Cowboy didn't hesitate. He opened the envelope and pulled out the small piece of paper inside. Even upside down, I could read the horrible scribble. *Burn, baby, burn!* After a brief pause, his eyes lit up with anger. "Fuck me. Why didn't you tell me you were receiving threats from them?"

"I didn't want to make a big deal out of nothing."

"Where are the other notes?" Cowboy grumbled.

I walked over to the oak desk in the living room and

pulled open the middle drawer where I'd been keeping them. Reaching inside, I grabbed the eight envelopes and then returned to Cowboy, placing them in his hand. I stood there staring at him as he quickly opened and read each one.

When he was done, his body was trembling with barely controlled rage. "I'm going to get dressed, go over there, and beat the fuck out of them two idiots."

"You can't do that."

"Oh, yeah? Watch me." He started to turn toward the bedroom, but I grasped his arm to stop him.

"You can't just go over there and accuse them of sending these. Besides, they'll probably just deny it anyway. It's just words on paper. Sticks and stones."

Cowboy paced a few steps away and laid the notes down on a nearby end table, while his brows slanted downward in frustration. "Sweetheart, you need to learn a few things about me. I can tolerate a lot of bullshit, but I won't put up with some asshole messing with my family, my friends, or my woman."

His words were serious, but I couldn't help the little smile that crept onto my lips.

And he noticed. "Something funny?"

"No, I just…well, you called me *your* woman." Then I grinned again. Surely he didn't mean that the way it sounded.

But he was still scowling at me. "Well, aren't you?"

Was he serious? I blinked at him, my heart hammering against the walls of my chest as he stood there waiting for an answer. *Oh my God!* He was serious. But it wouldn't work between us. Everything was going to come to a screeching halt the moment I left town.

Then I made the mistake of remembering how it had felt

waking up in his arms. Blissfully content. Safe and protected, like no one could ever harm me. And the benefits of having a smoking-hot, insatiable man like Cowboy in my bed for the next few months definitely outweighed the risks to my already fragile heart. For now, at least.

"I…um, guess so." It sounded more like a question than an answer.

"Okay, now we have a fucking problem," he grumbled, his eyes flashing with intensity and anger. He turned away from me and picked up his jeans off the floor. I couldn't see what he was doing, but I didn't want him to leave.

"Cowboy, wait."

He dropped the jeans on the floor and turned back to me, stalking toward me with a wicked gleam in his eye, while palming something in his hand. His strong, muscular body took on a lithe, almost predator-like posture and I actually had to tamp down the absurd urge to run. That didn't keep me from taking a few steps back, though. Or him from following. Even when my back came into contact with the wall, he continued to press forward. Wordlessly, he orbited in my personal space and the gravitational pull of his masculinity sucked all the oxygen out of the room.

I flattened myself against the wall and swallowed hard. "What problem?" I asked softly, not sure what had caused the sudden change in his demeanor.

But he didn't answer me right away. Cowboy stopped in front of me so close I could feel his warm breath caressing my face as I gazed up at him innocently. He pulled the towel gently from my damp hair and tossed it on the ground behind him. Then he gave me a menacing grin as he dropped his own towel from around his waist. His erection sprang free of the terrycloth and pointed directly at me, as if I'd done something worthy of accusation.

Our eyes met, and although I heard the soft crinkling of foil, I didn't look down to see what he was doing. Slowly, he lowered his mouth close to my ear, then loosened the knot tied in my robe before parting it open. "If you don't know by now that you're *my* woman," he whispered in a rough voice, "then I am obviously doing something very wrong."

His hands brushed across my scarred hipbones and his fingers slid just under the waistband of my cotton panties. One little tug and they were on the floor at my feet. I closed my eyes as a shiver shimmied through me. His intense eyes. His sexy morning voice. His imperceptible touch. It was all too much for me to handle.

Without warning, he gripped my hips and lifted me, wrapping my legs around his waist and entering me fast and hard in one smooth motion. I gasped and my eyes shot open at the delicious intrusion of my body. Grasping his shoulders, I tried to steady myself, but Cowboy wasn't having any of that.

Not giving me any time to adjust my position or even take a breath, he buried his face into my neck, licking and sucking, while thrusting his hips in long, slow motions. I banded my arms around his neck to hold on tight. Over his shoulder, I could see the muscles of his arched back flexing and tightening as the speed of his movements increased and he reached deeper inside me.

Lifting his head, he braced me against the hard surface at my back and supported my weight with his hands under my thighs. He smirked sexily as his pelvis ground against mine, creating a breathtaking amount of stimulation to my clitoris. It was as if he pressed my hot button over and over again and sounded the alarms in my body.

A seed of warmth grew inside of me and spread throughout my entire body. As the heat began to consume me, though, I clenched my inner muscles, stopping myself from flying over the edge. There was a problem. Nothing about this felt like a one-night stand.

He bit back a groan. "Baby, let go. I've got you."

Choking gasps burst from my strangulated lungs, making my chest ache. My body was on fire. Erotic flames traveled through me, licking at my insides, as a burning sensation simmered beneath my sensitive skin. As if Cowboy were holding a branding iron to my heart.

Oh God. He really did want more from me. But…

"No, I can't. It's too much, too soon."

His eyes focused on me with determination. "The fuck you can't."

As usual, Cowboy didn't like to be told no. He pounded into me harder, groaning and panting, as he clearly struggled for control. He caught my mouth, letting his tongue roll against mine in time with his thrusts before giving me a sharp nip on my bottom lip. "Tell me who you belong to," he said, rocking into me once again.

"You," I whispered.

"Still don't sound too sure. Maybe you need more convincing." He gripped my buttocks to rock into me with more force than before.

The exquisite angle had him hitting a toe-curling sweet spot, and I whimpered into his neck. "I'm yours," I gasped, reveling in the sensations he created. He was so far inside me, I'd almost swear his knees were hitting the wall beneath me.

"Say it again," he demanded.

My teeth chattered at the sheer power of his body stroking into mine as I surrendered to the emotions swirling inside me. "I'm yours, damn it! All yours," I cried out, digging my fingernails into his back as I blinked back unshed tears.

And just like that, the shuddering orgasm ripped through me. Trembling and convulsing, my inner muscles clamped down on him. He groaned in pleasure as he neared completion. Finally, he let himself go.

After a moment, he withdrew slowly and slid me down him until my feet touched the floor. My legs were limp, barely capable of holding my weight. Apparently, he was a little shaky himself because he planted one hand firmly against the wall next to my head to hold himself up. We stood like that for several minutes, breathing heavily and staring into each other's eyes.

It was only then I understood what he'd been doing. Cowboy had claimed me. Mind, body, and soul. *His*.

Chapter Seventeen

After work, I went straight home.

All day, I'd floated on cloud nine, reminiscing about how Cowboy had exquisitely tortured my body and left me deliciously sore from last night's marathon-inspired sexcapade. I had even worn a huge, stupid grin on my face, one I couldn't seem to wipe away.

But walking back into my home and seeing the wall Cowboy had taken me against earlier that morning ruined my good mood, and my euphoric state dissipated. Battling my emotions, I had to consider the previous night had been nothing more than one giant mistake on my part.

I'd yielded to my own feelings, allowing myself to fall even more for him, yet he didn't know I was leaving town. Or that by being with me, he was consequently putting a target on his back. But telling him that meant telling him everything, and I didn't know if I was prepared to do so.

As I tossed my keys onto the counter, I noticed the stack

of forgotten mail I'd placed there earlier in the day. Glancing at the clock, I sighed. Cowboy had said he'd stop by, but wouldn't be off work for another hour. Plenty of time to sort out the junk mail and take a shower before he arrived.

But as I sifted through the mail, I stumbled upon an official-looking envelope addressed from the Gib Lewis Unit Prison & Correctional Facility in Woodsville, Texas. My stomach churned, twisting with dread, as my shaky hands tore open the envelope and extracted the crisp letter inside. My fingers trembled as I unfolded it.

Dear Ms. Weber,

I have been notified by the Texas Department of Criminal Justice that the Victim Services Program has been unable to reach you using the Vine phone notification system. Therefore, I am sending this notice to your last known address, in hopes it will reach you at a forwarded address. This information is in reference to Stuart Nelson, prisoner no. 1018040.

The parole board originally determined the prisoner's earliest possible release would be August 22nd of this year, but due to overpopulation, the prisoner's lack of previous criminal record, and the model behavior he has displayed while incarcerated, the parole board has since moved his release day to March 1st.

Should you have any questions or concerns regarding this matter, please let me know or contact your local law enforcement agency.

Sincerely,
John P. Ellington
Warden, Gib Lewis Unit

Jesus. He was released early? I glanced at the desktop calendar, noting Stuart Nelson had been released from prison...*two weeks ago? Oh God!*

Instantly I recalled what Cowboy's friend, Junior, had said about the man I'd seen standing on the edge of my property. *Had to be someone else.*

Then I remembered the stack of threatening notes I'd received. That whole time, I'd thought the Barlow boys sent them. *But what if...?*

Lightheaded, I swayed on my feet. Fear and adrenaline shot through my veins, and my heart flopped around inside my chest like a dying fish. I reached over and twisted the deadbolt to lock the door. "I'm safe," I reminded myself out loud. "He couldn't have found me that fast. It's not possible."

But who was I kidding? It only took him a week to find me before, which also happened to be the last time I ever saw my moth—

The letter fell from my hands, landing on the counter. *It was him. He'd* been watching me, not the Barlows, not Junior. It was just like last time.

Panicking, I sprinted to my bedroom and yanked my large suitcase out of the closet, tossing it open on the bed. Returning to the closet, I ripped my clothes from their hangers until I had an armful, then raced back to the bed to stuff them inside the luggage.

I ran to the living room, extracting things from drawers, grabbing my research files, and sifting through personal items. Only grabbing what I absolutely had to have, I carried them all to the suitcase and placed them inside.

Next I went for the drawers, pulling them out of the dresser completely and holding them upside down to dump the contents of each into my suitcase. My undergarments spilled out, only half of them actually landing in the suitcase. The rest had fallen every which way and some even ended up on the floor. But I didn't have time to stop and pick them up. I closed the lid and zipped it up.

Reaching under the bed, I slid out a small black tote and threw the strap over my shoulder. The new identity inside would get me out of the country and the cash I'd stockpiled would keep me on the move until I found a good place to hide. I lifted the suitcase from the bed and headed to the kitchen, where my keys still sat on the counter. Just as I reached for them, a knock sounded at the door. My heart stopped and my stomach dropped. Setting my bags down quietly, I tiptoed to the door and peered out through the peephole.

Oh, no.

Cowboy stood on the other side of the door with a smile on his face. My body surged with guilt and remorse. I hadn't planned to tell anyone—including him—I was leaving. Not even when my six months were up, and certainly not now when my time had run out early.

After a few moments, his smiled disappeared and he knocked again. Harder this time. I couldn't pretend like I wasn't home. Surely, he had noticed my car in the driveway. But I couldn't bring myself to open the door, either, even when he banged on it a third time.

"Anna, I know you're in there. I can hear you breathing."

Figures.

I lowered my head, thunking it against the door as I let out a slow calming breath. All the running around I'd done had put my respirations in overdrive, and even though I was only softly panting, apparently it was audible. But I needed to get it under control if I were to face Cowboy without alarming him. I held my head up high, pushed a loose strand of my hair out of my eyes, and opened the door a few inches.

"Hi," I greeted cheerily, straining to keep my voice from cracking. He started to move forward, as if he were going to come inside, but I held my position and barred his entry. "I'm sorry, Cowboy. I'm going to have to cancel on you tonight. Something sort of came up."

I thought I'd done a great job keeping my tone controlled and light, but apparently it wasn't enough. He raised one eyebrow. "What's wrong?"

"Nothing. I've just been rushing around like a mad woman trying to get some stuff done. I had a busy day at the library and have things to take care of."

"What's this? You brushing me off?"

I shook my head. "No, I just…" Eager to escape the way he was looking at me, I tried to hurry the conversation along. "Look, I'm feeling a little strange about what happened between us and I need some time to process it all. I'll call you tomorrow, okay?"

"No, it's not fucking okay." He scowled. "If this is your way of sending me packing, then I want to know why."

"I don't want to talk right now. I just want to—hey!"

Without my permission, he shoved open the door and stepped over the threshold. His eyes took in the disheveled room until they finally zeroed in on the luggage I'd placed on the floor next to the kitchen counter. His green eyes flashed to me, but his expression was unreadable. "Going somewhere?"

"I…" My heart thumped against my rib cage. "Yes, I'm leaving town."

"You weren't even going to tell me?"

I cringed at the harshness of his tone. "No."

His mouth settled into a disapproving, grim line. "Why?"

"This is all happening too fast. You and me. I told you before we were too different. Our relationship is based solely on sex and I don't want—"

"Stop it, Anna. If you're going to stand here and give me a line of bullshit, then don't bother. This has nothing to do with us and you know it. So either tell me the truth or don't waste my fucking time."

"I…I don't want this, okay?" My voice warbled unconvincingly. God, I was such a bad liar. "I only want to be left alone to live my life as I see fit. I don't need the complication of a relationship." At least that part was true, but I knew it would take more than that to make him leave. "You're never going to be anything more than a playboy and I refuse to be another Kelly Deter."

"*Kelly Deter?* Who the hell is… Wait, the girl from camp?"

At least my eye roll was genuine. "I'm surprised you even remember her name at all."

"Well, why wouldn't I? She's the bitch who told everyone that she and I slept together the night of the bonfire. All I'd done was ask her out. I hadn't laid a finger on her. The next day, when I found out she spread the rumor among the other counselors, I called the whole thing off."

"But you weren't at the bonfire," I said, shaking my head

furiously. "I didn't see you there."

"I was on my way when I heard a commotion and ran to see what happened. I thought one of the kids had gotten hurt, but it was you. You were lying on the ground with all the kids standing around you as one of the other female counselors yelled for help. I picked you up and carried you to the nurse's station, then waited outside until I heard you were going to be okay. They'd told me you had a panic attack and fainted."

"Y-you carried me…" My heart squeezed and my eyes filled with blinding tears. I turned away from him. "I never knew. By the next morning, word had gotten around about what had happened and a few of the other counselors had started calling me 'Sparky.' I didn't want to be reminded of how I'd panicked and fainted in front of everyone when they'd lit the bonfire, so I packed my things and left."

"I know. I went to see you the following night to make sure you were okay, but Bobbie Jo told me you were already gone." He paused, then his tone laced with anger. "Guess that's what you do, though. You leave without saying good-bye."

I swallowed hard.

"Take care of yourself," he said solemnly. His boots clomped on the floor, the sound growing softer with distance as he made his way to the door.

Tears leaked down my face. I knew if I spoke again my shaky voice would tell him everything he needed to know. But despite everything I'd said, I wanted him. Now more than ever. He'd given me his trust. Maybe it was about time I did the same.

"I'm not," I whispered.

He must've stopped at the door because suddenly I couldn't hear his footfalls anymore. "Not what?"

It was a pivotal moment, dependent entirely on what words came out of my mouth next. Because if things went wrong… But I couldn't bear to let him think he hadn't been good enough for me. Even a guy with Cowboy's reputation deserved better than that. "I-I'm not okay."

"Anna…?" His voice registered concern.

I walked over to the counter and picked up the letter, not sure if I was doing the right thing. But now that I'd set the ball in motion, I couldn't seem to stop it. I turned and moved slowly toward him, clenching the letter tightly in my grip. Once he knew everything, there would be no going back.

His eyes flickered with confusion as I handed him the letter. "Who's it from? The Barlows?"

"Read it."

He did as I asked and then glanced up at me. "Is this who you're running from?"

"Yes."

"And you're afraid he might come after you?"

"I *know* he'll come after me. He always has. Even in my dreams he won't rest until he finds me."

Cowboy's eyes darkened with fury. "You know I won't let him hurt you, don't you?"

"That's the thing. You won't be able to stop him. No one can."

"Who is he?" he demanded. "Your ex-boyfriend or something?"

"No. H-he's my father."

Cowboy's eyes widened. "Why would your own father

try to kill you?"

"Because my testimony is what kept him in prison for the past twenty-two years. He murdered my mother."

"I thought your mom died in a fire. You said she was cooking dinner and went to answer the door. She told you to stay in the kitchen, but you didn't…"

I closed my eyes briefly. "That's true," I said, feeling the full weight of the guilt I'd held onto for years. "But what I didn't tell you was what happened after she opened the door and found my father on the other side." I rubbed my palms over my face and sniffled.

"Tell me."

"I could hear them arguing, yelling at each other at the top of their lungs, from the kitchen. He told her he wasn't going to let her keep his daughter away from him and that he was taking me home. Then, he must've pushed his way inside because my mom started screaming even louder for him to get out. The moment he hollered my name and demanded for me to come to him, I hid inside the pantry."

"You were scared of him?"

I nodded. "My parents divorced when I was six. I don't remember much of it, though. But Mom had warned me he wasn't a good man. He only wanted to take me away from her in order to punish her for leaving him. He hunted us down everywhere we went. That's why we moved around so much when I was younger. To keep him from finding us."

"Is that why you don't share the same last name?"

"Weber is my mother's maiden name. She didn't want me to have any connection to that man."

"Did he find you…in the pantry, I mean?"

I shook my head. "They came into the kitchen. Mom was

crying, begging for him not to take her little girl away, but he ignored her and continued calling out my name. It was like he didn't even care about my mother. He just wanted to hurt her." Pain and anger surged inside of me at the injustice of it all. "Had I just left with him, she would still be alive."

Cowboy's eyes softened. "Sweetheart, you don't know that."

"No, you're right. I don't know for certain. But I believe it's true." A lone tear ran down my cheek. "There was a scuffle. Glass shattered and my father cursed, then my mother released the most agonizing sound I'd ever heard. Moments later, everything went silent."

I shivered as my mind pulled me back in time and stuffed me back into my six-year-old body. Alone and trembling, I'd sat on the floor of the dark pantry with my arms curled around my knees until smoke eventually seeped under the door. I recalled the terror and confusion, the choking and gasping for breath, the way my eyes and throat burned. I made the decision to open the pantry door and face the awful truth about what had happened.

"By the time I opened the door, the kitchen was engulfed with fire and smoke. I could barely see anything as I tried to find a way out. Only when I tripped over something, did I realize what—or rather who—it was." I cringed at my own words.

Cowboy shook his head. "Anna, stop. You don't have to tell me any more."

I nodded. Of course I didn't. Because a fireman like Cowboy knew exactly what it was like to find someone in that capacity. A gruesome body, covered in flames and melting skin, lying in a fetal position, lacking any hair, and the smell of burned flesh in the air. With one look, he would have known my mother was past saving.

But I was only six.

"I tried to get to her…so I could help her," I admitted, barely able to hear myself over the visions of fire roaring in my head. "I tried to crawl toward her, but I never made it. A wooden beam in the ceiling had burned through and fallen on top of me, pinning my waist to the floor."

Cowboy's eyes narrowed and he breathed out through his nose. "That's how you got your scars?"

I nodded slowly. "I don't know how long I was trapped under it because I lost consciousness. The next thing I knew, I was being carried out by a fireman wearing a black helmet. I panicked and fought him, so he held me tighter and hummed to me all the way out to the ambulance. I guess I was in shock because I was pretty calm up until they rushed past me pushing a gurney with my mother wearing an oxygen mask."

"Jesus. She was alive?"

"Barely. I heard them say her pulse was weak and thready and that her throat was swelling shut. They were rushing her to the ambulance to intubate her. At the time, I didn't know what that even meant. I went wild trying to get up and go to her, but the paramedics gave me something to calm me down—a sedative, I suppose—and as I faded away, the last thing I remember was the fireman sitting next to me, humming a tune to keep me from being afraid."

"Chief Swanson?"

"Yes. I didn't learn his name until months later when he was called to testify in court. I wasn't allowed to be there, but my stepdad mentioned his name and said he was the one who carried me out of the house. Before they had discovered me in the kitchen, they found my father in the living room and pulled him out. He was arrested on the spot after neighbors confirmed he showed up at our house right before all the yelling started and the fire broke out. He never admitted what he'd done. Denied it, even after they charged him with murder. My mom died en route to the hospital."

"Did you see him in court?"

"No. Since I was a minor, the judge allowed my testimony to be recorded and shown to the jury in a closed courtroom. I was so badly burned that I was still in the hospital months later having multiple skin grafts when the jury finally found him guilty. Every day since, I have lived in fear he would be paroled and come after me. Now it's happening. He's not going to stop until he kills me, too."

"Anna, listen to me," Cowboy said, grasping my arms. "I'm not going to let that happen. You don't have to go anywhere. I can protect you from him."

I wanted to let him convince me to stay, but I couldn't put him in that kind of danger. "I can't ask you to do that."

"You didn't ask me. You're my woman, remember? It's my job," he said, dutifully. He smiled, obviously trying to settle my nerves. "Besides, you have enough FBI agents surrounding you here that you don't have anything to worry about."

"You mean Jake?"

"Jake isn't the only FBI agent around here. Hank is a retired FBI director, and Junior used to do some contract work for the Feds. And even though Ox, Judd, and I aren't FBI, we learned from the best. Your fath—Stuart Nelson—will have to go through all of us to get to you. Just tell me you'll stay."

"I can't do that. I always wanted to be surrounded by people who cared about me, and now that I am, I can't risk their lives by putting them in danger," I said, letting my head fall. "It's best if I just disappear."

He lifted my chin to gaze deep into my eyes. "That isn't what's best for everyone."

With my emotions running so high, I knew I wasn't thinking clearly. But his words filled me with a renewed sense of hope. All the years I'd spent running from my past had finally caught up to me. Would I be able to let all the fear go for Cowboy? For myself? I had to try, didn't I?

"Okay, I'll stay."

Cowboy drew me a warm bubble bath and made me some herbal tea to help soothe my frazzled nerves. When I was done, I started to dry myself off, but he grabbed the towel from me and took care of it himself. Afterward, he helped me into my flannel pajamas and then led me to the bedroom. He was pampering me, and I let him, because it felt good to have someone else to lean on for a change. No one had ever taken care of me that way before.

He held the covers up as I slid underneath, then lay down behind me, encompassing me with his warm body. It made me feel better, safer even, but it wasn't enough. The mental images I'd stirred up by talking about my past wouldn't stop replaying vividly in my mind. I needed him to make me forget completely, to make me forgo this feeling of doom hovering all around me.

"Cowboy, I…I need you."

"I'm right here, baby." He pressed his lips to my temple and held me firmer in his strong arms. "I've got you. No one is going to hurt you."

"No, I mean I *need* you…inside me."

I knew he wasn't sexually aroused. I could feel every bit of pelvic region pressing into my bottom through my flannel pajamas. He didn't have any problem sleeping in the nude, but I wasn't at the same comfort level. Yet the moment I spoke those words aloud, something must've stirred inside him. A long, hard ridge suddenly rested uncomfortably against me.

"Are you sure? We don't have to—"

"I need you," I whispered again.

His body shifted away from me a little and I considered it a sign that he was going to reject me, until the end table's drawer opened and then shut. The telling sound of a foil packet crinkled as he ripped it open. He seemed to understand what I was asking him for because, seconds later, he shoved me forward, settling me on my stomach, as he positioned himself between my legs.

He wasn't gentle. Which is exactly what I wanted. I needed him to claim me in a primal way, to disintegrate the images from inside of my head, as he screwed me senseless. Cowboy lifted my hips, yanked my pajama bottoms down to my knees, and plunged inside of me from behind. I whimpered, but my mind focused solely on him.

Gripping my hips with both hands, he grunted and groaned as he pulled almost all the way out and thrust himself back in once again. I gasped from the raw power of his body slamming against mine. Suddenly, he stopped.

Reaching around to find my clit, he applied just the right amount of pressure, which had me panting and hurtling toward a mind-numbing orgasm. But I bucked back into him, rocking hard onto his member. More than anything, I needed to feel him deep within me.

"Christ, darlin', you're going to make me come if you keep doing that."

Continuing to work my hips over his length, I gave as good as I got. The pace was frantic as he took me from behind, jarring my body forward and repeatedly jerking me back onto his length. The orgasm swept over me in much the same way, coming fast and furious, as Cowboy's own climax peaked. Not giving me one second to catch my breath, he rode me hard all the way to the end until he collapsed over me, breathing heavily onto my back.

After a few minutes, he rolled off me in a way mimicking an alligator's death roll and lay there, spent. "If we keep this up, I'm pretty sure you're going to be the death of me."

I winced, remembering the danger I was putting him in by staying.

God, I hoped not.

The moment Cowboy began breathing heavy, suggesting he was asleep, I eased away from him and slipped out of the room. I didn't want him to know I was still battling insomnia, so I closed the bedroom door to keep the light on the computer from waking him. At least one of us should be able to sleep.

I spent some time mulling over a few promising websites

and then settled on one to use for my research before I continued my search for Ned Swanson. An hour passed by with no new information. Same name. Wrong man. Each and every time.

My eyes grew weary and my body slumped in defeat with every click. So when I found a wedding photo labeled "The Swanson Brothers," I wasn't expecting much to come of it. I clicked on the thumbnail picture to blow it up to a sizeable proportion and took a closer look.

My heart stopped.

In the photo, a young Chief Swanson wore a black tuxedo and chuckled as he sprayed another man with a bottle of champagne. The other male also wore a tux and ducked to avoid the drops of liquid raining down on him. Unfortunately, his hand blocked out most of his face. Didn't matter, though. This was definitely Chief Swanson's brother, Ned.

Elated by my find, I zoomed in on the photo until I could make out the name on the building in the background. *Baytown Community Center.* I finally had a clue. Hoping to find an old address of his in the nearby Texas town, I typed the city name into a search engine, along with his, and gave it a go.

Within moments, my breath shuddered out of me.

The search results listed Ned Swanson as a *current* resident of Baytown, Texas. It couldn't be true. How could he have lived so close to his brother all these years without Chief Swanson knowing? It had to be an old address or something. But as I continued to scroll, I managed to retrieve a listed phone number…one that had been updated a week ago.

"I found him?" I said out loud to myself. "Oh my God!

I found him!"

Quickly, I scrawled the number on the notepad next to me like the information would somehow disappear from the computer screen if I didn't write it down elsewhere. Then I hurried to the bedroom to tell Cowboy the great news. But when I creaked the door open, he stirred and released a low pitiful groan. It was as if it pained him to rouse his tired body even in the slightest way.

Guilt washed over me.

Just because I couldn't sleep didn't mean he didn't deserve to get some rest. Especially after he'd spent the entire evening pampering and caring for me. With all the extra duties he performed as acting chief, he probably wasn't getting as much sleep as he needed to sustain his schedule. And with his investigation into the fire and the stress from the chief's death, it wouldn't be fair to disturb him or rob him of any more of it.

The good news could wait until morning.

I barely finished the thought when Cowboy rolled over, idly rubbing his hand over my side of the bed. The very idea that he was subconsciously seeking me out in his sleep made me smile. So I crawled carefully back into bed with him, slid under the sheet, and snuggled into his hard, masculine body.

"Mmm," he moaned, pulling me tighter against his warm chest and making me shiver. "Are you cold?" His raspy voice sounded thick, heavy with sleep.

"A little."

He angled away from me, letting his large hand move around to my waist to the front, then dipped his fingers beneath the waistband of my pajama bottoms. "Want me to warm you up?"

Holy hell. This man and his insatiable libido.

But remembering the news I hadn't yet shared with him, I grabbed his wrist to stop him. "Wait a minute," I said, while wondering why the hell the news couldn't hold out a little longer. "I have something to share with you."

His lips traveled up my neck and he nuzzled my ear. "Oh, yeah?"

"I found Chief Swanson's brother. Even got his phone number for you."

Cowboy yanked his head up and blinked at me. "What? When did you—"

"After you dozed off. I've been searching for him for over a week. But tonight when I couldn't sleep, I got back up and spent some time online doing research."

He frowned at that. "Anna, I'm glad you found him, but we need to talk about this sleep disorder you have."

"I don't have a sleeping disorder."

The look on his face told me he wasn't buying it. "Where's the number?"

"It's on my desk. I scribbled it on the notepad next to the keyboard. Why?"

"I need to call him."

I shook my head. "You can't call him at this hour."

"Sweetheart, his brother died. I don't think he's going to give a damn what hour it is when I call—"

A high-pitched alarm rang out, and my body jolted.

Cowboy unraveled his naked body from mine and sat upright, grabbing his pager from the nightstand and turning it off. He lifted his cell phone, read the screen, and quietly cursed under his breath. With the sheet still covering my waist, I sat up and leaned into his shirtless back. "What is it?"

"There's a structure fire on the south side of town."

"Oh," I said solemnly. An involuntary shiver ran through me at the thought of him leaving me here alone.

He must've felt it because he said, "Don't worry. I'm not going."

I didn't know which was worse: him putting off work commitments to make sure I was all right or me needing him to so I could breathe normally. I sighed. "You can't *not* go. You have a job to do."

"I'm not leaving you here by yourself."

"I'll be okay," I promised.

He groaned. "Then I'll get Jake to come over here and keep an eye on things until I get back."

"No, they have a new baby. I don't want you to wake up Emily and Lily by calling him in the middle of the night. Just go. I'll be all right. If nothing else, I'll stay awake until you get back."

"You sure?"

Though my heart raced and my thoughts ran wild, I managed to provide a convincing smile. "Yes, I'm sure. I may be a coward, but I can't keep you from helping other people. Now go. The sooner you leave, the faster you'll get to come back."

Cowboy slid off the bed and yanked on his jeans. He grabbed his shirt and hat and started to walk away, but then turned and came back. He clamped one brawny arm around my waist and lifted me high enough so that his mouth secured itself over mine. After a long, searing kiss, he pulled back and gave me a reassuring smile. "Well, I think you're brave. Especially since, if you'd turned me down one more time yesterday, I was planning to wring your pretty little neck." He winked at me, kissed the tip of my nose, and headed for the door. "When I get back, we'll talk about your sleeping disorder."

I hopped out of bed and raced into the living room, not bothering to turn on any lights. Didn't matter, though. The glow from the computer screen in the other room gave off enough light to see Cowboy tearing off the top sheet of the notepad on my desk.

"I don't have a sleeping disorder."

He glared at me. "Darlin', I'd love nothing more than to stand here and argue with you, but I have to go. We'll argue when I get back. That way we can make up," he said, shrugging his brows. Cowboy pecked me on the cheek and held up the piece of paper with Ned Swanson's phone number written on it. "Thanks for this. I'll call him on the way to the fire." Cowboy headed for the door and called out, "I'll be back soon. Lock the door behind me."

The moment he walked out, I shut the front door behind him and flipped the deadbolt to the lock position. I walked toward the couch to grab the remote, planning to watch some TV until he returned.

But as I reached for it, the floor creaked behind me and fireworks exploded behind my eyes.

Chapter Eighteen

My eyes flickered open.

I blinked a few times to clear my blurry vision, until I finally made out a faint glow of light. My head pounded, but when I tried to reach up and touch it, I realized I couldn't. My arms seemed somehow stuck behind my back. At first I thought I was paralyzed, but as I wriggled around, I felt the scratchy rope binding me twist painfully tighter.

Someone tied me up?

That knowledge sent a surge of fear running through me. I glanced around, searching for my captor, but all I could determine was that I was lying in a musty, hay-filled stall of an old, dilapidated barn, and there was no one in sight. As far as I could tell, I was completely alone.

That was, until someone banged loudly on something and a man's gruff, stale voice rang out. "Fucking idiot."

It sounded a little familiar, but I couldn't place where I'd heard it before.

Though the loud banging persisted, I couldn't see the man. Only heard him swear occasionally under his breath. Quietly, I tried to maneuver into a sitting position, but couldn't because my feet were bound, as well. Since I couldn't see my captor, I hoped like hell he couldn't see me—

Oh my God! I did recognize that voice. *Dan*, the not-exactly-homeless bum? But...why? What did he want with me?

Dread filled me, and my adrenaline kicked into high gear. Panicking, I rocked back and forth to gain enough momentum to allow me to sit up. But as I did, I knocked something over behind me in the process. The clanging noise echoed through the barn.

"Who's there?" Dan called out.

Who's there? Was he as deaf as he was blind? Or had he only pretended to be blind all along?

I shifted to see what made the noise, hoping to use the metal object as a weapon, but instead I gasped. An oil lantern sitting nearby had tipped over and leaked onto the ground, catching the musty hay on fire right next to me. Without shoes, I couldn't stomp it out, but I managed to scoot away from it. Unfortunately, that frantic move only ended up shoving more moldy hay into the flames. The fire grew larger.

I rolled to my side, twisting and pulling my arms to try and loosen the rope binding me, but it only tightened. Luckily, I managed to bend my arms back just enough to get the rope past my rear, where I tucked my knees to my chest and maneuvered my bound hands over my tied feet.

The fire was rapidly spreading and had already started working its way up the interior wall of the stall. I couldn't reach the tight knots between my wrists with my teeth, so I reached down and untied the knots at my feet.

I'd barely gotten the rope off my ankles and scrambled to my feet when Dan came into view outside the doorless stall. I backed away, watching him feel idly along the wall close to the entrance, as if he were looking for something, though there was nothing there to find. He didn't even flinch when he turned his head and looked right at me. Almost as if...he couldn't see me. Guess he's blind, after all. Which meant...

"Dan...?"

He nearly fell over from the shock. "Jesus fucking Christ! Who the hell are you and what the fuck do you want with me?" He'd had no clue I'd been there all along.

"Dan, it's me, Anna...Cowboy's friend."

"Who gives a fuck? All I wanna know is why you locked me in here. If you're here to rob me, you can forget it. The wife kicked me out again and I don't have no money."

"I...I didn't lock you in here." I considered having Dan try to untie my wrists, but then I took in the flames and gathered we only had a few short minutes to get out of the barn before the smoke overwhelmed us. With him unable to see the knots, it would take entirely too long. "Dan, we have to get out of here. The barn's on fire."

I hurried past him out of the stall and looked for the nearest exit. The fire had spread to the wall and door, which meant almost a quarter of the barn was already engulfed in flames.

"No shit, Sherlock. Just because I can't see the flames, doesn't mean I can't smell smoke. But I've been trying to get out ever since someone locked the goddamn door. No fucking use. It must be barred from the outside."

"No, you're wrong," I yelled over my shoulder, hearing the panic in my voice. To keep from burning my hands, I picked up an old piece of rotting wood and hit it repeatedly against the barn door. The door wouldn't budge. "Damn it. We're locked in."

"Told you that already," Dan said calmly, obviously not understanding the condition of the barn and the ferocity of the fire.

Toxic smoke filled the room, burning my eyes as I choked up. "No, please! I don't want to die!" I stood there frozen, shaking my head in disbelief. "This can't be happening. Not again. It's just a bad dream. Any minute now, you're going to wake up." Damn it, Anna, wake up!

Before I lost control, I closed my eyes and tried to block out the sounds of the fire roaring in my ears. But embers popped all around me, and my eyes opened to take in my surroundings. Sinister flames bowed the dry wood, and the old barn creaked, as if it were seconds away from caving in. I almost wished it would because I couldn't think of a worse death than being burned alive.

Until Dan coughed and gasped for breath.

I stared at him as he continued running his hands along the burning walls, searching for a way out. He was blind and doing everything in his power to get out, while the only person in the barn who could actually see stood there frozen, too terrified to do anything to help. His death would be my fault.

It was bad enough my mother died because of me. I couldn't let anyone else go through what she did.

I searched for a way out and spotted a large gaping hole

in the wall of the hayloft. We'd have to jump to the safety of the ground outside, but a broken neck or back somehow seemed more comforting than burning alive inside a building. It was our only chance. *I* was our only chance.

You can do this, Anna. Just breathe.

"D-Dan, over here," I shouted, gasping for a breath as I ran to the broken ladder leading to the hayloft. "Follow the sound of my voice." As he moved toward me, I encouraged his progress. "That's it, straight ahead." When he reached me, I took his hand and put it high up on the ladder. "Start climbing. When you get to the top, go to the right about ten feet. There's a large opening to the outside, though, so be careful. We'll have to jump. It's the only way out."

He frowned. "You should go first. You're the woman."

But I wouldn't be able to pull myself up easily with my hands tied together. "And you're blind," I said, desperately trying to loosen the knots again with my teeth as the flames worsened and blazed closer. The stifling heat etched its way under my skin.

"You sure love to point that out, don't ya? You know that makes you sound like a fucking asshole every time—"

"Dan, just go! I'm right behind you."

As he started to climb, I continued trying to free myself though I was coughing nonstop. The rope was too tight and I couldn't get a good grip, much less see what I was doing. It was taking entirely too long. If I didn't do something fast, I wasn't going to make it out.

Frustrated, I looked for something to cut them off, but the barn had obviously not been used for some time and there were no tools lying around. Just as I was about to give up hope, I spotted a rusty panel of roofing tin leaning against the far wall.

I covered my mouth with the inside of my elbow and stayed low as I made my way through the hazy gray smog in the room. Lining my wrists up on either side of the tin, I moved them back and forth in a sawing motion, allowing the rope to rub against the jagged tin as I held my breath.

Smoke burned my tear-filled eyes and heat from the hot tin seared into my skin. One faulty move had the rust slicing into my arm, and I let out a sharp yelp. Blood trickled down my wrist as I continued to use the jagged edge as a knife to cut through the binding.

The moment the rope gave, I stumbled back through the thick fog, groping for the rotting ladder that would lead me to safety. Once my hands found it, I climbed, hoping the shaky ladder wouldn't suddenly break and my slippery blood-soaked hands would hold me and keep me from falling back down into the fiery abyss.

A cry tore from my throat as pieces of the burning barn fell down around me. With every sure-footed step and every capable handhold I pulled myself up with, my chest burned more and more. I breathed deeper as I climbed, only ingesting more of the toxic air.

At the top, I crawled over the ledge and landed on my back, gasping for air. I wheezed, my achy lungs threatening to collapse with each breath. I grabbed the railing and pulled myself to my feet, turning toward the large window in the wall of the hayloft. Orange tendrils surrounded the opening.

I wasn't sure how far of a jump it was and had no clue how Dan managed it on his own, but he hollered from outside. He'd made it. Yet I stood transfixed by the fire, trapped on the upper floor of the barn, mentally preparing myself to jump through a burning ring of flames like a circus tiger.

I'd always had this chronic fear of being burned alive. Now, with the fire crackling around me, it was my worst nightmare come true. A self-fulfilled prophecy. But if I had any chance of getting out, I'd have to do it. Only one thought kept me from moving my feet.

Had my mother felt the same panic and desperation when she died?

Residual memories of my mother's smile and laughter washed over me. So vivacious and beautiful. Yet, my father snuffed out her light and crushed my soul. Cut all of our lives short by his callousness. His ruthlessness. His need to burn everything around him to the ground. Even the intense heat searing into my skin couldn't thaw that frozen image in my mind.

If he couldn't have me, then he'd burn us all to hell.

Taking a shallow, smoke-filled breath, I sputtered and gasped for clean air. Weakened by the lack of oxygen, I collapsed onto the wooden floor as the surrounding hayloft spun sideways. A knot formed in my sore throat, keeping me from swallowing. I wanted to cry, but my dry eyes seemed incapable of producing tears. There was no energy left in my body to get me to the opening, and as the lights in my eyes dimmed, I thought of the one person who mattered the most.

Cowboy.

The image of his face replayed over and over in my head like a looped recording, torturing me with his glittering green eyes and taunting me with his cocky grin. Pain seared through me at the devastating thought of never seeing him again.

No! I can't lose him now.

I blinked my stinging eyes to sharpen my focus and made out the blurry hayloft opening surrounded by fire. Only ten damn feet away. Even though the notion of moving an inch exhausted me, I had to make it out. For him. *For us.*

Using the only reserves I could muster, I lifted my body up and crawled toward the opening in the wall. My hands and knees skimmed the old wooden floor, collecting splinters from the desiccated planks as the breaths wheezed in and out of my chest.

As soon as I made it to the hayloft doors, I hung my head over the edge and gulped in huge breaths of fresh air as smoke billowed out above my head. My eyes focused on the ground, measuring the distance of my jump to safety, and nausea rolled through me. *Oh God.* The second story was much higher than I'd anticipated.

I started to shove myself back from the edge when my right hand pushed against something that moved. Peering back over the ledge, a sense of relief washed over me and I nearly cried. A small wooden ladder hung from the side of the hayloft doors, leading toward the ground.

Upon closer examination, though, my heart sank and my distress returned. Half of the decaying ladder dangled loosely to the trim by only one rusted nail, while the bottom half—the most important half—was missing altogether. I'd still have to jump.

But it wasn't like I had a choice.

Swinging my legs over the edge, I eased out onto the ladder while holding onto the building for dear life. If the shoddy ladder broke beneath my weight, I didn't want to go down with it. At least not right away. The rotting wood held, so I released my hand from the trim around the hayloft doors and grabbed onto the wooden pegs of the ladder. It wobbled a little, and I tightened my grasp.

I climbed down, executing a slow, careful descent, but it didn't matter. About a quarter of the way down, an eerily familiar voice yelled out my name. I faltered and my foot slipped. The wooden step broke beneath my weight, and I plummeted at least fifteen feet to the ground.

The sudden impact knocked the wind from my lungs, and an intense pain rocketed through my shoulder, radiating down my outstretched limb. I tried to cry out, but no air passed my lips. In silent agony, I cradled my injured shoulder to steady it and gasped for oxygen while the excruciating pain echoed through my arm. I couldn't move it.

But no matter how significant the blinding pain shooting through my system was, it didn't have anything on the crazy tricks it played on my fading consciousness. While I lay there on the ground, unable to move, a hazy figure came into view and hovered over me like an ominous dark cloud.

And I caught a glimpse of his face. "D-Dad?"

Then I swirled into darkness.

I couldn't breathe.

Choking and gasping, I awoke to something digging painfully into my stomach, expelling what little fresh air I managed to gulp in. My memory flashed back to the burning barn, but the searing pain in my left shoulder fast forwarded to the part where I fell off the ladder.

Then my head lolled, swinging back and forth in the air freely like a pendulum as something moved beneath me.

Correction: as someone carried me. My eyes shot open to see the back of a man's legs as his work boots kicked up dust with every step. Realizing I was upside down, my head spun and my stomach churned.

Each step he took sent a spike of pain into my throbbing arm. A man had thrown me over his shoulder and carried me away from the blazing building. But why? Where was he taking me? And who was this—no, I knew who he was.

My father, Stuart Nelson.

I struggled against him. I wasn't sure if that had anything to do with why he suddenly stopped in his tracks, but he bent and laid me down in the middle of a dirt driveway. He didn't hesitate to grab my incapacitated arm and flex my elbow out further. I cried out from the extreme amount of white-hot pain that shot through me.

My eyes glazed with tears and short breaths wheezed from my lungs, but I wasn't capable of fighting him off. Thankfully, as he rotated my arm and applied some pressure behind it, something in my shoulder popped back into place. The lingering pain was nothing compared to the immediate relief I found.

"Anna...? Baby girl, can you hear me?"

That voice... It had to be a hallucination. I couldn't fathom that the man who killed my mother was referring to me in terms of endearment. As if he hadn't ripped my heart out of my chest twenty-two years ago when he burned my mother alive and left me to live with the mental and physical scars his actions had caused.

Wailing sirens sounded in the distance and, out of my peripheral vision, I saw a speeding truck with flashing red lights barreling up the secluded road leading to the abandoned barn. Someone was coming to help me. That's when I realized Dan was missing. Was he okay? Had my father killed him to…get to me? A sense of dread washed over me. Oh God, no! Please let him be okay.

Anger, bright and hot, flashed through me.

As my father leaned over me, brushing my hair from my eyes, I shoved my foot into his chest and kicked out, catching him off guard and knocking him backward. I flipped over to scramble to my feet, but he quickly regained his balance and grabbed me by my ankle before I had the chance. "Anna, wait!" he growled.

Panting, I spun around and tried to hit him with my good arm, but he caught my wrist mid-swing. Those small efforts left me winded, but I had to do everything in my power to get away from him.

"Stop fighting me and let me help you."

I battled weakly against his grip as the roaring truck skidded to a halt only yards away from where my father held me captive in his tight grasp. The driver's door flew open and Cowboy leaped out, pistol in hand. "Let her go," he said firmly, lifting his arm and aiming the gun at my father's head to punctuate his demand.

Stuart glared at him. "You're making a big mistake."

Cowboy's eyes narrowed and his jaw twitched as he cocked the hammer back. "No, *you* made the fucking mistake by coming after her. Now step away from her, or it won't be your last." His even tone had a convincing edge to it.

My father released my arm and stepped back.

I scrambled to my shaky feet and stumbled toward Cowboy, who met me halfway. Out of breath, I fell just as he reached me. Wrapping his free arm around me, he tried to hoist me back up, but in my breathless state, I collapsed onto the ground and coughed violently.

He knelt beside me, keeping his gun trained on my father. "You okay, darlin'?" His voice was thick with fear and strained with worry. Tears of relief overwhelmed me, but I managed to nod. He pulled me tight against his chest and I moaned at the pain radiating up my arm. Loosening his grip, he looked me over, frowning. "Whose blood is that?" he asked, eyeing the dried red streaks running down my arm.

"Mine," I wheezed out.

Cowboy's eyes took on a wild, untamed glaze and shifted back to Stuart. "You sonofabitch!" His index finger curled around the trigger.

"No, d-don't," I whispered, my scratchy voice sounding strange even to me.

"Damn it, Anna! He tried to kill you."

"I didn't hurt her," Stuart said calmly.

The death grip Cowboy held on his pistol tightened even more. "I've seen dozens of scars on her body that beg to differ."

Stuart's face twisted with something strangely resembling pain or possibly agony as his eyes darted to me. "Baby girl, we need to talk about your mother. You need to know I—"

"You're talking to *me* now," Cowboy growled, cutting off Stuart's words. "Not her. Don't address her. Don't even fucking look at her." He stood and, taking a few steps forward, fine-tuned his aim directly at my father's head. "If you have something to say, you say it to me...and only me. Got it?"

The corner of Stuart's mouth twitched and amusement lit his eyes.

"Keep smiling, you sick sonofabitch. I dare you."

The overriding fury in Cowboy's caustic voice frightened me, and a shiver ran the length of my spine. His posture stiffened and his body quivered with undeniable rage. Intense green eyes held Stuart's as if Cowboy were waiting for the man to give him a reason to shoot him. But would Cowboy actually pull the trigger?

Several vehicles with flashing red and blue lights slowed out on the main road and turned onto the long dark driveway leading to the barn. But their howling sirens had nothing on the warning bells going off in my head.

From what I could tell, Stuart was keeping his distance and no longer posed a threat to anyone, including me. If Cowboy's wrath unraveled any more, it was possible he would snap and do the unthinkable. Not that Stuart Nelson didn't deserve it. He did. But I wasn't about to let Cowboy commit murder for me. Which is exactly what he would be doing if he shot an unarmed man.

"Don't," I said, though it came out as barely a whisper. "Please, Cowboy."

He didn't even look at me. "Why not? He deserves it after what he put you through. At most, it's justifiable homicide. He tried to kill you tonight."

I shook my head and cleared my raw throat. "H-he didn't. I don't know why, but…he pulled me away from the fire."

Cowboy paused. "Even so, if he wouldn't have started the fire to begin with—"

"*I* started the fire," I admitted.

Finally, he glanced over, his gaze meeting mine. "You set the barn on fire?" he asked, confusion slanting his lips.

Still trying to catch my breath, I nodded. "It was an

accident." I coughed so hard, I ended up gasping for my next breath.

Two Liberty County Sheriff cruisers, three fire engines, and an ambulance pulled onto the scene. An older sheriff with a mustache slid out of the car closest to me and pulled out the gun in his hip holster. He kept it lowered, but held it ready in his hand for any sign of trouble. "Cowboy, lower your weapon."

Slowly, Cowboy brought his arm down to his side, pointing his pistol at the ground, but kept his piercing eyes on Stuart.

"Now, would someone tell me what the hell is going on here?" the sheriff asked, as if he were puzzled as to why we were all standing around watching an old barn burn to the ground.

"This man is Stuart Nelson, a convicted murderer who was recently released from prison. He's been stalking Anna Weber, the only surviving victim of a fire this man started twenty-two years ago."

The sheriff's face hardened and his eyes zeroed in on me. "Is this true?"

Still coughing and feeling short of breath, I answered again with a quick nod.

The sheriff and the two deputies flanking him turned all their attention on my father. "Lie face down and put your hands behind your back."

"Maybe I can clear up some of the confusion," Stuart said, addressing the sheriff directly.

"On the ground. Now," the sheriff ordered, approaching him cautiously.

"Okay, fine," Stuart responded, dropping to his knees.

"But my daughter and her friend are in need of medical attention. They were both locked in the barn when the fire broke out. The old man is still lying in the field on the east side of the barn. I left him there in order to get Anna to safety. I think he has a broken leg."

Dan? He's alive? Thank God!

The sheriff motioned for his deputies to check on Dan and then his eyes cut to me and his brows pinched together. "Daughter?" he repeated.

With just that one word, my breath backed up into my chest and my body went numb. I gasped for air, but it was like my lungs didn't know what to do with it. Now that the perceived danger was gone, emotions overwhelmed me and tears of relief swept over me.

Without a word, Cowboy stalked past me to his truck and shoved his gun under the driver's seat. Then he returned, lifted me into his strong arms, and carried me toward the ambulance parked nearby.

I opened my eyes, blinking at the bright lights above me, as the oxygen mask made a hissing sound. Inside the ambulance, the paramedic hovered over me, strapping a blood pressure cuff on my right arm.

"Is she going to be okay?" Cowboy asked, his voice thick with fear and strained with worry.

"Let me finish checking her over," the paramedic replied. "She has some minor cuts and burns, but I think she'll be all right. The dislocated shoulder probably won't need surgery since that guy popped it back into place so soon after her fall. She'll most likely have to wear a sling for a short time, though."

I tried to speak Cowboy's name, but my throat was hoarse and too raspy to make out the word. Even though I had an IV hooked into my left arm, the paramedic handed me a bottle of water. "Sip this carefully. Only a little at a time."

I removed the breathing apparatus from my mouth and took a small drink. I might as well have been trying to ingest dust. The water trickled down my dry throat, and an explosion of deep coughs erupted from my chest. When the eruption went dormant, I tried to speak with my scratchy voice. "Cow…boy…"

"Don't try to talk, Anna. Lie still and let him help you. You're safe now. I got to you in time."

Barely.

"H-how'd you…find me?" I whispered, my voice straining to eke out the last two words.

Cowboy kissed my hand and then rested his forehead on it. "Someone called it in."

The inflection of his tone led me to believe things were not as simple as he stated. "Someone?" I croaked out.

He smiled warmly at me. "Shhh. Don't worry about that right now. Just concentrate on getting better."

I was so tired and felt safe, knowing Cowboy stood sentry at my bedside, so I allowed my eyes to flutter closed while the paramedic continued his medical assessment.

"Darlin', open your eyes," Cowboy said, pulling my hand into his. "We need you to stay awake."

I did as he asked, then gave him a weak smile as I squeezed his fingers to comfort him. Cowboy's expression was grim as his head dropped between his knees. "I'm sorry

I didn't get to you in time and couldn't rescue you from the fire." He shook his head with disgust and sighed. "I shouldn't have left you alone when I went on that fire call. This is all my fault."

"Y-you saved me…from my father," I said softly.

"That I did," he said, grinning. "Your own real-life Prince Charming, huh? And I didn't even need a white horse to do it." Cowboy winked at me, but I detected a touch of sarcasm in his tone.

Something was off with him.

"Sir, I'm going to have to ask you to step out of the ambulance for a moment," the paramedic said, addressing Cowboy. "I need to assess her without her trying to talk any more."

I tried to sit up, but Cowboy stopped me. "Whoa, tiger. You're staying firmly planted in this ambulance until you get checked out at the hospital." I shook my head back and forth and started coughing violently. "It's okay, darlin'. Let him do his job. I'll be outside and won't leave your sight. You're safe." Cowboy brushed my cheek with his hand, then kissed me on my forehead.

As he stepped out of the ambulance, there were two sheriff deputies standing just outside the ambulance doors, as if they were guarding us. Several other deputies combed the surrounding area searching for clues, as two paramedics wheeled Dan toward a second ambulance parked next to us. He was grumbling under his breath about kicking the shit out of the "stinkin' idiot" who tried to burn him alive.

Stinkin'? Since when did Dan refrain from using stronger words than that?

Firefighters hosed down the blaze, even though the

entire barn had already caved in. I caught a glimpse of Mandy running past the ambulance in full bunker gear. I wouldn't have known it was her if she hadn't been shoving her helmet on her head at the time I'd spotted her.

My gaze shifted as someone stepped into my line of sight. It was the mustache-wielding sheriff who'd pulled his gun out when he arrived. "Ma'am," the man said, tipping his hat to me. "I'm Sheriff Hunter Wells with the Liberty County Sheriff's Office. Would it be okay if I asked you a few questions?"

I nodded, but Cowboy shook his head. "Anna's been through enough tonight. Why don't you go question Stuart Nelson instead?"

"Mr. Nelson answered all of our questions already," Sheriff Wells said, his eyes zeroing in on me. "We released him ten minutes ago."

I gasped and shot straight up on the gurney, as if someone had erected a metal spike in my back. "What? You can't! H-he's going to—" I coughed so hard, sputtering to get the words out, that my head hurt.

Cowboy climbed into the ambulance, took my hand and squeezed it. "Damn it. Anna, you need to settle down."

"No, I—" I started coughing again.

His jaw tightened and he glared at the sheriff. "Want to explain why the hell you let the ex-convict go?"

"Sorry, Cowboy, but it looks like Stuart Nelson's not our guy. We don't have any evidence to hold him. Not only did he pull Miss Weber to safety by her own admittance, but he also was the one who made the 911 call. I had dispatch compare his cell phone number to the person who called in and it was the same...as he claimed it would be."

"Doesn't mean he didn't kidnap Anna."

Sheriff Wells shrugged. "Not sure what he'd gain by calling the cops on himself. Doesn't seem like something anyone with half a brain would do. Stuart Nelson doesn't seem to be the likely culprit here. He did, however, give us a lead to follow."

"What lead?" Cowboy asked.

"Miss Weber, do you own a blue Chevy Cavalier?"

I nodded slowly, unsure as to where Sheriff Wells was going with his question.

"Your fath—I mean, Mr. Nelson—said he arrived at your house just as a blue Cavalier pulled away and followed it out here. Since it was a dead end, he pulled over up the road a little ways and waited to see what you were doing."

"But I didn't—"

The sheriff raised his hand to stop me from continuing. "It's okay, we know that much already."

Cowboy glared at him. "Stuart Nelson is lying. Anna's car was still in her driveway when I got back from the fire call. Her vehicle wasn't stolen."

"He's not saying it was stolen. More like 'temporarily borrowed.'"

I shook my head. "None of this makes any sense. Why would the kidnapper take my car and then return it?"

"We have reason to believe the perpetrator wasn't aware the old man was in the barn," Sheriff Wells explained. "Nelson said your vehicle barreled out of here at a high rate of speed. He tried to follow it, but lost it a few miles down the road. Once he made it back to your home and saw your Cavalier sitting in the driveway, he drove back to the barn to find out what you'd been doing out here."

"And that's when he found the barn on fire?"

The sheriff nodded. "He called in the fire, then found your friend and moved him to safety. Said he hadn't even realized there was anyone else inside until the old man told him otherwise. He ran back to the barn and saw you climbing down the ladder."

"Well, that's just great," Cowboy sneered, pulling off his hat and scrubbing a hand through his hair. "So on his word alone, you let the ex-convict go."

"Didn't have a choice," the sheriff said. "We had nothing to tie him to the kidnapping. The only other suspects at this time are—"

"The B-Barlow b-brothers..." I wheezed, then stopped long enough to catch my breath. "It was them? They...did this?"

"That's what we're trying to figure out, ma'am."

Cowboy sighed and rubbed at the back of his neck. "Don't worry, sweetheart. We're going to catch whoever's responsible for this. No one's going to hurt you ever again." His cell phone must've buzzed because he stood and pulled it from his hip and looked at it. "I have to take this," he said, leaning down to kiss my forehead before hopping out the ambulance doors.

The paramedic glanced over at Cowboy. "We're ready to roll. If you want, Captain, you can follow behind the ambulance. Just be sure to turn on your flashers and emergency lights."

"Follow? Are you kidding? I'm leading this parade," he said, giving me a wink.

Chapter Nineteen

After arriving at the understaffed emergency room, I changed into a hospital gown, had a scan of my shoulder, and was eventually admitted to a room upstairs with Cowboy at my side. The nurses monitored me for any worsening signs of respiratory distress until the doctor on duty made his rounds and wheeled in a small surgical tray.

He examined me first, paying close attention to the sounds of my respirations, before moving on to my shoulder. The doctor explained how the results from my scan had showed no permanent damage, though I'd still have to wear a sling for a short period of time to promote healing. After adding a few stitches to the gash in my arm, he pushed the tray aside and told me he was keeping me overnight for precautionary observation due to the large amount of smoke I'd inhaled.

I wasn't the least bit surprised. Been there, done that.

When the doctor finally left the room, Cowboy kissed

my cheek and rubbed his calloused thumb along my jaw as he gazed down at my bandaged wrist. "I'm sorry, Anna. I wish I'd been there to protect you. I should've been. This is all my fau—"

I pressed my finger to his lips to silence him. "Don't say that. You can't stand guard over me every minute. The Barlows would have gotten to me sooner or later."

"It won't happen again," Cowboy said, deadly promise looming in his threat.

The door opened and we both looked up.

Sheriff Wells stepped into the room, followed by Mandy Barlow, who was no longer in her bunker gear. Neither of them looked happy. Not that I expected her to be after hearing her brothers were going to be arrested.

"Did you pick up Joe and Clay Barlow, yet?" Cowboy asked, apparently ignoring the shine of Mandy's teary eyes.

"No," the sheriff said. "That's actually what I came to talk to you about."

They didn't catch them?

The sheriff hesitated. "They said they weren't responsible for Miss Weber's kidnapping, and I have no choice but to believe them."

"It had to be them," Cowboy snarled, shaking his head in disgust. "If it wasn't Stuart Nelson, then they'd be the only ones left who had any connection to Anna and would want to do her harm. What about all the threats they sent her?"

Sheriff Wells wrinkled his brow in confusion. "Threats?"

Everyone shifted their eyes onto me and I sighed. "After I had a run-in with the Barlow boys, I started receiving hostile notes in my mailbox. I thought they were just trying to intimidate me, though."

"I want to see those notes," the sheriff said.

"I'll swing by Anna's and bring them to you in the morning," Cowboy stated, glancing over at Mandy. "I'm sorry. I know they're your brothers, but they need to pay for what they did to her."

Mandy shook her head. "That's what the sheriff is trying to tell you. It's not possible. They *couldn't* have been responsible for the kidnapping. Both of my brothers have been locked up in County Jail since last night. They started a bar brawl over at The Backwoods and were arrested. They're still in a cell."

"Wait," I said, trying to wrap my brain around this new information. "If what she says is true…"

"Then they both have rock solid alibis for their whereabouts," Cowboy finished for me. "Which means there are no more suspects to investigate."

"Actually," Sheriff Wells began, a somber expression taking over his face. "Sorry, Cowboy. I hate to ask this, especially right now, but…well, where were you earlier this evening when Miss Weber was abducted?"

Apparently, Mandy hadn't seen that one coming either because we exchanged a look of shock and confusion.

"Are you fucking kidding me?" Cowboy asked.

"You were the last one to see the victim before she disappeared, the one who reported her missing, and the first responder on the scene. Not only that, but the Barlow brothers claim you were yelling at Miss Weber and beating down her door more than once over the past few days. Like I said, I hate to ask, but…"

"Oh, fuck me," Cowboy said, rolling his eyes. "I left Anna's house around midnight after my fire pager went off, but it was a false alarm. After that, I went straight back to Anna's. Probably only took me half an hour at the most. She was gone and there was a lamp turned over, so I knew something had happened. That's when I called the sheriff's office and reported her missing."

"And then? Where did you go after that?"

"I was driving around looking for her. What the hell do you think I was doing?" Cowboy glared at him, but Sheriff Wells set his jaw and stared right back, as if the man were waiting for a full confession. "Oh, give me a fucking break! You think I kidnapped Anna, tied her up, and left her in some old barn so I could report her missing and then blame it on her father?"

The sheriff shrugged. "Crazier things have happened."

"Then how do you account for the blue Cavalier? I don't drive a car and I would have had to leave my truck at Anna's house."

"True. But like you said earlier, the man who gave us this information is an ex-convict. Doesn't hold a lot of weight at this point."

I scoffed. "I can't believe you're even considering Cowboy as a suspect. He didn't do it."

But the sheriff continued with his questions. "Were you alone when you returned to Miss Weber's home?"

"Yes, of course," Cowboy responded.

"So no one can verify your whereabouts around the time Ms. Weber went missing?"

Cowboy blew out a breath. "Guess not."

"Then that leaves me no choice," the sheriff said, shaking his head. "Cowboy, I'll need you to come down to the station with me for more questioning."

"You've got to be shittin' me!"

What? This couldn't be happening.

I ripped off my nasal oxygen tube and sat up, but Cowboy held me there, not allowing me to stand. "He didn't do this!" I yelled, my throat burning from the effort.

"It's okay, darlin'." Cowboy squeezed my hand and gave me a wink. "Don't worry. We'll get this all sorted out soon enough."

"This is absurd," I said, my voice straining against the ashes in my throat as tears leaked from my eyes. "He didn't do anything."

"Maybe not. But *someone* did. And it's my job to find out who." Sheriff Wells motioned for the door. "Let's go, Cowboy."

I watched helplessly as the sheriff led him toward the door.

When they reached it, Mandy suddenly spoke up out of nowhere. "Wait," she said, biting her lip. "I can vouch for his whereabouts. I...saw Cowboy earlier."

"You already told me you saw him at the station when he showed up for the false alarm. But that was *before* Miss Weber was kidnapped."

Cowboy and Mandy exchanged a look. I wasn't sure what it meant, but I saw worry in both of their eyes. "No, I saw him after that, too."

"You didn't mention seeing him earlier in your statement, Miss Barlow." The sheriff glared at her. "So if this is true, then why didn't you say that to begin with when I questioned you?"

Mandy's gaze flickered from Cowboy to me, then back to the sheriff. "Because he didn't want Anna to know."

"Didn't want me to know what?" I asked.

She looked down, keeping her eyes from meeting mine. "That Cowboy was with *me* tonight."

"What are you talking about?" I asked with an angry bite to my words. "No. You're lying. Cowboy, tell the sheriff she's lying." For a moment, there was nothing but silence. He didn't say anything in his defense. Instead, his gaze lingered on Mandy and he frowned. "Cowboy…?"

"I'm sorry, Anna," he said, not even having the gumption to look me in the eye. "It's true."

Hurt and confusion filled my heart. Cowboy had been with another woman. Even after he made the big play of pronouncing me as his and pretending we were ever anything more than a booty call. And I had believed him.

God, I'm an idiot.

"Why don't we give you two a minute alone," the sheriff said, motioning for Mandy to follow him out.

Once they cleared the room, Cowboy came toward me with an outstretched hand. "Sweetheart, I—"

I jerked away from him and tears filled my eyes. "Don't touch me, you…you cheating bastard. I trusted you!"

He sighed heavily and lowered his voice. "Anna, it's not true. I wasn't with Mandy tonight. I swear."

"Oh, really? Well, that's not what the two of you just told the sheriff," I sneered back at him.

"That was just her way of saving my ass. She was keeping me from going down to the station and getting my ass arrested."

"And you went along with it? Yeah, right."

"Darlin', look at me." When I wouldn't allow my eyes to meet his, he raised his voice. "Damn it, Anna, I can't sit in a goddamn cell at the county jail and leave you unprotected. The guy who did this is still out there somewhere. So I took a chance that you'd be reasonable and logical enough to allow me to explain myself before you thought the worst of me."

"Explain what? Why you just humiliated me in front of the sheriff by letting him believe a girl like me couldn't satisfy a man with your reputation?"

He cringed and ran a hand over his face. "I didn't mean to humiliate you. But that's always what it's going to come back to, isn't it? My reputation. Well, you know what? That road of trust drives both ways, honey. It sure the hell didn't take me much convincing on my part to get you to believe I wasn't faithful to you, but like you said…with my reputation and all." The sarcasm oozed from his voice.

"Don't you dare throw my words back in my face. It's not my fault you have a reputation as a playboy. What did you expect me to think?"

"I expect you to trust me. You should have at least given me the benefit of—" His cell phone buzzed on the nearby counter, so he lifted it and glanced at the screen. "I have to make a call. Can we argue about this when I get back?"

I nodded silently, feeling the awkwardness between us when he shifted his eyes away from me and headed toward the exit without so much as a good-bye. He swung the door open just as Dan filled the doorway, wearing a medical boot on his injured foot and lifting his hand to knock. When his knuckles only swept air, Cowboy chuckled and moved aside, allowing him entry.

Dan wasn't the least bit amused as he tapped his cane back and forth on the floor and stepped inside. "Very funny, asshole."

Cowboy looked back at me and grinned, long enough for me to feel the tension dissipate between us, then he disappeared out the door. I hoped that was his way of saying all was forgiven, but I wasn't entirely sure it was. But I couldn't worry about it right now.

"Hi, Dan. How are you?" I asked loudly, letting him follow the sound of my voice.

He found the chair next to me and sat. "Stop yelling. I'm blind, not deaf."

I coughed a little, which helped stifle my giggle. "How are you doing? You okay?"

"Fractured my ankle. Doc says I have to wear this fucking boot for a few weeks." He gave me one of his big rotten-toothed grins. "Since they released me, I came to see how you fared with our death-defying leap out the window."

"Actually, I didn't jump from the hayloft. Apparently, there was an old ladder on the outside of the barn. That's how I got out."

The smile Dan wore melted. "What the fuck is wrong with you, girl?"

"I, uh…beg your pardon?"

He shook his head in disbelief. "You let a blind man leap out a fucking two-story window while you climbed safely down a ladder?"

I tried not to smirk, afraid that he would hear it in my tone. "No, no, you got it all wrong. The smoke overwhelmed me before I could make it out. That's when I sort of stumbled upon the ladder. Had I known it was there, I never would have let you jump."

I sat quietly as Dan recounted his harrowing "brush with death," as he called it. I actually felt bad for the guy when he got to the part where he had to force himself to jump from the hayloft. Leaping out of a burning building would be frightening for anyone, but especially someone blind who couldn't see how high up they were or what they might possibly land on. Thankfully, he landed feet-first in an unruly pile of brush—hence the "brush with death" part—which cushioned his fall. Otherwise, his injuries could've been more severe.

Dan finally got to the part where my ex-convict father found him and moved him away from the burning building. He said he told the man there was a woman still inside and the man went silent, like he'd disappeared. Guess that was when my father ran to the barn to locate me.

But why? After everything he took from me and after my testimony had put him in prison, why did he—

"Can I borrow your pisser?" Dan asked.

"Of course."

He sat there quietly for a moment. "You gonna tell me where it is or do you want me to guess?"

"Oh, I'm sorry. The bathroom is directly behind your chair about five feet away."

Dan rose and tapped his aluminum cane back and forth on the tile until he found the bathroom. He disappeared from sight just as a light knock sounded on the room door. I didn't even have a chance to say "come in" before the large door pushed open and Mandy came into view.

She kept her eyes lowered as she approached my bedside. "I just wanted to apologize for my behavior," she said, shaking her head furiously. "I didn't mean to say anything. But I couldn't stand by and let Cowboy get blamed for doing something we all know he didn't do."

I was still upset, but considered her words carefully before answering. She obviously hadn't meant to cause any problems. And she had put her own ass on the line to keep him from becoming the sheriff's number one suspect. "Thank you, Mandy," I whispered, feeling like an idiot for not believing in Cowboy from the beginning. "I appreciate you standing by his side."

"Always." She offered me a sincere smile, but her brows quirked with confusion. "You know, you're taking this a lot better than I thought you would."

"It's okay. Cowboy already told me he wasn't with you. I understand why you would say that he was, though."

"No, I don't think you do. That's not exactly—"

The bathroom door swung open and Mandy shot out of her chair, wheeling around, as Dan tapped his way into the room. She obviously hadn't realized we weren't alone. She moved out of his way and around to the opposite side of my bed, allowing Dan to reclaim the chair. Staring blankly at me, Mandy chewed on her bottom lip. As if she wanted to say something, but stopped herself from doing so.

A sharp stab of anxiety cut deep into the pit of my stomach. Had Cowboy lied to me? Was that what she was going to say? No. That couldn't be it. No matter what he'd said earlier in front of the sheriff, I believed he was sincere when he said he hadn't cheated on me. But the moment I got Mandy alone, I planned to ask her for an explanation and clarify things once and for all.

The chair squeaked under Dan's weight as he shifted to get comfortable. "You know, you might want to have the nurse get maintenance up here," Dan said, leaning back in the chair. "The urinal in there is way too high."

"Um, Dan, there isn't a urinal in there."

"Huh. Well, then you might want to have someone give your sink a good scrubbing before you use it then."

My face must've warped with a horrified expression because Mandy giggled out loud.

Startled by the sound of a different voice, Dan sat a little straighter. "You got company or something?"

"It's Mandy Barlow. She came by to…check on me," I explained, though I was pretty sure her reason for stopping in had more to do with what she'd started to say before Dan returned from the bathroom and stopped her.

Sheriff Wells stepped back inside the room, interrupting my train of thought. "Pardon me, Miss Weber, but since we're running low in the suspect department, I think maybe it would be a good idea to go over your account of what happened once more."

"Guess that's my cue to leave," Dan stated, rising from the chair next to my bed.

"No, Dan, why don't you stay?" the sheriff asked him. "I'll need you to corroborate her statement."

"Okay, then," he agreed. "I'll just get out of the way." He tapped his cane and walked around to the opposite side of my bed until he bumped into Mandy's shoulder. "Sorry about that. Didn't hear you standing there." He grinned at his own stupid joke, moved over to give her some room, and sniffed the air. "That scent you're wearing…what is it?"

"Oh, I don't wear perfume," Mandy told him. "You're probably smelling my apple body mist." She looked at me and I grinned. Apparently, Dan was a ladies' man. Who knew?

Dan's mouth tightened into a firm, thin line. "No, that's

not it," he mumbled.

The sheriff took the seat Dan had vacated and focused his attention on me. "All right, Miss Weber, let's go through this one more time. What happened after you woke up in the barn?"

I prayed this would be the last time I'd have to go through all the details...at least for tonight. "I told you already. I was tied with my hands behind my back, so I maneuvered around until I managed to get my hands in front of my body and that's when I untied my feet. Had I known there was—"

I paused when Cowboy shoved open the door and entered the room with someone behind him, though I couldn't see who it was. Cowboy held up his hand. "Sorry, Sheriff, I just need to interrupt for a moment. Someone wanted to meet Anna." He stepped aside, revealing the shadow behind him.

"Oh my God!" I covered my mouth in shock. He looked much older than I remembered, but I would recognize his face anywhere. "C-Chief Swanson?"

"What?" Mandy exclaimed, backing up until she bumped into Dan, almost knocking him over. "Y-you're alive?" Clearly distraught, she braced herself by holding onto the foot railing of my hospital bed and covered her face with her free hand, rocking back and forth. "But...but you're dead," she whispered.

Chief Swanson glanced at the rest of us, and his brows furrowed. He stepped forward and put a hand on Mandy's slumped shoulder. "I'm sorry, but I'm not—"

Mandy reeled back at his touch, stumbling into the silver suture tray beside her. "No! It's not possible. I saw you!" she shrieked, shaking her head frantically back and forth. "You were dead. I know you were. I set you on fire and...I...I watched you burn."

A collective gasp sounded in the quiet room. Looks of horror and shock flicked across each of our faces at her confession and only then did Mandy realize her mistake. Her mouth dropped open and her eyes widened.

Cowboy's eyes cut to Sheriff Wells, but his expression remained bleak. "This man is not Ted Swanson. He's the chief's twin brother, Ned Swanson."

Mandy blinked. "W-what?"

But Ned didn't miss a beat. "You killed Ted?" he asked in disbelief.

She didn't say anything, just stood there staring at the man, as if the likeness of him to his brother had thrown her for a loop. The sheriff stood and took a step toward her. "Miss Barlow, I think you need to come with me."

I couldn't believe what I was hearing and sat there with my mouth hanging open, blinking and gawking at her in silence. Her bottom lip quivered as she backed slowly away. When she stumbled again into the silver tray behind her, she must've realized she was cornered and had nowhere else to go.

That's when I got a whiff of a familiar, yet unpleasant, odor and realized I'd been wrong the entire time. "Y-you did this? You sent me the notes, wanting me to think it was your brothers, but...*you* put me in that barn."

"No, of course not. I—"

"Don't bother denying it. It's faint, but I can smell the kerosene on you from here."

Dan's head snapped to me. "Kerosene! That's it!"

Though he couldn't see it, I nodded in confirmation.

But Mandy shook her head furiously, denying the accusation. "We're close to the same size. I couldn't have possibly carried you into the barn—"

"You're a firefighter, Mandy, which means you're trained to carry 150-pound manikins out of burning buildings. That's thirty pounds more than I weigh. Besides, who said I was *carried* into the barn?"

Panic flashed in her eyes. "I…guess I just assumed."

"Or you were there. I'm betting your whereabouts around the time I disappeared can't be verified." The last pieces of the puzzle linked together in my mind. "This was all you. That first night at the library, you weren't driving past when you saw the flames. You set the dumpster on fire and let me take the blame, didn't you?"

She stared at me with an unresponsive expression.

"In fact, I'm betting you started the fire at the chili cook-off, as well. You and I were the only ones standing close enough to have caused it. But you knew I'd look guilty. Because who would believe a firefighter started a fire they had to put out themselves? But there's still one thing I can't figure out." I paused momentarily, letting the words hang in the air. "Why? What did I ever do to you?"

She didn't respond verbally, but her gaze flickered over the end of the bed and directly onto one of the men. Instantly, her eyes filled with tears, revealing the unsaid truth.

"Cowboy?" I asked her. "He's the reason you did all of this?"

"We were going to be happy. The night Chief Swanson died, Cowboy held me in his arms and told me so. Said we'd get through it together. But then you came along and ruined it by making him feel sorry for you. Just like Janet did to Ted."

"Is that why you killed them?"

"It was an accident. When Ted called and told me he was leaving me to go back to his wife, I went to his house and found her there. I tied her up and left her upstairs so I could talk to him without her interfering. I only wanted to make myself a drink to calm down while I waited for him to get home. But the only thing I could find was a jug of moonshine. Ted showed up a few minutes later and we argued, so I threw the drink on him and he stumbled. If only he…hadn't been standing in front of the fireplace…"

"He caught on fire?" the sheriff asked, gently coaxing the information from her.

She nodded with tears streaming down her face. "I tried to help him, but he wouldn't stop screaming. I couldn't take it anymore. Everything started burning around me, so I…I…"

"What did you do?" Cowboy demanded, breaking his silence with his accusatory tone.

Her eyes cut to him and then closed as she lowered her head. "I left. But it wasn't my fault. He did this to himself."

"You threw the drink on him, and you left him to die," I said, cringing at her words. "You're the reason he's dead. You killed him. Every bit of that was *your* fault."

My comment must've pushed her over the edge because her eyes took on a glazed look as she turned her cold, steely gaze on me. "No. This is all *your* fault. If you would have just left after the first warning, none of this would have happened. For Cowboy's sake, I tried not to hurt you. That's why I put you in that barn…to get you out of the way. But I should have just lit your house on fire and killed you…

because you deserve to die!"

Without warning, Mandy grabbed something from the incision tray beside her, raised it high into the air, and lunged for me. Cowboy threw himself across me, blocking my body with his, as the sheriff and Ned hurdled over the end of the bed to subdue her. They grabbed her and, although she fought to free herself, managed to hold her arms behind her back as the sheriff handcuffed her.

Mandy screamed in protest and hatred filled her eyes. Then she stopped and grinned at me with a sinister look on her face that sent chills scattering through me. "If I can't have him, then neither can you," she sneered.

"What's going on?" Dan asked, confused by the scuffle he heard.

Cowboy groaned at her, obviously showing his exasperation. Though I couldn't see his expression, I could imagine him rolling his eyes at her.

"Hit the nurse's call button," the sheriff ordered me, clicking the last cuff on Mandy's wrist.

"It's okay, I'm fine."

He shook his head and I saw the fear in his eyes. "Cowboy isn't. Hit the damn button."

Uncertain as to what I missed, I shifted to get a better look and eyed a small pair of surgical scissors sticking out of his neck. "Oh my God!" I fumbled to grab the call button, though the weight of his body on top of mine made it more difficult. When I found it, I pressed the red emergency button over and over as tears squeezed out of my eyes. "No, no, no!"

Ned didn't wait for someone to come. He ran to the door and yelled, "We need help in here! Someone's been stabbed."

A doctor and two nurses rushed in almost immediately and began clearing the room. The sheriff dragged Mandy out, kicking and screaming, while a nurse led Dan to the waiting room, quietly explaining what had happened to Cowboy. Ned didn't make any attempt to leave. He just stood quietly in the corner, watching the scene unfold.

Once a gurney was wheeled in, a flurry of activity took place. The medical team quickly and carefully moved Cowboy off me and onto the other bed as they took his vitals and wheeled him from the room.

I tried to get up, but a nurse pushed me back down and ordered me to stay where I was as he was taken away. Upset, I began coughing violently, pulled out my IV, and tried to get up again. "No, I need to make sure he's okay."

She had at least fifty pounds on me, though, and held me there. "They're going to assess him first. Then he'll probably be taken up to the OR for surgery. You won't be able to see him anytime soon. I'll find out what's going on and come back and give you an update," she promised. "Sit tight."

The nurse glanced to Ned and he nodded. "I'll stay with her."

When she seemed sure I wouldn't get up again, she told him, "Hit the call button if you need anything."

I looked down at the white sheets on the bed and shivered. There was no blood. Anywhere. In fact, there wasn't a single drop on my hospital gown, the bed, or even the floor. Almost like it had never happened. I would have thought I was dreaming, but as the nurse closed the heavy door behind her with an echoing clang, I glanced around the sterile-smelling room and spotted the rolling hamper marked "soiled" on the outside.

Soiled. It was exactly how I felt.

A wave of dismay swept over my queasy stomach, dragging repulsion in its wake. Everything I thought I had known was now tainted by shock, stained with dread, and marked with violence. I wanted to remove any traces of the horror I'd just witnessed. But nothing could sanitize those memories of Cowboy lying helplessly across me, unable to talk, with scissors protruding from his neck.

Without a word, I leaned my head back against the pillow and sank into the bed, letting the tears leak down my cheeks.

God, please let him be okay.

It was an hour later when I finally stopped crying. Ned stood across the room, staring out the window and watching the sun rise. "Are you okay?"

I ignored his question and asked one of my own. "Why haven't we heard anything yet?"

"I imagine we will soon."

After sitting in silence a while longer, the door pushed open and I jumped to my feet. Bobbie Jo stepped into the room, followed by the rest of the gang. She rushed to my side, panic-stricken. "Oh, Anna. We came as soon as we heard."

My gaze flitted from Ox to Judd, then over to Emily standing there with Jake's supportive arm around her. I could see the worry in each of their eyes. Of course they'd come running the moment they found out about Cowboy.

He was their family.

"We don't know anything yet."

"Are they running tests or something?" Jake asked, looking puzzled. "You've had to have been here a few hours already. Why don't they know what's wrong with you?"

Me? He thought I was talking about…myself?

"And where the hell is Cowboy?" Emily asked. "He didn't even call us until after you were admitted. We're going to kill him for not letting us know about this sooner."

They were here for me? Which meant they didn't know about Cowboy's condition. And I had to be the one who told them. "I…thought…you knew," I whispered, my voice cracking under pressure.

"Knew what?" Bobbie Jo asked, rubbing her hand on my back.

"Cowboy was…injured," I said, unsure how to break the disturbing news. "Stabbed, actually…in the neck with a pair of scissors." They blinked as my words sank in and a few of their mouths dropped open. "We think he might be in surgery, but we're not really sure what's going on. No one has told us anything yet."

Emily looked up at her FBI husband with tears in her questioning eyes. "Jake…?"

"I'm on it," he said, his grim mouth turning down. He reached into his pocket and pulled out his badge as he headed for the door. "I'll be back when I find out something."

"What happened?" Ox asked, looking as confused as the rest of them. "Why would anyone go after Cowboy?"

My eyes misted over, but I cleared my sore throat and hoped like hell my words didn't come out as raspy as I thought they might. "It's my fault. He was protecting *me*." Their eyes widened as I started from the beginning and told them the whole story.

The moment I finished, Ox and Judd stepped out to call Cowboy's parents, who were visiting his grandmother in El Paso. Ned made himself useful by getting everyone coffee, while Bobbie Jo and Emily took turns wearing a hole in the floor with all the pacing they were doing. I, on the other hand, couldn't do anything but sit there on my hospital bed, feeling numb, waiting for news to arrive.

Another half hour went by before a nurse entered the room, her face weary and bleak. "The FBI agent asked me to give you all an update on your...er, friend," she said somberly, glancing at me.

Fear pumped through me. "He's not..."

"No, no, he's alive. Once we left here, we stabilized him and then he was taken up to the OR to remove the instrument from his neck. The blades missed a major artery by only a fraction of an inch and he's still in recovery, but he's awake and going to be just fine. He's a very lucky young man."

"Oh, thank God!" I breathed a huge sigh of relief and blinked back the moisture pooling in my eyes. "When can we see him?"

"It will be a little while. Agent Ward is with him right now and then we have to move him to a room. I'm not sure what your friend did, but if the FBI is questioning him, then he must be in a lot of trouble."

As she left the room, we all grinned. Jake wasn't on any official business, although he'd obviously led the hospital staff to believe something entirely different.

Everything was going to be okay.

Chapter Twenty

My airways had been singed and the doctor apparently felt like it was too early to give me any solid foods. So when the nurse brought me a small tray with some orange gelatin and some smelly broth, I sent everyone else down to the cafeteria for breakfast. Just because the hospital was starving me didn't mean they had to suffer the same fate.

But Ned declined.

I found it strange he wanted to stay, but could tell he had something on his mind. Once the others cleared the room, I gazed over at him. He seemed to be calmly mulling something over in his head. Everything had happened so fast after he'd arrived I hadn't even mentioned anything to him about Chief Swanson. "I'm sorry about your brother."

He nodded a thank you.

"I met him once…a long time ago. In Houston, where I lived with my mom. He pulled me out of a fire. I was only six at the time."

Ned grinned at that. "I know. You're Anna Weber."

My eyes widened. "Y-yes," I replied, confusion lighting my voice. "How did you—"

"Ted told me about you years ago. He was a rookie back then, fresh out of training, and you were the first person he'd ever saved. Said it made him feel like a hero."

"He *was* a hero."

"Yeah, I suppose so." He ran a hand over his wry face. "But he was also a jackass."

I glanced over at him, not sure how to respond to that.

He grinned in amusement at my blank expression. "I know that sounds heartless, especially coming from his twin brother who just found out he died. But that's not the way I remember him." He shook his head. "Ted may have been a hero to you, and probably many others, I'm sure...but, to me, he was a wife-stealing, no-good sonofabitch."

"You mean, Janet?"

He lowered his head as the pain smeared across his face. "We were married only a few short months when I caught them together. She was the only woman I ever loved. And I guess Ted must've loved her, too, since he was willing to forgo our family ties to be with her." He raised his head and his eyes narrowed. "But I didn't know that dumbass was going to end up cheating on her with that...monster of a woman."

His reference to Mandy made me cringe, but I remembered things Cowboy told me and wanted to be completely honest with him. "I don't know for sure, but from what I heard, the affair started after Janet left. Technically, Janet and Chief...er, I mean Ted, were still married, I guess, but when she came back into the picture and they got back together, he must've told Mandy it was over between them."

"And that's what drove her insane? Crazy enough to kill two people?"

I shrugged. "It's the only thing that makes sense."

Ned sighed and pulled an envelope from his pocket. "After I got the message from your boyfriend, I had to know what this letter said."

He held it out and motioned for me to take it. I did, though I wasn't sure why he was showing it to me. I slipped the paper out and unfolded it to read the chief's final words to his brother.

I may have been a hero once, but I haven't done a heroic thing since. I'm sorry about Janet. I didn't deserve her.

"My brother is...*was* a damn fool. When it came to women, he was always playing with fire."

After Ned left, I laid my head back and allowed my eyes to drift closed. The others hadn't returned from the cafeteria and the nurse said it would be a while before they moved Cowboy to a room. But as sleep claimed my tired body, I became restless and hyper-aware that my tangible surroundings had changed, morphing into something that resembled a young girl's bedroom.

It was dark.

A door creaked open, and then closed again, followed by the light sounds of slow breathing and the soft padding of bare feet across the wooden floor. I cringed, knowing what was coming next. It was always the same thing.

When the scratching started, I tried to hide under the covers only to have them ripped away from me. Whimpering,

I drew myself into a ball and wrapped my arms around my legs, burying my face into my knees.

I didn't want to look up, afraid of what I'd see: the thing that scared me the most. But I did anyway because, deep down, I knew the scratching wouldn't stop until I saw the explosion with my own eyes. It happened so often, almost nightly…and still, I was afraid.

This time, the scratching sounded only twice when the light burst in front of me, temporarily blinding me to anything else. The overwhelming sulfuric odor filled my nostrils and made me gag. But this time, something was different. As I jerked away from the fire, my consciousness returned to my body and my limbs stiffened from the vision.

It felt like a dream. The same one I'd had for years. But this time everything had been much clearer. Maybe it was because my subconscious was paying attention. As if a fog had been lifted.

That's when I realized that it wasn't a dream at all. It was a deeply embedded memory. One where I was five years old and witnessed matches being lit in front of my face while I tried to go to sleep.

Normally, I couldn't see the person's face, only knew they were there. The horrendous monster who would torture a scared little girl in her pink canopy bed. But this time was different. I recalled all the times that this very incident had happened to me, recollections I'd apparently blocked to keep myself from the pain of seeing the face of my tormentor.

But this time, I opened my eyes. And with that one innocent look, horrific, deep-seated memories rushed back to me at once. Memories a little girl had blocked to save her sanity. But as an adult, she'd never be able to push them back again.

As I opened my eyes, the haze cleared. A figure moved across the room and sat in the chair beside my hospital bed. "I've been waiting for you to wake up."

Recognizing the voice immediately, my body stiffened. I slammed my eyelids closed and clenched my jaw, not knowing what to say.

"Don't be afraid, baby girl. I'm not going to hurt you." My heart squeezed at the term of endearment I remembered from my youth, but I didn't respond. "Your friends are just outside the door. I asked them if I could speak to you alone."

I blinked several times to clear the fogginess in my eyes, but wouldn't allow my gaze to meet his directly. "And I guess they were okay with it…since you're here?"

"Not really. Two of them patted me down to make sure I wasn't armed, while the other did a federal background check on me. Once they realized I wasn't here to harm you, they let me in. You've got protective friends. I like that."

I didn't respond. Instead, I concentrated on pushing away the blinding pain and anger in my heart that waged war on the memories of my mother.

"I'm sorry I scared you the night you caught me standing outside your house. I wanted to talk to you then, but I was afraid if you knew it was me, you would run before I had a chance to explain."

I sighed. "Explain what? What do you want, Stuart?"

He winced a little at the use of his first name. "For you to finally know the truth."

I squeezed my eyes shut tight to keep out the images that

tried to squirm their way back inside my mind and released a ragged breath. The face I'd seen behind the match replayed over and over in my head like an eternal loop. "I…I already know the truth."

"No, that's the thing, honey. You've never known the truth about what happened that day. But that's my fault. I was only trying to protect you. But you're twenty-eight years old now. I think it's time you found out and got the answers you deserve."

Something landed in my lap and I opened my eyes. It was a thick, leather-bound journal, filled with tattered pages. "Look through this," he said, his voice wavering.

Hesitantly, I put my hand on it. "What's in it?"

"An explanation. Letters I wrote to you that I never mailed. Notes on things you can research. Other crucial pieces of information that will convince you I'm not the monster you think I am. My cell number is written on the inside. After you look through it, I'm sure you'll have questions. Even if you don't, but just want to talk, I'm here." He headed for the door, but turned back as he reached it. "I'm not going to push you, Anna. You're a smart girl. You know the truth about what happened." He smiled lightly. "I'm glad you're okay, baby girl."

Then he disappeared.

I lifted the journal and heaved it across the room. Papers fell out, fluttering to the floor. I didn't need to read the contents of that damn journal to know what was in it. It wouldn't tell me anything I didn't already know. And it wasn't something I'd soon forget, since I had the physical and mental scars to remind me daily what had happened.

I cried, letting the memories overwhelm me.

Visits to the mental hospital. The number of pills taken to keep the demons at bay. The excitement over fire. The exhilaration around flames. The number of burn scars marring perfect porcelain skin. The animated expression while lighting matches in front of a child's wide, fearful eyes. The panic-stricken scream after lighting one's self on fire.

All of which belonged to one person.

My mother.

My father hadn't been trying to take me away from her. He had tried to protect me *from* her. If only I hadn't suppressed the one memory that would have kept him out of prison twenty-two years ago. That the moment the scuffle in our kitchen had begun, I'd opened the pantry door to help my mother. But what I'd seen left me dumbfounded and in a state of shock.

My mother repeatedly attacked my father, biting and clawing at him, while he'd done nothing to defend himself. He'd never laid a finger on her. Then, in the midst of her raging fit, my mother had picked up a cast iron skillet and cracked it against my father's skull, knocking him backward into the living room.

Afterward, she calmly and quietly grabbed the bottle of cooking wine on the counter and poured it over her head before placing her wet sleeve over the open flame of the stove. She shrieked in pain as the flames consumed her, and I slammed the door on the pantry and curled into a ball, locking the images away in my mind.

Apparently, I'd blocked out the horror of what my mother had done to protect her memory, or possibly my sanity, but I couldn't do it anymore. My mom had not been murdered by my father. She was a depressed, suicidal pyromaniac who had not only tortured her only child, but killed herself to escape the seduction of fire.

And even though I'd witnessed the whole thing, I still sent an innocent man to prison for almost twenty-two years. I didn't know how he could forgive me for that. Or how I'd ever forgive myself.

An hour after my father left, a nurse came into the room. "Can I see Cowboy now?" I asked, still stewing in guilt over what I'd done to my own father.

"His parents just arrived, and he's only allowed two visitors at a time."

"It might be a few more hours, then?"

She hesitated. "Well it might be a little longer than that. But I'm sure you'll be able to see him in the next day or two."

"Day or two?" I blinked at her as she chewed her lip. "What are you not telling me?" My mind swelled with horrific images of me at Cowboy's funeral. "Oh God! Please tell me he's okay."

The nurse grasped my hand and gave it a hard squeeze. "No, no. He's fine, I promise," she said softly, looking as if she were mentally cringing at what she was about to tell me. "It's just that…well, he doesn't want to see you."

"What? What do you mean?"

"That's what he said. He said to tell you he was okay and that he'd talk to you in a couple of days once things settled down."

I shook my head. "No, you're wrong. You must've misunderstood him…or it's the pain meds he's on. Cowboy wouldn't—"

She squeezed my hand again. "I'm sorry, honey. I heard him say it myself. He's quite coherent and lucid about it."

"Where is he?" I demanded.

"I can't tell you that. He didn't give his consent to give out his room number and we have to abide by patient orders when it comes to their privacy." Her apologetic eyes gazed at me, trying to comfort me in my agitated state. "Just give him some time. I'm sure he'll come around after a few—"

I shot off the bed, ran out of the room, and down the long hallway, desperately yelling Cowboy's name. The nurse called after me, but I ignored her. Why would he say such a thing after everything we'd been through together? Had he been telling the truth about him and Mandy, after all? Had there been something between them?

As I made it to the end of the hallway, I was only vaguely aware of the hospital security guard behind me, chasing after me. He tackled me to the ground and held me there, while I fought against him, still screaming Cowboy's name until my throat burned and I choked on my coughs. Tears streamed down my face.

It isn't true. It isn't.

Moments later, a doctor showed up wielding a syringe and stuck me in the arm. Within seconds, my strength weakened, my vision blurred, and my screams quieted. The last thing I remembered was everything going black.

I rapped lightly on the outside of the office door.

"Go away," Cowboy said from the other side. "I'm

busy."

He might have left the hospital without saying a word, and avoided me for the last two days, but he wasn't going to easily dismiss me now, not without facing me one last time. He owed me that much at least. So I pushed the door open.

Cowboy was sitting at the desk, but stood up with a dizzying speed. "Goddamnit. I said I was—" He blinked, looking much like he didn't know what to say, then shoved his hands in his pockets. "Um, hey."

I stood at the door in a white sundress, twisting my fingers together nervously, not really sure how to respond, either. It was a moment I'd been dreading for days. Ever since I'd come to and was told Cowboy had checked himself out of the hospital early, against medical advice.

"Hi," I said, my voice coming out much weaker than I meant for it to.

"What are you doing here?" The sound of his cool tone gave me a sick feeling in the pit of my stomach. "I mean, are you well enough to be out of the hospital?"

Guess we're going to make small talk. Fine.

"I'm all right." I gifted him a halfhearted smile, which was much more than the bastard deserved. "I tire a little easier right now since I'm still recovering from the smoke inhalation, but I'm managing."

"Good. Glad to hear it."

There was a moment of awkward silence, so I gazed across the room at something that caught my attention. Worn helmets lined the wall on display like some kind of shrine. "Why are all these firemen helmets different colors?"

"Each color stands for a different rank." He walked over to the old, battered helmets lined up in a uniform row.

"Black is for the regular crew and trainees, red is for the lieutenant, yellow is for the captain, and white is reserved only for the chief."

"That's right. I remember seeing your yellow captain's helmet in your truck the night you gave me a ride home after the library fire."

He looked down somberly, as if that was the last thing he wanted to think about. Or maybe remembering how this whole thing started between us was what bothered him. Lord knows he hadn't been by to check on me after disappearing from the hospital two days ago.

As if that wasn't bad enough, Cowboy had left me completely in the dark as to what went wrong between us. No explanation at all. That's why I was here now. To ask him what happened. Problem was, I couldn't seem to do it.

He'd obviously made his decision to end things between us that day in the hospital when he refused to see me. Then he left me alone in the hospital and didn't return, as if we hadn't shared anything special between us. Like I meant nothing to him. So the least he could do was explain himself.

"I'm glad you stopped by," he said.

My brows lifted as my eyes met his. "Really?"

"Anna, I…I meant to come see you."

"Guess you were too busy."

He shook his head and rubbed at his neck. "I've just been thinking about things."

"Things?"

"Us, I mean. You and me."

I squinted at him in confusion. "What was there to think about?"

"I guess what I'm trying to say is…" He hesitated, as if

he were trying to predict the outcome of what he was about to say. *Just say it already.* "I've come to the conclusion I don't want to be one of those housetrained men."

I stiffened at his remark. "Housetrained? I don't think I follow you."

"You know, one of those guys who sit at home every night with their woman and never have much of a life. I need some excitement and am starting to feel like I'm being cornered."

Disbelief washed over me, and I blinked rapidly. "I don't really know what to say to that. I thought you were okay with the way things were going between us. You seemed to be."

"Well, I'm not." Though I tried to stop it, I had no doubt the devastation showed on my face. Cowboy frowned, then turned away. "Look, I'm sorry I wasted your time."

"Wasted my—" I paused, not believing what I heard. No way was he getting off that easy. "Are you serious? *That* was supposed to be your heartfelt apology?"

Cowboy turned back to me and sighed. "I know we're going to run into each other from time to time, with you being Bobbie Jo's friend and all, so I think we should try to at least remain friends."

"Y-you're giving me the friend card after all we've…" My voice warbled and tears formed in my eyes. "Do you not even care how much you're hurting me right now?"

His fingers gripped the corner of the desk until his knuckles turned white. "Damn it, I'm trying to give you a polite rejection, but you keep pushing. Anna, I'm not responsible for your feelings. We just got wrapped up in this and…" He squeezed his eyes shut, as if it pained him to continue. But that didn't stop him from doing so. "I'm starting to get bored, okay?"

My hand slapped across his face so hard, his head turned. Probably harder than I even intended, but the bastard deserved it. And I wasn't going to apologize. Not to him. Not after what he'd done to me. "You know, I guess you were right about one thing from the beginning, Cowboy. You *are* a piece of shit." Then I turned and marched out of the office, slamming the door behind me.

I held my tears at bay until I pulled out of the fire station parking lot. Then I couldn't stop them. Clenching the steering wheel tightly, I navigated the roads through misty eyes as I replayed Cowboy's words in my head. My heart burst all over again.

He hadn't felt anything for me the whole time. Only pretended long enough to get me into bed. Now that his mission had been accomplished, he was looking for a fun new toy to play with. Which kept me wondering if he hadn't really snuck off to see Mandy the night of the fire, after all. *Bastard.*

The vague, pathetic excuses had left me unsatisfied until I pushed him into telling me the real reason he'd dumped me. The novelty of our relationship had worn off. *Relationship. What a joke.* Meaningless sex was hardly referred to as a relationship. But it hadn't been meaningless. Not for me. Because I was in love with— Oh God! I was in love with…*a selfish, arrogant prick!*

Apparently, I had been for years. Only difference now was that I actually knew it. And there wasn't a damn thing I could do about it. Especially since I wasn't even sure what had gone wrong. Maybe I'd come across too needy. Or maybe I…

No! This isn't my fault. This is on him.

He had betrayed my trust, not the other way around. He had used me for sex and then calmly walked all over me like a doormat. Well, never again. Never again would I give my heart to a man…especially since I'd left all the broken pieces of mine at Cowboy's feet.

Chapter Twenty-One

Several days later, I was sitting in my kitchen dishing out lemon cookies and Gatorade to my two unexpected guests when someone tapped on my front door. I excused myself momentarily and opened it to find Bobbie Jo on my front porch.

Her worried expression sent a jolt of panic through my system. "Bobbie Jo, is everything all right?"

"That's what I was about to ask you," she replied. "Since you left the hospital, I've tried to call you several times, but you haven't answered. I guess I was just afraid you might have —"

"Left town?" I grinned at her, but shook my head. "Don't worry. I'm not going anywhere. I've decided to stick around permanently."

"What about Cowboy?"

Just hearing his name sent rage sloshing through my veins. Even though I walked out on him, he hadn't bothered to try and contact me. And since he wasn't willing to fight for me, I could only assume he was satisfied with letting me go.

"What about him? I don't need his permission to stay where I have friends. I know we're going to run into each other from time to time, and it will most definitely be awkward, but that's just too damn bad. If he doesn't like it, then *he* can avoid *me*."

He said he wasn't responsible for my feelings. Fine. Then I was sure as hell not responsible for his comfort level. *The jerk*.

"What about your father?"

"Oh, he's still in town. My dad rented an apartment with the money he saved by working in the prison on kitchen detail. As an ex-convict, he was having a hard time finding a job, but Junior hired him as a line cook."

"Are things…okay between you?"

"We've been talking and working through all of it. It's a lot to take in, especially after believing something that wasn't true for the last twenty-two years. But I think we're heading in the right direction. And we've even started proceedings to get my father's name cleared."

A clang from the kitchen had both of us leaning inside to see what was going on. Joe and Clay Barlow sat there, tiny teacups in their giant hands, looking rather sheepish. "Sorry, Miss Anna," Joe said. "We were fighting over the last cookie and this dipshit…um, I mean my brother…broke one of your plates. Don't worry. We'll clean it up."

"Thank you. I'd appreciate that," I replied, offering them both a sweet smile.

Bobbie Jo blinked as if she'd entered a different realm of existence. "The Barlow boys…in your kitchen…drinking herbal tea and…eating cookies?" Her brows raised a little higher with each pause.

"They're taking a break."

Bobbie Jo peeked inside again and the two hulking guys holding a broom and a dustpan gave her a quick wave. She shook her head and frowned. "A break from what… terrorizing you?"

"They didn't terrorize me. I only thought they did. The moment I got home from the hospital, the two of them came over and apologized for not only what their sister had done, but how they'd behaved as well. They had no clue Mandy sent me threatening notes, much less that she misspelled them on purpose to frame her own brothers. She hadn't known they were in jail when she kidnapped me, and I think they realize how lucky they were. It's changed them."

"What's going to happen to her? Is she going to prison?"

"No. She failed her psychological evaluation. Mandy Barlow will spend her years locked away in a mental institution. It's a fate worse than prison."

"More memories coming back?"

"They all sort of rushed back at once. My mother lived in a dream world and had brainwashed me into believing I lived there as well. She kept me away from my father because she was afraid of losing me, which is why I think I blocked out all of the bad memories of her. I was afraid of losing her too."

"Miss Anna, we're going to get back to work now," Clay said, lifting a large box from the living room floor and carrying it out the door past us. I smiled at them as Joe grabbed another and followed his brother out.

"Thanks, fellas. You're a big help."

Bobbie Jo grimaced. "So if you're staying, what's up with the boxes?"

"Oh, I'm donating all my books to the library," I said, motioning to the piles of cardboard boxes cluttering the walkway. "The boys are helping me with the heavy lifting and loading them into my car for me."

"You're truly okay, then?" she asked, eyeing me suspiciously.

"I'm fine," I said, letting out a small sigh. "I'm sorry I didn't answer my phone when you called. I guess I just didn't feel like talking to anyone. Especially about Cowboy. Besides, there isn't anything left to say."

Bobbie Jo leaned on the railing and snorted. "He's always been an idiot. This just proves it." She shook her head in disgust. "I am sorry it didn't work out. I don't know exactly what happened between the two of you, but I'm betting that somewhere in there, he's the one who somehow screwed this up and is kicking himself in the ass right about now."

"Doesn't matter. It's over." I gave her a non-committal shrug and watched Joe and Clay shove the remaining box into my backseat. "Maybe in time Cowboy and I can still be fr —" A jacked-up red truck coming down the road halted my speech. *Oh, great. Speak of the devil.*

As the truck drew closer, my eyes met Cowboy's. He slowed and waved, as if he were offering a friendly gesture to one of his neighbors. But if he expected me to wave back like we were friends, he could forget it. The only kind of gesture I was willing to give him consisted of one finger and wasn't usually considered all that friendly. *The jackass.*

I turned my back on him for breaking my heart and started inside.

But before I made it through the door, his truck screeched to a halt just past my driveway. I whipped around to see him throw it in reverse and drive backward into the middle of my yard. Cowboy jumped out of his truck, glaring at the Barlow boys as they made their way back to the porch. "You two get the hell out of here and leave Anna alone!"

"Whoa!" Joe said, as he reached the top of the stairs. "We're not here to cause problems. We're helping Miss Anna load up these boxes. Why don't you chill the hell out, dude?"

Cowboy marched past Clay and clomped his way up the stairs where I stood with Joe and Bobbie Jo.

I put my hands on my hips and glared at Cowboy. "That's not a parking spot!"

"Oh, yeah? Well, it is now!" he sneered.

"God, you're an even bigger asshole than I thought." I turned and marched inside, flapping my arms in frustration.

A growl burst from his throat. "Get back here," he demanded.

Surprisingly enough, I made it to the kitchen without him manhandling me. I'd fully expected him to be on my heels, but when I stopped and spun around, he wasn't there. Peeking around the corner, I found out why.

He had tried to follow me through the open door, but Joe had stepped into Cowboy's path and was now poking one large finger into his chest. "I think the lady wants you to leave."

I stood off to the side, just out of their field of vision, but where I could see and hear both of them. With rage burning in his green eyes, Cowboy measured up the big guy in front of him. "If you want to keep that finger attached, I suggest you remove it."

They stood there in an intense, heated stand-off that looked like it would never end. Thank goodness Bobbie Jo intervened, patting Joe on the arm. "It's okay, Joe. I've got this. Why don't you give us a minute?"

Joe nodded and walked by Cowboy, purposely bumping his shoulder as he passed. Cowboy rolled his eyes and started inside, but Bobbie Jo wasn't having it. She put her arm up and blocked the door, scowling at him. "You really did it this time, didn't you, Cowboy? Put your foot in it good."

"Ya know, I'd love to stand around here talking about how I screwed up, but I have something more important to do."

But Bobbie Jo persisted. "What do you want with Anna?"

Oh, I love having such protective friends.

"I just want to talk to her." He peered over Bobbie Jo's head and caught a glimpse of all the cardboard boxes in the living room. "What the hell is going on? Why are the Barlows loading boxes into Anna's car?" He ran a hand over his distraught face. "Sonofabitch. Don't tell me she's leaving town."

Bobbie Jo shrugged nonchalantly. "What does it matter to you? It's not like *you* care."

"What? I do care! Now let me in." But Bobbie Jo didn't budge. "Damn it, I need to find her. Get out of the way or I'm going to pick your ass up and move you."

Something resembling a smirk lifted the corners of her mouth. "She's probably in the kitchen packing up more boxes," she said nonchalantly, dropping her arm from the doorway.

As Cowboy stepped inside, I slipped out of view and pretended to be busy.

"Anna...?"

I poked my head out of the kitchen and frowned at him. "Why are you still here?"

"I want to know where the hell you think you're going."

"Beg your pardon?"

"You heard me."

I glared at him. "I'm no longer your concern, remember?"

Cowboy counted slowly under his breath, trying to gain control of his temper. "Stop this nonsense, woman. I won't sit by and let you leave town all because I—"

"Because you what? Used me? Took what you wanted and moved on? Guess you were bored with me. Isn't that how you put it?"

"That wasn't true and you know it."

"No, I don't know. As far as I'm concerned, that's exactly what happened. Now, get out."

"I need to talk to you. To tell you something. At the very least I owe you an explanation and an apology." When I crossed my arms and waited, he continued. "I was promoted to chief."

"Good for you. Now leave."

"Damn it, just listen. After I came out of recovery, the mayor stopped by to see me. I thought he'd heard about my injury and was coming to tell me he was appointing a new acting chief. But instead, he congratulated me for making chief."

"What the hell does that have to do with me?"

"I couldn't stand the thought of you living in fear that something would happen to me. That one day, I might be burned alive. You don't sleep as it is. I didn't want to give you any more nightmares."

My mouth dropped open. "So you didn't even fight for me because of *that*?"

"No, not just that. I…" He closed his eyes and breathed out slowly, gearing himself to say something he obviously dreaded. "I save people for a living. It's what I do. But I… couldn't save you. And to make it worse, the whole thing with Mandy was my fault."

"*Your* fault?"

"Before I saw you in the library that first night, I…I flirted with her. No more than I did with other girls, but I hadn't realized she was unstable and had taken any of it seriously."

"So you're saying you and Mandy *were* sleeping—"

"No. Of course not. Nothing ever came of it, but she got the wrong idea about me because *I* let her get the wrong idea. Just like everyone else around here." He shook his head. "No one takes a playboy seriously. And my behavior with the women in this town hasn't encouraged it. I'm sorry, sweetheart, but this was all my fault. I was doing what I thought was best…for you. To end things and let you move on without me." He glanced behind him at the boxes stacked everywhere before his eyes landed back on me and he frowned. "But I don't want you to leave. Damn it, Anna, I can't lose you."

Slack-jawed, I stood motionless and stared at him in silence for a full thirty seconds, waiting for a declaration of love or at the very least an honorable mention in the like department. But it didn't come. As the realization sank in that he might never admit his feelings for me, I only blinked at him, which apparently wasn't the reaction he expected.

He shifted his weight and sighed with annoyance. "Gonna

leave me hanging or are you going to say something?"

"I…um…I'm not leaving," I managed to say, watching the worry melt from his eyes. "Those boxes are filled with books I'm donating to the library."

"Oh, thank God," he said, the tension in his shoulders loosening. "When I saw them loading boxes into your car… well, you scared the hell out of me. I thought I'd lost you for good." Then he opened his arms to me.

But I didn't move into them. Even though I knew the truth, nothing had changed.

"So you think you can treat me like I'm nothing to you, then waltz in here with an apology? And then what? I'm supposed to just forgive you and get over it?" I scoffed under my breath. "No way in hell."

He dropped his arms to his sides. "Anna, I already told you why—"

"I don't care. Not only did you hurt me, but you embarrassed me. Made me feel bad about myself, as well as our relationship. And it was so easy for you. Then again, everything comes easy for you, right? Well, not this time," I said, starting past him.

Cowboy snagged me by the arm and raised a brow. "Are you saying you don't want me?"

"No, actually *you* said you didn't want *me*, remember?" I glared at him and even took it one step further. "I wouldn't want to *bore* you again, so we should probably keep things casual and see how it goes. Don't worry, though. If I'm feeling frisky, I'll give you a call. But only if my bed isn't already occupied by someone else."

His eyes narrowed and his grip tightened. "You don't mean that."

"Sure I do," I said, punctuating my indifference with a simple shrug. "After all, you're no Prince Charming. I wouldn't want you to get any wrong ideas about me falling in love with you. I guess I am grateful to you for teaching me how to make love, though. I can't wait to practice some more."

The insult must've hit home because Cowboy released my arm and said, "You want to wait around for Prince fucking Charming, then that's fine by me!" He turned and stormed out the front door.

The bottom dropped out of my stomach, and I stood there blinking like an idiot. *Oh, no! What have I done?* But by the time I came to my senses and made it to the door, he'd already slammed his truck door closed and was roaring out of my yard without even looking back. I swayed unsteadily in the doorway as my heart ripped apart at the seams.

I had only meant to show him how it felt to be tossed aside. How much it hurt for the person you loved not to love you back. But it all backfired and blew up in my face. Tears stung my eyes, but I refused to let them fall. My fairytale romance was over.

So much for happily ever after.

Thank goodness Bobbie Jo had been there when Cowboy ran out on me. I'd needed the comfort of a good friend. And she was, indeed. Not the least bit fooled by my silence, she made me some chamomile tea to soothe my broken heart.

She handed me a steaming cup. "I don't understand

Cowboy. I only let him inside to talk to you because I thought he was here to fix things with you." She shook her head in disgust. "Now I'm going to have to kill him."

"No, Bobbie Jo, it was my fault," I told her, twisting my fingers together. "He tried. Really, he did." Unshed tears clogged my throat, but I managed to rasp out the rest. "I guess I wanted to give him a dose of his own medicine and show him how much he had hurt me. It didn't work out quite how I thought it would."

"He's a big boy. If he wanted to fight for you, then he should've stayed and done so." Bobbie Jo frowned as she looked to be pondering something. "I hate to even say it, but the one thing I've learned from dealing with Jeremy is that some relationships aren't…"

"Meant to be?" I asked.

"I'm sorry, honey. I shouldn't have said that. I'm sure it doesn't help."

"No, it's a fair statement. And true, too. Like you and Jeremy. Some people don't belong together." I sighed wearily. "I guess I just thought Cowboy and I might."

Suddenly, something popped loudly outside, startling us both. Bobbie Jo and I exchanged glances, then I closed my eyes. "If those Barlow boys are setting off fireworks again, I'm going to—"

Another pop sounded, followed by a horn honking, and something that sounded like a dull roar. With puzzled faces, we rose from our chairs and headed to the door. I threw it open, stepped onto the porch, and gasped.

In what looked like a traffic jam, vehicles were lined up along both sides of the road out front of my home. Horns blaring. People cheering while standing in the back of their trucks or on top of their hoods. The Barlow brothers took turns shooting off fireworks over my house from my own front yard. *What the…? Now they have an audience egging them on?*

I double-timed it down the stairs and glared at them with my hands on my hips. "What the hell is wrong with you two?"

"Oh, hey, Miss Anna," Clay said nonchalantly, setting off a chain of pops that exploded in colorful disarray above us. "What do you think? Pretty, right?"

Bobbie Jo joined me and nodded to the familiar faces on the edge of the driveway. Emily rocked Lily while Jake held wide-eyed Austin in his arms. They stood next to Ox, Judd, Hank, and Floss. All of them wearing wide grins. "What's going on, guys?" Bobbie Jo asked, as confused as I was.

"Just came to watch the show," Jake said with a wink. "Heard there'd be fireworks here tonight."

I glared at Joe and Clay. "I thought you two weren't going to do this anymore? You promised me!"

Joe set off another shrill whistle which combusted into a huge ball of blue lights in the sky and grinned. "Your boyfriend asked us to. He knew it was one way to get you outside."

"My boyfriend? I don't have a—"

The clomping of horse hooves sounded in the distance and my head—along with everyone else's—spun in its direction. A white horse came into view, bobbing its head proudly. *Hank's colt, Ruckus?*

Cowboy was on the back of the trotting, once-wild stallion he'd tamed, whirling his white Stetson in the air. The crowd went wild, applauding and wolf-whistling as he grew closer.

Good grief. What the heck was he doing now?

Gravel crunched under the horse's hooves as Cowboy steered him up my drive, then stopped in front of me. He rested an arm over the saddle horn and leaned forward, tipping his hat back and giving me a wicked grin. Then he offered me his hand.

"Have you gone insane?"

"Darlin', the only thing I'm crazy about is *you*." Cowboy scooted back in the saddle and gave the other guys a quick nod. "Boys, why don't you give the lady a boost?"

"No, I don't want—" But Ox and Judd grabbed a hold of me and gently lifted me into Cowboy's waiting arms. Balancing on the front of the saddle with my legs hanging off one side, I wrapped my arms around his waist to keep from sliding off.

Everyone quieted and stared at the two of us, waiting for one of us to speak. Not used to being the center of attention, I felt my cheeks heat and lowered my gaze to avoid all the prying eyes. "What are you doing?" I whispered.

"I'm laying claim to what's mine," he said, lifting my chin. His intense eyes reminded me of the last time he'd "claimed" me.

My heart sped up and a tingling sensation rocketed through my lower abdomen, but there was still no way he was getting off that easy. "You can't just come here and take whatever you want. It doesn't work that way."

"Wanna bet?" Cowboy wrapped his large hands around the back of my neck and roughly pulled my mouth to his.

Briefly, I froze. But the moment his tongue slid into my open mouth, the fever kicked in. My frenzied hands swept up his back, knotting his shirt in my fist, as he kissed me silly. So much for me playing hard to get.

A round of applause sounded, reminding me that not only were we on a horse, but there were others present, watching us make out. I was the first to pull away. Touching my swollen lips with my fingertips, I glanced around at all the smiling faces, wondering if they could all see what I was feeling.

I glanced up at Cowboy. "You're sure you want me?"

"No, darlin', I don't want you," Cowboy said, making a lump form in my throat and tears burn behind my eyes. "I *need* you. And only you." He lifted my hand and kissed it. "I love you, Anna."

My heart ballooned in my chest, filling with more joy than I could have ever imagined. "I love you, too."

"Then what would you say if I told you I wanted to marry you and give you that happily ever after you deserve?"

Tears fell from my eyes, landing on my cheeks. "Really? You mean that?"

"Hell, yeah, I mean it! I may not be scaling a wall, slaying a dragon, or even be much of a prince, but I'm damn sure on a white fucking horse, aren't I?"

"Then I guess I'd say I'm feeling pretty jubilant right about now."

"Sonofabitch." He groaned in frustration. "Woman, you know damn well I don't understand what the hell that means. Was that a yes or a no?"

I smiled at him and gave him a quick kiss. "That was definitely a yes!"

Epilogue

"You sure you don't need any help?" Cowboy called out from the living room over the low rumblings of our family and friends.

"No, I've got it."

I placed the leftover sheet cake into its box, but before closing it, I swiped one finger across the corner, scooping the white frosting, and popped it into my mouth. A low moan escaped my lips as I sucked the icing off. Delicious.

When I turned to grab a napkin, I realized I wasn't alone. Cowboy stood in the doorway, his eyes focused on me and one brow raised, as if he caught me red-handed. "Very unladylike," he reprimanded.

But his smirk told on him.

"And you loved it."

"Damn straight," he replied, then continued standing there with his eyes burning with uncontrolled intensity.

For a moment, all I could do was stare back. Even after

a year of marriage, it amazed me how his watchfulness still affected me. Warmth crept up my neck, as if my body was a thermometer and heat from his pointed gaze caused my mercury to rise. Then his eyes flickered down to my chest and my swollen nipples hardened.

"W-what are you doing?"

"You mean, besides looking at my beautiful wife?"

I glanced down and caught sight of the bulge in his jeans. Just my luck. His wick was lit. "Yeah, right. We both know what that look of yours leads to." I crossed my arms over my chest, hoping the disarming gesture would slow his roll. "Put away the weapon of massive proportions," I told him, lowering my tone to a whisper. "We have guests."

Cowboy groaned. "This is going to kill me, you know?"

I smiled. "You'll live."

He stepped into my space and cinched his arms around my waist. "You sure about that?" he asked, dusting his lips across mine and then nipping gently.

My ragged breath caught in my throat and my pulse raced. The force of attraction between us bonded us together in a way I couldn't explain and it still blew me away. Cowboy's high libido was definitely going to be problematic over the next—

"For the love of God, Cowboy!" Bobbie Jo exclaimed from the doorway, holding an empty plate. "You think you could give the poor woman a few weeks before you start trying to sex her up again? She just had a baby, for goodness sakes."

Maybe Cowboy should have felt deeply ashamed for his behavior, but he just chuckled. "Can I help it if she tastes so sweet?"

The sugary aftertaste still coated my tongue. "Frosting," I explained to her. "He was just helping me put away the leftover cake."

"Well, I just came to tell you we're leaving. I'm sure you're exhausted and would like to get some rest." Her eyes cut to Cowboy and narrowed slightly.

Cowboy raised both of his hands in the air and smiled innocently. "Hands off, I swear."

I rolled my eyes at him and gave her a quick wink. "Don't worry. I know how to handle this cowboy if he gets too frisky."

We walked into the living room, where most of our friends and family had gathered quietly in a semicircle around Dan. He must've sensed us approach because he turned and grinned wide. "Sure is a hefty little guy, isn't he?"

Seeing our newborn son sleeping in Dan's arms made me smile. "He's beautiful, isn't he?" Then I cringed at my words. Crap. It slipped out.

Cowboy came up behind me, placed his lips near my ear, and whispered, "Who's the fucking doofus who passed the baby to the blind man?"

I elbowed him into silence and motioned to the others standing around Dan. Every one of them were on guard, watching for any little mishap that could possibly occur. I had no doubt our son was perfectly safe and secure.

"He's healthy and has a good, strong name," Dan said. "That's all that matters."

Everyone smiled at that. When we'd announced we were naming our son Daniel, the old man automatically assumed we'd named our child after him. He had no clue we actually named him after a little boy named Danny who wanted to be a fireman and never got the chance to fulfill his dreams. Or that it was also my father's middle name. None of us had the heart to correct him.

"Here ya go, little fella," Dan said softly. "Go back to your mommy." Then he handed our baby boy to Bobbie Jo.

We all bit our lips to keep from laughing, but no one said anything. Bobbie Jo shrugged and gently laid Daniel in a nearby bassinet, patting him lightly to get him back to sleep. Seconds later, he was out again.

"Thank you for throwing us a welcome home party," I said, tearing up a little. "It was very sweet of you."

"No problem," Bobbie Jo said, offering me a hug. "Any woman who can convince Cowboy to give up his bachelor status deserves a hell of a lot more than a party."

"Yeah, yeah," Cowboy cut in. "Just wait 'til the right guy comes along and you find yourself in the same position."

She smiled and gazed over at Austin playing on the floor with Lily. "Not going to happen," she said. "There isn't a man out there who can undo the damage Jeremy caused when it comes to my low opinion of men."

"Hey!" Jake, Ox, Judd, and Cowboy said in unison.

"Sorry. You know what I mean." Bobbie Jo laughed as she strolled over, lifted her son into her arms, and headed for the door. "Anna, if you need anything, let me know."

Emily picked up Lily and carried her toward me. "Same goes for me, sweetie." She gave me a quick hug, then strolled out the door.

Jake, Ox, and Judd shook hands with Cowboy, then each gave me a kiss on the cheek, congratulating us on our new addition. Then they all stepped out, as well. Dan was riding with Ox and Judd, yet he was the last to walk through the door, tapping his cane in front of him. We followed him only as far as the front door, but I was worried about him falling off the porch.

"Watch your step, Dan!"

Ah, damn. Cowboy stifled a laugh while I covered my face with my palm. I needed to stop saying things like that. But Dan just shook his head and continued down the porch stairs, not bothering to respond.

Jake pulled his black Silverado out onto the road, but stopped as Emily motored down the window and leaned out. "Oh, hey, Cowboy! I almost forgot today is May first," she said, giggling. "So much for Bachelor of the Month. Guess who's not getting any for the next six weeks?" She grinned as they drove away with the sound of Jake's laughter echoing behind them.

Cowboy's eyes narrowed. "Think Jake would care if I kicked out her two front teeth?"

"Cowboy!"

He flashed me a grin. "Oh, come on. You know I'm just kidding."

"Still, you shouldn't say things like that," I said in a chastising tone and turned to walk inside. "It's not nice."

"Oh, like what bigmouth said was any nicer?" Cowboy stepped inside and kicked the door closed with his boot. "They're never going to let me live this down. I'm going to be harassed daily by those assholes for the next six weeks. I should know. We did the same thing to Jake after Emily had Lily."

I reached up behind my head and unclipped my hair, letting the red strands tumble around my shoulders, then removed the glasses from my face and set them on the counter. Smiling sweetly, I sauntered toward him, grasped him by the collar of his shirt, and pulled him close. "I'm not Emily. As I told you once before, I *know* how to use my mouth."

He smirked. "Dear God, I love it when you talk dirty to me."

Acknowledgments

There's always so many people to thank and never enough space to do it in. But I'll try.

To my husband, Denny, and my boys, Matthew and Andrew, thank you for your encouragement, support, and for ordering pizza on the nights I'm working. To my mom, my dad, Annita, Becca, Amanda, April, Andrea, and the best mother-in-law I've ever had, Terry, thank you for being there when I needed someone to listen to my ramblings.

A huge thank you to my critique partner, Heather Boey, for convincing me that Anna was a perfect heroine in her own right. This story wouldn't have seen the light of day had you not given me the confidence I needed to follow my heart.

Big hugs and kisses go out to my other amazing critique partners who gave me awesome notes, great advice, and all the smiles — Carol, Joy, Sam, Sonya, Rebecca and the two gals who make up Elizabeth Hayley. Also, big thanks to

Samanthe Beck, who is a gem for giving me a fantastic cover quote and for not turning me away when I sent her one of those "out of the blue" emails.

Thank you to my adorable super-agent, Andrea Somberg for always being there for me and for listening to me ramble on the phone. It's okay, I know I do it. Thank you to Robin Haseltine for your hard work and, most importantly, your friendship. I'm still jealous of this lake view you speak of. Huge thanks to Candy Havens for jumping in with both feet, helping to polish up this diamond in the rough, and making it sparkle. Also, thanks to my cover artist, Louisa Maggio, and anyone else at Entangled who helped bring this book to the published world.

A group hug goes out to my fantastic five PAs (Barbara Campbell, Dana Leah, Crystal Wegryznowicz, Cindy Yocum, and Tessa Walters) as well as the other awesome members of my Pure Bliss Street Team. Not only do you guys support my books, but you also promote positivity, laughter, and friendship within our group. I adore you all and want you to know there's no one else I'd rather eat checkers with. Home of the romantically insane lives on!

A very special thanks to Stacey Z. Thornton for choosing Hunter Wells as the sheriff's name in the character naming contest. Couldn't have picked a better one myself.

Last but never least, thank you to all the bloggers, reviewers, and readers who have helped spread the word about my books! Much love to you all!

About the Author

As the youngest of five girls, Alison Bliss has never turned down a challenge...or been called by the right name. Her writing career *may* have started out as a dare by one of her sisters, but Alison hasn't put her pen down since.

She grew up on a small island off the Texas Gulf Coast, where most of her childhood vacations consisted of camping or hunting trips to the deer lease. Although she'll always be a Texan at heart, Alison currently resides in the Midwest with her Iowa farm-boy husband and their two sons. With so much testosterone in her home, it's no wonder she writes "girl books."

Alison is an animal lover, a closet video game enthusiast, and believes the best way to know if someone is your soul mate is by canoeing with them because if you both make it back alive, it's obviously meant to be. She's an avid romance reader who enjoys penning the type of books she loves to read most: fun, steamy love stories with heart, heat, laughter,

and usually a cowboy or two. As she calls it, "Romance…
with a sense of humor."

To learn more about Alison Bliss, visit her website at
http://authoralisonbliss.com, where you can sign up for her
newsletter to keep up with her latest book news. You can
also email her at authoralisonbliss@hotmail.com or connect
with her on social media. She'd love to hear from you!

Discover the **Tangled in Texas** *series…*

RULES OF PROTECTION

Rule breaker Emily Foster just wanted some action on her birthday. Instead she witnessed a mob hit and is whisked into witness protection, with by-the-book Special Agent Jake Ward as her chaperone. They end up deep in the Texas backwoods. The city-girl might be safe from the Mafia, but now she has to contend with a psychotic rooster, a narcoleptic dog, crazy cowboys, and the danger of losing her heart to the one man she can't have. But while Jake's determined to keep her out of the wrong hands, she's determined to get into the right ones—his.

Made in the USA
San Bernardino, CA
06 September 2017